"A fresh take... nd real moral di... ne who likes their fae modern, their stakes high, and their property damage extensive."
—Seanan McGuire, *New York Times* bestselling author of the October Daye novels

"Combines top-notch writing and world-building with characters you'll adore . . . and the star-crossed lovers may just break your heart . . . If you enjoy fae urban fantasy, then don't miss this splendid debut. Loved it. Can't wait for the next book."
—Ann Aguirre, national bestselling author of *Endgame*

"When facing this stubborn, smart escape artist of a heroine, watch where you walk, as every footstep leaves a shadow and every shadow tells a longtime reader like McKenzie Lewis the truth . . . whether she wants to know it or not."
—Rob Thurman, *New York Times* bestselling author of *Doubletake*

"Fantastically fun urban fantasy! One of the best debuts of the year . . . [It] checked off all my urban fantasy wish-list boxes, and I can't wait to read the sequel."
—*All Things Urban Fantasy*

"A gutsy heroine and plenty of fae lore."   —*Library Journal*

"Fun and fast-paced."   —*Fantasy Cafe*

"Fantastic . . . filled with action and suspense. I was constantly on the edge of my seat."   —*Urban Fantasy Investigations*

continued . . .

Ace Books by Sandy Williams

THE SHADOW READER
THE SHATTERED DARK

THE SHATTERED DARK

Sandy Williams

ACE BOOKS, NEW YORK

THE BERKLEY PUBLISHING GROUP
Published by the Penguin Group
Penguin Group (USA) Inc.
375 Hudson Street, New York, New York 10014, USA

Penguin Group (Canada), 90 Eglinton Avenue East, Suite 700, Toronto, Ontario M4P 2Y3, Canada (a division of Pearson Penguin Canada Inc.) • Penguin Books Ltd., 80 Strand, London WC2R 0RL, England • Penguin Group Ireland, 25 St. Stephen's Green, Dublin 2, Ireland (a division of Penguin Books Ltd.) • Penguin Group (Australia), 250 Camberwell Road, Camberwell, Victoria 3124, Australia (a division of Pearson Australia Group Pty. Ltd.) • Penguin Books India Pvt. Ltd., 11 Community Centre, Panchsheel Park, New Delhi—110 017, India • Penguin Group (NZ), 67 Apollo Drive, Rosedale, Auckland 0632, New Zealand (a division of Pearson New Zealand Ltd.) • Penguin Books (South Africa) (Pty.) Ltd., 24 Sturdee Avenue, Rosebank, Johannesburg 2196, South Africa

Penguin Books Ltd., Registered Offices: 80 Strand, London WC2R 0RL, England

This is a work of fiction. Names, characters, places, and incidents either are the product of the author's imagination or are used fictitiously, and any resemblance to actual persons, living or dead, business establishments, events, or locales is entirely coincidental. The publisher does not have any control over and does not assume any responsibility for author or third-party websites or their content.

THE SHATTERED DARK

An Ace Book / published by arrangement with the author

PUBLISHING HISTORY
Ace mass-market edition / November 2012

Copyright © 2012 by Sandy Williams.
Map by Adam F. Watkins.
Cover art by Gene Mollica.
Cover design by Lesley Worrell.
Interior text design by Kristin del Rosario.

ISBN: 978-1-937007-81-2

ACE
Ace Books are published by The Berkley Publishing Group,
a division of Penguin Group (USA) Inc.,
375 Hudson Street, New York, New York 10014.
ACE and the "A" design are trademarks of Penguin Group (USA) Inc.

PRINTED IN THE UNITED STATES OF AMERICA

10 9 8 7 6 5 4 3 2 1

ALWAYS LEARNING   **PEARSON**

For Mom.
Thank you for always believing in me,
especially when I didn't believe in myself.

ACKNOWLEDGMENTS

•◆•

People say second books are harder to write than first books. That's especially true when you have twins a few months before your deadline. This book wouldn't have been written if it weren't for a few awesome people.

My mom, who made the five-hour trip between Houston and Dallas more times than I can count. Thank you for watching the boys so I could work. The same gratitude goes to my husband, who was on baby duty every evening and weekend for months, and to my grandmother, who helped keep me sane on the days I was home alone, juggling the babies and a deadline. I couldn't have done this without your sacrifices and support!

I also have to give a shout-out to Rissa Westerfield, who has taken such great care of my boys. I don't think any of us would have survived without you!

Mega gratitude goes to my beta readers, Shelli Richard and Renee Sweet. Renee, your comments are always spot-on, and they never fail to make me laugh. Thanks so much for knocking some sense into McKenzie!

To my agent, Joanna Volpe—wow! You always know exactly what to say to keep me from totally freaking out. Thank you for your guidance and your many last-minute reads! Also, much appreciation goes out to the illustrator, Adam Watkins, who endured many "final" tweak e-mails from me to create a kick-ass map of the Realm.

And to Kat Sherbo, my editor: Thank you for being so incredibly understanding while I learn how to be both a mom and a writer. Your patience made it possible for me to make this the best book it could be.

Lastly, big hugs to my boys, who still love me despite the number of hours I've spent banging away at my computer. Your smiles brighten the gloomiest days!

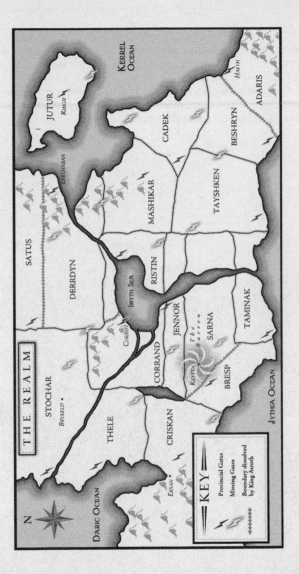

ONE

-•-

I HAVE FIFTEEN minutes to grab what I need from an apartment I lived in seven years. Sadly, that's more than enough time. My walls are bare except for a single abstract painting, and the sofa and coffee table are secondhand, just like a college student's furniture should be. This place was always supposed to be temporary. I used to think that would be because I'd graduate and move on to a real job, a nicer apartment, and, well, a nicer life. But war will ruin anyone's plans.

Instead of turning on the lights, I open the blinds as a courtesy to my guards, two fae named Trev and Nalst. They're here as a precaution even though it's extremely unlikely that the remnants of the king's fae will choose *this* moment to come here. We took the Silver Palace two weeks ago. They've had plenty of time to ransack my place, but everything is where I left it. Most likely, they have no clue where I live. Back when I worked for the king, my identity was one of the most tightly guarded secrets in the Realm, and the few people who knew my name are now either dead or, like me, they're working with the rebel fae.

"Hurry," Trev orders. A bolt of blue lightning strikes down his neck, disappearing beneath his *jaedric* armor. A fae's chaos lusters grow more active, more frenzied when they're near human tech, but that's not why Trev is anxious. The rebellion needs every sword available to keep its enemies from retaking the palace. He and Nalst need to return to the Realm ASAP.

They wait in the living room while I head to my bedroom. I grab a suitcase from my closet, throw in my favorite pair of jeans and a few shirts, then I reach up to the shelf above the clothing rod and grab a leather-bound sketchbook. Half its pages are filled with my messy shadow-readings. The chicken scratches look more like a lunatic's drawings than maps, but if I show them to a fae and name the location out loud, he or she will be able to travel to the place I've drawn. That skill and my Sight are the reasons I was pulled into the Realm's wars. Few humans can see the fae; fewer still can read their shadows.

This is the sketchbook I always used when shadow-reading for the king's fae, but I didn't have it with me when the rebels abducted me from my campus a little over a month ago. I shouldn't have needed it because I was *supposed* to have the day off.

I toss it into my suitcase, glad to have the sketchbook back. I like the broken-in look of the leather, and the long strap allows me to wear it across my body like a messenger bag, so it's easier to hang on to than a normal notebook. With the way the war in the Realm is going these days, I need that little convenience. I can run faster when my hands are free.

Leaving the suitcase open, I walk to my desk to take my wallet out of the middle drawer. There's actually money inside. Sixteen dollars to be precise. That's probably more than what I have in my bank account. Back when the king was alive, he gave me a small monthly allowance for tracking down criminals. Many of those fae were truly horrible, but some of them? Some of them, I recently learned, were not.

I make sure my driver's license and Social Security card are inside the wallet. They're the real reason I'm here. Every year I worked for the king, my human life slipped further and further away. I lost my friends, my family, and my best chance at a college degree, all because I put my work for the fae before myself. I can't do that anymore. I'm starting over, and this time, I'm determined to find a balance between my human life and my life working for the fae. The license and Social Security card will help me do that. A start-up news aggregation Web site offered me a job in Las Vegas, and I need to give the identification to the owner, Brad Jenkins, to finish the employment process.

A part of me can't believe I'm setting down roots in Vegas—the city is too flashy for my tastes—but that's where I'm sharing a hotel suite with another Sighted human, who actually likes the city. I guess I'm lucky, though. Jenkins is probably the only editor alive who's going to take a chance on a college flunkout.

I slide the wallet into my back pocket, then grab a photo album off a shelf. I don't open it. I hardly ever do. It contains pictures from a different life, a life back before I became entangled in the Realm's wars. I haven't seen or talked to my parents since I was seventeen. I didn't plan for that to happen. I planned to go back home after I graduated from college. I needed the degree to prove I wasn't wild or irresponsible or any of the dozens of other things they accused me of being, but maybe I can accomplish the same thing with a job. If things go well, I might finally find the courage to give them a call.

I *want* to give them a call. I miss them and the safe, comfortable life they provided.

After I tuck the album into the suitcase, I add my laptop and power cord. Trev and Nalst will be extremely annoyed if they see the tech, but the laptop's battery is completely dead. It shouldn't affect their magic much, certainly not enough to prevent them from fissuring me back to Vegas.

The suitcase zips up with plenty of room to spare. I survey my room again, feeling like I should have more memories to take with me, when my gaze rests on the small, wooden box sitting open on my desk. I hardly ever wear jewelry, so the box doesn't contain much. There's just a thin gold necklace, a beaded stretch bracelet, a few other trinkets and . . .

My breath catches. There, neatly curled at the bottom of the box, is a name-cord. It's a string of onyx and *audrin*, a smoky, quartzlike stone found only in the Realm. Fae used to wear name-cords braided into their hair, but only the most prominent families keep the tradition now. This one belonged to Kyol. He gave it to me with a kiss and an embrace the day the king made him his sword-master. Back then, neither one of us could have predicted he'd one day kill that king.

I should leave it behind. I miss what Kyol and I had together, but I chose to leave him. I chose to take a chance on somebody who risked everything to be with me. Honestly, though, I miss Aren, too.

Something flutters through my stomach. It's hard to tell if the feeling is worry or want. It's been almost a week since I last saw Aren. He was alive then, but it only takes a moment to die, and he and Kyol and all of the fae supporting the rebellion haven't had a moment's rest since taking the Silver Palace. Somebody's organizing what's left of the king's fae—the remnants, we've been calling them—and if we don't find out who it is soon, they're going to overtake us.

I pick up the name-cord. I've never seen Kyol wear it, but it's a family heirloom. The least I can do is give it back to him.

I slip it into my pocket, then grab my suitcase and roll it into the living room.

"I'm ready," I tell the fae.

Trev is fidgeting with a piece of *jaedric* that's peeling up from his armor. The bark is pulled off *jaedra* trees in long strips, then applied in layers to a molding. The former Court fae's armor is always a dark, even brown, well oiled and with a thirteen-branched *abira* tree etched into the cuirasses, front and back. In comparison, the rebels' are discolored, unadorned, and overall, pretty shoddy-looking. They're functional, though, which is most important.

Trev lets go of the *jaedric* snag and nods. A chaos luster strikes at an angle across his nose, and a muscle in his cheek twitches, making the sharp angles of his face stand out even more. Fae don't feel the lightning unless they're touching a human, but I'm sure he saw the blue flash. His hand tightens just perceptibly on the hilt of his sheathed sword, and his eyes narrow enough to give him shallow wrinkles at the outer corners. Trev looks like he's in his midtwenties, but the

Realm ages people slower than Earth does, so it's difficult to guess exactly how old fae are. Those tiny wrinkles on an otherwise smooth face are a giveaway to me, though, and I'd bet he's at least fifty.

He heads for the door. I follow but stop when I see the stack of mail on my kitchen table. The top letter is from my college. I can't resist the temptation to open it even though I'm sure I don't want to read what it says. I make it to the line, "We regret to inform you," before I stop and frown.

The frown isn't because I've flunked out of school. The rebels found me when I was taking my very last final exam, and back then, I thought they were the bad guys. I ran out of my English Lit class—a class I had already failed twice—because I couldn't let them kill or capture me, so I'm not at all surprised I've been expelled. I'm surprised because I don't know how this letter—how any of these letters—got here. No one has a key to my mailbox and apartment except Paige, my only human friend. She puts up with my frequent absences and weird behavior. When I worked for the king, I often didn't show up when we agreed to meet somewhere, and more than once, I left in the middle of a conversation. I had to make up all sorts of crazy excuses for my actions, but Paige always shrugged her shoulders or gave me a look that contained just a hint of doubt . . . and then, she let it go.

This time, though, I think I've flaked out too much even for her. I've been calling Paige every other day for over a week to apologize for disappearing at her sister's wedding, but she hasn't answered the phone. If she's that pissed, I can't see her coming over here to check on my place.

But she must have. I spread out the mail, searching for a note or letter from her. There's nothing, and I'm about to go to my phone and call her yet again when I see the purse resting on a halfway-pulled-out chair. When I pick it up, a tingle runs up my arm.

"McKenzie?" Trev calls.

Goose bumps sprout over my skin. This is Paige's purse and . . .

And oh, crap!

"I broke a ward." I drop the purse as if I've been burned.

That tingling sensation was more than regular goose bumps; it was a magical trip wire that will signal the fae who created it.

I spin away from the kitchen table and sprint for the front door. I don't have to explain anything more to Trev and Nalst. They know as well as I do that a remnant must have created that ward.

"Go," Trev orders. Nalst nods, and a strip of vertical white light rips through the air beside him. He steps into it, disappears.

With effort, I wrench my gaze away from the shadows the fissure leaves behind. Only shadow-readers like me can see the rippling afterimages, but this time I don't need to draw out their twists and turns to know where Nalst has gone. Even though the remnants shouldn't know where I live, we made a contingency plan. He'll bring back help from the Realm.

But we're not going to stand around here waiting for it.

Trev draws his sword as I yank open the door. I rush out first, turn right, and run across the cement breezeway to the staircase.

My apartment's on the third floor. Ignoring my racing heartbeat, I focus on the steps as I fly down them two at a time. Trev stays with me, keeping pace despite the fact that he can move twice as fast or simply fissure to the parking lot below. I make it all the way down without any remnants appearing. Maybe they're becoming disorganized, and no one's prepared to fissure here. Maybe the fae who created the ward is dead. Maybe they—

Slashes of light rip through the air to my left. I curse, round the corner of the building . . .

And plow into a man. Even though he's a good foot taller than me and extremely overweight, I have enough momentum to make him stagger into one of the cars parked outside my building. He's human. The three beings appearing around us are not.

"McKenzie," the man says. I almost don't hear him because the two nearest fae lunge at Trev. He deflects the first remnant's sword with his own, then fissures out of the way of the second's attack.

Another fae, a woman, watches me and the human, who I finally recognize as the apartment manager when I notice his clipboard. He's the only thing keeping her from killing or capturing me. I don't know how long that will last, though. The king's fae used to go out of their way to remain undetected by normal humans, but less than a month ago, they launched an attack in the middle of a neighborhood near Vancouver without any regard for human lives or property. She might decide I'm worth the collateral damage.

Collateral damage. Is that what Paige has become?

"Your rent's late again," the manager says, oblivious to the woman stepping around him with her sword raised. Without the Sight, he can't see the fae unless they choose to be seen.

"Where's Paige?"

My demand makes the fae hesitate. She looks at the manager when he follows my line of sight. While he's distracted, searching the parking lot for something he can't hear or see, I grab his clipboard, turn, and throw it at the head of the shorter fae attacking Trev.

My aim is perfect, and Trev is good enough with a sword to take advantage of the distraction, finding the weak area on the side of the remnant's cuirass and plunging his blade between his enemy's ribs. The remnant cries out, then disappears into a fissure. Whether he survives that injury or not, I don't know.

"You're copping an attitude?" The manager grabs my arm. "I've already let you slide three times this year."

"Sorry," I say, watching the fae behind him. When it's clear she's moving toward us, I use the manager's grip on my arm to try to pull him away. "We need to go."

"You need to pay your rent."

The fae lifts her sword.

"Move!" I yell, this time throwing my shoulder into him in an attempt to shove him out of the way.

"I'm calling the cops—"

The fae slams the hilt of her sword into the side of his head. He drops, pulling me down with him. His hand goes limp when he lands, though. I'm off-balance, but I'm free.

I scramble back as the fae approaches. A quick glance over my shoulder shows that Trev is still occupied with the taller remnant. I'm unarmed. If they wanted me dead, I'd be thoroughly screwed. The fact that I'm still alive means I might have a chance—and I think I might be able to buy some time. She knocked out the manager—I *hate* that he was caught up in this—so there's a good possibility she doesn't want to draw the attention of normal humans.

Before she reaches me, I slam my heel into the nearest car. Its alarm blares a second later. It's loud—loud enough to startle me even though I'm expecting it—and it stops the fae in her tracks. She shuffles back, staring at the car as if it's about to attack.

I throw myself over the hood, scramble off the other side, then sprint deeper into the parking lot before she realizes the alarm isn't a huge amount of tech—it's not going to screw with her magic. I'm near the apartment building on the opposite side of the lot when my skin tingles.

A fissure opens to my left. Trev. He steps to my side just as two more bright slashes of light rip through the atmosphere, one in front of us, one behind. The remaining male remnant stalks forward, bloody sword raised. I glance behind us and see the woman, who's trying to gauge if she can get to me without Trev interfering.

I look at Trev, see blood gushing from the gap between the lower part of his cuirass and the *jaedric* armor protecting his right thigh. Shit.

"Get out of here," I tell him. He'll bleed to death if he doesn't get the help of a fae healer soon.

He shakes his head and takes an unsteady step forward, putting himself between me and the approaching remnant. For one brief moment, I consider letting them take me. Trev could fissure out, and it would be the quickest and easiest way to get to Paige. But then, I have no way of knowing if she's alive.

My throat tightens, but I force my worry for my friend down as I face the woman. When she raises her sword, I say, "There's tech trained on this parking lot. It's recording everything. Drag me out of here, and the whole world will see." My words might be true. I'm sure a few security cameras are trained on the parking lot, but I have no clue where they are or how many.

"They'll see only you," she says.

Yeah, me being hauled across the parking lot kicking and screaming. People would most likely write me off as crazy rather then guess that fae exist, but she doesn't need to know that, so I start to point out how suspicious that would look when half a dozen fissures erupt around us.

Rebels. Nalst has fissured back with more fae wearing shoddy *jaedric* armor. The woman recognizes whose side they're on the same instant I do. She opens her own fissure and disappears before Nalst, the nearest rebel, can attack. The remnant fighting Trev isn't as lucky. He opens a fissure, but isn't able to leap through it before Trev kills him.

"The shadows," Trev says, his voice strained. "Read them."

Since the dead fae disappeared into the ether—into the fae afterlife—and not into a fissure, those misty white soul-shadows tell me nothing, but the shadows from the woman's fissure are weaving themselves into a pattern. I focus on them, my fingers itching to draw a row of . . . houses? Storefronts? Without actually sketching the shadows, I can't be sure what they are or where she went. They don't really become concrete unless I draw them out. All I know is she's gone to the Realm. Possibly someplace in the north.

"I need a . . ." My sketchbook. It's in the suitcase left behind in my living room, but even if it was safe to go back for it, the shadows wouldn't remain in my memory long enough to map them.

"There's no time," Nalst says, stepping to my side. "The remnants will return with reinforcements." To Trev, he says in Fae, *"Go."*

Trev nods, then fissures out as the rebels Nalst brought with him take up positions around me. I don't recognize anyone else, but that's not surprising. A month ago, I was the rebels' prisoner. They didn't exactly make a lot of introductions.

"The nearest gate's ten minutes from here," I tell Nalst. A gate is the only way I can enter a fissure with a fae and survive. They're places in the atmosphere, always over water, where fae can enter the In-Between while escorting a human, or anything else they can't wear or hold themselves. The magic of how to make more is lost, so we've always had to work with the ones that already exist.

It would take me twenty minutes to get there if I walked, but I head to the north side of my apartment complex at a run. If a fae doesn't have an anchor-stone imprinted with a location, or if they haven't been to a place before, they can only fissure within their line of sight. My apartment is still within view. I need to get the hell out of this parking lot before a new wave of remnants arrives.

I'm just a few strides away from the walkway between the buildings when I sense the fissures. A second later, just as I'm darting into the narrow space, I hear them opening. I have no clue if they've seen me, but I'm certain they've seen the rebels, so I force my legs to move faster, stretch farther.

I reach the back of the building, sharp *shrrips* and flashes of light erupting behind me.

"Get to the gate!" Nalst orders. A tall, thick hedge lines the back of the property, so I have to cut to the right. The hedge is to my left as I run. The rebels hold their position at the junction of the back alley and the gap between the buildings—that's where the remnants have to be to get a glimpse of me. If they make it there, they'll be able to re-appear at my side.

I'm at a full sprint, passing another gap between buildings, when a strip of white light splits the atmosphere directly in front of me. Not only does it cut off my escape route, it's so close, I nearly run into it. I lose my balance evading it, but I'm not able to avoid the fae stepping into this world.

My fist rises instinctively, aiming for the fae's face, until I recognize Aren. Even though my heart thuds at the sight of his silver eyes and wild, disheveled hair, I'm tempted to keep swinging. His fissure could have killed me.

He grabs my fist in the air, then uses his body to maneuver me out of the back alley and into the narrow space between the buildings.

"You're missing something, *nalkin-shom*," he says before I can yell at him for opening his fissure so close to me.

Missing something? "My suitcase? That's hardly import—"

He ushers me farther down the walkway. "I gave you a weapon."

I scowl at him over my shoulder. The sun is directly overhead, so even though we're hiding between two tall apartment buildings, his light brown hair is streaked with gold. It doesn't quite touch his shoulders, which are protected by *jaedric* armor, but it's long enough that, if we had more time, I wouldn't be able to stop myself from touching the slightly curled ends.

"You gave me a sword, Aren. Where am I supposed to hide that?" He can run around this world all he wants with his sword waving about, but I can't. Not even the strongest fae illusionist can make a human invisible.

"Then you should have asked for a dagger," he says, coming to a stop just before we reach the front edge of the apartment building.

"My apartment was supposed to be safe."

"Shh." He puts a finger to my lips as he presses me against the side of the brick building and, of course, that's when the *edarratae*, the chaos lusters, decide to react. The blue lightning leaps from his fingertip to my lips. I suck in a breath. It's an involuntary reaction to the hot, addictive sensation traveling down my neck. It sinks into my core, making my stomach tighten, and even though I try to hide how much the sensation affects me, Aren sees it.

The tiniest smile pulls at one side of his mouth. A month ago, that smile would have infuriated me. Now? Now, I recognize the spark in his silver eyes. He doesn't just want me because I'm an asset that can help the rebels keep the Silver Palace; he wants me because he's fallen in love with me.

He's fallen in love with me in less than two months. It's insane considering we were enemies for the majority of that time.

He takes hold of my hand, keeping me in place while he cautiously peers around the edge of the building.

"The closest gate is back in the other direction," I whisper.

"The remnants know that, too," he says. Then, he loops

his arm around my waist and inches me forward. "See anything?"

Only a human with the Sight can see fae who are hidden by illusion, so I scan the parking lot, searching for anyone Aren can't see. A car is slowly driving around, probably looking for a specific apartment—the numbers on the sides of the buildings are tiny—but that's to our advantage since the remnants apparently don't want to cause a scene. As long as Aren remains invisible to normal humans, the driver shouldn't take notice of anything unusual.

"It's clear," I say. I check over my shoulder to make sure no remnants are in sight. I can hear them fighting somewhere in the back alley, but the rebels must be doing their job, keeping the former king's fae engaged long enough for me to escape.

Aren unhooks a sheathed dagger from his belt. Then, meeting my gaze, he hands it to me and says, "Don't go anywhere unarmed again."

No one should be allowed to have eyes like his. You can get lost in them. The silver-gray irises are flecked with light, and they're darker on the outer edges. A fae's eyes darken and lighten with emotion, and right now, Aren's are as determined as steel. He expects me to use the dagger if I'm threatened.

I wrap my hand around the weapon's hilt. I've killed before. It wasn't deliberate—I wanted to ward off the fae attacking me, not slash open his stomach—and I hope I never have to again.

Aren draws his sword, then we step off the narrow walkway. The car cruising the parking lot circles around again. We walk past one row of parked vehicles and are almost to the next when my skin tingles. Fissures, four of them, cut through the air to our left. Aren curses and disappears into his own slash of light just as an arrow whistles through the air. It vanishes when it hits his fissure, and before I have time to duck or run or come up with another plan, Aren reappears on my other side.

He lunges behind me. The sound of swords clashing rings in my ears. A cry tells me Aren's killed or injured a remnant, but I remain facing the pair in front of me. They press forward.

I draw my dagger out of its sheath. It looks tiny compared to the fae's swords, but it's all I have.

The fae on the left disappears. I spin around, knowing he'll reappear behind me, and slash out with my dagger. The remnant is just far enough away to avoid my attack. He grabs my arm before I can bring my weapon around for a second swing.

I gasp when he digs his fingers in between the tendons on my wrist, trying to force me to drop the dagger. I hold on to it, try to pivot its point toward him, but he's ten times stronger than I am, and his grip *hurts*.

He brings his sword up, issues a threat in Fae.

In my peripheral vision, I see Aren charge forward. The remnant notices him, too, but not soon enough. Aren rams into us, sending both me and the remnant stumbling across the parking lot.

Across the parking lot and into the path of the approaching car.

I swear to God the driver speeds up. It hits hard, sending me and the fae onto the hood. Pain shoots through my thigh, then through my ribs and right arm, as the sky spins.

It's still spinning when the driver slams on the brakes. I'm suddenly sprawled on the asphalt in front of the car. I try to push myself up to my hands and knees, but before I reach my feet, Aren's there, yanking me up. He jerks open the vehicle's door and shoves me into the passenger seat. I tumble awkwardly inside, look up in time to see a remnant fissure in behind Aren just after he slams my door shut.

"Watch out!" I shout, but the remnant's sword is already swinging.

TWO

•-◆-•

THE SWORD CRASHES into the car, shattering my window and cleaving into the doorframe. I cover my face with my arms, shielding my eyes from the flying glass.

"Hold on!" someone says from the driver's seat as the car's tires squeal.

I look at Shane, the human who's driving, as he spins the wheel, throwing me against the damaged passenger door. The car makes a wild left turn out of the parking lot and onto the road.

I grab the oh-shit handle above the door, my heart pounding. "Did he fissure out?"

Shane nods, straightening the wheel. "Just after he ducked. Crazy bastard dove headfirst into the light."

The wind whips into my side of the car, throwing tiny shards of glass at me and tangling my hair. I brush it back with my fingers and hold it in a ponytail while I try to slow my breathing.

"Here," Shane says, taking a pink scrunchie off the gear-shift and handing it to me.

I stare at it a second, then glare at him. "You stole this car."

"You want to hold your hair the whole way to the gate, or do you want to use this?" he asks, not a hint of regret in his voice. I guess that shouldn't surprise me. He doesn't have a problem accepting the money the fae give us—money that's stolen from U.S. banks—to pay his bills, so why should he care about stealing a car?

I take the scrunchie.

"It was Aren's idea," Shane says, resting his right hand on the gearshift. His shirtsleeves are pushed up, so the long, wrinkled white scar on his forearm is visible. It's worse than any of the scars I have. He won't talk about how he got it, but I'm sure a fae had something to do with it.

"You should be thanking me."

I lift my gaze from his arm to give him a skeptical look. "Thanking you? You hit me with a car."

"I saved your life," he points out.

I roll my eyes but don't argue. I don't know Shane well despite being roommates these past two weeks. He's not a shadow-reader like me, but he worked for King Atroth, too, using his Sight to see through fae illusions. I first met him just a few weeks ago, right after the rebels traded me to the Court for one of their own. I spent one restless night in his mansion before I returned to the Realm and had my world turned upside down. That's when I stopped being the rebels' prisoner and started to have serious doubts about working for the king.

"Did you come from the palace?" I ask Shane. He wasn't home when I left our Vegas suite. For him to get here as quickly as he did, he must have been with the rebels.

"Yeah," he says, slowing down. "I talked to Lena."

Lena, daughter of Zarrak. She's in charge of the rebellion and claimed the silver throne after King Atroth was killed. We both wanted to see the other dead not so long ago, but now, I'm desperate to keep her alive. She's the best hope I have for ending this war with my friends still breathing.

Sometimes, I still can't believe Lena and I are working together.

"You finally agreed to help us?" I ask.

Shane shrugs as he accelerates. "I was getting bored."

I manage to keep my mouth shut. Barely. If excitement is the only reason he's joining the rebellion, nothing will stop him from switching allegiances if the situation in the Silver Palace gets even uglier than it is now. I'm sure the remnants wouldn't hesitate to take him back. The rest of the humans who worked for the king are already helping them. Lena and the rebels didn't move quickly enough tracking them down. The only reason we got Shane is because he was at the palace when we invaded. Afterward, Lena set him up in the suite with me because she thought I might be a good influence on him, like my choice of allegiance would spread to him like a cold or something.

He turns onto a feeder road, and I try to relax. I'm out of danger for now. My heart rate should be slowing down, but it's not, and I think I know why. With the whole fleeing-for-my-life thing, I've been able to ignore the worry gnawing at my stomach. I can't ignore it any longer. The remnants have Paige.

Paige's purse was warded. The rebels checked out my place before Trev and Nalst fissured me there. If the remnants had placed a ward in the typical places—on a door or in a hallway—Trev or Nalst would have found it, but they didn't go around digging through my drawers or picking up every object in my apartment. They had no reason to touch Paige's purse. Placing the ward there was a cunning move on the remnants' part.

I tuck a strand of hair that escaped from my ponytail behind my ear as I stare out my broken window. We're passing the turnoff for my college. My *former* college now that I've been kicked out. God, I still want that degree. I want a normal job and a life where I don't have to worry about someone killing me or the people I care about.

I pinch the skin between my eyes, trying to release some of the pressure building behind them. Is there any possible way I could be wrong about Paige? Few people from the king's Court knew my name or where I lived on Earth. The remnants shouldn't know a thing about Paige. Maybe she left her purse at my place, and the fae thought it was mine?

"Don't get on the highway," I say suddenly, grabbing the steering wheel to keep Shane from veering toward the on-ramp.

"Hey!" He swipes my hand away but stays on the access road. "We're meeting Aren at the gate north of the city."

"We're going to my friend's house first. It'll only take a minute." I have to be certain Paige is really gone.

I'm kind of surprised when he doesn't argue. We might be on the outskirts of Houston, but traffic is horrendous. It's impossible to get through a single intersection in one minute. He follows my directions, though, and half an hour later we pull up in front of a town house that's in the middle of a row of attached homes that all have the same white shutters, small balconies, and miniscule front porches. The only thing different is the color of the front doors. Paige's is pink. I tell Shane to wait in the car as I climb out of the passenger seat.

It takes a few steps before my muscles loosen up. They're sore from the fight at my apartment, and my right leg throbs under my jeans when I put weight on it. Nothing's broken, though; I think I just have a deep bruise on my thigh.

A knot of dismay tightens in my stomach when I reach Paige's pink door.

"Please be home," I whisper as I knock. After a few minutes pass with no answer, I step into the flower bed to the right of the porch and peek in through the window. Only a sliver of the living room is visible through a part in the curtains, but the little that I see doesn't look good. Broken glass and something blue are scattered across the floor. It takes me a second to realize the latter are hundreds of tiny blue pebbles, the remains of Paige's fishbowl, I think. She has a betta named Phil or Max or Johnny or something. She has trouble keeping them alive, so I can never keep track.

"Is your friend not home?" Shane asks from the porch, not from the car where I told him to wait.

"The remnants took her," I say.

Shane frowns. "Come again?"

I step out of the flower bed, feeling sick. Since the fae don't belong in this world, they're able to turn their visibility on and off with a thought. Only humans who have the Sight are able to see them all the time; the rest of the world has no idea they exist. Paige won't have any idea. I don't know how she'd react if she was grabbed by invisible fae. She might think she's caught in a nightmare or that she's lost her mind or that she's possessed or something. But maybe the remnants will let her see them. Maybe they'll explain who they are and what's happening.

Or maybe they'll just kill her.

No, I tell myself, pushing that thought aside. She's more valuable alive. Alive, they can negotiate a trade.

"Her purse was at my apartment," I tell Shane, trying the doorknob. It doesn't turn, of course. "I broke a ward when I picked it up. That's why the remnants came."

"Hmm," he says. He presses his lips together, but there's no worry or sympathy in his expression. I clench my teeth to keep from saying anything. When I first met him, I had the impression he was a bit egocentric. He's living up to that assessment.

Stepping away from the door, I scan up and down the street. An occasional car passes by, but no one is outside. I can probably time a break-in so that I don't get caught.

I pick up one of the rocks lining the flower bed.

"You know," Shane says, "if the remnants do have your friend, it's highly possible they know where she lives."

"You're worried about them showing up?" I heft the rock in my hand. "Why? You can just switch allegiances. I'm sure they'd pay you whatever you ask."

"Ouch," he says, sounding genuinely insulted.

I hurt his feelings? Whatever. He's only involved in this war because he gets paid. This shouldn't be about money. Our actions have consequences. I didn't realize just how dire those consequences were until a month ago. Back when I worked for the king, I thought the Court captured most of the fae I tracked. They didn't. It was easier to kill them than to put forth the effort to take them as prisoners. If I'd known how much blood was being shed because of my shadow-reading, I wouldn't have become so deeply involved in the king's wars. I've caused more pain than I can stand thinking about.

Before my thoughts darken further, I search the street again. It's a weekday. Most people will probably be at work, but I make sure I check the windows of the nearest homes. It's hard to see through the sun's glare on the glass.

"Here." Shane grabs the rock from my hand. "You keep standing around, and eventually someone's going to notice." He launches the rock through Paige's window.

"And, yes," he continues. "I took a while to make up my mind, but that doesn't mean I don't give a shit." He grabs the curtain from inside the town house, yanks it off its hanger, then uses it to knock out the rest of the glass and clear off the windowsill. "I'll open the door."

He climbs inside, and, of course, I feel guilty now. It wasn't easy for me to change allegiances; why should it be easy for him? Still, I don't apologize when he opens the door. If he really does give a shit, he should act like it more often.

As soon as I enter Paige's apartment, it's obvious there was a struggle here. In addition to the shattered fishbowl, the narrow table behind Paige's couch is on its side, and it looks like someone tried to throw a floor lamp across the room. It's still plugged in, but the lampshade is crushed. I step over it and head to her bedroom. She fought there, too, launching her jewelry box at her attacker. Its contents are scattered through the doorway and into the hall, where shards of glass litter the floor. Paige put up one hell of a fight.

She shouldn't have had to put up a fight. She wouldn't have had to if she wasn't connected to me.

"Are you sure the remnants took her?" Shane calls from the front of the town house. I turn away from the bedroom and head back his way.

"I wish I wasn't, but yeah. Why?"

He's standing at the kitchen counter staring into a large, yellow mixing bowl. "There's a fish in this."

I frown, walk to his side, then peer down at a bright blue and very much alive betta.

"If the remnants kidnapped her," Shane says, "it seems odd that they'd stick around to take care of her fish."

"Maybe one of them really likes fish?" I say, even though he has a point. It doesn't make sense at all.

I scan the living room and kitchen. Looking for what, I don't know—evidence, I guess—but there's nothing here except the overturned furniture and shattered fishbowl. Maybe I should have searched Paige's purse before dropping it on the floor of my apartment. The remnants could have left a ransom note in it.

"We should go," Shane says. He's found a little container of fish food and taps some into the mixing bowl. "Aren's waiting."

I don't say anything; I just keep staring at Paige's apartment.

He sets the container down and looks at me.

"The rebels will help you find her," he says gently, as if he's trying to reassure me.

They *might* help me find her. The last two weeks have been rough, though. We won control of the palace, and Lena has claimed the throne, but convincing the high nobles—the fae who run the Realm's thirteen provinces—that her bloodline is pure enough to become their queen isn't going so well. Not only that, but the high nobles are hesitant to break tradition and allow a woman to sit on the silver throne. They're postponing a vote on the matter, probably hoping a better option will step forward.

The headache I had on the way here doubles in strength as I head for the door. The delay on the vote wouldn't be such a big deal if the remnants weren't taking advantage of the uncertainty. They're launching attacks on the silver walls surrounding the palace almost daily, and we're fairly certain they're encouraging the protests and near riots that are occurring throughout the Realm. If we could just figure out who's organizing them, arrest or kill or make a deal with him or her, then maybe Lena and the rebels could have a break. They need a break. We all do.

FOR a people who tend to live a century and a half, the fae are incredibly impatient. It's one of the side effects of being able to fissure from city to city or even world to world in a few seconds' time. The drive from my apartment to the outskirts of the city would have taken about twenty minutes without our detour. With the detour, it's been close to an hour.

Aren whips open my door before the car completely stops. He isn't as afraid of human tech as most of the fae are, but

I'm still surprised he didn't wait the few seconds it would have taken for me to open it myself. *Edarratae* protest the contact by flashing up his forearm. They keep flashing when he takes hold of my elbow. His eyes scan me head to toe, looking for injuries, I'm sure, and when he doesn't see any— at least, he doesn't see any that are serious—he visibly relaxes.

"Did my directions send you in circles?" he asks, looking past me to Shane, who's turning off the engine.

"No, they were surprisingly good for a fae." He opens his door and gets out.

I swivel in the seat to face Aren. "The remnants have Paige."

He's down on one knee, so his silver eyes are level with mine. "Who?"

"Paige," I say. "My friend. You met her at the wedding."

"The wedding?" His gaze dips to my mouth, and I can almost taste him. That was the first time we kissed. I was still in love with Kyol, but my emotions were a chaotic mess. Aren was making me doubt everything—even how much I hated him—and before he turned me over to Kyol, he left me with a diamond necklace imprinted with a location. I could have betrayed him with that necklace. I didn't. I didn't because I was beginning to fall in love with him.

And I'm still falling.

I clear my throat. "I have to find her, Aren. She doesn't belong in this war."

"You're sure they have her?" he asks, refocusing on my eyes.

"The ward was on her purse."

His jaw clenches, and I almost wish I hadn't said anything. His role in this war is changing. Before the rebels took the palace, he was always on the offensive. He's used to launching brief surprise attacks on the king's fae, on supply depots, and on the gates that are required to fissure anything more than what a fae can carry. Now, Aren's trying to keep the remnants from doing the exact same things he did. With as few swordsmen as he has at his disposal, he's doing a good job, but I don't want to add to his responsibilities.

"She doesn't know anything about us?" he asks.

"No," I say. Few humans do unless they have the Sight. Keeping their existence secret has been a law in the Realm for centuries. If humans ever learn about the fae, there's no doubt war would break out. Not all humans would be content to leave the fae alone. Some would want to kill them. Others would want to capture them. They'd want to find a way to enslave them for their magics. King Atroth enforced the secrecy law just as strictly as the previous kings, and whenever the fae decide to approach a human who can see them, they do so with caution.

Most do so with caution. My introduction to their world was anything but gentle. A fae named Thrain abducted me. He starved and threatened me, demanding that I use my Sight to point out fae hidden by illusion. I did so once, the first day I was in his custody, and he slaughtered that fae right there in front of me.

Aren draws in a breath. When he releases it, it's like all his responsibilities fall away. I know they're still there, still weighing on his mind, but he hides them behind a haphazard smile and confident attitude.

"We'll find her," he says, pulling me out of the car. His confidence is contagious to other fae—I think that's half the reason the rebels were able to win the palace—but I'm human, and I stopped believing in miracles years ago. Paige could be anywhere in the Realm or on Earth. The chance that we'll just stumble across her is virtually nonexistent.

"Hey," Aren says, tilting my chin up with a finger. "I found you, didn't I?"

The half smile on his lips is cocky but reassuring. It's sexy as hell, too, and despite all my worries, my stomach flips. I'm trying so damn hard to be smart about this. I'm trying to take things slowly, to carefully wade into this relationship because, God knows, we didn't meet under the best circumstances. I don't want Aren to be a fling or a rebound, but I tend to forget caution when he looks at me like this, like I'm the only thing that exists in this world.

A chaos luster leaps to my skin, traveling along my

jawline until it reaches the nape of my neck. Whether he leans in toward me or I lean toward him, I don't know, but our lips touch then—

"Aren."

It's not Shane who speaks. I peer around Aren's shoulder and see a fae—an illusionist named Brenth—stepping through the thin tree line that separates the road from an empty field. He's one of Kyol's swordsmen, a former Court fae who's sworn to protect Lena. His armor isn't shoddy like the rebels'. It has a smooth, even texture and an *abira* tree etched into its surface, but he's added four branches to it, one for each of the provinces Lena plans to reinstate.

"Perfect timing," Shane mutters, just before Brenth says in Fae, *"We were out of time ten minutes ago."*

"It will be fine," Aren tells the latter.

I'm already following Shane to the tree line because I need to walk off the tingling sensation that's swept across my body. I'm hoping the heat I'm feeling doesn't reach my face or, if it does, the others think it's a result of the bright Texas sun overhead.

"So anxious to get away from me?" Aren asks, a note of amusement in his tone as he falls into step beside me. He knows exactly why I needed to move.

"Call it a habit," I retort, but I let the smallest of smiles bend a corner of my mouth when I slant a glance his way. I spent the first few weeks I knew him trying to escape. I was almost successful a number of times, but he just wouldn't let me slip away.

He chuckles. "I promise not to make you wear a blindfold this time."

A blindfold? We step through the tree line and into the field on the other side, but I don't recognize this place until I spot the small pond off to my right. This is where he brought me after he abducted me from my campus. I had no idea— and, more importantly, the Court fae had no idea—that this gate was here, and I thought . . .

I turn to Aren. "I thought this place was hours away from my apartment."

He lifts an eyebrow.

"When you kidnapped me," I say, "it took at least three hours to get here."

"Ah." His gaze goes to my left temple. That's where he hit me with the pommel of his dagger less than two months ago, knocking me out so I couldn't call the police. "We had some difficulties getting you off campus without any humans seeing you."

I snort. Yeah, that would have looked odd, me being carried over the shoulder of an invisible man. With the cops searching the building and Kyol still looking for me, it couldn't have been easy getting me away from there.

We reach the pond just after Shane and Brenth. The gate is just a blur in the atmosphere to the fae's left. Brenth turns to it, then scoops up a handful of water. The water is necessary to connect with the gate, and the fissure opens gradually, the stream of water turning into a stream of white light as it pours between his fingers. A second later, a deep rumble signals the connection to the In-Between. He hands an anchor-stone to Shane, then Shane grips the fae's forearm, and they disappear into the light.

It takes an effort to wrench my gaze away from the shadows the fissure leaves behind, but Aren takes my hand and leads me to the blur at the edge of the pond. He presses an anchor-stone into my palm. He can fissure to locations he's memorized without it, but if I want to go along with him, I need it. Otherwise, I'd become lost in the In-Between.

Aren reaches into the pond, opening his own gated-fissure. Before he pulls me into it, his hand tightens around mine, and he says, "I've missed you, McKenzie."

Then he finishes the kiss Brenth interrupted.

THREE

•◆•

I'M BREATHLESS WHEN we step out of the fissure. That's probably the In-Between's fault, but I'm blaming Aren. He kissed me until his chaos lusters slid into my skin, making me forget everything but him. Then, just when the lightning built to a level where I swear I was seconds away from losing control, he pulled me into the In-Between.

The *icy* In-Between.

Going from hot to cold like that was both divine and torturous.

As soon as I'm able to stand without swaying, I glare at him. He gives me a maddening grin in return.

My hand is still in his, the anchor-stone still pressed between our palms. The lightning darting between our clasped fingers is white in this world, not blue, and it originates from me. Even so, it's as hot and tantalizing as his is on Earth.

I slip my hand free before the lightning builds further—it's already difficult enough not to press my lips to his again—then scan the cobblestoned area outside Corrist's silver wall. Brenth must have taken Shane back to Vegas because they're not here. No one else is, either, and that makes me uneasy. Two weeks ago, this place was filled with fae haggling and making purchases in the shops to my left.

We call the thirty-foot buffer zone between those shops

and the silver wall a moat even though it's level with the rest of the city and not filled with water. Kyol and the Court fae fissured me to this area hundreds of times over the last ten years, but it's never felt so wrong to stand here. The pale yellow stone of the shops facing the silver wall is usually tinted blue at night, but no one has lit the orbs topping the streetlights, and I'm pretty sure most of the buildings are deserted.

Deserted by the merchants, at least. Remnants have used the abandoned buildings for cover during their attacks. Some of the shops are two or three stories tall, and from down here on the ground, there's no way of knowing if a fae is hiding on a tiled rooftop or behind closed curtains.

"Any later and you would be dead, Jorreb," someone shouts in Fae from the silver wall, using Aren's family name.

"Then my timing is perfect!" Aren shouts back, turning his grin on whoever's watching us from one of the spy holes above the lowered portcullis.

I clench my teeth together. Since the remnants have been launching random attacks on the wall, Lena's issued an order not to wait to identify the fae who step out of opening fissures; the guards on the wall are to shoot immediately except at the "safe" fissure locations. Those locations change every half hour. Lena and Kyol devised a rotating pattern, a code of sorts, that only the people they trust the most know.

"Let us in," Aren says.

We duck under the rising portcullis. It's made of pure silver. The metal doesn't prevent fae from using their magic inside the wall—it only prevents them from fissuring in or out, or around inside the Inner City and the palace. Necessary of course, to keep us safe from attack, but it's a significant handicap given that the fae are so used to being able to appear and disappear at will. Aren looks completely at ease, though, when he crosses to the other side.

Two swordsmen emerge from an opening in the wall. More are on watch inside, I presume. The wall is eight feet wide and hollow between the stone blocks that support the heavy silver plating. Wooden stairs and narrow platforms allow the fae to stand guard inside the wall. I've stood guard inside it recently as well, making sure no one hidden by illusion was attempting to enter the Inner City.

I wrap my arms around myself, trying to hold in what little warmth I have left, while Aren exchanges a few words with the shorter of the two fae swordsmen. The taller fae is carrying a *jaedric* cuirass and a cloak. He hands them both to Aren, who brings them to me. He helps me slide the cuirass on over my head, then tightens the bindings on the sides.

I'm more thankful for the cloak than the armor, and not just because I'm cold. The chaos lusters are bright on my skin. Supposedly, the fae who have remained in the Inner City support Lena or are neutral in this war, but it's not like we've had time to interview every individual to see if that's really true. Without the cloak, the lightning would draw too much attention, so I pull it on over my cuirass and adjust the hood so that my face is hidden beneath it.

"One more thing," Aren says, holding a third item I didn't see before. He takes the two ends of the long strap in his hands, then buckles them around my waist, under the cloak. "Think you can keep up with this one?"

I reach behind my back, feel the hard *jaedric* casing that, I'm assuming, holds a dagger. It's about the length of my hand and sheathed so that the weapon is almost parallel with the ground.

I can grab the dagger's hilt with my right hand relatively easily.

"Don't trust me with a sword?" I tease.

"They didn't have a spare," he returns, a small smile playing across his lips. And that's all it takes, that slight curve of his mouth, to make warm, tingling happiness flare through me. I've missed our playful disagreements.

We don't take a direct route to the palace. Instead, one of the swordsmen leads us to a narrow passageway between the buildings to the west of the *Cavith e'Sidhe*, the Avenue of the Descendants. Aren stays at my side, his gait more a saunter than a walk. If his hand wasn't casually resting on the hilt of his sword, I'd say he wasn't worried at all about a possible attack. But the hand *is* there, and his head is cocked slightly to the side as if he's listening for an extra set of footfalls or the soft scrape of a blade sliding free of a scabbard.

My stomach tightens with unease. My hearing isn't nearly as good as a fae's, but I'm listening and watching for an attack, too.

Moss and red-flowered plants grow out of cracks in the stone walls on both sides of us. On Earth, that would be a sign that this part of the city isn't well taken care of, but here in the Realm, it adds a certain beauty and exoticness to the twisting passageway.

The Inner City is where the wealthiest fae live and where the high nobles have their secondary residences away from their provincial estates. We reach one of those residences soon. Kyol pointed it out to me once before, saying it belonged to Lord Kaeth, elder of Ravir and the high noble of Beshryn Province, one of the fae we have to convince to support Lena. The gardens surrounding his home are still green despite it being late fall here.

We turn right at the edge of a meticulously trimmed hedge, then left when we reach the Avenue of the Descendants. Blue light from the magic-lit lampposts makes it easy to see the cobblestones beneath our feet. They're level except for the parallel indentions where *cirikith*-drawn carts have weathered away the stone. None of the beasts, which look like a thin version of a stegosaurus with horselike hooves and haunches, are out now. When the sun goes down, they fall into a minihibernation. It takes a hell of a lot of effort to keep them awake through that, and even if you do, the *cirikiths* move so sluggishly it's hardly worth the effort.

Despite how well this is going so far, goose bumps break out on my arms, and the nape of my neck tingles. Out here on the avenue, there are plenty of places for the remnants to hide.

"Relax," Aren says beside me. "They'll come after me before they do you."

I pull my cloak more tightly around me. "That's supposed to be comforting?"

"It would have been a few weeks ago." My hood is too far forward for me to see him, but I can imagine the amusement in his eyes. That's just like him, shrugging off the fact that people want to kill him, but I hate that he's a target. I might be trying to take our relationship slow, but losing him would devastate me.

The avenue curves to the left, and now I have goose bumps for a completely different reason. It doesn't matter how many times I've walked up this road, the view at its end is still staggering.

The Silver Palace is more like Neushweinstein Castle than an impenetrable fortress. It's impractical for defensive purposes, but aesthetically? Aesthetically, it's freaking beautiful. Six blackwood turrets, all lit by the fae's magic, rise into the night sky. The palace is built against the base of the Corrist Mountains, so the silver-edged spires in the back reach higher than those in the front. The *Sidhe Cabred*, the Ancestors' Garden that only a few privileged fae were allowed to enter under King Atroth's rule, climbs up the steep cliffs marking the mountains' southern edge.

We reach the end of the avenue and step onto the huge, tiled promenade in front of the castle's main gate. The palace has three entrances, but this one is the most impressive. The slate blue stone that makes up its walls is imported from a province in the southeast, so the lighter color stands out dramatically against the deep red-brown of the mountain behind it.

We don't enter through the carved blackwood gate—it's gargantuan and takes forever to open and close—we enter through a nondescript door to its left, and I relax a little. The palace is filled with fae loyal to Lena. Only a few watch from their posts in this chamber, but somewhere above us, archers stand guard, ready to kill and raise an alarm if the remnants attempt another attack.

I pull my hood back. As soon as I do, I see two fae heading our way. One is a rebel swordsman whose skin, despite the chilly air, glistens with sweat. The other is the impeccably dressed assistant to Lord Kaeth, the high noble whose home we passed. Their accents are thick and, when they reach us, they both start speaking at once. I can't decipher what they say. I began learning their language only a little more than a month ago, and while I'm picking it up quickly,

I struggle when fae speak too quickly or if I'm distracted by other things.

Aren holds up a hand. *"Not now."*

The swordsman swallows his words, then respectfully bows his head before he retreats.

The assistant isn't as easily dismissed. *"Shall I tell Lord Kaeth you're with the human?"*

That, I do understand, but there must be more meaning in the words or the fae's tone because Aren stiffens.

"You can tell Lord Kaeth I'm with the queen." His response is way too calm, but the fae doesn't seem to notice.

"She isn't the queen," he says. Then, with a disdainful glance in my direction, he turns on his heel and walks away.

Aren's eyes don't leave Lord Kaeth's assistant, not until he takes my arm to lead me down a side corridor.

"What was that about?" I ask.

"Nothing," he answers.

"Aren."

He squeezes my hand, keeps walking. "It's nothing, McKenzie."

Which means it's definitely something, and I'm 99.9 percent sure I know what it is. Lena and the rebels might have won control of the palace, but that doesn't mean everyone in the Realm is suddenly okay with our races being together. King Atroth forbade relationships between humans and fae. That was something that always held Kyol back, but it hasn't deterred Aren. He and the rebels are much more accepting of humans than the Court fae ever were. The problem is, the rebels don't make up the majority of the population. Most fae still think humans and human culture damage the Realm's magic.

Aren looks at me. He must see that I've figured it out because he says, "I'm not him. I won't pretend I don't have feelings for you."

Him. Kyol. I spent the last decade pretending I didn't have feelings for him in front of the Court fae. It was a ridiculously long time to stay in love with a guy who put the Realm and his king's wishes before me.

I don't respond to Aren; I just keep pace next to him as we

step into the palace's sculpture garden. It must be late—maybe close to the middle of the night—because only a few fae are gathered here. This is a serene place that reminds me of a movie version of a Roman forum, a beautiful, open space adorned with carved-stone statues and vibrant green plants, where people can meet and talk. Some of the fae watch us with curious expressions as we pass through its center. Their looks say they want us to stop, to answer questions or provide information or gossip, but nobody actually calls out to us.

The huge, gilded doors to the king's hall are shut. Or is it the queen's hall now? Lena's made very few changes these last two weeks. She's waiting until the high nobles confirm her lineage and approve her taking the throne so that her decrees will be considered official. Nobody knows when—or if—that vote will happen, though.

A guard—one of Lena's rebels—opens a smaller door that blends into the larger one's design. I follow Aren in, and we walk side by side down the plush blue carpet. It's only after Aren curses under his breath that I notice no swordsmen or archers are in here. Just Lena. She's sitting with her shoulders slumped on the top step of the silver dais at the end of the hall, not on the silver throne that crowns it. It's a constant battle, trying to get Lena to act like a queen.

She straightens as we approach, but it's a weak attempt to look strong and alert. Her normally perfect, glowing complexion is marred by the dark circles under her eyes, and her long, blond hair doesn't seem as silky as usual. She's wearing a white tunic that fits snug around her slender frame, and something that I can only describe as half of a long skirt is tied around her hips. The lean muscles in her outer left thigh are visible, but her entire right leg is hidden under the skirt's thick layers of blue and white feathers. Lena's father, the elder of Zarrak, was the high noble of Adaris, one of the provinces King Atroth dissolved to gain the throne, so she usually dresses like she's highborn, but this has to be the most ornate and impractical thing I've ever seen her wear.

"No one's in here," she says defensively.

"That's the other problem." Aren stops at the foot of the dais. "There should be. Where are your guards?"

"I sent them to the *veligh*." Her expression is stony, as if she's daring him to question her decision.

Beside me, Aren stiffens. "The remnants?"

"Of course," she says.

Veligh translates into waterfront. Most of the buildings of the Inner City are to the south and west of the palace. To the east, there are no homes or stores, just a sliver of land before you reach the silver wall. The Imyth Sea is on its other side, and because that part of the wall and palace would be so difficult to penetrate, Lena's kept only a minimal guard on watch. Apparently, the remnants decided to take advantage of that.

"Their numbers are growing, not shrinking," Lena says, directing an empty stare at one of the tall, arched windows lining the wall to the left of the throne.

My gut tightens. The remnants haven't met with much success these last two weeks. Sure, they've hurt and killed a good number of us, but we've hurt and killed a good number of them, too. They should be losing support, especially since Lena wants to make changes that will benefit the majority of the Realm. She's promised to do away with Atroth's unpopularly high gate taxes, and there will be no more special exemptions and favors for the fae who kiss noble ass—my words, not Lena's. Fae will no longer have to worry about swordsmen invading their homes on hunches, and they will no longer be required to register their magics. I honestly don't understand why the remnants are willing to kill to keep Lena from the throne.

"Do you think they've found another Descendant?" I ask as I take off my cloak. A Descendant with a traceable bloodline back to the *Tar Sidhe*, the fae who ruled the Realm centuries ago, might have a stronger claim to the throne than Lena. I might—*might*—be able to understand their behavior if that's what has happened.

The palace archivist showed me Lena's heritage after the king was killed. It confirmed that she's a Descendant, and that she and her brother, Sethan, would have been high nobles if their parents weren't murdered and their province dissolved.

Lena turns away from the window, but before she can respond, another voice answers my question.

"If they had a Descendant, they would have told the high nobles by now."

It's Kyol. His voice still affects me, sending a warm, anxious tingle through my body. It's impossible to ignore his presence. Even without turning, I know where he is. It's like the air itself recognizes his authority, and it's difficult to describe what I'm feeling. Kyol is the man I loved for a decade, and what we had together didn't just disappear overnight. I still care deeply for him, but I haven't seen him in two weeks, mostly because I've been avoiding him. Or we've been avoiding each other. The last thing I want to do is hurt him, and I'm worried that seeing me, especially seeing me with Aren, will do just that.

But it will be obvious I'm uncomfortable if I don't acknowledge his presence, so after setting my cloak down on the lowest step of the dais, I finally turn and see him striding toward us. His dark hair lies damp with sweat against his forehead, and there's a smudge of dirt or ash on his left cheek. *Jaedric* covers his shoulders and torso, his forearms, thighs, and calves, and even though it's obvious he's been fighting the remnants, he's almost more presentable than Aren, whose *jaedric* armor is slipshod in comparison. Aren would be the first to receive a new, well-oiled set of armor if he wanted it, but he chooses to wear these patched-together pieces.

Kyol stops a few paces away and gives me a slight nod. It's the way he always acknowledged me in front of Atroth and other Court fae. Detached but respectful.

"We didn't tell the high nobles about Sethan," Aren says. His posture has changed. Before Kyol entered, he was annoyed at Lena, but he was relaxed. He's not relaxed anymore. His left hand, which was resting casually on his sword's hilt, has dropped to his side, and his right is now loose and open, ready to draw the blade if he needs to. He won't need to, though. Kyol has sworn to protect Lena, and he'd never do anything to hurt me. Aren knows that. I don't think he's aware of the subtle change in his posture.

"We didn't tell them about Sethan because we knew Atroth would attack Haeth if he knew who we were," Lena says, referring to the city she and her brother grew up in. Sethan was the fae the rebels intended to put on the throne, but he was killed by the Court fae outside of Vancouver. If he were still alive, I think the transition to a new ruler would be going much more smoothly. He was prepared to be king, wanted it. Lena's a different story.

"Maybe no one is convinced you would be different," I say to Lena. "They might be afraid you'll attack their homes and friends just like they attacked yours." Then, reluctantly, I add, "They associate the rebellion with Brykeld."

Mentioning the city's name puts the taste of smoke on my tongue. Aren's known as the Butcher of Brykeld. That's one of a dozen reasons why I hated him when we met. He wasn't actually there when one of his men gave orders to seal families inside their homes and burn the city, but most fae don't know or don't believe that. I didn't believe it until I got to know him better, until I saw the pain of the memory in his eyes.

He looks at me now, his expression uncharacteristically closed off. He knows I have issues with some of the things he did to overthrow King Atroth, and I think he's afraid I can't get over his past. I'm working on it. This world isn't my world. It's more violent, more archaic. On the one hand, I understand that. On the other, doing things like exposing fae to tech until they break or turn *tor'um* is wrong. The sudden loss of magic makes them go mad. That's why human technology is banned from the Realm—too much exposure cripples them for life.

I can't accept Aren doing that or anything like it ever again. It's one of the many reasons I'm trying to take things slowly with him. We still have things we need to talk about.

"Perhaps we're dealing with a false-blood," Lena says into the silence, a silence that grows heavier as we consider the possibility. That's something we don't need to deal with right now. I've hunted many false-bloods in the last decade, all in an effort to prevent them from gaining enough support to overthrow the king. Most of them were easy to capture.

Most couldn't prove they were Descendants of the *Tar Sidhe*, so they never had a big, loyal following. But for some false-bloods, that lack of proof didn't matter. They gained enough support, with either cunning or brute force, to be dangerous. Thrain, the fae who found me ten years ago, used plenty of both.

Kyol shakes his head. "The remnants wouldn't follow a false-blood so easily. We're dealing with a fae who is charismatic and smart. I think it's likely he was one of Atroth's officers or he was rising in the ranks quickly. He's looking for a Descendant who can rival your bloodline, but he hasn't yet found one who's willing to take the throne."

No one here misses hearing the "yet." We're on borrowed time. I don't know how Lena's going to make the high nobles confirm her as queen, but she needs to come up with something soon. I wish I had a suggestion, but fae politics are beyond me. Plus, I have another problem to add to our list.

"There's something else we need to talk about," I say. "The remnants abducted Paige."

Out of the corner of my eye, I see Kyol stiffen. He looks at me, but I keep my gaze focused on Lena, and say, "They put a ward on her purse and left it at my apartment for me to find. That's why they showed up when I was there."

"And Paige is . . ." Lena asks.

"My friend. We went to her sister's wedding." "Went to" is stretching it. We were there for, like, five minutes because Aren wanted a public place—one filled with humans—to exchange me for Lena after the Court captured her. "I need your help finding her."

She stares at me for a good five seconds before she turns and sits on the top step of the dais. If she didn't look so weary, I'd be annoyed by her lack of reaction. Still, I have to get Paige back.

"What do you want me to do?" she asks. "Assign a hundred fae to search the entire Realm for a single human? Shall I assign a hundred more to search Earth?"

"Lena," Aren interjects, stepping to my side.

"What?" she snaps. "The remnants attacked the palace because they knew I'd divert resources to save her."

I manage to draw in a slow breath and count to three before responding, but only because I know she's stressed and hasn't been getting much sleep.

"You could offer a trade," I say. "They took her for a reason. You could at least attempt to—"

"And who should I trade?" she demands. "You?"

Lena and I have never been friends. We probably never will be, and our tolerance for each other has its ups and downs. If she didn't need my shadow-reading talent and I didn't need her to bring some kind of stability to the Realm, we would have nothing to do with each other. But the fact is, she does need me, and I need her. I need her to end this war so that I can have some hope of living a seminormal human life.

"If it comes down to that, yes," I tell her.

I feel Aren turn toward me—I'm sure he has a few things to say about a trade—but I don't look away from Lena, not until her gaze focuses behind me. I glance over my shoulder and see Jacia, daughter of Srillan, limping our way. She's a former Court fae, one of almost a hundred Kyol convinced to support Lena. She also happens to be the woman King Atroth wanted Kyol to form a life-bond with. That never happened because he was in love with me. I wonder if it's a possibility now. She's strong and beautiful, with long, black hair braided over one shoulder and the brightest silver eyes I've ever seen.

"We need a healer," she says in Fae. Her voice is monotone, but not tight, which is a surprise since she's left a trail of blood behind her. The *jaedric* armor protecting her left thigh hangs on by just one lace.

"There's still fighting at the veligh*?"* Lena demands. She rises from her seat on the dais's top step to glare at Kyol. *"Why are you here?"*

"I needed to . . ." He stops, glances my way before clearing his throat. *"I needed to know what was happening here."*

Translation: he needed to know I was safe.

Almost as an afterthought, he adds, *"You sent your guards to the* veligh. *I'm here because you cannot be left unprotected."*

"One thing we can agree on," Aren mutters as he walks

to Jacia and peers down at her injury. He pulls off the *jaedric* leg shield, then slips his hand through the rip in her blood-soaked pants so he can heal the gash in her leg.

Only Aren, Lena, and a handful of other fae have the ability to heal. It's one of the only endangered magics that I wish was more common. Some of the others, like the ability to read minds or to cast darkness, are less beneficial, more terrifying. The king and the majority of the Realm think humans and our culture and artifacts have been weakening the fae's magic over the generations. They blame my people for making gate-building and a few other magics—magics that I'm not certain ever existed in the first place—extinct.

Jacia's gaze moves from Aren to me. I have no idea if she knows why Kyol rejected a life-bond with her. We tried to hide our feelings for each other, but I'm sure some people were suspicious. But then, maybe life-bonds are rejected often? Fae are able to sense each other through the magical bindings, and if it's a good pairing, they're able to use more magic without becoming exhausted. The biggest drawback is that life-bonds are permanent; even if the couple splits up, the magical bond remains. I'm pretty sure the only way to end one is for one of the fae involved to die. That would definitely discourage me from agreeing to one.

"Jacia," Lena says. *"What's happening at the* veligh?"

Jacia says the situation is under control, but if I'm translating her words correctly, the remnants were close to breaking through our defenses. A portion of the silver wall was damaged from flames thrown by a fae.

That fae had to be powerful to be able to manipulate fire like that. Trev is a fire-wielder, one powerful enough to throw flames, and Lena can do something similar with air, but most fae who are able to manipulate the elements can only create small, temporary flames or a soft puff of wind. I hate knowing that the remnants have such powerful people supporting them.

When Aren finishes healing Jacia, Lena questions her further. They'll need to erect a scaffold to support the wall until a more permanent fix can be made. Aren and Lena discuss who will be in charge of that project, then they switch to another subject, then another. When they start talking about the books that contain a registry of fae names and magical abilities, I glance at Kyol, but he seems very determined *not* to look my direction.

A resigned sigh escapes from me. It's a familiar feeling, being pushed to the side like this.

Without a word, I leave the king's hall.

FOUR

❖

For ten years, I kept my human life separate from my life as a shadow-reader. I let my parents believe I was crazy because it was forbidden to tell them about the fae, and I was on academic probation almost my entire time in college because I couldn't keep my grades up. Except for Paige, I've been friendless this entire time. But I accepted all of that. I accepted everything because it was best that humans not know anything about the fae. It would endanger the Realm, and I didn't want to drag anyone else into its wars.

My precautions and sacrifices did a hell of a lot of good. They didn't protect Paige.

"McKenzie."

I'm surprised to hear Aren's voice behind me, but I don't slow down. I pull at the bindings of my cuirass as I stride through a corridor that follows the palace's exterior wall.

"Hey," he says, forcing me to stop when he cuts off my path. "Hey. Lena will help you."

I sidestep around him, pulling at the bindings again. The damn knot tightens.

"I'll talk to her," he says, falling into step beside me.

"Don't bother."

Aren grabs my arm, turns me toward him. "She's exhausted.

She misses Sethan, and the nobles aren't cooperating with her on anything, but she will help, McKenzie. *I'll* help."

"Lena won't help because she shouldn't." I pull my arm free but don't try to move past him again.

Aren tilts his head to the side. "She shouldn't?"

"No." The air whooshes out of my lungs. Sometimes, I really hate being reasonable. "She has to think about what's best for the rebels—for the entire Realm, really. Paige is only one person, and she's human. She's not Lena's responsibility. She's mine."

"McKenzie." Aren's voice is laced with a warning.

"What?"

"Don't try to get her back on your own," he says. He reaches out to help me untie my cuirass's bindings.

"I wasn't planning to."

His silver eyes meet mine. "I know that expression, *nalkin-shom*. You have a plan."

Nalkin-shom. Shadow-witch. The title should irritate me. Instead, it makes my stomach flip. The fae have called me *nalkin-shom* behind my back for years. I didn't know that until Aren told me fae children have nightmares about me. Their parents tell them no one can escape the *nalkin-shom*, that if they misbehave, I'll read their shadows, I'll suck their magic dry. I still think he's exaggerating. I might be the best at what I do—when I read a fae's shadows, they almost never escape—but I'm not a monster.

Aren's not looking at me like I'm a monster. Somehow, he makes *shadow-witch* sound like a term of endearment.

"I don't have a plan," I tell him. Not yet, at least.

He raises an eyebrow.

"I don't," I say, maybe a little defensively. Aren just shakes his head with that little half smirk I used to find infuriating. It's not infuriating anymore. It's alluring.

The bindings of my armor finally loosen, and Aren helps me lift it over my head. My hair gets caught on something. Aren gently pulls it free before setting the cuirass aside, then he lets my loose ponytail slide from his hand. When he does, his fingertips graze my neck. It's a brief, accidental contact, but my *edarratae* react instantly. By the way Aren's gazing down at me, it's obvious he felt the lightning's heat, too.

"Jorreb," someone says, surprisingly close to us. Fae have better hearing than humans, but Aren stiffens just enough to indicate that the nearness of the fae startles him, too. He takes a step away from me as he turns toward Jacia.

Her silver eyes move briefly to me before settling back on Aren. *"Lena wishes for the shadow-reader to speak to Naito."*

A muscle in Aren's cheek twitches. *"It's only been two weeks."*

Two weeks since Naito's lover, Kelia, died. My throat tightens. Kelia was the rebel fae who taught me to speak their language. She was almost a friend, and I envied her relationship with Naito, a human shadow-reader. Despite some bumpy times, they were happy together—they were *good* together—but Naito's father, a hateful man determined to eradicate the fae, killed Kelia the day we took the palace. Naito hasn't been the same since.

"Lena needs him in the watch rotation," Jacia says. *"And she needs him to read the shadows."*

"I'll talk to him," I say, even though I agree it's too soon. But I haven't seen Naito in several days. I want to see how he's doing.

Aren looks at me. I think he wants to protest. Instead, he says, "I need to help secure the *veligh*. I don't know when I'll see you again."

This is the problem with starting a relationship in the middle of a war. Including today, I've seen him only three times since I ended my relationship with Kyol. For us to work out, I need time to get to know him. The thing is, it's very possible we won't have that time. Despite the way Aren acts sometimes, he's not invincible. I'm certainly not, either.

My gaze goes to Jacia. I don't know her at all. I don't know her view on human and fae relationships or if she would rat us out to a high noble if I wrapped my arms around Aren. That's what I want to do. I want to forget our responsibilities and run away to somewhere remote and quiet, someplace where we can be normal and sit and talk and . . . do other things.

Aren must know the direction my thoughts are heading. The half smile he gives me is both an apology and a promise. "I'll find you as soon as I can."

After he leaves with Jacia, I have to assure myself a dozen times that he's going to be okay and that I *will* see him again. Then I start looking for Naito. Surprisingly, he's difficult to find. A human with lightning-covered skin kind of sticks out in this world, but I check his room, do a quick walk-through of the sculpture garden, and search a few other locations where he's likely to be, all without any success. I finally start asking the English-speaking fae—we decided it's best that the high nobles don't know I've learned their language—if they've seen him. After half a dozen negative responses, someone tells me Naito's in the royal archives. I clarify that with the fae more than once, though, thinking he must have misunderstood me. Humans aren't allowed in the archives. At least, they weren't under Atroth's reign. Eventually, though, I head in that direction because I don't know where else to look.

"McKenzie." Kavok smiles when he opens the door. I can't help but smile in return. I've always liked the archivist. He's dedicated to his job. So dedicated he didn't leave the palace when Lena gave the Court fae the opportunity, and when I worked for the king, he was one of the few fae who was always willing to talk to me. That's mainly because he's so curious about humans. Whenever he had the chance, he questioned me about my life and my world, and sometimes, he told me a few things about his.

"Hi, Kavok," I say, looking into archives behind him. Drawers line the walls of the large room. The symbols on them are illuminated by hanging orbs, which are lit with magic. The combination of blue and white lightning inside them creates a steady, slightly tinted glow that doesn't damage documents like the sun or lights from my world would. But that's not the only thing that preserves the records in here. Kavok can, to a certain extent, control the weather. It's a useful magic, one that's in high demand. Farmers employ fae who can tweak the weather if there's a drought, and the former king used to use them to darken the sky when he thought it would give the Court fae the advantage during an attack. Kavok, though, uses his ability to regulate the temperature of the archives. He keeps humidity out, too, and from what I've heard, some documents in here look like they were created yesterday even though they're centuries old.

"It's good to see you," he says. Then, his face brightens even more. "I found an earlier reference."

I have no idea what he's talking about, but he turns to the desk that's just to the left of the door. At least, I think there's a desk under the mountains of papers, thick, leather-bound tomes, and haphazard stacks of anchor-stones. An entire alcove in here is set aside for storing the latter. Locations both here and on Earth are kept in drawers in case the king needed fae to fissure somewhere they'd never been before.

After a minute of shuffling through the piles, Kavok looks up.

"Come in," he says.

Carefully, I step over the threshold. I feel the atmosphere change when I do. It's dryer and cooler than the corridor. "I thought humans weren't allowed in here?"

He shrugs. "New ruler, new rules. Ah, yes. Sixteen hundred ninety-one years ago—our years, not yours. That's the earliest mention I've come across. It corresponds with . . ."

He begins describing some kind of agricultural process, but I'm only half listening because I'm trying to figure out what reference he's referring to. I haven't spoken to him in months. He might have an impeccable memory, but I don't. I can't even remember the topic of our last conver—

Oh.

"You found a reference to a shadow-reader?" I ask.

"Yes!" He looks up from the huge book in front of him and grins. "It's 350 years earlier than Faem thought."

Faem, I think, was the previous archivist. The silver in Kavok's eyes practically sparkles. His giddiness makes him seem even younger than he already looks. If he was human, I'd guess him to be in his midtwenties, so that means he's probably pushing fifty, still a relatively young age for a fae. His hair is blond, just a few shades darker than Aren's—most likely because he locks himself in here all day, every day—and it's just long enough to be frazzled.

In short, he's the geekiest fae I know. I keep expecting him to push wire-framed glasses up on his nose.

"What does it say about the shadow-reader?" I ask, interrupting his lecture on agricultural practices.

"Oh, yes." He clears his throat. "It doesn't say this is the first shadow-reader, and I can't validate the text's authority, but it appears that there is little difference between his abilities and yours. The shadows only told him where a fae exited the In-Between, not where he entered it, and he, too, had to draw what he saw and name the nearest city or region out loud. But then, we come to a small discrepancy."

"Discrepancy?" I move closer to his desk, but he closes the text and rises.

"Not with your abilities," he says. "With ours. According to the author, only a few fae were able to fissure to the locations the shadow-reader mapped and named."

Now, *that's* interesting.

"Is it something fae learned to do over time?" I ask.

"It's implied that the fae who could follow the maps had more . . . er, more contact with humans." Kavok doesn't meet my eyes.

"Sex?"

He lifts a shoulder, says almost apologetically, "It's implied."

Everyone who has the ability to fissure can make it to the locations I sketch, and since most of those fae would rather not touch a human at all, sex definitely doesn't have anything to do with it.

"That's all I've discovered," Kavok says. "I found the reference a few weeks ago, but you were . . . Well, you were . . ."

"Things were different then," I say, hiding a smile. It's almost cute, how easily flustered he is. "I'm looking for Naito."

He seems grateful for the change of subject. "Of course. He's there."

He points to an alcove that splits off from the main room.

After he takes a seat at his desk, I walk toward the alcove he indicated, and there, sitting at a table heaped with papers, books, and a few boxes, sits Naito.

He doesn't notice me. He's staring at whatever is in front

of him. His left hand is clenched in his black hair, helping to
hold his head up, and his forehead is creased. He's wearing
the same jeans and white T-shirt I saw him in a few days ago,
and his shoulders are rounded and slumped. Oddly, though,
he looks better than he did before. I can't quite put my finger
on why. Maybe it's the lack of anger in his expression. Maybe
it's the amount of concentration, of focus, in the way his eyes
move back and forth, reading, I presume. Or maybe it's just
the fact that he's not demanding someone fissure him back to
Earth so he can murder his father.

"Hey," I say when I reach his table.

"Hey," he responds without looking up. I wait a moment
then, when he still doesn't glance away from what he's reading, I pull out the chair across from him and sit.

My gaze sweeps across the table.

"You can read this?" Everything is written in a jumble of
symbols and marks. I can speak Fae fairly well now, but even
if I had years to study, I don't think I'd ever be able to make
sense of their written language.

"Kelia is teaching me," Naito says.

I bite my lower lip, unable to ignore the fact that he's still
talking about her in the present tense. "Naito—"

"I understand enough to get by," he says. His tone is firm,
now, and his eyes have hardened.

Everyone's been tiptoeing around Naito these past two
weeks. I don't want to make him hurt any more than he
already does, but I think it's time someone convinces him
that he'll never see Kelia again. She's well and truly gone.

I ignore the way my throat burns when I swallow, then
say, "Kelia would want—"

"To be with me," he interrupts again. There's steel in his
voice. It's as if he's daring me to claim otherwise. Before I
can do just that, he turns the book in front of him around so
that it's right side up for me.

"Banek'tan," he says, pointing to a jumble of tiny lines.

The word sounds familiar—I'm pretty sure it's a type of
magic—but I say, "I can't read that."

He raises his eyes to meet mine. "It means 'one who
retrieves the departed.' A banek'tan can bring Kelia back."

Really?

I stare down at the book as an almost giddy feeling takes over me. A *banek'tan* could undo so much. With one's help, Naito and Kelia can be together again. They can have their happy ending, and we could bring back the innocent fae who were caught up in this war: the merchants who were in the wrong place at the wrong time, the families who were burned inside their homes in Brykeld, the swordsmen on both sides of the war who were only following orders.

We could bring back the fae I inadvertently killed in Belecha.

We could resurrect Sethan.

But just as quickly as those hopes appear, they vanish. What the hell am I thinking? If that magic existed, Lena would have already tried to bring her brother back from the ether. And someone would have tried to bring back the king.

I close my eyes as a rush of pity flows through me. It's tinged with pain, and it takes everything in me to keep it locked down tight. I swallow, trying to loosen a tight and raw throat, then, carefully, I ask, "Is that an extinct magic?"

Naito's gaze doesn't waver. It's almost as if he's waiting for the pity or skepticism to reach my face, but after a handful of heartbeats, some of the tension leaves his shoulders. "These documents are filled with references to *banek'tan*. And some of them are recent. This one"—he grabs a loose parchment from one of his stacks—"is only twenty years old. A false-blood's bond-mate was killed. She came back."

I bite the inside of my cheek and watch as he picks up another paper.

"Same thing with this one," he says. "It's a little older, but there were dozens of witnesses. A fae died in the silver mines of Adaris. His bond-mate was able to bring him back. I've found twelve stories like these from the past century. Twelve. There has to be some truth to them."

There's so much hope in his voice, I almost want to let him believe this. Would it be so wrong to? This is the best he's looked in weeks. He has a reason to live, but these . . . these stories are just that. Stories. They're rumors. Dreams.

I want to believe them, too, but I've learned the hard way that life isn't a fairy tale. People don't come back from the dead.

No. I was wrong before when I thought it was too soon for him to go back to work. He needs the distraction. He doesn't need to sit around researching dreams that can't come true. It isn't healthy.

"What happened to them?" I ask.

His brows lower. "What do you mean?"

"These fae who came back from the ether. Where are they now?"

He blinks, then stares down at the pages in front of him. "I'm not sure."

I wait a moment, letting him think things through. "Naito, the *banek'tan* don't exist."

He looks up again, his expression hardening. "Neither did the *ther'othi*."

And one point goes to Naito. Fae aren't supposed to be able to walk the In-Between, but Micid could. He was a cruel, sick fae who worked for the previous king and his lord general, Radath. Instead of going through the In-Between, the freezing space fae pass through when they fissure, he waded in, taking me with him into a dimension within a world. We were invisible to everyone, but could still move and interact with the world. I suppose I can see why Naito is clinging to this hope, but it's so, so thin. If a fae was ever brought back from the ether, there would be more evidence than what's hinted at in these documents.

I draw in a breath, let it out slowly, then go for a not-so-subtle subject change. "Lena's having a hard time keeping the palace secure."

"Hmm," Naito murmurs, leaning back in his chair and pulling a book closer. "She needs more fae to guard the *Sidhe Tol*."

"The *Sidhe Tol* aren't the problem," I say. They're not entirely the problem. A *Sidhe Tol* is a very rare and very special type of gate that allows a fae to fissure into an area protected by silver. We know the locations of three of them, but rumor has it there are more. No one's been able to find them, and until two weeks ago, no one but the king and a few trusted advisors knew where they were. *I* wasn't supposed to know where they were, but Kyol fissured me through one once. I gave the rebels its location, and then, they learned where the other two were as well. They used the *Sidhe Tol* to take the palace. Now, we have to guard them to make sure the former Court fae don't do the same thing to us.

"The remnants are launching organized attacks from within the silver walls," I tell Naito. "They have illusionists and all of the humans who used to work for the Court. Lena needs—"

"Not all of them," Naito interrupts. "They don't have you. I hear they don't have that Shane guy, either."

So he *is* aware of some of the things that are going on around the palace. That's good. It means he isn't completely lost in his research here. "Lena needs your help."

"I'm busy."

"Naito."

"I said I'm busy." His glare comes off as a warning not to press the issue further.

Too bad. I have to.

"And how much time do you think you'll have for your research if we lose the palace?" I demand. "Do you think the remnants will just let you hang out here?"

His bottom lip twitches.

"You need to join the rotation," I say. "With you and Shane, there are six of us working for Lena. We can keep all the entrances watched."

Naito's gaze grows distant, focusing somewhere behind me. "It won't make a difference. We can't keep watch indefinitely. Lena needs to take out the remnants' leader. She needs to go on the offensive."

It's hard to argue with that because it's true. The rebels' other Sighted humans and I are almost burned-out already. We need a break, and while Naito and Shane will help lighten our workload, it's only a temporary solution.

Naito is still staring behind me. I look over my shoulder just as Kyol reaches our table.

"I need a shadow-reader," he says. "Quickly."

I rise automatically, not noticing until I'm already standing that Kyol isn't focused on me. He's focused on Naito.
Naito meets his gaze but doesn't say a word for a good six
seconds.

"I'm busy." He returns to reading the documents in front
of him.

I don't know if it's obvious what Naito is researching—I
feel like it should be—but Kyol's face remains expressionless, even when he eventually looks at me. "Will you come?"

It's a question I was rarely asked when King Atroth was
alive. The fae always assumed I would drop everything and
help them, and most of the time, I did. My own fault. I should
have stood my ground more often, made more time for
myself.

"Yeah, I'll go," I tell him. Jenkins doesn't need my driver's license and Social Security card until 5 P.M. on Friday,
two days from now. I have more than enough time to help
Kyol and get back to Vegas, and I *want* to help him.

I turn to Naito. "You'll have to cover my watch."

He doesn't glance up.

"Naito," I say again, sharper this time. I see his jaw clench
once, twice. Then, when I think he's going to ignore me
indefinitely, he finally says, "Fine."

I'll have to trust he'll follow through on that because Kyol's
already heading for the door. I was avoiding Kyol these past
two weeks only because I didn't want to hurt him, but it doesn't
look like being near me fazes him at all. Maybe I'm a fool to
think he still wants me. Maybe he's completely over me.

I follow him out the door, breaking into a jog when my
legs can't keep up at a walk. Usually, Kyol would slow down
for me, but when we exit the archives, he increases his pace.

"We might lose him if we don't move quickly."

The urgency makes my stomach tighten. The last time I
shadow-read with him was two weeks ago in Montana. It
didn't go well. A lot of fae died securing the *Sidhe Tol* and
fissuring into the Silver Palace. They've been dying ever
since, and while I want to believe we've made it through the
bloodiest days of this war, my gut tells me we haven't. More
lives will be lost before the high nobles accept Lena as queen.

FIVE

❖

KYOL ISN'T THE fae who fissures me out of Corrist. He hands me a cloak, a sketchbook, and an imprinted anchor-stone, then lets Taber, his second-in-command, take me through the slash of white light. As soon as the gated-fissure fades away, I release Taber's arm, trying to ignore the heat swirling in my palm. He doesn't look bothered by our contact. I'm sure he is, though. The majority of the Realm's citizens believe humans and human tech damage their magic. Chances are none of the three fae with me now want to get too close to me; they're just too professional to show it.

They're all former Court fae who served under Kyol. I've worked with Taber before, but not the other two, though I have met Brayan, the tall but stout fae standing to my left, once. He was one of the men guarding the storage room where Kyol was holding Naito and Evan, another shadow-reader, during the war. I haven't seen him since then, but being with the three former Court fae makes this assignment seem so familiar, I almost feel like nothing has changed these past few weeks. Nothing, that is, except our target. We're not hunting Aren anymore.

"We're hunting Dyler, son of Jielan," Kyol says when he joins us. The shadows from his extinguished fissure twist in the air behind him. Fae can't see them. They don't feel the itch to sketch out their peaks and valleys. They don't need to know if the tiny swirl in the middle of the black haze puts us on the east or west side of the river that cuts through the city. I do, though, and my fingers tighten on the sketchbook in my hand. I wish I had the strapped sketchbook I packed in my suitcase, but this one will work, and it will take only a few seconds to slip the pencil from the spiral and draw what looks to be a marketplace just north of the swirl. If I—

"McKenzie."

I blink. Kyol's voice is firm, like he's called my name more than once.

I give my head a little shake so I can focus on him and not the shadows dancing over his shoulder. In the last ten years, I've only tranced out a dozen times looking at them. Two of those times have been in the last week. I think sleep deprivation and constantly being on edge is finally getting to me.

"Are you sure you can do this?" His silver eyes don't soften like they usually would with that question.

"I'm sure," I say, keeping my voice neutral as well. We both know I'm the best person for this job. "You said we're looking for . . . ?"

"Jielan," Kyol says.

I recognize the name. I read the shadows for him just a few months ago. We were looking for Aren in Jythkrila, but the rebels set a trap for us. For me, really. They'd killed and replaced the inspectors at the city's gate. The inspectors' job was to make sure the fae who used the gate paid taxes on the goods they took through it. They'd never approached me before, but one did that time. He feigned interest in the sketchbook I carried. By the time I realized something wasn't right, he locked his hand around my wrist.

Jielan saved me from the rebels. They were my enemy then, so I was grateful. I thanked him. Now, I'm here to help Kyol capture or kill him.

"Up here," Kyol says, motioning me toward a ladder. It's only then that I really take in my surroundings. My impressions from the shadows were wrong. We're nowhere near a marketplace. The ladder climbs up the side of a gray-and-black brick wall. The building is big, stretching more than fifty feet to either side of me. It's plain, though, with a flat façade and what looks like a flat roof. My guess is it's a *bregorm*, a stack house, which is basically the Realm's equivalent of a UPS. *Jaedric*, wood, textiles, and other bulk items don't just appear in merchants' stores. They have to be brought there, and the fae who harvest or create them don't have the time to fissure what they're selling in small armloads to every merchant who might want them. So they bring them here, stacking them in their local *bregorm*, where other fae agree to the tedious job of hauling them to the nearest gate.

The stack house is the only building I can see. I don't know what's on its other side, but there's nothing but an open field at our backs. It was near midnight in Corrist, but here, it's maybe late afternoon, which means we're a good ways to the east of the Silver Palace.

I grab the first rung of the ladder and start up, thinking maybe I'll recognize the city when I have a better view. It's close to a three-story climb, but I make it to the top quickly. As I pull myself onto the roof, I notice the thick band of silver edging the building. The metal prevents fae from fissuring up here or inside, but that's not the only reason we emerged from the In-Between at the base of the ladder. One of Kyol's swordsmen lies flat on his stomach on the far edge of the roof. His head is pointed away from us and tilted at an angle that presumably gives him a decent view of the door to the building that's across the street. From where I'm crouched by the ladder, I can only see a roof and the top edge of a window. No one inside should be able to see me, but if we'd fissured directly up here, there's a chance they might have seen the flash of light.

I stay low and let my gaze sweep across the rest of the area. We're on the outskirts of a town. Most of the buildings are spread out, but a strip of structures built closely together is off to my far right. I'm guessing they're stores of some kind, maybe with a few small residences scattered among them. The street they're on snakes back and forth, and I think I was wrong about a river cutting through the city. That road is the wavy line I saw in the shadows.

"Is he still here?" Kyol asks in Fae, climbing onto the

rooftop behind me. Taber and the other two fae remain on the ground below.

The swordsman lying on his stomach nods. His brown hair is cut short enough to see a black cord hanging around his neck. *"Yes, lord general,"* he says. *"He and three others."*

Lord general. The title puts a bad taste in my mouth. I'm not used to Kyol being called that. I don't think he fits the role. The previous fae who held that position was overbearing, arrogant, and in the end, cruel. Kyol isn't any of those things.

To me, Kyol says, "The house is protected by silver. Jielan will most likely fissure as soon as he exits, but if he doesn't, you'll need to be ready to move."

"There isn't a back way out?"

"There is," he answers, "but he doesn't know we're here. He has no reason to exit the other way."

Staying low, I inch forward until I'm at the edge of the roof. Kyol does the same.

"Where are we?" I ask, moving the buckle of the belt Aren fastened around me so it's not so uncomfortable to lie on. That moves the sheathed dagger a little more to the left on my back, but I can still reach it fairly easily.

"Spier," Kyol says.

I stare at him without saying a word. Each of the Realm's provinces has a capital city with a gate, but Spier is nowhere near any of them. And unless there's a Missing Gate—a gate not on the public maps—that I don't know about, the nearest place for me to safely fissure is half a day's walk from here.

"I needed a shadow-reader," Kyol says without looking at me. Usually, his tone would be apologetic—he always hated keeping me away from my human life—but it's firm now, just as it should be. I never needed to be coddled, and as frustrating as it is to be stranded so far away from a gate, it's good that I'm here. Jielan could lead us to the other remnants. He could lead us to Paige.

I open the notebook on the roof in front of me, taking the pencil out of the spine so that I'll be completely ready when Jielan comes out. The quicker I sketch his shadows, the more accurate my map will be. I just hope we don't have to kill him.

"There he is," Kyol says sharply.

My gaze snaps to the front door. Jielan's there, stepping outside without so much as a glance at his surroundings. He immediately disappears into a fissure. The light winks out, leaving behind a twist of shadows.

My hand is already dragging my pencil across the sketchbook, dipping into a shallow valley near the continent's southern coast. Jielan's stayed in the Realm. He's even still in Cadek Province, most likely. I scratch down a few more broad strokes—an ocean to the east, a fairly dense forest to the northeast—then flip the page as my mind zooms in on his location. A part of my brain registers that the other three fae who were inside the house have exited as well, but they don't obscure the shadows. I keep my pencil moving, and within seconds, I identify a dark swirl to the west of a river. It cuts through a village that . . .

No, wait. It's not a river. It's a street. It's *the* street.

"Watch out!" I shout, pushing up off the rooftop and spinning toward the ladder. My warning comes too late. One of the swordsmen waiting below lets out a bellow and the sound of clashing swords rings through the air.

"Stay with her!" Kyol orders, already moving. The fae wearing the black necklace takes up position at my side, sword drawn. I know Kyol wants me to stay up here, to stay safe, but as he disappears over the side of the roof, I grab my sketchbook and scramble to the ladder. Jielan might fissure away. If he does, I need to map his shadows.

I peer over the building's edge just as Taber deflects a hard swing from Jielan, then counters with an attack of his own. Both their swords move impossibly fast, diving and slicing and stabbing through the air. Taber retreats a step, stumbling. He doesn't look injured, but I'm certain I see red on Jielan's blade. I don't know if it's from Brayan, who's scrambling back to his feet, or from—

I spot a wisp of white shadow. Yes, the blood must be from the other fae. He's nowhere to be seen now because he's dead. Jielan killed him. All that's left to mark his existence in this world is his soul-shadow, and even that disappears when Taber lunges through it, his blade narrowly missing Jielan's shoulder.

Then Kyol's there, leaping off the ladder and drawing his sword. Jielan sees him. He has to know he's outmatched and outnumbered, but when he fissures, he doesn't leave the fight. He emerges from the In-Between only a few feet away from where he disappeared. It's the perfect position to snake his arm around the neck of a still-unbalanced Brayan. Jielan pivots, pressing his back against the wall and using Brayan as a shield.

"Taltrayn." Jielan uses Kyol's family name, not sounding surprised or concerned.

Kyol advances slowly now, moving away from the ladder in deliberate, measured steps. *"You'll lose this fight,"* he says, stopping several paces away from Jielan.

Taber holds his position to Kyol's left, waiting for his commander's order. Kyol and his swordsmen are the most disciplined soldiers in the Realm. They're all duty and sacrifice, and even though I can't see Brayan's face from my rooftop position, I'm sure it's as unreadable as the others'. He'll accept whatever action Kyol takes, even if it leads to his death.

But Kyol has never been one to needlessly sacrifice his men, not if there's another way to achieve his goal.

"Release him, Jielan," he orders. *"We don't have to be on opposite sides of this war."*

Jielan lets out a sharp laugh.

"The daughter of Zarrak does not belong on the throne," he says. *"She and her fae should be banished from the Realm, but you're supporting her. You're supporting her despite her refusal to turn . . ."*

I don't understand the last part. It's something about a king or a Descendant, but the conjugation doesn't make sense. It doesn't matter, though. It's clear Jielan is firmly against Lena and anyone who supports her.

"The high nobles choose who sits on the silver throne," Kyol says. *"Not you or I. Drop your sword."*

"Nobles can be bought and blackmailed. No, lord general." He makes the title sound like a slur. *"You've chosen your side. It's the wrong one."*

The air erupts with a staccato of *shrrip, shrrip, shrrip*s as three fissures flash into existence. The three other fae who were in the house step out of the slashes of light.

I realize this is a trap at the same moment Kyol grates out, *"Taber!"*

He doesn't have to say more than that—it's clear he's ordering Taber to go for help—but before the fae can open a fissure, Jielan says, *"Brayan dies if he leaves. So does the shadow-witch."*

The hair on the nape of my neck prickles. I start to turn, but a sword presses into my back. It's the fae wearing the black necklace.

I close my eyes in a silent grimace. It had to happen eventually. Aren argued against allowing any former Court fae to remain in the palace, even if they swore fealty to Lena, but Kyol vouched for them. He trained them and trusted them, and he said that they would protect her with their lives. He was wrong.

The scabbard belted around my waist moves when the fae behind me confiscates my dagger.

"Down," he orders. Even if I couldn't understand his language, his meaning would be clear. I grip the part of the ladder that attaches to the roof, then start down before the traitor decides to draw blood. My mind works furiously on the descent. The fae doesn't have his sword on me now—he can't because he's following me down—so I'm safe for a very limited amount of time. We're outnumbered, though, and I'm human and I'm unarmed.

I'm three rungs from the ground when I decide I have to act. I leap off and to the left, landing on Jielan's shoulder. He snarls as he swings his fist, not his sword around, aiming for me. It's a mistake. His blade is no longer against Brayan's neck. I let go of Jielan when Brayan grabs his wrist and flips the remnant over his shoulder. Then, almost in synch, every other fae vanishes into fissures.

I back against the stack-house wall. The fae reappear an instant later, all in different locations. With the shadows replacing the white light, I'm disoriented. I have no idea who's where, not until Kyol grabs my arm.

"That was foolish," he grates out, pulling me alongside the building.

Alongside the building and directly toward a fae who's standing ready with his sword.

"Straight ahead. Illusionist."

No need to say more. Kyol lunges forward, sword slicing out in front of us. The attack takes the remnant by surprise, but he's still able to deflect Kyol's swing. Touch breaks a fae's illusions, though, so Kyol can see him now, and in two efficient moves, he kills the fae.

As soon as the soul-shadow rises into the air, I turn, searching for more remnants who might be invisible. The only way to tell if Kyol and his swordsmen can't see someone is to watch where they look. If they don't react when a remnant approaches, I assume they're hidden. I think there was only one illusionist here, though. Everyone's fighting somebody. Unfortunately, the remnants outnumber us, and one of them focuses on me.

Shit.

I don't call out for help—I don't want to distract the rebels. Instead, I turn and run, sprinting around to the front of the stack house.

Its door is a few strides away. I pray it's unlocked, reach out for it . . .

. . . and hear a *whoosh* fly past my left ear. I throw myself to the right, hit the ground as something slams into the stack house.

Heat explodes behind me. On hands and knees, I scramble away from the burning door, look to the right for the remnant who must have thrown the fire. Taber is occupying him.

I leap back to my feet and make a dash across the thirty-foot stretch of land between the stack house and the building Jielan and his cohorts emerged from. The outside walls have silver mixed in with the paint. The fae won't be able to fissure inside.

Lights erupt around me as I run, but I ignore the fighting fae. As soon as I reach the front door, I turn the knob, shoulder it open, then slam it shut behind me. Almost instantly, I realize I'm not alone.

SIX

•◆•

I'VE ALREADY LOCKED the door. My back is to the dimly lit room, but I hear the softest *tap, taptaptap, tap* behind me. In my rush to get inside, I didn't even think about the possibility of there being another fae in here. I draw in deep breaths, trying to calm my racing heartbeat. I listen for movement—the pad of a footfall, the swish of clothing, or creak of *jaedric* armor—but the only other sounds come from outside, and while I'm standing here trying to decide what to do, they, too, fade away. It's silent except for the rhythmic tapping.

I stare at the door handle. It'll take a couple of seconds to unlock it. Some gut instinct tells me not to try it, that it might trigger the person behind me. Slowly, carefully, I turn.

In the center of a sparse living area, a tall, slender fae woman stands between two backless couches. She's ramrod straight except for her right arm, which is fully extended so she can rest her hand on the hilt of her sword. Its blade is pointed straight down, digging just a little into the surface of a low, wooden table. Aside from one index finger drumming down on the pommel over and over again, she doesn't move; she just stares.

I stare back, not daring to breathe. Pale, wavering bolts of lightning fade in and out on her face and hands. We're in the

Realm. She shouldn't have any chaos lusters here, but she's not a normal fae. Even if the lightning weren't visible on her skin, I'd know she was *tor'um*. Something about her feels off.

Her inky black hair is pulled back into a high ponytail, and she's wearing *jaedric* armor. The treated bark is dark, well oiled, and molded to the curves of her body. Etched across her chest is an *abira* tree with thirteen branches, the symbol of Atroth's Court. Does she fight for the remnants? She's standing there silent and unwavering, projecting the feeling that she's competent with her sword, but *tor'um* are so magically handicapped that they can't fissure. That makes her odds of surviving a fae swordfight not much better than a human's.

"Your skin is bright."

The bluntness of her statement makes me stare down at my arms. White lightning bolts around my left wrist. Another one scurries up to my right elbow. Chaos lusters always appear and disappear quickly, but I guess my skin could be considered bright. I just don't get why it's important enough to say out loud, or why it seems to annoy her.

"I told him you wouldn't turn it off."

Turn my skin off? I frown at the lightning again, and that's when I realize: she's speaking English. It's a skill very few fae have. Usually, only those who work with humans learn my language. Maybe she lived somewhere on Earth for a time? That's what the *tor'um* in Vancouver did before King Atroth attacked their homes.

I focus on her again, watch as she tilts her head to the side, wrinkles her nose, then tilts her head back upright.

Understanding sweeps through me. Some fae are born unable to fissure. They're magically handicapped, but they're sane. This fae isn't. She lost her magic sometime during her adulthood and, now, her mind is broken. Whether that makes her more or less dangerous, I don't know.

Without warning, she's in front of me, grabbing my wrist. Her cold touch makes more chaos lusters shoot down my arm. They pool beneath her hand, almost as if they're trying to keep my skin from turning to ice. I attempt to pull away, but she's strong, and her dull, dark eyes are locked on me.

"You're not Paige."

I go still. Her Fae accent is faint; I'm certain I heard her right. "You know Paige? Where is she?"

"Why aren't you Paige?" Her hand tightens to the point where it hurts. My back is against the door. I can't move away when she leans forward, her face coming within inches of mine. Her eyes are narrowed, agitated. "You feel like Paige."

"McKenzie?" Kyol's voice from the other side of the door. He pounds on it, jiggles the handle.

The *tor'um* hisses, then swings me around with so much momentum, my feet leave the floor. My hip hits the table, sending a sharp lance of pain down my leg, and I slide off the other side.

A dagger is on a couch cushion, not ten inches from my face. I grab it, spin toward the fae, and slash at the air.

The *tor'um* isn't near me. She's standing above me with that same mix of anger and confusion in her eyes. My gaze moves to the sword in her hand. Her knuckles go white then back to normal as she tightens and loosens her grip. Then, all of a sudden, she looks 100 percent sane.

She whispers, *"Nalkin-shom."*

"Kyol!" I yell, scrambling away because I'm certain she's going to kill me.

"McKenzie!" There's a loud *bam* as Kyol rams into the door. I reach it and manage to get it unlocked before the *tor'um* leaps forward.

The door slams open and Kyol is there, putting himself between me and the fae. His sword is raised to deflect her attack, but there's no need to. She swings her blade well short of us, then stands there, looking utterly perplexed. After glancing around the room, she scowls at her feet.

"My fissure is broken," she mutters.

Kyol's muscles were already tense in preparation for her attack, but his stance changes. He's somehow stiffer now.

The *tor'um* stomps a foot on the ground as if that will make a fissure appear.

"Outside," Kyol whispers in my ear. I don't protest. I back through the doorway, keeping my eyes on the *tor'um* until

Kyol gently shuts the door. He stares at it a few seconds before he turns to me, then he takes a step back, looking for injuries I presume. That's when I notice the wound just above his right elbow. A remnant aimed perfectly, slicing at one of the few areas not protected by *jaedric*. Kyol's undershirt is dark with blood, but he doesn't seem to be favoring the arm any.

"She knows Paige," I tell him. His gaze returns to my eyes. His mouth thins before he nods once, then he motions Taber over. They speak quietly in Fae. I don't catch everything that's said, but Taber's eyebrows go up briefly, and he stares at the house. They have to be talking about the *tor'um*. They know her, I'm sure of it.

A dozen of Kyol's swordsmen are standing alert and ready in the space between the *tor'um*'s building and the stack house. They're spread out in a honeycomb pattern. If a remnant fissures into the clearing, he'll be surrounded by no less than four of Kyol's men. I want to order them to break their pattern. We need someone watching the back door so the *tor'um* can't escape. She may already have.

"They'll take care of the *tor'um*," Kyol says.

I stop midnod. Fae have told me some form of that sentence often over the past ten years. I assumed it meant that Kyol and the Court fae would fissure after and arrest a fae, but that wasn't always the case.

"They'll fissure her to the palace," he says, as if he can read my thoughts. He can't; he just knows me well enough to know how I think. "We need to leave before the remnants return."

This time, I finish my nod. I slip the dagger I found in the house into the scabbard at my back. Fortunately, it fits, and less than two minutes after exiting the house, we're on our way, heading east. I've memorized a map of the Realm, so I'm fairly certain we should reach the outskirts of a forest in an hour or two. After hiking through it, the river curves its way to the north. A gate is on the western bank. It's one of the gates that was lost during the *Duin Bregga*, an ancient war that resulted in the loss of a good portion of fae history, and the locations of an unknown numbers of gates. This gate isn't labeled on any public maps, but I don't think fissuring from there is going to be as safe as it used to be. It's likely that at least one of the remnants was high-ranked enough to know the locations of all the Missing Gates Atroth knew about. I wouldn't be surprised if they tried to set up an ambush there.

I glance at Kyol. He doesn't seem to be worried about an attack. He never once looks over his shoulder to check for pursuers, and only three of his fae are traveling with us. Even if he thinks we're safe, I'm surprised he hasn't brought along more guards. My jeans and T-shirt mark me as human. I usually change into fae clothing when I'm in the Realm, but I didn't know I'd be needed to shadow-read so soon.

Despite how tired I am, I'm able to keep up with Kyol. We've worked together long enough for him to know the quickest pace he can set. Any faster, and I'd wear out too quickly. It helps that I'm anxious to get away from the city. I was lucky twice today. The remnants could have killed me at my apartment complex, or they could have killed me just now in Spier. They had the chance, but Jielan chose to swing his fist, not his sword, at me, and that last remnant was definitely trying to capture me, not end my life.

"Why do the remnants want me alive?" I ask Kyol. There's the briefest break in his stride, like his thoughts were wandering and he's just now remembering I'm here.

"They can use you against us," he finally responds.

"They already have humans helping them, and even if they didn't, they should know I won't shadow-read or uncover illusions for them." At least, they should know it if Kyol is right about their leader being one of Atroth's high-ranked officers. Those officers know I willingly betrayed their king.

"That's not why they want you," Kyol says. "They know what you mean to Jorreb. They know what you mean to me."

This is the first time since I broke things off with him that he's mentioned how he feels about me, and the admission makes my chest hurt. He doesn't look like he regrets his words, though. His expression is serious, but not pained, and I'm not sure how to respond. I don't even know if I should.

Before the awkward silence stretches too long, a fissure opens a few yards ahead of us. One of the fae Kyol sent after the *tor'um* steps out of the light. I listen to his report and hope I'm misunderstanding him.

"Keep searching," Kyol orders. The fae nods, then steps back into the In-Between, returning to the house, I assume. We're still within line of sight of it.

I look at Kyol. "The *tor'um* disappeared?"

"Yes."

"But *tor'um* can't fissure."

"Most of them can't," Kyol confirms. "A few of them can. The ones who manage it aren't able to fissure far or often. The small amount of magic they possess takes months to regenerate. Most likely, the *tor'um* ran or hid."

I stare at the grass beneath my feet, feeling the small glimmer of hope that we'd get Paige back soon disappear.

"I know what Paige means to you," Kyol says after a moment. "We'll find her."

"You recognized her, didn't you? The *tor'um*?" I focus on the swath of dark green that marks the edge of the forest some few hundred feet in the distance, but when Kyol doesn't respond, I slant a glance his way. Kyol is twice my age but still young for a fae. His dark hair doesn't have a streak of gray, and his broad shoulders, his back and torso are more toned and muscled than most humans' in the prime of their lives, but tiny lines appear at the corners of his eyes. I look at the gash above his elbow again, wondering how bad it is.

"Yes," he finally says. "I recognized her."

The wound is barely bleeding. I don't think it's hurting him, so it has to be the *tor'um* that's weighing on his mind.

"Who is she?"

Another long pause. I think he's not going to answer until he draws in a breath, and says, "She almost became Atroth's sword-master."

This time, I break stride. "His *sword-master*?"

Kyol's a few paces ahead of me now. He looks over his shoulder and slows, waiting for me to catch up.

"She wasn't *tor'um* then," he says, when I'm at his side again.

I almost ask what happened to her, but I don't think I want to know. It's possible for fae to burn out their magic, but it's extremely rare. They know their limits and the consequence for pushing too far, so I'm almost certain that's not what happened to her. No, chances are, overexposure to human technology killed her magic.

I don't realize I'm clenching my teeth until I feel Kyol looking at me. I try to force my jaw to relax, to act like nothing is bothering me, but he sees right through my façade.

"It was years ago," Kyol assures me.

The muscles in my shoulders relax, and my next breath comes a little easier. We started hunting Aren just under a year ago. It's unlikely he was the one who turned the woman *tor'um*. I know that shouldn't matter—Aren stripped others of their magic—but Kyol knew the fae. They were colleagues— they might even have been friends—so I'm glad Aren isn't the one who made her insane.

Of course, that leaves the question of who did make her *tor'um*, but it's obvious the memories bother Kyol, so I let the subject drop. We spend the next few minutes in silence; then, just when we reach the outer edge of the forest, Kyol catches my arm, making me stop and turn toward him. His touch excites my *edarratae*, making the lightning come quicker and intensifying their heat, but I don't pull away. His brow is ever so slightly creased. No one else would notice it, but I've learned that's a sign that he's worried about something.

"McKenzie," he says. "You've escaped the remnants twice now. They won't let that happen again. The next time they find you, they'll kill you. You have to be careful. More careful than we were today." He pauses and glances at the three fae who've stopped a respectable distance behind us. When he speaks again, his voice is even lower than before. "Someone in the palace told the remnants that I was bringing you here. *You* specifically, not another shadow-reader. Vinn isn't the only traitor."

Vinn must be the fae from the roof, the one wearing the black necklace. Even after ten years, it's hard to wrap my mind around the fact that anyone would want me dead. I mean, I *do* get it. My shadow-readings keep fae from being able to fissure to safety, and that makes me at least indirectly responsible for the deaths and captures of hundreds of fae over the years, but I still feel like a relatively normal person, and normal people don't have enemies who want to slit their throats.

But normal people *do* have jobs. They have homes and families and friends they don't pull into wars. I need at least some of that if I'm going to stay sane. That's why I have to make it back to Vegas. Despite the walk to the gate, I should still be able to make it in time to turn in my paperwork. But then, a part of me thinks that maybe I should give up on having a human life and concentrate on helping Lena secure the throne, instead. I don't want to be responsible for anyone else getting involved with the fae.

I rub at the headache growing behind my eyes. Everything will be simpler once this war ends.

"You're going to have to send the former Court fae away," I tell Kyol. "I know you don't want to."

He releases my arm, walks a few paces away, then stops with his back to me. "We'll lose the palace without their help."

"The way things are going, we'll lose it with their help, too. We have to be able to trust the fae who are helping us."

"I know," he says. He grows quiet again, and it's incredibly hard not to put my arms around him. I want to comfort him, but I don't know how much that would help. Plus, three of his swordsmen are standing nearby. Even if we were together still, I wouldn't touch him.

"Are you okay?" I ask instead.

"It's a shallow wound, McKenzie. It will heal quickly."

My gaze drops to his elbow. It's still bleeding, but not enough to cause concern.

"That's not what I meant," I say. "Are you *okay*?"

He opens his mouth to say something, but then closes it again when he realizes what I'm asking. I stop breathing because, if he says he's not okay, that I'm hurting him and that it's painful to be around me, I don't know what I'll do. I can't love him like I did before, but I'd still do just about anything for him. I want him to be happy.

Finally, the most miniscule of smiles breaks his expression. "I'm okay, McKenzie. It's . . ." He pauses, his gaze goes to the left as if searching for the right words. "It's different . . . being around you now. I still care for you. I still feel the need to protect you, and I don't want to hurt or worry you. But, yes, I am okay."

Another smile, slightly bigger this time, and something inside me uncoils. I feel a smile tug at the corner of my own mouth. This is going to work, us being around each other. I don't have to be careful around him or feel awkward or guilty. He's okay—*we're* okay—and it's the biggest relief in the world.

We start walking again, but less than a minute later, he says, "I need to speak with Lena. You should reach the gate by nightfall. I'll make sure it's protected. You'll be okay."

I can't tell if that last part is a question or not. In the past, it would have been. But then, in the past, he most likely would have stayed with me and sent another fae to deliver his message.

"I'll be fine," I assure him.

His gaze moves from me to the three swordsmen trailing us—they'll make sure I make it safely to the gate—then, without any other farewell, Kyol opens a fissure and disappears. It's only after I blink the shadows from my vision that I realize I still have his name-cord in my pocket.

SEVEN

◆◆◆

I STEP OUT of the In-Between and into the Vegas suite I share with Shane. Kyol underestimated the amount of time it took to reach the gate. It was closer to the middle of the night before the fae and I arrived. Fortunately, the remnants didn't show up. Maybe they sent a scout who saw the thirty swordsmen and archers Kyol had sent to guard the gate. That force would deter most fae.

It wouldn't have deterred Aren, though.

If Aren were leading the remnants, he would have found a way to achieve his goal. That was his specialty, attacking against the odds. He and Lena are having a tougher time now that they're on the defense.

After my fae escort leaves, I glance inside Shane's room. I don't see him sprawled across his bed, so my best guess is he's in the Realm, making himself useful. The alarm clock on his nightstand says it's just after 1 A.M. Thank God. I can take a nap and still have time to take my driver's license and Social Security card to Jenkins. He needs it by five o'clock tomorrow, but I don't want to wait until then. I need to mark that off my list today so I can concentrate on finding Paige.

I fall into bed, too tired to do anything more than take off my shoes and socks and unbelt the scabbard from around my waist. Twenty minutes later, though, I'm still lying here

exhausted, but awake. My mind won't shut off. I'm worried
about Paige. The *tor'um* knew who she was. If I had any
doubt the remnants had her, I don't anymore.

Opening my eyes, I stare at the ceiling. I hope the remnants have let Paige see them. I hope they've tried to explain
things to her. But even if they haven't, even if she thinks she's
trapped in a bad dream or that she's snapped, I can fix it. I'll
tell her everything. King Atroth forbade it when he was alive.
He thought he was preserving the Realm's magic by keeping
the human and fae worlds as separate as possible, but that's
not the only reason I kept silent about them. The one time
I tried to tell a Sightless human about the fae, I ended up in
a mental institution. That's where I met Paige. She hated
Bedfont House as much as I did. She won't want to go back.

I roll to my side, pulling my covers over my head.

"I think I'm crazy," I tell Paige as I stare at the white wall
across from my bed. The counselors at Bedfont House leave
it bare and encourage us to decorate it however we want. I
haven't lifted a finger to do so. When I first arrived, I thought
if I put up a picture or poster, it would be like I'm admitting
that I belong here. Now, I'm thinking maybe I do. I haven't
seen any lightning-covered fae in more than three weeks.
Maybe I made them up. Maybe I made it all up.

"Everyone here is crazy," Paige says, not looking away
from her handheld mirror. Her eyes are opened wide while
she puts on glittery mascara. Her side of the room *is* deco-
rated. She painted it black. How the hell she got a hold of
black paint, nobody, not even the staff, knows. They didn't
make her repaint it, and they've said nothing about the post-
ers of cemeteries and creepy old houses she's put up. The
wall is accented with red: a scarf hanging near the door, a
crimson teddy bear sitting on her dresser, the bright silk pillow that's between her and the wall at her back. She has bats
in her blond hair. Six of them. They're tiny black clips with
glitter on the wings.

We've been rooming together for two weeks now, and if

you ask me, this whole Goth thing isn't really her. I think she's putting on a show to screw with the staff.

I return to staring at my blank wall. In the corner of my vision, I see her put down her mascara. She sits up, swinging her legs off the side of her bed so that she's facing me.

"Okay, fine," she says, sounding impatient. "Why do you think you're crazy?"

I frown. Did I say I was crazy? I can't remember. My mind feels heavy, sluggish. The white wall across from me is oppressively bright. It's almost as hard to look at as a fissure opening.

Ah, a fissure. The fae. That's right. I *do* think I'm crazy. I hope I am, at least, because if I'm not, if the fae do exist and I can see them and read their shadows, then I was taken advantage of. I helped Kyol and his king hunt down the false-blood Thrain, and now that he's dead, they're through with me.

Kyol's through with me, which means he never cared about me in the first place. None of them did. I was just a tool to help them win their war.

My chest aches. I want to go back to their world. I want to be needed and important, and I want to see more of the Realm, meet more of the fae. I want . . .

I want Kyol. If he's real, I want him.

Paige's bed squeaks when she stands. I hear her sigh then, a few seconds later, my bed sinks as she sits beside me.

"Here," she says, handing me a glass of water. "You should stop taking the meds."

I stare at the water's rippling surface. "They make me take them."

"They make all of us take them," she says. "They only watch us for five minutes afterward. Go to the restroom and throw up. Most of it won't make it into your system."

I take a sip of water, then force myself to focus on her. It's more difficult than it should be. "That's what you do?"

"Yeah. Ironic, isn't it? I get thrown in here after downing a bottle of cold medicine and here they are forcing pills down my throat. Now"—she takes back the glass and sets it on my nightstand—"tell me. Why do you think you're crazy?"

I haven't told any of the other girls why my parents sent me here. I guess I'm sane enough to know how crazy it sounds. The meds must really be messing with my judgment now because, without hesitating, I tell her, "I see things. People."

"Dead people?" she asks.

I give her an are-you-kidding-me glare.

"Just checking," she says, grinning. She has a cute face, pixieish. I've lucked out with her as a roommate. She's easy to get along with, and she doesn't judge. Plus, she's not a raving lunatic like some of the others here. She's not a raving lunatic like me.

I squeeze my eyes together, trying to think through the fog in my mind. The details of the past few months, of the king and his fae and the false-blood and his devotees, are too vivid to be fake. And Kyol . . . I couldn't have made up someone like him.

"Hello, McKenzie?" Paige says, waving her hand in front of my face. "Maybe I was wrong. Maybe you are nuts."

"I'm sorry, what were you saying?" I ask.

"I think we should break out of here tonight. Hit the town and party. There's this guy I know. He can pick us up and . . ."

I jerk awake when something scurries up my leg.

I'm across the room before I have time to scream. This isn't a cheap hotel. This is a fifteen-hundred-square-foot suite that costs over $500 a night. There should *not* be rodents here!

Heart thudding, I stare at the bed, waiting for the comforter to move. It doesn't. Could I have dreamed that? It's possible, but my calf still tingles where the thing touched me. It was furry, and even though I'm still wearing jeans, I'm sure I felt tiny feet.

The comforter wiggles, and I slam back against the wall. The thing is *not* tiny. The lump under the cover is close to two feet long, the size of a skinny pillow, and it's shifting, rolling to the left, then to the right, almost as if it's trying to burrow into the mattress. That's not the way a rat behaves, is it?

I feel my eyes narrow. Pushing away from the wall, I take

the three steps back to the bed, grab the edge of the comforter, and whip it off.

Something silver darts off the other side of the mattress. I hiss out a breath between my teeth, throw the comforter back down, then walk around the foot of the bed.

"Sosch."

Two big blue eyes blink innocently at me, and silver fur fades to white as I watch.

"How did you get here?" I ask as I kneel down and extend my hand. *Kimkis* aren't pets—they're an endangered species in the Realm—but they tend to bond to certain people. This one bonded to Aren. Sosch can find him anywhere. *Kimkis* aren't able to create their own fissures, but they can scurry into ones opened by fae. From there, they navigate the In-Between to their favorite people and places. This isn't the first time Sosch has found me, but it's the first time he's found me in my world.

I slide my hand down his long body, watching as his fur flushes silver under my palm. *Kimkis* do that when they're near scents they like, and they tend to like the smell of Sighted humans and gates. The fae use them as detectors. I'm pretty sure a *kimki* led Thrain to me all those years ago, and I know Sosch has helped Aren discover a few of the Realm's Missing Gates. I don't know if he's bonded to me. It's obvious he likes me, though, and I have to begrudgingly admit that he's just a little adorable.

Sosch lets out a sound that's a cross between a chirp and a squeak, then uses my outstretched arm as a springboard to my shoulders. He looks at me and does some weird, crinkly thing with his nose.

"Are you hungry?" I ask. What the hell do *kimkis* eat?

I spot the snack-sized bag of Goldfish on my dresser. That probably won't hurt him. I open the bag and hold up a fish to Sosch's mouth. He eats it, then his nose crinkles again.

"Good?" I reach inside for a second tiny cracker, but this time, he turns his head away, and his mouselike ears twitch. He leaps off my shoulder and rushes out of my bedroom one second before there's a knock on the door to the suite.

"Housekeeping," a maid calls. Shit. Humans can't see the

fae unless they want them to, but I'm pretty sure they can see a *kimki* that's wandered into our world.

"Sosch!" I try to grab him, but he's much too quick.

"No thanks!" I call out, hoping the maid will move on. She shouldn't be knocking on our door at all. Shane and I leave the DO NOT DISTURB sign hanging on the handle when we're gone. I didn't take it off when I was fissured here.

Sosch lets out another chirp.

"Shh," I say. Then I see the DO NOT DISTURB sign on the *inside* of the door. Crap.

"Sosch!" I yell, but it's too late. The door is already opening. The *kimki* flushes silver with pleasure, then darts past the maid's feet.

"Sosch!" I call out again.

The maid lets out a squeak very similar to the *kimki*'s, then hops back. Her head turns, following his progress down the hall.

"What *is* that?" she asks.

"It's a . . . a . . . an Egyptian otter," I stammer as I move past her. Sosch scurries under the housekeeping cart. I grab the handle to move it out of the way.

"We don't allow pets in this hotel," the maid says.

"I'm sorry," I say again. "I'll get him out of here."

Sosch looks over his shoulder, and I swear to God, he gives me the *kimki* equivalent of a grin before darting down the hallway. I'm going to kill him, and after I kill him, I'm killing Shane for leaving the DO NOT DISTURB sign on the wrong side of the door.

"He doesn't shed, does he?" The maid has a look of horror on her face as she stares into my suite.

"I have no idea," I mutter. I grab a pillowcase off the housekeeping cart and chase after the damn *kimki*. A chime rings and, just as I round the corner, I realize what the sound is.

"No, not the—"

Sosch scurries inside an elevator as a startled woman gets out. The doors slide shut right behind him. I sprint forward, try to hit the button to open the doors again, but it doesn't work.

What the hell am I supposed to do now? If animal control picks him up, they'll figure out that he is definitely *not* an

Egyptian otter. There's no telling what they'll do with him then.

Grumbling under my breath, I punch the button for the second elevator. I should let Sosch fend for himself, but I can't stand the thought of him ending up in the hands of biologists or scientists or anyone else who wants to figure out what he is or how his fur flushes between white and silver.

I fist the pillowcase in my hand as I watch the numbers above Sosch's elevator count down the floors. Of course, it doesn't stop until he reaches the ground floor. The image of hotel guests screaming as bellboys throw themselves across the floor, trying to catch the *kimki*, leaps into my mind. This could be really bad.

The second elevator pings. I step inside, punch the glowing number one, then jab the DOOR CLOSE button half a million times.

Sosch had a nonstop trip all the way down. Me? I stop at two additional floors and pick up six hotel guests before the doors finally slide open on the ground floor. I slip past the others with an apology, then scan the lobby.

It's less chaotic than I feared. No women screaming or bellboys on the floor, but Sosch definitely passed through here. Everyone's looking to the left, where a set of glass doors are propped open. Clenching my teeth, I stalk in that direction. You'd think the damn *kimki* was native to this world, he navigates it so well.

Hot summer air envelops me as soon as I step outside. The Vegas Strip is about a hundred feet ahead. It's packed with people. No way am I going to push my way through that crowd searching for Sosch. Never mind that I probably won't be able to find him, I'm not wearing shoes, and once I get out of the shaded entrance, the concrete will toast my feet.

A chirp-squeak comes from the decorative fountain a few paces to my left. Perched on the marble edge is the *kimki*. He happily nibbles at a cracker a young girl gives him. Fortunately, the girl's parents aren't paying any attention to her.

I've changed my mind. The *kimki* isn't adorably cute; he's a hideous rodent who doesn't belong in my world.

I wait until the girl holds out a second cracker before I

step out of the shade. The concrete is as bad as I thought it would be, but if I keep moving, my feet might not turn to ash. I sprint to the fountain and make my move, sweeping Sosch up with one arm while pulling the pillowcase over his head with my other hand.

"Thanks for finding Sosch for me," I tell the girl when her mouth falls open. She stares up at me, and I swear to God she's about to break down into tears.

"Really sorry," I say, hopping from foot to foot as I back away. The apology doesn't help. Her chin quivers.

I spin around and take off before she can point me out to her parents. Just as I'm merging with the crowd on the Strip, sobs ring out behind me. I feel like crap for making the girl cry, but I didn't have a choice. I have to get Sosch out of here.

And I have to find some shade.

I refrain from slinging the pillowcase over my shoulder. Instead, I hook my arm under Sosch's belly and keep him pressed to my side, making sure the pillowcase stays open so he can breathe. I don't know what I'm going to do with him. I can't take him back inside the hotel.

The concrete isn't so bad in the middle of the crowd. So long as no one steps on my foot, I might be okay.

At least, that's what I think until my skin prickles. I look over my shoulder, searching for the chaos luster I think I saw leap across someone's hand. There's a group of girls wearing flashing crowns walking the other way. The battery-powered blue lights are bright even under the blazing sun. Maybe my brain interpreted those as a fae's *edarratae*?

Someone runs into my shoulder, wrenching it hard. I ball my hand into a fist as the guy turns toward me.

"Sorry," the human slurs, drunk even though it's not even noon yet. His friends laugh as they guide him away.

Yeah. I'm definitely paranoid.

I try to force myself to relax as I continue on, but my skin is still crawling. It's not a feeling I get often in my world, and it's ridiculous to have it here, in the midst of all the flashing lights, the billboards, the humans with all their electronic devices. A fae's *edarratae* would be going crazy. They'd be easy to see. And that's why Shane and I are staying here, in a hotel on the Strip. Aside from the rebels dropping us off or picking us up, it should be fae-free.

My feet freaking hurt, but I keep going, making my way toward the south end of the Strip. The only place I can think of to go is to the gate. It's on a stretch of road that connects the city of Vegas to Lake Las Vegas. It's relatively rural, and since *kimkis* are attracted to gates, there's a chance Sosch might stay there for a while.

I can get there by bus, but the stop I need is ten blocks east of Las Vegas Avenue. It'll take twenty minutes to get there. As I turn down a side road, I readjust Sosch on my hip. I swear he's fallen asleep, and somehow, he's made himself weigh twice as much as usual.

Only a handful of locals and a few tourists who've wandered away from the Strip share the sidewalk with me. With the smaller crowd, it's easy to see that no one—no fae at least—is following me. After checking over my shoulder for the tenth time, my anxiety level finally lowers. Exactly one second after that, I hear the *shrrip* of a fissure opening behind me. Before I'm able to turn, I'm yanked into an alley.

I drop Sosch as I twist toward my attacker, swinging a fist at . . .

"Lorn," I grind out when I recognize the impeccably dressed fae plucking my fist from the air.

"McKenzie," Lorn returns with a smile. That smile disappears when an obviously pissed-off Sosch shoots out of the pillowcase, wraps himself around Lorn's left leg, then bites him just above the knee.

"Ahg. *Off!*" Lorn snaps in Fae, kicking out with his leg. Sosch thuds against a grimy door.

"Hey!" I glare at Lorn as I scoop the *kimki* up in my arms. "What are you—"

I stop because we're not the only people in this alley. A human is leaning against the wall, smoking a cigarette.

"What's that?" he asks, eyeing Sosch, as the *kimki* climbs up onto my shoulders.

"Otter," I mutter.

Lorn laughs. I clench my teeth together, adding Lorn's name to the list of people I'm going to kill.

EIGHT

•◆•

ONCE THE HUMAN is out of sight, Lorn breaks into a shop that's either gone bankrupt and was shut down or it's just been purchased and is being renovated. There are dozens of retail spaces in a similar stage of transition scattered all over the city. In this one, huge sheets of white plastic cover the glass windows, and the walls are missing Sheetrock. Empty clothing racks are tangled one on top of the other in the back corner, and the store's checkout counter is crooked and covered in an even thicker layer of sawdust than what's on the floor.

I set Sosch down. He makes a beeline for a stack of collapsed cardboard boxes, leaving a trail of tiny footprints behind him.

"What are you doing here?" I demand, when Lorn goes to the window. With one finger, he moves aside the plastic so he can peek out. I haven't seen Lorn since he fissured me to Vegas just over two weeks ago. He set me up in the hotel room and hasn't been back since.

"I came to see you, of course," he says, letting the plastic fall back into place.

"You could see me at the suite."

"I did see you," he says, scanning the shop. His lips pinch together as if the disorder and dinginess disgust him. Heaven forbid he get a smudge on his pristine white shirt. He's wearing it under a brown vest, which I think is made from *jaedric*, though it's not as thick as the *jaedric* in a fae's armor. The scabbard holding his sword on his left hip is darker than the vest; so is the messenger-style satchel that's slung over his shoulder. "I saw you right before the metal doors locked you inside the . . . the moving box."

"Elevator," I say. He saw me get into the elevator. He must have fissured into the suite when I was in the hallway; I was just too distracted chasing after Sosch to notice. "What do you want, Lorn?"

He manages to look offended. "What makes you think I want anything? Maybe I just want to visit with my favorite shadow-reader."

I meet his eyes, wait. Everything is a game to Lorn. The problem is, you never know if you're competing with him or against him, especially now. He has—*had*—a life-bond with Kelia. Lena and Aren think that's the only reason he provided them with supplies and information while they fought against the king, but I'm not so sure about that. I think Kelia was more of a convenient excuse for him to help them. He's more involved with the rebels than he has to be. In fact, after Sethan was killed, he was the first person to speak up and suggest that making Lena queen wasn't a bad idea.

When he doesn't give up the charade and tell me why he's really here, I say, "Take Sosch back to the Realm. It's not safe for him to be here."

I make my way back to the door to the alley. It has a window in it. I didn't realize it before because it's covered in such a thick layer of grime. I reach for the handle.

"I need you to shadow-read, McKenzie," Lorn finally says.

I look over my shoulder. "You came to my world just to ask me that? You could have found me in the palace."

"I could have," he agrees, clasping his hands behind his back as he walks to the checkout counter. "But Lena and I have had a . . . disagreement. I'm not welcome in the palace at the moment."

That doesn't surprise me at all. Lorn hasn't exactly been

forthcoming with information since the rebels took over the capital.

"What did you do?" I ask.

"It's insignificant," he says with a dismissive wave of his hand. "How long will it take you to get to the gate?"

"I haven't agreed to help you yet," I say, turning to face him fully. I shouldn't even consider it. I already have too many responsibilities: a friend I need to find, a watch rotation I shouldn't skip out on, and a job I need to finish applying for. I don't have time to shadow-read for Lorn.

"You will." The corner of his mouth slants up into a smug smile that gets under my skin.

"I'm sorry," I say. "I can't help you."

"Oh, I think you can." He sounds so pleased with himself that I'm about to turn and leave just to spite him, but before I do, he adds, "Rumor has it a friend of yours is missing."

My blood runs cold. He knows about Paige? How? I only learned she was missing yesterday.

"You know where she is," I say.

His smile widens. "I'll give you her location after you shadow-read for me."

I should have contacted him as soon as I learned Paige was missing. He has resources—spies, if I want to be accurate—everywhere. He probably knows more about what's going on in the Realm than Lena does, but still, I'm not sure if making a deal with him is the wisest thing to do, not without consulting Aren first.

"Must I remind you that you owe me?" A bolt of blue lightning slashes across his face, drawing attention to the circles under his eyes. They're not dark—I didn't notice them before the chaos luster—but they don't belong there. He's tired, and even though there isn't any active tech in this room, I'm sure it's not the most comfortable place for a fae. He probably has one hell of a headache.

"I'm aware of that," I say, staring at the plastic-covered window. Lorn saved my life in a tavern in Belecha, and he paid for the Vegas suite until Shane took over the bill a few days ago. The high nobles haven't allowed Lena access to the palace's treasury, and Shane has an extremely large rainy-day fund because he demanded a ridiculous amount of money from the king for his services. I hate being in anyone's debt, so the opportunity to make things even with Lorn is tempting. Plus, to some degree, I trust him. He acts like he's concerned only about information and profit, but he cared about Kelia. Her death and the loss of the life-bond have affected him more than he lets on.

I study Lorn. No one's been forthcoming with the details of that bond. As far as I know, Kelia and Lorn never loved each other. They bonded because they were a good match, and the connection made their magic stronger. Now that she's dead . . . ?

I *want* to help Lorn. It'll probably push my meeting with Jenkins to tomorrow, since I'm on the watch rotation at the palace later, but he won't leave the office until 5 P.M. I'll have all day to get there.

And I need to find Paige. If Lorn knows where she is, I have to help him.

"Who do you want me to track?" I ask, hoping this isn't a mistake.

He smiles. "Her name is Aylen. She's an associate of an associate."

"What do you want with her?"

"Just to talk," he says smoothly. "I'll meet you at the gate, shadow-reader."

"Wait," I say, as he opens a fissure. "We only have an agreement if you take Sosch with you."

"Sosch?" He stares at the *kimki*, who's sniffing at an exposed pipe in the wall.

"I can't keep carrying him through the city."

"He's not my *kimki*."

"He's not mine, either."

Lorn raises an eyebrow. "Really? Then why did you chase after him?"

I scowl back. "Just take him with you, Lorn."

"He's free to use my fissure if he wants to leave," he says, opening a slash of light between him and Sosch.

Sosch glances at Lorn, then returns to sniffing the pipe. I roll my eyes as I walk to the *kimki*. His fur turns silver when

I pick him up, but by the time I place him in Lorn's arms, he's stark white again. I don't think he's too pleased with this arrangement, either.

"Take him with you," I say again, ignoring Lorn's overly dramatic sigh.

IT takes more than an hour to get to the gate. That's mainly because I took a detour to buy a pair of socks and sneakers from Payless. I put them on after scrubbing my feet in the restroom sink, but they're still sore and a little black from walking on the hot concrete.

The bus driver questions me when I ask him to stop. He's the third driver this week I've had to convince to drop me off here, a good distance off the bus's actual route. We're twenty minutes outside the city, and there's not a building in sight. That works for me, though. I hate trying to fissure when humans are around.

After the bus leaves, I step off the road. The ground is all dirt and dead grass. It crunches under my feet, but a few dozen yards away, the landscape turns green along the banks of a stream. Lorn is there, sitting with his eyes closed and his back against a tree. He looks like he has all the time in the world to take a nap. So does Sosch. The *kimki*'s sunbathing in the blurred atmosphere that marks the gate's location.

"The idea was for you to take Sosch back to the Realm."

Lorn cracks open an eye. "Took your time getting here, didn't you?"

"I don't want Sosch with us when I shadow-read."

"He's perfectly happy where he is," Lorn says. That's true. The *kimki* hasn't so much as budged since I got off the bus.

"He doesn't belong on Earth." It's unlikely a human will stumble across him out here, but he's stuck in this world until a fae opens a fissure close enough for him to scurry into.

"If he doesn't use my fissure this time, I'll send someone to pick him up. Here." He hands me an Earth-made sketch-book. I wish I had mine with me, but it's stuffed inside my suitcase back at my old apartment. This one looks like it belongs to another shadow-reader. The first half already has maps drawn in it. At least, I'm assuming they're maps. I can't decipher them, so I have no idea what the lines and scribbles mean. Whoever drew it would know, though.

"Whose is this?" I ask, but as I turn another page, I know. Kelia stares back at me. Unlike me, Naito can actually draw. He's made his fae lover look delicate. Her hair is long and loose, shaded in with the edge of a pencil, and her eyes are soft and mesmerizing. Somehow, he's managed to capture her otherness on the page.

I close the sketchbook and hand it back to Lorn. "I don't feel right using this."

"You can rip out the pages you use," he says. "After that, I want you to return it to Naito."

"You can return it to him."

He still doesn't take it. "I did mention I've been banned from the palace, didn't I?"

"Lorn . . ." I fade off, fingering the sketchbook's worn cover. Naito might appreciate having it back. It's actually a pretty sweet gesture.

"He won't mind," Lorn says, standing. He pulls at his cuffs to straighten the barely there wrinkles in his sleeves, then he reaches into his pocket and hands me an anchor-stone. It's smooth and the color of snow-white quartz.

"Where will this take us?" I ask. The stone is warm, a sign that it's been imprinted with a location.

"Worried I'll abandon you in the Realm, miles away from a gate?"

"Pretty much. Yes." I'm not up for another six-hour walk through a forest, and tomorrow is Friday. I *have* to have my driver's license and Social Security card turned in to Jenkins by then.

"Fortunately for you, the city we're traveling to does have a gate." He dips his hand into the stream. The water pours between his fingers before it turns into a strip of white light. He holds out his other hand to me.

"Where, Lorn?" I'm not stepping into the In-Between until I know.

"Nashville," he relents.

"Tennessee?"

He tilts his head to the side. "Ten of what?"

"Never mind," I mutter. There's a gate in Nashville, so I'll assume that's where we're going.

After I take Lorn's hand, he adds, "My apologies in advance."

I stiffen, but he pulls me into the fissure before I have a chance to back out. The cold air hits me, freezing my breath in my lungs. That's not unusual, but the sharp pain in my chest is, and it doesn't disappear when I stumble out of the light, hitting the ground hard.

Lorn's on his knees beside me. Chaos lusters flash erratically over his clenched jaw. He's having just as difficult a time trying to breathe as I am, and I realize that *this* is the real reason he didn't take Sosch to the Realm. It's difficult for him, working any magic. If he fissured back and forth between his world and mine, he might not have had enough energy left to take me through the In-Between.

If I'd known just how weak he was, I might not have agreed to come. Most of the time, fissuring doesn't affect me like this. As long as my escort isn't overly tired or hurt, their magic shields them from the drain of passing through the In-Between. Lorn's magic hasn't shielded either of us.

I squeeze my eyes shut, cough, then force myself to rise to my feet. I'm light-headed, and I notice the human standing a few paces in front of me only after the fuzzy black spots clear from my vision.

"Did you . . . were you . . ." He looks down at my knee. My bleeding knee. My jeans are ripped. "Are you okay?"

The man is holding a set of car keys in one hand, a brown paper bag that looks like it's holding a bottle of alcohol in the other. He's probably in his late thirties, a family man, and, if his black slacks and tucked-in white cotton shirt are any indication, he's some kind of businessman.

And he obviously saw me appear out of nowhere.

"I'm good," I say as lightheartedly as possible with a queasy stomach. "I just need to watch where I'm going. Tripped over my own feet."

I start walking before he can say anything else. I'm not

about to give him a chance to ask what he wants to. If he's like the handful of other humans who have seen me appear out of nowhere over the years, he'll doubt what he saw. He's probably shaking his head now, thinking he needs some sleep or to check his vision or something.

"You could have warned me," I hiss at Lorn, when he falls into step beside me. We're on the back side of what appears to be a strip mall. Looking around, I think that one human might have been the only person who saw me. Most likely, the cars on the road to our left were driving too quickly to notice the girl stumbling into the parking lot.

"I believe I did warn you, my dear," Lorn says. I think he's trying to keep his tone light, but he doesn't succeed.

"You could have been more specific." I'm still feeling unbalanced, but at least the queasiness is fading, and my chest doesn't feel quite so tight. "And was this your idea of a safe place to fissure?"

"It's the only location I have memorized aside from the store," he says. Then he lengthens his stride. "Now, hurry, please. We might have already missed our opportunity today, thanks to your delays."

A human woman is walking toward us, so I stifle my response and follow as Lorn leads the way around the row of connected stores. Once we're on the front side of the strip mall, he points to the corner retail space. The sign above the door is simple: it's plain white with the words *A Taste of Ether* written in a sophisticated cursive script. Sunlight reflects off the store's glass windows, making it difficult to see inside. The only thing I can make out for sure is a few wooden crates in the windows.

"Is this a wine store?" I ask, thinking there might be an arrangement of bottles sitting on top of those crates.

Lorn nods. "A human named Sara works here. Don't let her know what you are. She'll be absolutely furious."

"She knows about the fae?" I ask, surprised.

"She has the Sight."

"Really?" I stare at the storefront again, trying to see inside. I know the five other humans who are working with the rebels. None of them is named Sara. Could this be one of Atroth's humans? I only knew a few of them. She could be working for the remnants now or—

"Don't get any ideas," Lorn says, eyeing me. "This is another reason I'm not going through Lena. Sara isn't some stray waiting around to be recruited. She's mine."

There's a warning in his voice. It's completely unnecessary. If she's not helping the remnants, I'm not about to pull her into the war. I wish I hadn't been pulled into it. I want nothing to do with the death and the violence, but I've been involved too long to just walk away. I care about too many people now, and I have too many mistakes to account for.

"A Sighted human is working in a wine store?" I ask Lorn. King Atroth wouldn't have ever allowed this; he'd see it as a waste of her talent.

"Profit, my dear," he responds, his tone lightening. "Nobles love their luxuries, and your world produces a delicious grape. I've tried transporting the vines to my farms, but our soil doesn't have the depth and personality that yours does."

I slant him a glance. "You have farms?"

"Vast areas of fertile land suitable for the raising of crops and livestock? Yes. I have several."

I try picturing Lorn as a farmer and fail.

"What do you grow?" I ask.

"Cows."

"Cows?"

"All quite illegal, in fact."

"You have illegal cows?"

"I do," he says with a pleased smile. "And the Realm hasn't imploded yet."

Obviously, Lorn isn't concerned with damaging the Realm's magic. It's mostly the high nobles and extremely conservative fae who want to keep human goods and culture out of their world. King Atroth appeased them, ordering his people to arrest merchants who were caught with human goods or with anchor-stones that were imprinted with Earth-based locations. The only exception, of course, was for his own swordsmen who had to escort Sighted humans through the In-Between. But I guess I shouldn't be surprised Lorn didn't follow the rules.

"Maybe Lena will lift the ban on nontech human goods," I say.

"I should hope not." Lorn gives me a look of exaggerated horror. "Wine and cows won't be worth half as much if she does."

Sometimes, I think Lorn is a halfway-decent fae being. Other times, I think he's exactly as selfish as he seems.

Lorn taps a finger on the sketchbook I have tucked under my arm. "Make sure your map of Aylen's shadows is accurate. I'll fissure inside as soon as she leaves."

"I want Paige's location first."

"I'm sure you do," he says. "But that's not the way I work. I'll give you her location after you read the shadows."

I cross my arms. "I don't even know if you really have her location."

"So little trust," he says, tsking. "I always keep my word."

I let out a sigh. He better know where she is. "How long until the fae shows up?"

"No idea. Could be in ten minutes. Could be in a few hours."

"And I'm just supposed to hang around until then?"

"Yes."

I roll my eyes. "What am I supposed to say when Sara asks why I'm there?"

Lorn smiles. "You'll figure something out."

NINE

-•-

A BELL ABOVE the door chimes when I walk in. Sara is younger than I am, early twenties probably, and wearing black slacks and a burgundy top with ruffled sleeves. She has a creamy, dark complexion—African-American and maybe a hint of something else? Bottles of red wine are in neat rows on the shelf in front of her, but she straightens them anyway, making sure each label faces out, before she turns to me.

"Can I help you with . . . something?" Her tone changes drastically after she takes in my T-shirt and ripped jeans, and about that same time, I realize this isn't some little Podunk wine store.

I swear there's not one trace of dust on the bottles, and each display has been set up with meticulous care. There's a lot of floor space, and more than one bottle has a small table to itself in the middle of the floor. Those bottles might as well have spotlights on them. They're displayed in small wooden boxes and cradled in a bed of black shredded paper. I don't see a price tag anywhere in the store. That's a flashing sign that says I can't afford this stuff.

So, what am I supposed to say to her? I look around the store, searching for an idea.

"I got in a fight with my boyfriend," I say. It's the only

thing I can think of to explain my ripped jeans and the dried blood on my knee. "Do you mind if I hang out here for a while? Just to be sure he's gone?"

She folds her arms, cocks her hip. "I assume he's your *ex*-boyfriend?"

"Soon to be, yeah. Definitely."

Her posture becomes much more casual. "Then, honey, you can stay here as long as you want."

"Thanks." I pretend to stare out the window, looking for the asshole who skinned my knee. After a couple of minutes pass, I see Sara's reflection approaching behind me.

"Here," she says, handing me a glass of red wine. "You look like you need to relax."

That's an understatement.

She looks out the window. "Is he out there?"

I take a sip of the wine. "I think I saw his truck a second ago."

"Should I call the cops?"

"No." I cough. "No. That's okay. I'm sure he'll go away soon." Before she asks more about my imaginary ex-boyfriend, I ask, "Do you own this place?"

She takes a sip of her wine, then shakes her head. "Not yet."

The bell above the door jingles, and a man walks in. Sara gives me an inquiring look, and I shake my head no. That's not the ex.

She helps him pick out the perfect wine for his anniversary. Another customer comes in after him, and she helps him, too. While she's working, I nurse my wine. Half an hour passes. I think Sara is getting annoyed, but just when I think she's about to kick me out, my skin prickles.

Sara definitely has the Sight. She tenses when the fissure cuts through the air. The woman who emerges is about my height, which is short for a fae. She's not wearing *jaedric*, just a turquoise tunic over fitted black pants. The pants are tucked inside a pair of black boots that are embroidered with a pattern of gold half circles and diamonds. The design matches the scabbard holding her sword at her left hip. I'm surprised to see the name-cord in her hair. I wish I knew what kind of stones they were. If I did, I might be able to place where she's from, but I don't think I've seen these before. They're two different shades of red with smaller black stones that might be onyx between them.

The fingers of my right hand start to tingle. I want to sketch the shadows, but they always tell me a fae's exit point, not where they've come from, and since I already know where we are, there's no need to draw out their curves and angles. Plus, I don't want to get caught staring at something I'm not supposed to be able to see. I down the rest of the wine to distract myself and try not to make a face when it tickles my nose.

"Finished?" Sara asks, her tone clearly saying she wants me out of there. I can empathize. I hate trying to communicate with fae when Sightless humans are around.

I hand her the empty glass. "I think my ex is gone, but can I use the restroom?"

She presses her lips together. I think I'm going to have to find another excuse to stay, but finally, she says sure and points to a back room.

"Thanks," I say. The restroom is on the left side of the storeroom. I open and shut the door without going inside, making sure it's loud enough for her to hear, then I tiptoe back to the open doorway of the storeroom and listen. I don't really care to hear what they say; I just have to be able to see Aylen's shadows when she fissures out.

"Quick," Sara says. "Before she gets back."

I peek around the doorframe, see Aylen tip open a draw-stringed pouch. Strands of gold slide out. Necklaces. Thin bracelets. A couple of plain rings. If Sara makes deals like this with fae often, she must be making a fortune.

"It's behind the counter," Sara says.

Aylen nods. She opens a fissure as she walks behind the register, but it's not until after she bends down to pick up a crate of six bottles that I realize this isn't going to work. Half her shadows will be hidden behind the counter when she fissures out.

My sketchbook is already open and I'm halfway across the store when she disappears. Sara's back is to me, so I give in to the urge to scratch down what I see. A swoop of black tinged with shades of gray fades in and out in the upper part of my vision. Aylen's gone to a coastal city. I've drawn the waves on the top of the page, so she's on the southern edge of a body of water.

I turn to the next page, draw a craggy spine down the left side of the page. She's gone to Criskan Province. There's a city that's bordered by mountains to the west and the Daric Ocean to the north. It's called . . .

I frown, trying to recall my mental map of the Realm. I don't have every single city memorized, but this is a major port town with a gorgeous beach and a dense population. I should know it.

I close my eyes. I'm going to have to remember the name of that damn city before Lorn will give me Paige's location. What is it?

"You didn't flush."

My eyes snap open. Sara is standing directly in front of me.

"What?"

"The toilet," she says. "It sounds like a tornado when it flushes. You didn't flush."

"Oh. Um." I look over my shoulder at the opening to the storeroom. "Sorry, I'll—"

Her gaze drops to the sketchbook in my hand. My map is a mess of wavy lines and lopsided trees, but it's clear she knows exactly what it is. She looks at my drawing, then up at me, then over to where the fae disappeared, then back at my drawing.

"Son of a bitch," she says. "Who the hell are you?"

Well, crap. The game is up. Might as well be polite.

"I'm McKenzie," I say, holding out my hand for her to shake. She doesn't take it.

"Who sent you?" she demands.

As if on cue, a fissure opens to my left.

"Lorn," Sara all but snarls when he steps out of the light. "You brought her here?"

"She didn't stumble upon you all by herself," he says, staring at the map, not at her. "Where is this?"

Good question. I still can't remember the name of the city.

"It's at the northern part of the Jythia Mountains," I say. "The big city on the coast?"

He glances up at me, then stares down at the map. "*This* is Eksan?"

That's it. "Yeah. That's where she went."

Lorn raises an eyebrow, waiting. He's probably memorized at least one location in Eksan, but he needs me to say the city's name out loud to have any chance of fissuring close to where Aylen did, and I'm not about to name it. Not yet.

"My customers trust me, Lorn," Sara cuts in. "They don't expect to be stalked by their competition."

Lorn laughs. "Aylen is hardly any competition for me." He turns to me. "Now, name the city."

"Don't," Sara says, her fists clenched at her sides. "My business is none of your business."

"No one will know I tracked her from here. The city, McKenzie."

"Tell me where Paige is first."

His lips flatten into a thin line.

"You gave me your word," I remind him. "And you *always* keep your word."

"I promised to give you her location," he says. "And I will. Just as soon as I learn where that location is."

He doesn't know. Damn it.

Sara *hmmphs* as if I should have known better. I did know better. I came here on a gamble that didn't pay out, but I'd do it again. I'd do it again because I owe it to Paige.

"The deal is off," I tell Lorn.

"The deal is not off," he says, a warning slipping into his tone. "You have ten seconds. If you don't name the city, I'll leave you stranded here and your *kimki* stranded in Las Vegas, and you'll never find your friend."

"You're not my only option," I say.

"If I don't want you to find her, you won't find her. Five seconds."

I grit my teeth. I don't know if he can see that threat through, but I definitely don't want to make him my enemy. "You swear you'll try to find her?"

"I do."

Another second passes. I curse, then finally relent. "Eksan."

Lorn gives me a curt nod as he tugs at the cuffs of his sleeves. "I'll let the rebels know where to find you. Have a good day, ladies."

Shadows fill the space he occupied. I squeeze my eyes shut until my hands stop itching to draw them. When I reopen them, I'm able to focus on Sara.

She glares at me through the twisting shadows. "Get the hell out of my store."

TEN

•◆•

I'M NOT ABOUT to rely on Lorn to send a fae back to get me, so I ask a man on the street to use his cell phone. Unfortunately, Shane isn't at the suite when I call. I leave a message telling him where I am, but I don't know if he'll notice the tiny red light on the hotel phone when he gets in.

At least Lorn stranded me in my world, not the Realm. I blend in here, and if my bank account weren't at zero, I'd have the option of booking a flight back to Vegas. I suppose if worse comes to worst, I can go into my overdraft protection. I shouldn't have to, though. Either Lorn will keep his word and send a fae for me, or I can stake out Sara's wine store until another fae shows up. I might be able to talk whoever it is into fissuring me to Corrist on the promise that they'll be well paid if they do.

So, I decide to spend the rest of the afternoon at the cafe two doors down. It has outside seating, and I have just enough change in my pocket to order a cup of coffee. That ends up being a mistake. It makes me jittery. I'm no closer to finding Paige, and with each passing minute, I worry more about her and about what's happening back at the palace.

An hour passes. Then another. I flip through Naito's sketchbook. Two more pictures of Kelia are sketched on its pages. One of them is in the corner of a shadow-reading.

Naito's ten times the artist I am, but his maps look like a child's scribbles just like mine do. I wish I knew where this one leads to—he's drawn an elaborate frame around the entire page, so it's probably somewhere important—but shadow-readers can't decipher anyone's maps but their own.

I miss Kelia. It's weird, admitting that. I only knew her for a few weeks, but we were close to being friends. I think she was honest with me, and I think we'd get along well if she were still alive. I could ask her about Aren. I miss him, don't know if I'm doing the right thing with him. I don't know him any better than I did two weeks ago. For us to work out, we need to spend time together, time where we're not running for our lives or tracking somebody. Not for the first time, I wonder if it's a bad idea to try to start a relationship right now.

Sara locks up the wine store. I think about following her, but a flicker of blue light in the corner of my vision catches my attention. It's Trev. The last time I saw him was yesterday back at my apartment. Blood was gushing from a bad leg wound then. Aren or Lena must have healed him because he's not even limping now.

He doesn't see me until I close Naito's sketchbook and stand. His gaze travels down to my feet, then back up. "You're not injured?"

A couple is sitting at one of the other tables, so I just shake my head, tuck the sketchbook under my arm, and start walking.

"How did you find me?" I ask when I'm far enough away.

"The *kimki*," Trev says. "He came to the palace with an anchor-stone and your name tied around his neck."

Looks like Lorn kept part of his promise. Maybe he'll keep the rest of it and find out where Paige is.

Trev increases his pace. I'm *barely* able to keep up. It's annoying—he knows humans are slower than fae—but I don't complain. Trev isn't my biggest fan. He puts up with me when he has to, but he's never exactly liked me. I helped the king hunt down his friends and family. Like most of the rebels, he has a reason to resent me. Those reasons didn't disappear just because I joined their side of this war.

My feet are sore, but I jog to catch up with him when I fall too far behind. "For what it's worth, I'm sorry."

He glances my way for a whole half second. "Lena healed me."

I frown, then realize he's talking about the remnants' attack at my old apartment. He almost bled to death because of me.

"No, not for that," I say, then I grimace. "Well, yeah, for that, too. But I'm sorry for what happened before I met you. I didn't know everything that was going on."

"You're forgiven, of course," he says. His accent makes it difficult to pick up the sarcasm in his tone, but I'm certain it's there.

I don't jog to catch up with him when I fall behind this time. He can either slow down, or I'll meet him at the gate. That's where we're heading. I've never been to Nashville before, but I've seen Atroth's maps of the U.S., and while I haven't memorized every single gate known to exist in this country—there are way too many to keep track of—I do remember one being on the lake to the east of the city. I'm pretty sure the highway up ahead runs to the west of it.

It takes twenty more minutes to reach a small, wooded cove on the lakeshore. Trev dips his hand into the water without a word. After the fissure rumbles open, he reaches into the draw-stringed pouch tied to his belt and takes out an anchor-stone. Chaos lusters flicker over his hand when he imprints it. He hands it to me, then holds out his arm.

It's awkward, touching a fae who hates you, but I wrap my fingers around his forearm and brace myself for the In-Between. Cold, harsh air clenches around me, squeezing for what feels like an eternity, before it spits us back out. My body is stiff and sore and pissed at me for traveling so soon after Lorn's hellish fissure. My vision turns white, the world tilts, and I have to hang on to Trev in order to stay on my feet.

I'm still freezing. I don't realize why until I let go of Trev's arm and force my eyes to focus. I expect to be in the Realm; I don't expect to be in a city that is not Corrist. It's night here, but the streets are white with snow except for the circles of blue beneath the magically lit street orbs. Long, thin icicles cling to the eaves of the row houses lining the street. They're single-storied, but there's quite a distance between their front doors, which means they're big. We're in an upscale part of this city, and something about the architecture—the curved rooftops and pale blue stucco of the walls—is familiar. I think I've been here before.

An uncomfortable, nervous feeling pools in my gut.

"Where are we?" I take a step away from Trev and lock my gaze on the shadows from our extinguished fissure. I dropped Naito's sketchbook when we stepped out of the In-Between. I bend down to retrieve it from the snow-covered ground, my heartbeat picking up its pace because I don't know if I can trust Trev.

"We're in Rhigh," he says.

The sketchbook slips from my fingers. A gust of wind flips it open before I recover. I slap it shut, dust off the snow that sticks like powder to its cover. This place is familiar because I *have* been here before. With Thrain.

I hug the sketchbook to my chest as if it can keep me warm. It was cold ten years ago, too, but I was wearing long sleeves and a jacket when Thrain abducted me, not a thin, short-sleeved T-shirt. After three days in this weather, though, the extra layer of clothing didn't matter. Thrain didn't warm the air in the house he imprisoned me in. I would have frozen to death if Kyol hadn't found me.

Trev starts walking down the street, toward a multistoried, ornate building. The high noble's home, maybe? Rhigh's gate is in the other direction.

"Trev," I call out. Either he doesn't notice my reaction to this place, or he doesn't care. It's probably the latter. He hasn't asked why I was in Nashville or who took me there.

I hate being on this street with him—there's no telling who might be watching from a window—so I grab his arm and pull him into a narrow walkway. If he didn't want to move, he wouldn't, but he doesn't shake free until after we're off the main street.

"Why aren't we in Corrist?" I demand.

"Lena wants you here," he returns. That's it. No elaboration.

If this wasn't Rhigh, and if I didn't need a fae to fissure out of here, I'd turn on my heel and leave. With the exception of Kyol and a few others, this was how the Court fae treated me. They were usually more considerate than Trev—they never would have brought me here without a cloak—but they were mum when it came to explanations. When I was a teen, I didn't have the confidence to demand more information from them, then it became a bad habit, doing what they said without knowing the reason why. I'm not putting up with that from the rebels.

"Why does she want me here, Trev?"

"Because I asked for a shadow-reader." Aren's voice comes from my left. A tingle runs through me when I see him. He wasn't on the main street before, but he must have seen Trev and me slip between these buildings. And he must have been outside somewhere because the wind has made his hair even more disheveled than usual. He doesn't look like a bum or an unkempt *tor'um*, though. He looks good. I don't know how he pulls that off. Maybe it's the armor hugging his torso and his arms and legs, or maybe it's the way his silver eyes drink me in. Whatever it is, it makes him undeniably attractive.

His gaze drops suddenly, following the path of a chaos luster down my neck, I presume, then he frowns down at the rip in my jeans. My knee is scratched up and sore from stumbling into the parking lot in Nashville, but it hurts less than the bruise on my thigh that I got when Shane hit me with a car. Neither is serious enough to need healing. Aren must realize that, but he closes the distance between us as if I'm two seconds away from dying.

"Sidhe, *Trev. She can't keep warm,*" he says, placing his hands on my shoulders.

His *warm* hands. I step closer, breathe in his cedar and cinnamon scent, then shiver when his touch sparks through me. I'm sure he feels the lightning, too, but he's still glaring at Trev.

"*Are you trying to make her sick?*"

"*I forgot—*"

"*That she's human?*" Aren cuts him off.

Trev opens his mouth to say something else, but swallows his words when he focuses behind me and Aren.

"Lord Hison," Trev says instead, with a shallow dip of his head.

Lord Hison, elder of Dice and high noble of Jutur Province, stands only a few feet away. His midnight blue cloak is embroidered with gold leaves. It looks warm and heavy, a sharp contrast to his silver eyes, which are cold and so light they almost look white. That's the snow reflected in them, I think.

Aren's tense. He moves back slightly, and I see the battle he's fighting with himself. He doesn't want to keep his distance from me, but like Lord Kaeth, we need Hison to vote Lena to the throne. I've met the high noble a few times before. He barely tolerates the presence of humans in the Realm. He definitely wouldn't approve of Aren's relationship with me.

I make the decision for Aren, taking a long step back. A brief wince appears on his face before the stiffness leaves his posture, and he turns.

"Lord Hison," he says. *"I didn't expect you to follow."*

Hison is focused on me. Normally, I'd avert my gaze. I don't this time. I'm in his world trying to end the war that has spilled so much blood these last few years. I'm *helping* him and his people. He's going to have to accept that I'm here.

"Be careful with that," Hison says, his gaze still on me. *"Rumor is she seduced Taltrayn. She may try to do the same to you. Atroth should have discarded her years ago."*

The only reason I don't react is because he doesn't know I understand Fae, and I want to keep it that way.

"She is bewitching, isn't she," Aren says smoothly. *"I'd caution you against touching her."* His tone is light, but there's an edge to it, too.

Hison stiffens.

"The nalkin-shom *needs to be inside,"* Aren continues, before the high noble decides to take offense at his words. *"Humans are susceptible to the elements."*

Fae are susceptible to some extent, too—they can't use

their magic to keep warm indefinitely—but I don't complain. I'm twice as cold as I was before Aren touched me.

"Send your man for a cloak," Hison says. *"She'll survive until he returns. We'll continue on."*

Aren's eyes narrow just perceptibly, but Hison is already moving.

"I'll return quickly," Trev mutters. Then he opens a fissure and disappears.

I'm so cold, I'm numb to the pull of his shadows. I'm not numb, however, to Aren's next words.

"Lena shouldn't have sent you."

All the warm, fuzzy feelings I had when I first saw him vanish. "It's good to see you again, too."

"I didn't—"

"Was I not clear that I want you to come along?" Hison asks, peering back down the walkway.

Aren draws in a breath. I start walking before he lets it out, partly because I'm hoping moving will warm me up and partly because I'm just a tad bit hurt. I've been worried about him. Has he been too busy to worry about me?

He's fighting a war, I remind myself. He has more important things on his mind.

"Are you okay?" he asks, falling into step beside me. His gaze dips to my bare arms.

"I'm fine," I say. I intend my response to be short, but it comes out harsher than I wanted. It's the weather's fault. My face is going numb. I *am* going to get sick if Trev doesn't return soon. I'm sure he's staying in this world; he shouldn't have to wait too long before he fissures back.

"You know I didn't mean it that way," Aren says, keeping his voice so low I wonder if Hison understands English. Two fae are with the high noble. Only the woman is a guard, I think. She's on Hison's right, trailing slightly behind him. The fae on Hison's other side wears a name-cord in his hair. He's carrying a sword, too—all fae carry them—but he doesn't seem as ready to use it as the woman does.

"I've missed you. I've been wanting to see you, too, just not like . . ." He stops, clenches his jaw, then continues. "Not here. Not like this."

He almost sounds pained. I scan him, searching for injuries. He looks okay, but he looks different. He's not the same Aren who held me captive. That Aren was cavalier and sly, always ready with one of his infuriating half grins. This Aren is tense. Stressed-out. I want to help him, but I don't know how.

Not for the first time, I'm struck by just how little I know him. I was his prisoner for two weeks. I've been his ally for two and a half.

His ally. Is that all our relationship is? It feels like it sometimes, but I want to be so much more than that.

"This province has been unstable since we took the palace," Aren says, keeping his gaze straight ahead. "Hison issued a curfew to try to keep things under control."

A curfew. That explains why the streets are empty.

"It's not working," he continues. "The gate isn't being monitored. Merchants are fighting over who gets to use it first, and while their backs are turned, fae are stealing their goods. They're breaking into their stores, too. Hison should be able to take care of it, but the gate guards were paid by Atroth. Even if they're willing to work for Lena, we don't have the *tinril* to pay them. The high nobles won't send the gate taxes to us because they haven't voted Lena to the throne."

I frown. I think I do, at least. My face is so numb I can't tell for sure. "Sethan was against taxing the gates."

Aren looks at me. "No." His gaze drops to my bare arms again. He seems agitated. "We wanted fair tolls. Atroth's were designed to keep him in power. He let merchants from the provinces he dissolved fissure for free so they wouldn't protest. The gates need to be taxed, but we don't have enough fae to spare to monitor them and . . . And I can't watch you freeze like this."

His arms are around me before I process his last sentence. I look at Hison. He's still walking, but he could turn around any second.

"Screw him," Aren says.

I'm too cold to step away. Instead, I meet Aren's eyes. "Did you pick that phrase up from Naito?"

The corner of his mouth tilts up. "From you, actually."

The nervous feeling in my stomach disappears. It's replaced with a warm, tingling sensation.

His smile widens. "I really have missed you, *nalkin-shom*."

That smile disappears when he takes my hands in his. "*Sidhe*, your fingers are ice."

"Yeah." I look back the way we came. We're still in line of sight of where Trev and I fissured in. I'm assuming that's where he'll reappear, but there's still no sign of him. How long does it take to get a freaking cloak?

I turn back to Aren. Past his shoulder, I see Hison staring at us.

"We need to keep walking," I say.

Aren scowls, but we turn and follow the high noble. Aren doesn't stop touching me. He runs his hands up and down my arms, then alternates cupping first my right, then my left hand between his. The contact helps. The lightning distracts me—*he* distracts me—and somehow, I'm as hot as I am cold. My body isn't numb anymore. I'm all too aware of just how much I want him.

"You didn't say what we're doing here."

Aren's thumb massages my palm. "Hison captured a fae who's been encouraging the disorder. He's outspoken against Lena, the corruption of the palace, the war. We think he's close to the remnants' leadership. We're going to let him escape. We need to know where he goes."

Hison leaves the street, taking a narrow path between two tall stucco buildings. The shadow-reading should be simple. This is the type of assignment I was given almost all the time when I worked for the Court. It's safe. The target never even knows I'm there unless something goes wrong.

Like something went wrong back in Spier.

"You trust Hison?" I ask.

"Not at all," he replies. Then, "Here's Trev."

Trev must have either known where we're going or seen us turn down this path. He jogs toward us, carrying a white cloak. Maybe that's what took him so long. Most of the fae's cloaks are dark colors—deep blues and various shades of gray and black. This one will help me blend in with the snow.

Aren takes it from him. He runs his hands over it twice before he opens its folds and places it around my shoulders.

I very nearly moan. It's like being tucked inside a blanket taken directly from the dryer.

"God, I love you . . . you're magic." Shit. That was a bad stumble. Humans throw those words around so casually, but I don't know if he knows that, and I'm not ready to tell him I love him, not while we're fighting a war and not while our relationship is so new and unstable.

He pulls my hood over my head. Keeping a grip on the front edges, he pulls me close.

"Careful, *nalkin-shom*," he whispers conspiratorially. "I might think you're starting to like me."

I'm grateful he's making light of my slip. My shoulders are defrosted enough that I manage a shrug. "I might not hate you quite as much as I used to."

He smiles, then lets go of my hood to run his hands over the cloak again. A new wave of warmth envelops me. Seriously, fae magic is pretty awesome sometimes. I could melt inside this cloak. It's heavy enough to block the wind and it has huge, wide pockets on the inside that I can slip my arms into.

Aren's palm glides down my back . . . and stops just above my waistband. That's where the dagger he gave me should be. It seems like forever has passed since I left the Vegas suite, but that's where the dagger is, uselessly parked on my dresser. Unless the maid called the authorities.

"It's Sosch's fault," I mutter.

Aren lifts an eyebrow as if to say, "Really?" There's an entertained glint in his silver eyes that makes my stomach flip again.

He unhooks a short scabbard from his belt. "Lena's not going to be happy when she learns you're depleting the armory."

He lifts the back of my shirt to slide it—

"Cold!" I squeak as soon as the scabbard touches my skin.

"Oops," he says, sliding it into my waistband, but he's grinning. He sobers a second later, though. Softly, he asks, "You're okay?"

I pull the cloak more tightly around me. "Yeah, this is warm enough. Thanks."

"No. Are you okay with being here? In Rhigh?"

I'm not sure what he's asking. He knows Thrain was the false-blood who pulled me into the Realm. Does he know Thrain held me here? I don't see how he could. This was only one of Thrain's bases, and I don't think Atroth or any of his fae went around telling others this is where they stumbled across me.

Trev—I almost forgot he was here—clears his throat, then mutters the warning, "Hison."

"Is there a problem?" Hison has doubled back and is standing only a few paces away.

Aren focuses on the high noble and says, *"Lena expects her humans to be taken care of. McKenzie's well-being is my priority. I want her out of the elements."*

"It's not much farther," Hison practically spits. It was so much easier to work for the fae when I didn't realize just how much some of them hated me.

It takes less than a minute to reach our destination, a small, detached home near the city's marketplace. I can't see it from here, but that marketplace is on the river. That's where the gate is, too. Kyol fissured me through it when he stole me away from Thrain.

I'm uncomfortable being back here, but I don't let it show. I follow Hison and Aren through the door and into the living area. The room is dark, lit only by the moonlight coming in from a window, but I can still make out the blue silk shimmering overhead. It's a common fae custom to pin thin drapes to the ceiling. They're soft and light, moving like waves when we walk beneath them. They're supposed to be relaxing, but I still feel tense, which is stupid. Thrain is dead. Dead, dead, dead.

Unless Naito is right and *banek'tan* do exist.

I don't know why I let that thought creep into my mind.

I'm 99.9 percent certain no one can bring fae back from the dead.

"Is this close enough?" Hison asks. He's standing in front of a window.

"It's close enough," Aren answers. He motions me forward. "The fae will come out of that door."

That door is barely ten feet away. It's just across the narrow street and nearly hidden behind the snow-covered branches of a leafless bush, but it won't be a problem to draw the fae's shadows; the problem will be to do it without the fae seeing me.

"This is fine," I say, taking the pen out of the spine of the sketchbook tucked under my robe. Now that we're out of the weather, I'm much warmer. I don't take my hood off, though. If a chaos luster flashes across my face when the fae steps onto the street, he might figure out this is a setup.

Hison orders his assistant, the one with the name-cord, to go. From what I understand, he's to check on the fae prisoner, then "accidentally" leave a door unlocked.

I sink down to one knee beside the window and wait.

Aren squats beside me. "Trev and I will fissure after him."

That will leave me alone with Hison and his guard. Lovely. "How am I getting back to Corrist?"

"I shouldn't be gone more than a few minutes," he says. He looks directly at me. "McKenzie—"

The door across the street swings open. I don't have time to see the fae's face; he disappears into his fissure the instant he steps outside.

I flip open Naito's sketchbook, rest it on my knee, and start sketching. I draw three thick, wavy lines at the top of the page. It's the Daric Ocean. I frown at the shadows, scratch down a few bottomless triangles. It's the same mountain range, too. The fae didn't fissure to the exact location Aylen did, but it's close enough to be extremely coincidental.

I flip to the next page, narrow down my map. He's close to a winding street on the west side of the city. He might even be on it, but I'm not 100 percent sure. I wait for the shadows to shift, see a thin dark line appear in the center of my vision.

An intersection. I mark an "x" where the shadows tell me he exited, then turn to Aren.

"He's gone to Eksan," I say. "I just drew—"

Trev fissures out.

"Thank you." Aren rests his hand briefly on my bent knee before he rises.

"Aren—"

"I'll be back soon," he says. Then he disappears into a slash of white light.

ELEVEN

※

I'M ANNOYED. SO annoyed, I don't get drawn in by Aren's shadows. I get that he needed to go, but it was obvious I was trying to tell him something. Trev had already left. Would it have killed Aren to wait five seconds? I'm sure it's just a coincidence—Eksan is a huge city—but it's possible there *could* be a connection between the remnants and Aylen. Between the remnants and Lorn. He called Aylen an "associate of an associate." That could mean anything.

"What do we do with this?" Hison's guard asks. She's staring at me.

I'm so close to saying something because, really, what are the consequences if they learn I speak Fae? Hison will be pissed at Lena for letting me learn the language, but he's already not happy I'm here in his world.

I look at the spot where Aren disappeared. How long until he gets back? He said "soon," but if the fae didn't fissure directly to the remnants, Trev and Aren will have to follow him. And then, there's always the chance the fae will double fissure—that's how Aren evaded us for so long. Toward the end, we had a second shadow-reader standing by at a gate. After I mapped the fae, one of Kyol's men would fissure to that human, then take him or her through the gate to the location I sketched out. It wasn't a perfect solution, but we did come closer to capturing Aren that way.

That's probably why he started fissuring more than two times. It's an impressive talent. After traveling a substantial distance, most fae have to wait two or three minutes before they're able to enter the In-Between again.

"Jorreb will come back for her," Hison says. *"If she didn't lead him into a trap."*

"You think she's feeding information to the remnants?"

Okay, so maybe this is why I don't want them to know I can speak Fae. People are loose with their tongues when they don't think I can understand them. Also: what the hell? I've been working my ass off for the rebels.

"It would explain why she tolerates being near the protégé of a false-blood."

I stare down at the sketchbook still propped on my knee. I retrace one of my marks, clenching my teeth together so I don't say anything. Sethan wasn't a false-blood. Lena isn't either. They're Descendants of the *Tar Sidhe* just like Atroth was. I confirmed that with more than one former Court fae after we took the palace.

"Humans don't care about false-bloods," the bodyguard says.

"This one does."

I can feel Hison's gaze. He's waiting for me to look up. If I don't, I think it will be suspicious, so I raise my eyes from the sketchbook and meet his. I'm through with letting fae intimidate me.

"What?" I stand, so my demand has more of an impact.

Hison doesn't look away. *"Did you understand Jorreb's conversation with her?"*

"Some of it. He told her why she is here," the bodyguard tells him.

"No mention of Thrain?"

The name makes my blood turn cold. No, no, no. Kyol killed him—I saw his soul-shadow—and *banek'tan* do not exist. Thrain is dead. Aren would tell me if he wasn't.

But Aren did say Lena shouldn't have sent me here. Is this why?

"You speak Fae."

Hison's statement pulls me out of my near panic. I shake my head, clearing my mind, and focus on the high noble. My thoughts obviously showed on my face, but Thrain in Fae is the same as Thrain in English. His conclusion that I speak his language is a guess.

"What about Thrain?" I ask.

The bodyguard translates what I said. Hison's eyes narrow. He looks directly at me when he says, *"Jorreb is his protégé."*

Aren? It takes everything in me to look confusedly back and forth between the two fae. Inside, though, I feel sick. Is it true? Hison could just be trying to get a reaction from me, but this could explain why Aren asked if I was okay in Rhigh. If he's connected to Thrain, he could know Thrain kept me here.

Hison takes a step closer. *"You do understand me, don't you?"*

I furrow my brow further. Then my skin tingles. A second later, Aren steps into the living room. I let myself give in to the urge to stare at his shadows because it's an excuse not to meet his eyes.

"That didn't take long," Hison says, sounding disappointed. *"Were you successful?"*

In my peripheral vision, I see Aren nod. *"He led us to a home where three others were meeting. They'll be taken to Corrist."* He turns to me. "We can go now, McKenzie."

I should win an Oscar. I meet Aren's eyes, and I smile. "Back to the suite or to Corrist?"

Maybe the smile is too much. His gaze drops to my lips, and his brow wrinkles slightly as he frowns. "Corrist, if that's okay."

"It's great," I tell him cheerily.

"Your shadow-witch isn't as terrifying as the stories make her out to be," Hison says.

Aren glances at the high noble. *"That's because she's not your enemy. Lena will contact you if we learn anything from the fae."* He takes my arm, and I'm thankful for the protection the cloak offers against his touch. I can't deal with any chaos lusters right now.

"I heard Thrain discovered her ten years ago," Hison calls after us. *"Is that true?"*

Aren tenses. He turns his head to the side but doesn't quite look over his shoulder. *"I've heard that as well."* He reaches for the doorknob.

"It's a shame Atroth stole her from you," Hison adds.

Aren looks down at me. My face is expressionless when I meet his eyes, and that's all he needs to know that I know.

"I didn't know her then," he says, then he opens the door.

"CAN we talk about this?" Aren asks, keeping pace by my side. That pisses me off even more than I already was because I'm walking as quickly as I can. If he were human, he wouldn't be anywhere near me. I don't want him near me right now.

"I didn't know you then," he says, when I don't respond. "I swear I never saw you. I broke ties with Thrain about the same time he took you."

"So you claim." I stuff Naito's sketchbook into one of the big pockets on the inside of my cloak. The snow is beginning to fall faster, but I'm too angry to feel the bite of the air.

"I've never lied to you, McKenzie," Aren says. "Never."

"And I'm supposed to take your word on that?" I stop at the end of our narrow, curvy passageway and peer both ways down the main street. Two cloaked fae look our way. They're breaking curfew. Technically, so are we. I bury my hands in the pockets of my cloak, trying to preserve what little warmth they have left.

"The gate is to the left," Aren says.

The two fae watch as I turn that way. I return their stares and, surprisingly, they drop their gazes. Even with the occasional *edarratae* flashing across my face, I don't think I'm very intimidating. Most likely, Aren's glaring at them over my shoulder. He's just behind and slightly to the right of me, walking through the night fully armored in *jaedric*. His sword, sheathed at his left hip, is easily accessible. He could kill both men before they throw aside their cloaks to get access to their weapons.

"That's the shadow-witch?" the shorter of the two fae asks. The other doesn't respond; he just backs away. Which is ridiculous, considering I'm on the opposite side of the street from them.

I just shake my head and keep walking. I try not to think, because when I do, I either flash back to ten years ago or think about the fae—the fae I barely know—who's trailing me. Aren was Thrain's protégé. It's so hard to believe, and not just because my heart breaks a little when I think about the connection. Anyone who was associated with Thrain should be mentally unstable. They should go from calm to irate in two seconds flat. They should issue threats, dole out punishments with their fists, and be abusive both mentally and physically and . . .

The scar on the side of my neck throbs, and I freeze. It's the remains of a horrible moment, when Aren and I were still on opposite sides of the war, when he threatened me . . . Maybe Aren *is* like Thrain. Maybe I've just been too blind to see it.

"I'm not a mistake, McKenzie," he says softly, stopping beside me. His voice is soothing, reassuring. My chest tightens, and a warm, tingling sensation rushes through me. That scares me. I've told myself to take this relationship slowly, but my heart refuses to listen. I'm growing too attached to him too quickly. I shouldn't be on the brink of falling in love with someone I know so little about. I shouldn't want to believe every word he says. That's what happened with Kyol. I loved him so blindly and so completely, I put my life on hold. I never questioned anything he told me, and I regret that so much.

I swallow down a lump in my throat. "You should have told me about him."

"When?" Aren asks, and for the first time, impatience creeps into his voice. "Including today, I've seen you four times since we took the palace, McKenzie. Four."

"That's not my fault." I start walking again, but he grabs my arm.

"You're not being fair," he says.

"Of course I'm not," I yell, turning toward him. "You're as bad as Kyol was about not telling me the complete truth."

His nostrils flare. The comparison hurts. I'm almost sorry

I made it—almost—but I'm sick of people withholding information.

I meet his gaze. "Anything else you want to confess?"

That gets under his skin. The silver in his eyes seems to sharpen, and he takes a step forward, pressing his body against mine so that I have to move back.

"The complete truth, McKenzie, is I'd do anything for you, but you ask for nothing. You won't confide in me. You won't rely on me. You're so preoccupied trying to decide if you can trust your feelings that you won't consider giving in to them."

I back against a stucco wall. He's breathing hard. So am I, and I have to admit it's not only because I'm hurt and angry. There's some truth to his words. I don't trust my feelings for him, but there's good reason for that. Learning about his connection to Thrain proves it.

I put my hands on his chest to push him away. He doesn't budge. Instead, his grip on my arm tightens.

"Let go, Aren."

He shakes his head. His eyes are narrowed.

"Seriously, let go." I twist this time, trying to slip free, but his arms go around me, pulling me more tightly against him.

"Aren—"

"Shh," he says. Then, when I keep struggling, he looks down at me. "You can be angry, McKenzie, but don't be careless. Listen."

I don't allow myself to relax in his arms, but his hearing is better than mine, so I turn my head to the side and listen. At first, all I hear is his heartbeat. It's a steady, almost hypnotic *thumpthump. Thumpthump.* But then I hear something else. A raised voice. A shout. A crash. It's all coming from the direction we're heading.

"I thought there was a curfew," I say.

"There is," he answers. "Stay close."

I don't protest when he places a hand on my back, just next to the dagger he gave me, and urges me forward. Rightly or wrongly, I trust Aren with my life. Even when we were enemies, he took care of me; my gut tells me he'll take care of me now. I might be disturbed by his origins, his past, but that's something I have to deal with later. Right now, I need to deal with what's going on here.

The shouts and noises grow louder as the snow under our feet turns from a soft, white blanket to a wet, dark mush. People have been through here recently. Lots of people. At the end of our alley, an orb-topped lamppost turns the stucco walls a brighter shade of blue. We stop at the corner and peer out at the scene.

Standing between us and the river, some two hundred feet away, is what I can only describe as an angry horde of fae. They're massed around the location where I remember the gate being. By the number of sleepy *cirikith* standing scattered throughout the marketplace, my guess is that half of the fae are merchants. I don't know who the other half are. Not innocent bystanders. They're pushing and shoving to get at the crates laden onto the carts the *cirikith* pulled here. Others are pushing and shoving just for the hell of it, I think. Aren said the people of Rhigh were almost rioting. I don't think there's any *almost* about this. They're out here breaking curfew and looting just because they can.

I jerk back into Aren's chest when there's a crash to our right. It's followed by an excited shout, and by the time I find the source of the noise, fae are pouring through the broken window of a store no more than ten feet away from us. The fae look like they're the age of human teenagers, but they could be as old as thirty.

One of those fae slips in the slosh of melted snow and dirt. The whole marketplace is one giant mud pit. It's been ten years, but I remember Rhigh's riverfront looking like one of my world's touristy boardwalks. Even in my delirious, half-starved state, it hit me as ironic because Rhigh shouldn't have looked like a vacation spot. From my experience in it, it should have looked like a ghetto outside a prison.

It looks like a ghetto outside a prison now.

A strange-sounding wail cuts through the air to the left. A *cirikith* lies on its side, straining to get back to its feet, but its haunches are stuck beneath a broken cart. It's bleeding from its neck. Even from this distance, I can see that its huge, opalescent scales have turned crimson. *Cirikiths* aren't pretty beasts, with their oversized heads and thick, hooved legs, but I can't help but feel sorry for it. *Cirikiths* are strong. The only reason this one hasn't regained its feet is because it's hurt, and it's fighting off its nightly hibernation.

Aren rests a hand on my shoulder. "We should wait until things calm down to use the gate."

"Wait where?" I ask, backing away from the chaos.

He takes my hand, turns me back down the alley. "Hison should have a place . . ."

Two fae are walking toward us. They're wearing *jaedric* over thick woolen shirts and pants. Their gloves and heavy animal-skin boot coverings look warm but tattered. Well before they reach us, I move aside. Aren doesn't. His posture relaxes, and he stands his ground. That's when I notice the two newcomers don't exactly seem surprised to see us.

"We heard you were here with an asset," the fae on the left says. Interwoven feathers are braided through his hair, almost as if they're taking the place of a name-cord.

"Did you?" Aren replies lazily. He slips an arm inside the folds of my cloak, and I feel him slide the dagger out of my waistband.

"You know them," I say.

It's not quite a question, but he responds with, "You know that past you're holding against me?"

Great. This can't go well. I throw him a glare but take the hint and wrap my hand around the hilt of the dagger, making sure I keep it hidden beneath my cloak.

"Also heard you're with the daughter of Zarrak," the second fae says. *"You know how to get inside the palace. Useful information, that is. Valuable."*

"I'm sure you've heard many things, Vent," Aren says. He squeezes my arm gently beneath the cloak. Telling me to be ready?

Feather-braid takes a step forward. *"We control the gate, now."*

Aren throws an exaggerated look of surprise over his shoulder where the marketplace is. *"I can tell."*

Feather-braid scowls. *"You can either pay for the human or turn her over to—"*

Aren appears beside the fae. I'm just as startled as they are because I didn't sense or see the slash of light until he was already gone. But there he is, swinging his sword through the shadows from his exit fissure and cleaving into Feather-braid's shoulder. Feather-braid is nothing but a soul-shadow a second later.

Vent reacts quickly, fissuring out of Aren's way. Aren pivots, his sword arcing around, and kills the fae as he exits his slash of light. His soul-shadow joins his companion's.

An instant later, Aren's at my side, taking my arm. "We're leaving."

"Good friends of yours?" I ask. The fight started and ended so quickly. A spike of adrenaline is just now pumping through my veins.

"The best," he answers, leading me back the way we came. "We have to get to the gate."

I slant a wide-eyed glance his way. "The gate? Now?"

"Yes," he says. "Unless you have another idea."

"I can probably come up with something that doesn't include a horde of pissed-off fae." Seriously, he's crazy to think that we can make it to the gate, the same gate everyone else is trying to fissure through, with the crowd standing in our way.

"You can't stay in Rhigh," he says. He's walking so quickly I have to run to keep pace. "If Vent and Tyfin know you're here, then the others do as well. They'll be looking for you."

"Who were they?"

"A local . . . gang?" He looks at me to confirm he used the correct word. "Thrain paid them to do minor jobs. They're idiots, but they can be dangerous."

We reach the end of the alley again and stop. Aren curses under his breath. I don't have to ask why. The marketplace is crammed with twice as many fae as before.

"And exactly how are you planning to get to the gate?" I ask.

He doesn't answer immediately. His face is pinched, and I can practically see the thoughts churning in his head. His brow lowers. Then, he must lock on an idea because the tension running through him evaporates. He looks at me, and he grins.

TWELVE

❖

"WE'RE GOING TO use what?" I ask. I had to have heard him wrong.

"We're using your reputation," he says. "Take off your cloak."

"It's minus a million degrees out here. I'm not taking it off."

"They need to see the *edarratae*." He pulls the cloak off my shoulders. I'm just able to catch the hood before the whole thing falls into the mud.

"Can't you fissure to Corrist for help?"

"I wouldn't be able to bring back more than three or four fae, and it would leave a section of the wall more vulnerable to attack. This plan is better." He tugs on the cloak.

"That's the only thing keeping me from freezing to death," I snap, refusing to let go.

"This won't take long, I promise."

"This is crazy."

He laughs. "I know, but it will work. The fae in Rhigh are superstitious. They'll see you and make room."

"Like Vent and his friend made room?"

His smile finally fades. He looks directly into my eyes, then says, "Trust me, McKenzie."

He has a lot of nerve asking me to trust him after not

being forthcoming about his connection to Thrain. I should be stubborn about this, tell him to come up with another solution because this is the most ridiculous idea ever, but Aren has a reputation for crazy plans that work. Plus, I really don't like being back in Rhigh. I want out of here.

I let go of the cloak. "This doesn't mean I'm forgiving you."

The grin returns to his face. "You will, *nalkin-shom*."

He moves aside so I can see the crowded marketplace. "Count to thirty, then walk directly toward the gate."

"That's it?"

"That's it," he says, and before I can question his sanity again, he's gone.

I swear to God if this plan of his gets me killed, I'm haunting him for the rest of his life. I hug myself, trying to trap in what little warmth I have left, and count.

It's hard as hell to force myself to step out of the alley once I reach thirty. There's still a mass of fae around the gate, and nearly every window in the marketplace has been broken. The fae are preoccupied looting and yelling and fighting each other, but it doesn't take long for them to notice me. I tighten my grip on my dagger and keep my eyes focused on the gate as I stride through the melted snow.

I usually don't notice the *edarratae* unless I'm touching a fae, but I'm aware of each strike of lightning across my skin. So is everyone else. This never happens. A human doesn't just walk through the Realm unescorted. It's strange and unusual, and it's obvious the nearest fae don't know what to make of me. They back away. I hear *nalkin-shom* whispered more than once. I don't know if that's a guess—maybe they'd think any human female is the shadow-witch—or if Aren's described me in those rumors he's spread.

When I near the thickest portion of the mob, I think my luck has run out: These fae aren't moving. They're not even looking at me. They're too involved in cursing out the people around them or stealing the food and clothing and everything else the merchants were transporting.

Just when I think I'm going to have to stop or turn back, something happens. The shouts lessen, and more than one fae's gaze goes toward the night sky. I look up, too, but I don't see anything except faint stars.

"Quickly." Aren's voice comes from my left. "Follow me."

He shoulders his way into the crowd, carving a path. The fae glare at him when they're shoved aside, but then their gazes lock on me. Their eyes go wide. They look back up into the sky, then move out of my way.

"What are they looking at?" I ask, striding behind Aren.

"A lightning storm."

An *illusion* of a lightning storm. No wonder the fae are backing away. Lightning is extremely rare in the Realm. Some people think it's a sign that the *Tar Sidhe* are angry at the presence of humans and human culture. Others think it's just a random, natural occurrence. Either way, I can see how the fae would be nervous, seeing a lightning-clad human beneath a lightning-struck sky. But Aren can't be doing this. He's a healer. It's a powerful, endangered magic, and while illusionists are more common, creating a lightning show impressive enough to catch this mob's attention would require a huge amount of skill. I don't think Aren has the ability to create tiny, short-lived illusions, let alone something on this scale.

The crowd splits. I see the gate on the riverbank. Or rather, I see the flashes of near-constant light that are being opened where I think the gate is. Technically, Aren doesn't have to create a fissure of his own to get me out of here. We can travel through another fae's. The slashes of light are rips in the atmosphere that lead to the In-Between; I just need an anchor-stone and a fae escort to live through it.

Aren discreetly hands me an anchor-stone. My hands are so cold and numb, it feels like it scalds my palm, but I clench my fist around it. Just a few more steps to the riverbank. Aren's plan is actually going to work.

"Tchatalun."

I've blocked out the whispers of *nalkin-shom*, but that one word whispered from somewhere to my right rings in my ears. It means "defiled one" but it's basically synonymous with "human." The last time I heard it, I was in Lyechaban, and it was uttered by fae who wanted me dead.

I can't identify who said the word now, but there's a

change in the mob. It's as if they've suddenly realized my destination. Their surprised and almost fearful expressions vanish. Aren must sense the change, too, because he hooks his arm around me, pulling me against his side.

Only a few more feet to the gate.

Aren takes my hand. He shoves someone aside.

Someone shoves back. I stumble, but manage to stay on my feet. Two more steps, and we'll be at an opened fissure.

The crowd surges around us. I tighten my grip on Aren and throw my weight forward. The fae in front of me move when I do so. My momentum carries me to the riverbank. Aren's hand slips from mine. I try to turn back to find him, but my sneaker hits the edge of the frozen river. I lose traction. Slip.

I put out my hands to catch myself, but I'm falling all wrong, and the river isn't completely frozen over. The fae have hammered through the ice surrounding the gate.

My shoulder hits first, and I can't stop my head from slamming down, too. Pain explodes through my temple. Aren calls my name. I push up to all fours, trying to focus on the ice beneath me.

The ice that's cracking beneath me.

I lunge toward the bank, but I'm too late. The slab beneath me breaks off, plunging me into the dark, cold depths of the river.

I arch my back, trying to free myself from the restraints around my wrists, but the nurse is at my side, tightening them further. A tingling sensation runs up my arm, then it starts itching. It's the saline solution still, but the drugs the nurse added to the IV bag will enter my bloodstream soon.

We tried sneaking out of Bedfont House. One of Paige's friends was parked just outside the center's gate. He took off when the security guards caught us. We were in enough trouble for that alone, but the staff also figured out that Paige and I weren't taking our meds. Instead of being reprimanded and sent to our room, we were reprimanded and sent to separate observation cells. The isolation doesn't bother me, but I don't want my mind to fog over again. The drugs make me feel like I really am crazy.

After I stop struggling, the nurse leaves the room. There's no way to take the IV out of my arm. My eyelids grow heavy, my vision blurs. I fight against the haze, but I lose the battle.

"McKenzie." Kyol's voice near my ear. A hallucination? That's what I've been told I experience. I started agreeing with the counselors weeks ago. It seemed like the quickest, easiest way to get back to my life.

"McKenzie." I'm afraid to open my eyes, afraid I'll see nothing but the darkness if I do.

A soft, sweet pressure on my lips.

"Kyol?" I whisper. He's here, leaning over me in a silhouette that's etched in lightning. One hand cups my face, the other rests just above my left wrist. His touch is tender, but hot—tantalizing—and something stirring and electric runs through my body.

"You're real," I breathe. This must be how Snow White felt when her prince kissed away her sleep.

"I couldn't find you," he says, his thumb sliding over my cheek. "I thought another false-blood had taken you."

I try to lift my arm, but I can't. When he sees me struggling, he takes out his dagger, slices through the material binding my wrists, then he lifts me into a sitting position.

It's too quick. Black spots swirl through my vision. I bite my lip, waiting for the dizziness to pass. When I'm able to focus again, I'm staring at my cut restraints. "They were Velcro."

"What?" Kyol asks.

"Velcro." Strong Velcro, but the dagger wasn't needed.

I look up. Kyol stares at the IV bag, at me, then at the IV bag again. He grabs the plastic tubing and cuts through it. I watch the liquid drip onto the floor.

"What is it?" he asks.

"Medicine."

His brow creases.

"We don't have healers so we . . . we put plants in our veins." I laugh, then cut it off short. God, my head is spinning.

Too much of the drug made it into my system. The needle is still taped to my arm. I pull it out.

"Are you okay, McKenzie?"

I stare at the blood welling out of the tiny hole in my wrist. I don't think I took it out right.

"I'm fine," I say, swiping my arm across my clothes. I'm wearing Bedfont House's standard-issue nightgown. It's ugly, not much better than a hospital gown. "The door locks from the outside."

"I've unlocked it."

The knob turns smoothly. Since I'm wobbly, he puts an arm around my waist and guides me out of the cell. I enjoy being close to him way too much. He's wearing fae armor—*jaedric*, I think it's called—but it doesn't hide the power in his body. He's warm, safe, and even though we're forbidden to be together, I'm almost certain I'm in love with him.

We're almost to the door at the end of the corridor when my brain starts to function again. I tell Kyol to wait.

"I can't leave without Paige."

"What page?" he asks, following my gaze back down the hall.

"She's my friend." The only friend I have here. Probably the only friend I have period. Jessica, Kelly, all the people I used to hang out with abandoned me months ago. I can't blame them. I stopped showing up at school meetings and quit two committees that really needed my help.

Not to mention I flunked English, my favorite subject, and ended up in In School Suspension for skipping classes.

"She should be in one of these rooms." I squeeze my eyes shut, trying to remove the fog lingering in my vision, then I drag him back down the hall. He doesn't protest. He would if he realized that the tech making his *edarratae* vibrate so strongly is the building's security cameras. There are at least two recording me. I might have no more than a minute or two to find Paige and get out of here.

She's three doors down from where I was imprisoned. It's locked from the outside with a simple dead bolt.

"Paige," I whisper as I slip inside.

She doesn't respond, just lies there strapped down to the hospital bed. They're giving her drugs, too.

"Paige, wake up." I carefully remove the tape holding her IV in place.

Her eyes flutter open. "McKenzie?"

"We're getting out of here." I yank at the Velcro securing her wrists. It's freaking hard to get off, but I do it, then help her sit up. "Can you walk?"

More of the sedating drugs made it into her system than mine. She blinks. Then grins. "A breakout? Seriously? McKenzie, you fucking rock."

She stands. Wobbles. Yeah, she's definitely worse off than I am. I try to help her balance, but I'm not entirely steady, especially when I reach out to open the door. I miss the knob.

Kyol opens it for us. Paige doesn't even notice the door moving seemingly on its own.

The hallway is still clear, but the door at the other end seems to stretch farther and farther away as we hurry toward it. When we're finally only a few paces away, it opens. Security. Shit.

Paige and I stop. Kyol doesn't. He grabs the edge of the door, then slams it back at the guard, hitting him in the face.

"Go!" Kyol orders.

I pull Paige past the guard, who's clutching his nose. He grabs at my leg, but Kyol kicks his hand away.

"That was lucky," Paige slurs, turning to look back.

"Come on." I pull her after me, try to make her run, but her legs are so uncoordinated, I'm just throwing her balance off. I settle for a really quick walk, then turn left when an EXIT sign points the way to our freedom.

The door is right there. Kyol's in front of us. Before I can warn him, he presses the bar to open it.

The building's alarm is deafening. It's not exactly a lot of tech—it's just a lot of noise—but Kyol flinches. A frown creases his forehead, and he's squinting as if he has a headache. He recovers quickly, though, checks outside, then motions us through.

Kyol heads to the left. I follow with Paige, hugging the side of the building until he leads us away from it. The edge of the property is lit by bright floodlights. A tall wrought-iron fence keeps Bedfont House residents inside. It has two entrances: a gate up front for visitors and clients, and a gate in the back for personnel and deliveries. Kyol isn't leading us to either of those. I'm about to ask where he's going when he turns, stiffening.

I follow his line of sight and look behind me. Three of the night guard are exiting the building with flashlights in hand. They haven't seen us yet, but they're moving this way. Right before their flashlight beams reach us, I grab Paige and yank her to the ground.

"Ick," she says, staring at the dew-covered grass an inch from her nose.

"Shh!"

The ground is cold and wet, but I don't let her get up. We're in a shallow ditch. If they don't walk all the way over here, they might not see us.

I hold my breath until they turn away.

"Jesus, McKenzie," Paige whispers. "Have you had Special Forces training or something? You're a little too good at this."

"Paintball," I say, though I've only done that once.

"Next time I need to run from the cops, I'm totally calling you."

She's sounding more coherent now. Good.

"Hurry," Kyol says.

We almost make it. I see the bent bars in the fence. Kyol must have planned ahead, using his magic to heat and bend the metal. They're just wide enough for Paige and me to slip through, but just when I'm about to increase our pace, I skid to a stop instead. Two guards shine their flashlights directly on us.

"Damn," Paige whispers.

They must have been walking the perimeter. They move away from the fence now that they've spotted us.

"Girls," the guard on the left says. "Don't move."

Kyol steps to my side, but he looks agitated, uncertain.

"McKenzie, I shouldn't . . ." He doesn't finish his thought. He just goes quiet, his jaw tightening.

He shouldn't take down a human when another human is

watching. The fae king doesn't want anyone to become suspicious that they might be in this world. I don't think that's likely to happen just from Kyol knocking someone out. They'll blame it on me, somehow.

Kyol steps forward. He's going to ignore that rule. He's going to ignore it to save me.

My stomach tightens. I swear, he loves me—*me*, not just the feel of the *edarratae*—but he refuses to admit it.

Beside me, Paige straightens. "Go. I'll distract them."

I shake my head. "We can both make it."

She laughs. "No, we can't. I can barely see straight."

She doesn't know about Kyol. He'll make sure we make it.

"Seriously, go," Paige says. "My eighteenth birthday is in a few months. They have to let me out then. I'll look you up. We can be roommates or something."

"I'm not letting you take the fall for this." She'll be in twice as much trouble because of this escape attempt.

"It's my fault we were caught sneaking out in the first place," she says. Then, before I can come back with another argument, she rolls her eyes, shoves me forward, then takes off across the field. Both guards take off after her.

"Paige!" I yell, when they tackle her.

"We have to hurry, McKenzie," Kyol says at my side. He ushers me toward the fence. I look over my shoulder, watching as she kicks and flails at the two men holding her down. God, I'm the shittiest friend ever, leaving her behind like this. I owe her, not only for distracting the guards but for keeping me sane while I was here.

Kyol grabs one of the bent bars on the wrought-iron fence. "You can repay her later."

I meet his eyes. He's right. Staying behind accomplishes nothing.

I slip through the gap in the fence and run. Kyol stays at my side, directs me to veer left before we reach a road. Bedfont House is out in the country—the rural setting is supposed to be relaxing—but even though there's a serene little stream to the south of the institute, I don't think there's a gate on it. I wish there were because I can't run any longer. My side hurts, and it's too hard to focus.

I have to stop. I bend over, intending to rest my hands on my knees, but my legs are like jelly. I sit. Kyol lowers to the ground beside me.

"Are you okay?" he asks quietly, not even winded.

No, I'm not—I feel like crap for leaving Paige behind—but I just nod. I'm going to owe Paige for the rest of my life for this.

He lets out a sigh. We're knee to knee in the dew-covered grass. Leaning forward, he rests his forehead against mine and cups the back of my neck with one gentle hand.

His touch sends a bolt of heat down my spine. I'm aware of how close his lips are. Is he aware of mine? Does he know how much I need to close that distance between us? To kiss him? It takes everything in me to stay completely still. He rejected me the last time we kissed, said he couldn't be with me, couldn't touch me tenderly anymore.

He's touching me tenderly now.

The lingering drugs in my system make me brave. I tilt my chin up, whisper, "Kyol."

"Kaesha." The word comes out as a sweet sigh. He's called me that only a few times before, and though he says there's no translation for it, the affection in his voice is absolutely clear. Tension leaves his body. He gives in, pressing his lips against mine. The cool air doesn't touch me anymore. There's only him. His touch. His heat. His chaos lusters. But I know before he deepens the kiss that he's going to end it soon. His arms move to my shoulders, tighten as he battles with what he wants to do and what he should do.

I try to hold on to him, make him hold on to me. It doesn't work. Just when the kiss reaches the point where it might turn into more, he pulls away. *Now*, he's breathing hard.

I draw in a deep breath, trying to calm my racing heart. "I was starting to believe you weren't real."

He helps me to my feet. "I'm sorry I didn't find you sooner."

"It's okay. I . . . Thanks for finding me. For taking care of me."

He gives me one of his rare smiles. "I'll always take care of you. Always."

THIRTEEN

•—◆—•

I'VE RELIVED THE same memory a dozen times now. Something's wrong. Instead of feeling hot from Kyol's touch, I feel numb, cold, and oddly distant.

I turn my head to the side. It's dark that way, too, but I feel a presence there. Someone's gaze. My confusion finally begins to dissipate, and by the time I realize all I need to do to get rid of the darkness is to open my eyes, I remember Rhigh.

My eyes snap open. I'm in my room at the palace. This is where I've always stayed when I've remained in the Realm overnight. It's not a large space, but there's enough room for the bed, a nightstand, and the chest of drawers that's pushed against the wall beside a small bathroom. It's simple and it's comfortable, and ever since the rebels took the palace, I've started to think of it as mine.

"Here," Lena says. I slowly turn my head to the right, see her sitting in a chair beside my bed. She's holding out a glass.

"Cabus?" I ask. She nods. My hands shake as I take it from her. I hold my breath, take a sip, and do my best not to spit it out.

"It's not that bad," she says.

It *is* that bad, but I'm parched, so I force myself to take another sip. It burns down my throat. It's not an entirely unpleasant sensation considering how cold I am. *Cabus* is used to replenish a fae's energy if they overexert themselves by fissuring too quickly or using too much magic. It's supposed to help rehydrate and reenergize humans, too. Personally, I think a glass of Gatorade would do the same thing, but I can't exactly run out to a convenience store to buy some.

"Where's Aren?" I ask.

"I sent him away."

I lift an eyebrow.

She scowls. "He wasn't doing you or anyone else any good sitting here waiting for you to wake up."

"How long was I out?"

"A few hours," she says dismissively. Because, you know, people fall into icy rivers and lose consciousness all the time.

"What were you doing in Nashville?" she asks.

Nashville? It feels like it's been days since Trev picked me up from there. And what did he tell me? That Sosch went to Lena with a message attached to a collar. Apparently, Lorn didn't sign that message.

"I was repaying a favor." I roll to my side, then try to sit up. I'm surprised when my body actually cooperates.

"A favor to whom?" Lena asks.

I'm a little dizzy. I wait for the room to settle then focus on her. She's dressed in a long, white dress. A wide *jaedric* belt encircles her slender waist. A series of *abira* trees are etched into its surface at even intervals. They each have seventeen branches, one for each of the Realm's provinces, including the ones Atroth dissolved years ago.

"Lorn," I tell her. By her lack of reaction, she already knew that. "He said you guys had an argument."

She *hmmphs*, and her already unsmiling face turns stony. She reaches up and tucks a long strand of blond hair behind her ear. It's an action I've rarely seen her do, and it makes her look . . . *Softer* is the best word I can think of.

"You read the shadows for him, I presume." After I nod, she asks, "Whose?"

"A fae named Aylen."

"And who was this Aylen?"

"According to Lorn, an associate," I say. Then, I remember the connection to the fae in Rhigh. "She fissured to Eksan."

Her perfectly sculpted eyebrows go up. "The same Eksan that's on the southern edge of the Daric Ocean?"

"I tried to tell Aren, but he fissured out before I could. Then we had to figure out how to get out of the city and—"

"And you found out about his connection to Thrain."

That's not what I was going to say, but now that it's out there, I shrug. "Yeah."

There's a knock on my open door. A magically lit orb on the corridor wall outlines Aren's lean frame in a soft, blue light. He looks like something out of myth standing there. Appropriately so.

"Is it okay if I come in?" he asks. There's a cautious note in his tone, like he's afraid I'll say no and send him away.

Lena rises before I answer. I try to stand up, too, but my head spins when I lean forward.

"Easy, McKenzie," Aren says, coming to my side. He places a hand on my shoulder, keeping me still. "You hit your head hard when you fell."

His palm warms my skin through my thin, fae-made shirt. I've been changed out of my wet clothes. The pants I'm wearing are black, loose, and comfortable. I sit on the edge of the bed and face Aren, feeling my strength slowly seeping back into my muscles.

"You scared me," he says. There's a glimmer of leftover fear in his silver eyes. I don't know what happened after I went under the water, but I know I didn't get out of the river on my own. He must have dragged me out, dragged me through the gate, and brought me here.

"I told you your plan was insane," I say.

A small grin. "I thought we'd have a few more seconds before they reacted."

If I wasn't still a little dizzy, I'd roll my eyes. Instead, I give him an exaggerated glare. His smile widens, then his gaze goes to my lips. Suddenly, I'm conscious of them. I'm conscious of just how close he is. His hand is on my side instead of my shoulder now.

There's an exasperated sigh from the doorway.

"We're meeting with the high nobles after sunrise," Lena says. "Don't be late."

Aren just nods, not taking his eyes off me. When she leaves, closing the door behind her, he asks softly, "Are we okay?"

"I don't know," I tell him. It's the truth. I haven't had a chance to process his connection to Thrain yet. What kind of person follows a false-blood? The only answers I can come up with are the foolish and the cruel. Aren doesn't fit the first category—he's smart and observant—but he doesn't fall into the cruel category either. He's always taken care with me, and he's a healer. He helps people by taking their pain away.

"I just . . . I need time, Aren." Time. That's what I've been asking for these last two weeks, and it's the one thing we don't have much of. He said he understood, but if the shadow that moves through his eyes is any indication . . .

I want to make that shadow leave his expression. I want to lean forward, press my lips against his, and let my *edarratae* chase away his fears, but kissing him is dangerous. I wouldn't want to stop, and as ridiculous as it is to be a twenty-six-year-old virgin, I need to be 100 percent sure about Aren before we're together. So, instead of closing the distance between us, I slowly push my way to my feet. Aren moves back to give me room to do so, but he stays close enough to help me when I sway.

The dizziness passes in just a few seconds. I actually don't feel that bad. I think I'll be fine if I walk some. My equilibrium will return.

I start to tell him that but stop when my gaze settles on the chest of drawers beside the restroom. Or rather, when it settles on what's on top of the chest of drawers.

"Is that my . . ." I stop because it's not *just* my favorite pair of jeans. It's my favorite pair of jeans, my sketchbook, and my photo album. Not the entire contents of my suitcase, but it's the important stuff.

I cross the room, pick up my photo album.

"It's all I could bring without risking some of it being lost to the In-Between," Aren says behind me.

The In-Between can be temperamental. In general, it lets a fae fissure with what they can easily carry, but if they start trying to take armloads of clothes or boxes stuffed full of food or supplies, it'll steal random things. It's safer to use a gate if you're carrying multiple items. "I can go back if you need something else."

I turn to face him. "You went to my apartment?"

"Trev told me you'd packed a suitcase. I was there and back within a few minutes." His gaze drops to the photo album in my hands. "I flipped through that. I hope you don't mind."

I look down. I've opened the album to a random page. My mom and dad are there, both holding shovels in our backyard. They're planting a tree—a peach tree, if I remember correctly. I was twelve or so, and I'd just gotten a camera for my birthday. A photographer, I am not. My parents are off center, and the whole image is crooked, but the memory makes me smile. I was young then. Happy and innocent. I miss that life. I miss my parents.

"I would meet them," Aren says.

I clap the album shut. "What?"

"I would meet your parents," he says, taking a step toward me. "If you wanted me to."

God, this man loves me, and all I can do is stare at him, feeling my heart thump against my chest. Every time I start to question why I want to be with someone like him, he shows me why. He shows me he loves me, and underneath his half smiles and his laid-back attitude, he's considerate and caring. Maybe I shouldn't be asking why I want to be with him. Maybe I should be asking why he wants to be with someone like me.

"You've only known me a month," I say, placing the photo album back on top of the chest of drawers.

"Yes," he says, giving me a small smile that suggests he knows where I'm going with this.

"How can you be so sure of the way you feel about me?"

"You're human," Aren says. "You're the weakest person I know."

The warm, fluttery sensations in my stomach disappear. "Geez, thanks."

He laughs and takes my hands in his before I turn away.

"And that makes you the strongest. The most courageous. When I found you on your campus, you fought me. You didn't give in even though you knew you were outmatched. I was halfway in love with you before we reached Germany."

And the sensations are back. His touch excites my chaos lusters, making them spark across my skin. He reaches up, touches the side of my face. It's so, so hard to keep my distance from him. Back in Rhigh, he told me he wasn't a mistake. Maybe I should just take his word on that. Maybe now is the time we should be together.

A warm, pleasant ache flares up low in my stomach.

"When is sunrise?" I ask, moving closer to him.

"Soon," he says. "Now, probably."

Which means we have zero time together. I close my eyes, stifling a curse.

Aren's thumb traces the line of my jaw. "Come with me."

My brow furrows as I try to make sense of his words. "To the meeting?"

"Yes," he says.

I raise an eyebrow. "The meeting with the high nobles?"

"Yes."

I reach up to take his hand away from my face so I can think about something besides his touch. It doesn't help much, though, because he doesn't let go of my hand.

"They'll hate that," I say.

He responds with a smile.

Ah, I see. He doesn't want to go play politics. "That's okay. I'll pass."

"You can think about it on the way," he says, as if I didn't just answer. "It could be entertaining."

He uses his foot to nudge something out from under the bed. Tennis shoes, the ones I bought on the way to the gate in Vegas. I let out an exaggerated sigh but grab a pair of socks and shove my feet into the shoes. They're dry. I don't think they've had enough time to do that on their own, so I'm guessing a fae evaporated the rest of the water using magic.

Aren opens the door. I finger-comb my hair, pull it back into a quick ponytail, and ask, "Will Lena let me sit in on the meeting?"

"We'll see, won't we?"

If Atroth were still king, it wouldn't be a question. He would never have considered letting me stick around for even an informal conversation with a high noble. Oh, he would have been polite about it, maybe even apologetic, but he would have sent me back to Earth the moment I finished whatever task he gave me to do.

Things aren't that way with Lena and the rebels. I've made it clear I want to know what's going on in this war, and I won't let them keep me in the dark like her predecessor did.

Aren and I are passing through the sculpture garden, and I'm imagining all sorts of reactions from the high nobles if I decide to sit in on that meeting when Lena steps out of the north wing of the palace. She stops beside a carved pillar, looking almost startled to see us.

"Is the meeting canceled?" Aren asks, sounding hopeful.

Lena's gaze moves back and forth between us before it settles on Aren. "It . . . No. No, it's not canceled."

"Then you're running away?" he asks, letting the question hang there.

Her expression turns cool. "No. I came to get you. I want you to look like a sword-master at this meeting. There's new armor waiting for you in your room. Go change into it."

"I don't think what I wear will make a diff—"

"Go, Aren," she says.

He clenches his jaw as he nods once, reluctantly accepting her order before he turns and leaves. I actually agree with Lena. Aren and the rest of the rebels should look like they belong in this palace; they shouldn't look like they're . . . well, rebels. This is just an odd time to insist on the clothing change.

I'm struck by how exhausted Lena looks. Her hair, usually shiny and smooth, is pulled back into a simple ponytail, and the silver in her eyes is dark. They don't have that sharp edge that they used to.

"When was the last time you slept?" I ask.

As if she's suddenly conscious of her appearance, she

straightens. "When was the last time you slept?" she fires back.

"I just woke up," I point out.

"Unconsciousness doesn't count as sleep." The almost petulant note in her tone reminds me of Kelia, which is a comparison I really don't want to make. Lena and I are allies. It's best that I think of her as a queen and a means to keep the people I love safe.

"So tell me what's wrong."

"Everything," Lena says. She draws in a breath, lets it out. "The high nobles. They insist I tell them who . . ." She stops, closes her eyes and begins again. "They're insisting I tell them who killed Atroth."

Kyol killed Atroth. She's keeping that from them? "Does it matter who did it?"

She gives me a look. "It's illegal to kill a king."

"Okay. And?"

"And nothing," she says, almost dismissively. "Let's not talk here."

She turns to head back inside the north wing of the palace. I have to jog to catch up with her.

"I received a message today," Lena says, when I reach her side.

When she doesn't elaborate, my gut tightens. "What did it say?"

She looks at me a moment before focusing ahead. Her face is rigid when she says, "If I let you go, I have to let them go. It could be a trap, and . . ." She sighs. "And nothing can happen to you. I'll lose both of them if you die."

I grab her arm, make her stop walking. "What did the message say, Lena?"

She easily shakes free of my hold as she faces me. Then she hands me a folded piece of paper she removes from beneath her *jaedric* belt.

I open it.

"Shane said it gives Paige's location."

A good number of fae can speak my language, but I don't know of any who can read it. What looks like a UK address is written in the center of the paper. Below it is Paige's name. That's it. No explanation.

"Who's this from?" I ask.

Lena's lip twitches. "It's anonymous. It came with a stack of other correspondence."

I sniff. Of course. I look back down at the writing. It could be from Lorn. It could also be from the remnants. "How do we know it's not a trap?"

"We don't. That's why you can't go."

Refolding the paper, I slip it into my pocket. "I can't *not* go."

"I know that, too." After a moment, she adds, "Most of the time, these tips turn out to be nothing."

"And sometimes they turn out to be solid. London is a big city. Humans will be everywhere."

"I can't send you there alone, and I need Kyol and Aren both at this meeting. We might be able to force the high nobles to vote."

My eyebrows go up. "Really?"

"The fae you tracked to Eksan," she says. "We were able to recapture him and the three fae he met. Two of them confirmed that the remnants don't have a Descendant they can put on the throne."

"That's good," I say. An understatement. It's *really* good, and a tension I didn't realize I felt slowly lifts from my shoulders. If the high nobles approve her, things should get better soon.

Lena nods. "I need my lord general and sword-master with me when I talk with them. They respect Kyol's opinion, and Aren is good at reading people. I won't be able to send them with you until after the meeting."

I play with the scrap of paper in my pocket. "Any guess how long Paige might be at this location or how long the meeting will last?"

"On how long Paige might be there, no. On how long this meeting will take? Forever."

I'm not sure how much of an exaggeration that is.

"How long have you had this?" I ask.

"It just came."

"And there's no way of knowing how long ago it was written," I say.

"No," she answers, even though I wasn't quite asking a question.

"Can you send a couple of other fae with me?" Without knowing more about the tip or Paige's condition, I can't convince myself to wait for the meeting to end.

Lena nods. "I can. But what am I supposed to tell them if you don't come back?"

"I'll come back," I say. "If there are too many remnants in London, we'll leave."

She looks at me dubiously. "You'll leave even if you see your friend there?"

"I don't have a death wish," I say. That's not exactly answering the question, but Lena doesn't press it.

FOURTEEN

· ◆ ·

L ENA SENDS SHANE with me. Apparently, he lived in London for a year before moving to Houston. He says he knows the area of the city where Paige is, possibly, being held. That will save time. If the tip doesn't pan out, we should be back in Corrist before Aren or Kyol know we were gone.

The stretch of the Inner City between the palace and the silver wall is shortest in the northeast corner. That also happens to be where Corrist's gate is. Lena said she'd have two fae meet us in the antechamber, so Shane and I wait there for our escorts.

"I found a house we can rent in Vegas," Shane says, leaning against the wall and playing with something in the pocket of his jacket. The jacket is made from a soft, expensive-looking black leather. I grabbed a longer coat from the palace's supply of human clothing. It's white and a little big, but it hides my dagger, and I didn't have much else to choose from. Atroth kept only a limited amount of my world's textiles here. It's ironic he kept any at all considering how adamant he was about keeping our cultures separate, but there were enough occasions when he needed his fae to be visible on Earth that he decided to keep a stash here.

"Where?" I ask Shane.

"It's on the west side of the city," he says.

"Is that an expensive side of the city?" His place back in Houston was huge. At the time, he worked for Atroth the same as I did, but he demanded the king pay his mortgage along with an insanely high monthly allowance. I was happy in my little apartment—it was my home for almost eight years—and I've never been comfortable with accepting more money than I need to get by. All I need is attention from the IRS. Honestly, I don't know how Shane hasn't set off red flags with his lifestyle.

"About that," Shane says, hooking his thumbs in the pockets of his jeans. "You have to ask Lena for a raise. She won't pay me more than she pays you."

Good for her, I think. Out loud, I say, "We'll be fine in an apartment."

"*You'll* be fine in an apartment. Not me. I need space."

"Get a job," I tell him. Then, I curse.

A job. That's exactly what I'm supposed to be getting.

"What day is it?" Damn it, I don't even know where my driver's license and Social Security card are now. If they survived my dip in Rhigh's river, they're in my old jeans.

"In Vegas? Thursday afternoon, I think," he says. "Why? You have a date?"

That leaves me around twenty-four hours to meet with Jenkins and finish my paperwork. If everything goes smoothly, it's doable, and I *want* that job. I need to feel like a normal human every once in a while—I can't live and breathe war twenty-four/seven—but finding Paige and making sure she's okay is more important than that. Way more important.

"It's nothing," I tell Shane. If I can't make it to Jenkins's office by five tomorrow, I'll just have to convince him I had a crisis that couldn't be avoided.

Shane doesn't have a chance to press the issue. Trev steps into the antechamber. He's raided the king's stockpile of human clothing, too, and is wearing khaki pants and a sweater loose enough to hide a good-sized dagger underneath. Since we're going to a city with a dense population, there's too much of a chance that someone would bump into the fae if they were invisible, so I insisted our escorts allow the humans to see them. Their chaos lusters will still be invisible to anyone who doesn't have the Sight, and as long as no more than two or three fae are visible at once, people tend to overlook their otherness. They don't notice their silver eyes or their slightly exotic faces.

"Looks like you're stuck with me again," I say to Trev.

"Not exactly." He gives me a half smile, and I swear that's the first time I've seen him do anything but frown. He steps farther into the antechamber, making room for . . .

Aren. I keep my face expressionless as he approaches. It's not easy, though, and not just because I feel like a teenager caught sneaking out at night. Aren, too, is dressed in human clothing. The only time I haven't seen him in fae garb was when he wore a suit to Paige's sister's wedding. He was gorgeous then. He's gorgeous now even though he's just wearing a pair of relaxed-fit jeans and a simple, black shirt with the sleeves rolled up to his elbows. *He* won't blend in on Earth. He'll draw attention from every woman around.

It takes me a second to find my voice. "Shouldn't you be meeting with the high nobles?"

"I should be," he acknowledges. "But I'm not letting you walk into a trap."

If his clothing wasn't a clue that he knows exactly what I'm doing, that statement certainly is. Someone told him about London. Who? Not Lena. If she was against me going after Paige, she didn't have to tell me about the tip in the first place.

"The remnants might not be there," I say. I feel my eyes narrow as I look at Trev. He doesn't like me. He was almost killed back at my apartment, and I know he wasn't thrilled to be tasked with picking me up in Nashville. Plus, he and Aren are friends. I wouldn't be surprised if he ratted me out.

"Paige might not be there," Aren counters, taking a step forward. "And don't blame Trev, *nalkin-shom*. I made Lena tell me what was going on."

Lena *did* cave? I know Aren can be persuasive, but, seriously, she's supposed to be the ruler of the Realm. He's supposed to cave to her wishes, not the other way around.

"I'm going," I tell him. "I don't know how the remnants

have treated Paige. She might be hurt. She might think she's—"

"I'm not trying to talk you out of going, McKenzie," he interrupts, holding out his hand. I stare at it while his words sink in. Sometimes I forget he's not like Kyol. He doesn't decide what I should and shouldn't do. He lets me choose. He supports me; he doesn't control me.

And that's one of the reasons why I'm taking a chance on him. He doesn't put me inside a padded box to protect me. He gives me my freedom. He lets me be me.

I take his hand. His grip is strong, comforting.

"Shouldn't you stay for the meeting?" I ask, needing to make sure it's okay if he leaves. Rescuing Paige is important, but so is securing Lena's place on the throne.

"Lena underestimates herself," Aren says, turning me toward the exit. "She can handle the high nobles on her own. Plus, she has Taltrayn at her side."

Despite his distaste for politics, Aren knows the high nobles and the game they're playing better than I do. I give his hand a light squeeze before I slide my fingers free from his. I'd rather keep holding it, but we're not alone, and Shane and Trev both look annoyed and impatient.

It doesn't take long to make it to the gate. Within fifteen minutes, we cross the Inner City and reach the silver wall. Just on the other side, a river flows down from the Corrist Mountains. A relatively flat area of land lies between the wall and the rapidly rising foothills. No homes or shops are built on it, so we have a clear view of the gate as soon as we pass under the wall.

When we stop beside the river, Aren dips his hand into the water first, and a deep thunder rolls through the air. After his fissure opens, he slips an imprinted anchor-stone between our clasped palms, and I hold my breath as he pulls me into the In-Between.

A second later, we emerge into a stale-smelling room. A broken chair is visible in the instant before our fissure winks out. Then the room plunges into complete darkness. Well, complete darkness except for the blue lightning on Aren's skin. The chaos lusters look agitated, a sign that we're in the middle of a major city. There might not be any tech on in this room, but there most certainly is a good amount nearby: streetlights outside, wi-fi in the air, mobile phones placing and receiving calls. Heavy, pounding music grows louder, then fades away. A car driving by, most likely. This isn't like hanging out at an abandoned inn in the middle of Nowhere, Germany, like the outpost where the rebels first kept me captive. A few hours here, and all the fae will have migraines.

Which makes this city a really odd place for the remnants to hold Paige. I feel the odds of her being here dropping with each erratic flash of lightning across Aren's skin.

A slash of light nearly blinds me when it pierces the darkness. Trev and Shane step into the room. As soon as Shane releases Trev's hand, he reaches into his pocket and takes out a cell phone. Trev scowls as Shane holds down the button to turn it on. Apparently, Shane didn't mention the tech to the fae.

"Paige isn't that far away," Shane says. "We don't even need to take the underground."

Paige isn't that far away *if* she's at the address we were given.

"Good," Aren says. "If anything goes wrong, we'll meet at the gate. You both know where it is?"

On a map, yes. Finding it in person might be a little more difficult, but Shane and I both nod. Hopefully, we won't get separated. And, hopefully, this won't take long. Trev is already rubbing his forehead as if he has a headache.

Shane leads the way out. I follow him down a narrow staircase, and Aren and Trev descend after me. It's dark, but I can still see stains on the thin carpet covering the steps. I keep my hands close to my sides. This is the kind of place where you don't want to touch anything. At least this is a safe place to emerge into my world. The archives only had three anchor-stones imprinted with locations in London. According to Kavok, one would have taken us directly to the gate, which is out in the open on the northern bank of the Thames, and the other one would have taken us to Westminster. Shane said Westminster wasn't anywhere close to the address we have, though, so we chose this one because Kavok suggested it was a discreet location. He was right about that. No one's around to see us.

Shane reaches the door at the bottom of the stairs. He opens it, exits the building. It's dark outside. Streetlights reflect off the damp sidewalk, and there's a chill in the air. I'm grateful for my jacket, but I'm wishing I'd put on something heavier than a thin, long-sleeved T-shirt beneath it.

I stuff my hands into my pockets, then turn, waiting for Aren and Trev to exit the building. The room we fissured into is above what looks like a real-estate agency. Pictures of flats and quaint-looking houses that cost upward of a half million pounds are taped to the window. A couple of doors down the road, a small group of men are standing outside a pub, smoking.

"It's this way," Shane says when the fae join us. I fall into step beside him and attempt to not look like a tourist. You'd think that would be easy since I've spent so much time in the Realm, which is definitely a more foreign location than this city, but this is *London*. There's so much history here. And never mind that this is the homeland of Shakespeare and Jane Austen, King's Cross Station is somewhere around here. I want to see Platform 9¾. I swear, one of these days, I'm going to have a fae fissure me here for a vacation.

"You're alive in this city," Aren says.

"What?" I ask, turning. I was walking beside Shane, but I must have slowed down to take everything in. Aren's beside me now. Trev and Shane are a few paces ahead.

"You're more mesmerized by this place than by any place I've seen you in the Realm."

"That's because no one's trying to kill me here," I say.

No one's trying to kill me here *yet*. I'm surprised Aren doesn't point that out, but he just smiles as he watches me, and my stomach does a little flip. It's as if seeing me here like this makes him happy, and just for a moment, I let myself think about what it would be like to walk down this street with Aren without any worries about the remnants or Paige. That's what we need, time to be together without all the pressures of the war.

"That's the address," Shane says, pointing to a section of a brick building about thirty feet in front of us. We pass a tiny convenience store and an even tinier restaurant serving lamb and chicken kabobs. A long line of people blocks its entrance, but they're not waiting to order anything. They're waiting to get into the white-walled building just ahead. By the way the humans are dressed, it has to be a club or a rock concert. I really don't get the girls' clothing choices. It's *cold* out here, and they're all dressed in short skirts and skimpy tops.

Shane stops before we reach the front of the line, staring down at his phone before looking back up again. A metal door is set into the plain brick wall. It's dented and has orange rust stains at the top and a streak of something black and sticky-looking in the middle. It's the kind of door you don't touch because you're afraid of what you'll find on the other side.

I look up at the second story. The four evenly spaced windows are dark. The building is probably deserted— *completely* deserted. If the remnants were here, they'd have a light of some sort, either a candle burning or a magically lit glass orb. We've come this far, though, and I need to be certain Paige isn't on the other side of the door.

When I step forward, Aren stops me with a hand on my arm.

"Behind me," he says.

I was going first just so I could get us through the line of humans, but he parts the crowd with his shoulder. He's careful not to let his skin touch anyone else's. A few girls protest, thinking that we're cutting in line, but Aren flashes them a smile, and says, "Just passing through."

Of course, they don't protest then. One of them even returns his smile. She reaches for his arm and says in a heavy British accent, "No need to hurry off."

He barely manages to dodge her touch. I'm beside him the next instant, and the girl's expression turns sour. My action was more to keep them separate than to claim him as mine, but I don't mind if that's the way she's seeing this.

Her gaze shifts to Trev, but before I have to rescue the other fae, the line moves. She forgets about us the second she turns away.

We reach the door, and Aren looks down at me. "Are you sure you want to go inside?"

I could let Aren go in without me. He could do a quick search and be out here in no time. But if I'm wrong and the remnants are actually here and one of them happens to be an illusionist, Aren and Trev won't see an attack coming. I won't let them be vulnerable like that.

"Yeah," I tell him. "I'm sure."

His jaw clenches, but he discreetly takes out a dagger from under his shirt.

"Shane, wait out here," he says. "Warn us if you see fae."

He reaches for the door but doesn't turn the handle. He looks back at me. "Tell me you're armed."

I'm so, so close to saying I'm not just to see how he'll react, but it's not the time to kid around. I reach behind my back and take my dagger out, keeping it concealed beneath my coat.

He nods once, then twists the handle.

I don't expect it to move. I expect us to have to break in somehow, but the door swings open without a sound, a fact that creeps the hell out of me. The door looks old and heavy; it shouldn't glide open like a well-oiled hinge.

I have to force myself to step inside the dark, musty-smelling room. When I do, I'm immediately on edge. This place doesn't feel right. The air is dense. It tastes like a warning, and the way the door clicks shut behind Trev triggers a memory. That's how the door to the girls' locker room sounded ten years ago when I entered it. Volleyball practice was over. I'd forgotten my gym bag and had to borrow the key from the janitor. I couldn't find the light switch, so I blindly felt my way along the lockers, counting them off until I reached the sixth one. It took only a second to grab my bag, but when I turned around, I wasn't alone.

That wasn't the first time I had seen Thrain, but it was the first time he knew I saw him. Even though I didn't know anything about him then, when he smiled in the dark, the way the *edarratae* flashed across his sunken eyes and the hollows of his face made him look menacing.

"McKenzie?" A whisper from Aren. He's stopped just in

front of me. Chaos lusters flash across his face, and I squeeze my eyes shut to block out the remainder of the memory, reminding myself that this isn't my high-school locker room. It's an empty foyer to what must be a bankrupt hotel or apartment building. I think we came in the back entrance because a glass door is on the opposite side of the room. The glass is painted black. A few scratches in the paint let in a miniscule amount of light. Now that my eyes are adjusting, though, that light is enough for me to see what might have once been the check-in counter a few paces to the right of the door.

"Upstairs?" I whisper back to Aren, nodding toward a narrow staircase on the left side of the room. A tiny elevator with a gated door that you manually open and close is next to it, but even if tech didn't bother fae, I wouldn't want to use it. It doesn't look extremely dependable.

Aren studies me. I try to force the tension out of my shoulders and to relax my grip on my dagger, but I'm sure he notices how stiff I am. He looks relaxed, but alert, and by the slight tilt of his head, I can tell he hears every creak and groan of the building despite the rumbling bass from the club next door.

Trev walks past us and climbs the stairs. I give Aren a tight-lipped smile and follow, feeling the beat of the music on my skin as I step into a long hallway. This hotel must extend over more than one shop. A slant of street-light comes in through a boarded-up window, providing just enough illumination to see a dozen closed doors lining both sides of the hall.

Aren stops beside the first door, puts a finger to his lips, then slowly reaches for the handle.

It gives the softest click as it turns.

I hold my breath. I don't know if it's better for him to throw the door open or to open it slowly, hoping that if someone *is* on the other side, they won't hear him enter.

He opts for the second method. The door silently moves, inch by inch, until the whole dank, empty room is revealed. A single bed occupies more than half of the space inside. It's made, but the flowered comforter is faded and moth-eaten. At the foot of the bed, a sliding door leads to a bathroom barely big enough for a sink, toilet, and stand-up shower. It's obvious no one's here. No one's been here for months, maybe years.

"Check the other rooms," Aren whispers to Trev.

Trev moves to the door opposite us and turns the handle. Just like the first one—and just like the metal door we entered through—it turns without the least bit of resistance. Goose bumps prickle across my skin because that's *wrong*. Even if the owner deserted this place at the last minute, he or she would have locked up. There should be some sign of a break-in. Honestly, there should be some sign of life. This is definitely not a Hilton, but if I had no place to live, I'd stay here. London is a big city; there should be squatters in an abandoned building like this.

Aren moves to the next door. Once again, it opens and, once again, the room is empty save for a bed. Trev's second room is the same, but it's not until they're both opening their fourth doors that I breathe a little easier. If the remnants were here, they would have made an appearance by now. I don't know if I'm more frustrated or relieved. I want to find Paige, but I'm glad we're not going to start a fight in the middle of this city.

I walk to the other end of the hall. A second staircase occupies the space where Aren's last door is. It's steep and narrow, and I think it leads directly outside. Maybe an emergency exit or something.

I slide my dagger back into its scabbard. Aren is still opening his doors quietly, but Trev has given up caution. He holds his dagger ready in his left hand as he pushes his last door open with his right.

No remnants leap out, but Trev just stands there in the doorway.

I move to his side.

I stare inside the room.

It takes a millennium for me to process what I see.

"Oh, God," I choke out.

FIFTEEN

◆·◆

MY HAND COVERS my mouth. I stare at the four blood-soaked bodies just long enough to know they're all human, then I have to turn away.

I hold on to the doorframe, digging my fingernails into the painted wood. The smell . . . It's sour and stagnant and sickening, and suddenly, the air feels too hot. Too humid. It's like the spilled blood has moistened everything. I look at my arms, expecting to see my skin misted red.

"McKenzie?"

I barely register Aren's voice. It sounds distant, cavernous. I can't respond; I just turn back to the tiny hotel room without saying a word. I focus on the body nearest me because I can't look at the one that's sprawled across the bed, the one that's missing its skin. The cuts on the body near my feet aren't straight lines. They're small and jagged, like tiny bolts of red lightning. I've seen death before—fae who were beheaded before entering the ether, humans who were caught in the cross fire of the Realm's war—but I've only seen this kind of twisted torture once. It was in Lyechaban, a city on the eastern coast of the Realm. The fae there loathe humans, and when I was in the city with Kyol nearly seven years ago, two humans were tied up on a dais. The Lyechabans tried to cut the lightning from their skin. I thought they were dead until one of them twitched and . . .

With horror, I force myself to focus on the person on the bed. Please, *please* let him be dead.

"What's wrong?" Aren freezes beside me. He's close, but I don't feel the warmth of his body, just a bone-chilling dread that makes my stomach churn. Is the guy's chest moving?

"Sidhe," Aren whispers.

I think it might be moving, but the way the light from the room's single window slants across his chest, it could be my imagination.

Aren takes my arm. "We're leaving. Now."

Did a lip twitch? I hold on to the doorframe, refusing to move.

"Aren," I say softly. "Make sure they're dead. Please."

"They are." He urges me to move again; I stand my ground. Two of the bodies are female. One has hair bleached the same shade of blond as Paige's. She's propped up against the foot of the bed, but her face is turned away. I can't tell if it's her.

Aren squeezes my arm. "Okay." He kisses my temple. "Okay."

He steps into the room. The soles of his shoes leave tracks on the blood-drenched floor. He's wearing casual, high-ankled fae boots. I didn't notice them before, but they look odd paired with his jeans and shirt. Foreign. Atroth didn't include shoes in his stash of clothing. I should tell Lena to add footwear to the collection.

Why the hell am I thinking about shoes?

I shake my head, attempting to reboot my mind so I can focus. Aren is squatting by a body. He touches a wrist, checking for a pulse. Jaw visibly clenching and unclenching, he rises then moves to the next body. When he squats beside that one, I swear I see movement from the next, the blond girl who looks like Paige.

I take a step toward her. I *know* I saw movement, but she's in the same position as she was before. I don't know what . . .

Oh. Her hair. A lock of it flutters, caught by the draft

coming in from the window. The window's lower portion is pushed out, allowing air in. Allowing air out, too. How is it possible the people on the street can't smell this death? How could they not hear the screams? The humans had to have screamed. None of these deaths were quick. They were slow, painful.

"Look at me, McKenzie," Aren says. He's standing in front of me. He cups my face between his palms, and *edar-ratae* tickle down my neck. "We have to get out of here. You can't panic right now. Do you understand?"

I feel a crease wrinkle my forehead. I don't think I'm panicking.

"These are the missing humans," he says. "The ones who worked with Atroth."

What?

"Are you sure?" I ask. The remnants need Sighted humans as much as we do.

"I'm sure," he says, "The walls list their names."

My stomach churns, but I look over his shoulder at the blood painting the walls. Now that I'm focused on the smears of red, I recognize the Fae symbols. I still can't read it, but it's definitely their language.

"Why would the remnants slaughter them?" I ask, focusing on the blond girl. I recognize her now. Her name is Anya. She is—*was*—Russian. Sixteen years old. The same age I was when I began working for the Court, only she started when she was fourteen. While working for the king, I met fae who disapproved of my presence in the Realm, but they accepted it because I hunted down the Court's enemies. I can't imagine any of those fae doing something like this. This is beyond barbaric.

My nostrils flare. I clench my fists at my sides and feel the fury sink in with each blood-tainted breath I take. Lena has been trying to make contact with the remnants to negotiate with them, but screw that. Anyone who can do something like this can't be reasoned with. Once we find out who's organizing them, I'll track him and his supporters down. I don't care how long it takes. I won't let something like this happen again.

This time, when Aren urges me to move, I do, turning my back on the desecrated bodies. We retrace our steps down the hall and are no more than four paces from the staircase when Shane's voice rings out, "They're here!"

He sprints into our hallway a second later. "They saw me."

"The other staircase. Go," Aren orders, pushing us down the hall before taking up position in front of the steps Shane just ran up.

I stumble, brace a hand against the wall, then turn, looking back at Aren and Trev. Trev remains in this world only for a second more, then he disappears into a fissure.

I turn to Shane. "How many remnants—"

"Come on!" He cuts me off, grabbing my arm and forcefully yanking me down the hall. I shake him off but run for the second staircase. Trev will bring back help, and Aren won't fissure out until I'm safely away from here.

My heart beats in time with the hard, fast music pounding next door. We sprint to the other end of the corridor then down the stairs. Shane reaches the bottom first. A glass door leads outside, but, of course, *this* one is chained shut.

Shane doesn't hesitate. He sidekicks his foot through the glass. I'm right on his heels, ducking under the chain after he does.

We don't exit onto a street. We exit into the tiniest courtyard I've ever seen. There's just one door, wooden and curved on top, in the wall opposite us.

Shane runs to it, grabs the handle, attempting to pull it open. No luck.

I scan the area, feeling boxed in by the four brick walls. The music is louder out here. Between drumbeats, I think I hear fissures opening in the building we just left.

Shit.

My gaze locks on a metal ladder. It's almost hidden behind an outcropping of a chimney. It climbs the wall, stopping at a small platform one level up. There's a door there, cracked open.

"Shane. Here." I jump, grabbing the highest rung I can reach, then I climb, making it to the platform in a few seconds. I make sure Shane's following me before I slip inside.

Strobe lights flash in the dark. I'm in the club. Backstage. Thick curtains hang from floor to ceiling to my right. To my left, a writhing, screaming horde of people crowds the floor.

"Go!" Shane yells, slamming into me. "Go!"

I run, sprinting for the packed dance floor. It will be easy to get lost in the mass of revelers, and with the near-deafening music and all the tech in this room, the fae will be disoriented.

We have to jump down from the side of the stage to the floor. I catch a quick glimpse of the band as I do. The bassist, a tall, skinny guy covered in tats, is headbanging as he plays. A cord runs from his bass to the equipment behind him, a cord that, apparently, a remnant doesn't see. It rips out of the instrument as the fae trips over it. The last thing I see before I shove into the crowd is a baffled look on the human's face.

"Go! Go!" Shane yells, shoving me deeper into the crowd. I'm trying, but the place is packed. I slip between two dancing girls, then look over my shoulder.

Shane's gone. I have no idea where, but I keep moving, trying to get to the center of the dance floor. Everyone is pushing and dancing and not making it at all easy for me to get anywhere. Somehow, I end up near the front of the theater. I look up at the stage, see a remnant standing there. He's in fae clothing and holding a sword as he scans the crowd. I have to assume he's invisible since security isn't doing anything to remove him.

I think I might be safe where I am. I can't see the fae spotting me here. When the concert ends, I can file out with the crowd. I should be able to avoid the remnants.

If I survive the concert.

Despite the cool air outside, it's hot in here. I can barely breathe in this mass of people. My nose wrinkles when someone lights up something that's definitely *not* a cigarette nearby. The smoke gets into my lungs, makes them itch.

Suddenly the song ends. The lights go out. The crowd becomes a sea of lit-up cell phones and . . .

A flash of blue lightning strikes across a face, right in front of me.

I reach for the dagger hidden under my shirt while I back

up, pushing against the crowd as hard as I can, but the crowd pushes back. I can't get the dagger free. The remnant doesn't have the same problem. When the lights flash back on, they glint off the short steel blade in his hand. He stabs toward my stomach, but at that exact moment, the crowd reacts, surging around us and making the fae miss.

Miss me. Not the girl who's tripped into the space I just occupied. Her scream is lost under the fierce, pounding notes of the next song. She collapses to her knees. Instinctively, I reach out to help her, but everyone is still moving, shoving back at people who shoved them.

I manage to grab the girl's elbow. I'm pulling her up and looking for the remnant at the same time. Someone shoved him. Unintentionally, I think, since it's obvious no one else can see him. He shoves back, then his eyes lock on me once again.

I need to run—the fae won't miss me a second time—but if I can somehow get the girl to Aren, he can save her.

"Come on!" I have to yell at the girl so that she can hear me over the music.

She takes one step, then her knees buckle. I strain to keep her on her feet, but her arm slips from my grasp. No one else helps her. They don't notice the blood soaking her clothes.

The remnant is only a pace away. That's when the anger takes over. Anger at the unfairness of the girl's impending death and the brutal torture of the Sighted humans in the building next door. With a scream that nobody hears under the roaring music, I attack the remnant.

It's clear he doesn't expect it. There's a moment of shock in his expression as I ram into him, my fingers reaching for his silver eyes. My nails scrape down the side of his face instead.

I scramble for the hand that was holding his dagger a moment before, but can't find the weapon. I look at the cement floor to see if he dropped it, but he grabs a fistful of my hair. He jerks my head down, brings his knee up.

Tiny glints of silver dance through the air. *Stars,* I think, as he slams his knee into my face again.

When my vision clears, I'm on my hands and knees, still

alive somehow. Breathing makes my face hurt, but I draw in the hot, smoke-tainted air and look up. Aren is here. He's wrestling with the fae. Neither of them has his weapon in hand; they're trying to kill each other with their fists.

Aren dives for the remnant's knees, gets underneath him, then lifts. I think he intends to body slam the other man, but the fae gets his arm around Aren's neck, throwing him off-balance. They fall recklessly into the crowd, taking two guys down with them. The humans can't see what happened; they have no idea what's going on, but they make assumptions. The first guy throws a fist at the second. Someone jumps in to help, and all of a sudden, the whole place becomes one giant mosh pit.

When someone steps on my shoulder, I realize I'm going to be crushed if I don't get back to my feet. I stagger forward, half crawling, half standing until I trip over the girl the remnant stabbed. She's still breathing. Still crying.

Grabbing her arm, I heave up. I have her halfway to her feet when an elbow to the ribs sends a sharp pain down my side. I'm shoved back to the ground. I make an effort to get up again, but people are stepping on the edge of my open coat, pinning me down. The crowd presses in, and the gap I once occupied disappears.

I can't breathe. Someone steps on me, then someone else. I'm lying on top of the girl, almost cheek to cheek with her. Her eyes are open, glassy. A reckless foot kicks her head. She doesn't blink or cry out.

The screams from the crowd are actual screams now. I manage to slip out of my coat, then try to get off the ground yet again, but there are too many people around me, on top of me. I'm going to be trampled to death.

Then I'm wrenched back to my feet. I look over my shoulder, expecting to see Aren. It's not him. It's a human. Someone I don't know and who doesn't know me. Just a random stranger saving my life. I want to thank him, to make sure he gets out of this okay, but I lose sight of him when the crowd surges again. We're all converging on the exit, an exit that's far too small to accommodate this many people. Everyone's screaming and yelling and shoving and pushing. No one will make it out that way.

I shove backward and sideways at the same time, manage to slip through the thinnest gap in the crowd. Adrenaline and a desperate urge to survive are fueling me now. Everyone's trying to escape the club, so the farther I get into it, the less resistance I meet.

To my left, a trio of girls have broken a window. They're climbing out of it. I start to head that way when something on the stage catches my eye.

Paige.

A fae has a sword in one hand, my friend in the other. He wrestles her behind the thick, black stage curtain.

"Paige!" I scream, even though I know she can't hear me. I don't see any other fae in the club. They could easily have fissured out, so I run, jumping on the stage and sprinting for the split in the curtain where I saw them disappear.

There's an exit back here. I run through it, scan up and down the street. I don't see Paige or the remnant, just humans, some who were obviously in the club and others who are watching the rest of us spill out the exits. Some of the women are sobbing. The men look disoriented, too, and the sound of sirens grows louder as the authorities respond to the scene.

Then I hear something else, something I've heard far too much lately: the sound of fae fighting.

It's coming from a side road to my left. I run that way, stop at the corner of the building to peek around its edge. Trev brought back help. He and Aren and at least ten other rebels are fighting an equal number of remnants.

"McKenzie!"

I turn to see Paige sprinting toward me. Before she reaches me, fissures open up all around us.

"Paige!" I scream when a remnant appears out of a slash of light right next to her. She doesn't blink or swerve away from the fae. Normal humans can't see the battle taking place in the middle of a London street; she has no idea how close her enemy is.

Fortunately, the remnant doesn't pursue her. He intercepts a rebel's attack, swinging, then fissuring and swinging again.

She reaches me. I take hold of her arms as she takes hold of mine. She has a scrape across her left cheek, but otherwise, she looks okay.

"This way," I say, pulling her to the right at the same time that she pulls me left, and says, "Over here."

"No, Paige—"

"Come on!" she yells. "We have a plan."

"A plan? Who's we?" I demand, but she's still pulling me down the street. "Paige, what are you doing?"

She turns back to me.

"What does it look like I'm doing?" she says. "I'm saving your ass."

SIXTEEN

•—◆—•

*S*HE'S SAVING *ME?*

My gut tells me I know what that means, but I don't have time to ask what the remnants have told her. A police officer or cop or whatever it is they call the authorities here approaches us.

"I need to see your identifications," he says in his lilting British accent. Lights from the city's emergency vehicles make his neon vest bright. They also disorient me. I tense with every flash in my peripheral vision, but I don't see Aren or Shane or any of the remnants. Where the hell did they go?

"Now," the officer demands, taking a step forward and resting his right hand on the baton at his hip.

Paige and I take a step back.

"I left my ID in my other jeans." Totally true, but the cop either doesn't believe me or he doesn't care. He slips his baton an inch out of its holder. I don't know what his deal is. Hundreds of people were in that club. He should be asking if we're okay. He shouldn't be treating us as if we're . . .

Criminals. As if we're armed.

I *am* armed, and if the bodies in the building next door have been discovered, the cops are probably searching for the killers.

"Keep your hands where I can see them," the officer says.

Paige suddenly loops her arm around my waist, throwing her weight against me with enough force to make me stagger.

"Call an ambulance!" she says, her bright blue eyes going wide. "Can't you see she's bleeding?"

Bleeding? I look down, see that my shirt and jeans are covered in blood. I'm not hurt, though. Not badly, at least. This is all from the girl in the club.

The *dead* girl in the club.

"You have to help us," Paige says, forcing me to move toward the officer. "Please."

Paige is a great actress, but the cop isn't buying it. His baton slides all the way out of its holder, and he shouts a name, calling for backup, I presume.

I look toward the right, where the rest of the cops are congregated, helping the injured or setting up barricades to keep out traffic and the decent-sized crowd that's developed.

Speaking of that crowd, it surges toward the sidewalk, making room for a black sedan to pass. The car hits the opposite curb, nearly clips the post holding up one side of the canopy in front of the theater's entrance before returning fully to the street. Completely ignoring the barricade the police are moving into place, it heads straight for us.

It has to be Shane. Thank God he made it out of the club okay.

I grab Paige's arm, removing it from around my waist and using it to pull her toward the approaching vehicle. Then I remember the last time Shane came to my rescue. He plowed into me. I don't want a repeat experience, so I backpedal toward the sidewalk.

"Hey!" the officer in front of us shouts, moving forward. He notices the car a second later. I tense, hoping Shane doesn't intend to run him down—hitting a remnant is so much different than hitting a human who's only doing his job—but the officer staggers backward, out of the way.

The car screeches to a stop between us. I grab the handle of the back door, jerk it open, and am halfway inside before I realize the driver isn't Shane.

He is human, though.

His dark brown eyes meet mine. "You have two seconds to make a decision."

He shifts into first gear. Paige shoves me from behind. I'm not in the mood to see the inside of a British jail, so I scurry across the seat. Paige barely has time to fall into the car beside me before the driver takes off.

Or rather, he sort of takes off. I'm thrown back, then forward and back again as the transmission protests. This is a standard. Whoever this guy is obviously doesn't have much experience with them.

"Let me drive," Paige says, putting her hands on the shoulders of the front seats to crawl over the center console.

"No," the driver answers. After another rough stop and start, he gets moving. For about ten seconds. The car coughs and dies.

"You're going to strip the gears!" she says, grabbing the hand he has on the stick shift.

There's a muffled yell outside the car. I turn in time to see the officer slam his baton into the driver's window. The safety glass fractures but stays in one piece.

The cop raises his baton again just as the car roars back to life. We lurch forward. I turn around, looking out the back window to see the officer running after us with the baton raised again. He swings. This time, he misses.

But we are *so* not out of danger yet. A car parked beside the crowd of onlookers starts moving, heading toward us with its lights flashing.

I face forward again, see that the street is clear ahead, but I've seen enough police chases on TV to know that this won't end well. We might be in the UK, but I'm sure they have helicopters and cameras the same as we do in the U.S. The only way we might—*might*—get away with this is with fae help. We need to get to the gate.

The guy driving brakes as he makes a sharp left. The turn goes well, but as soon as he tries accelerating again, the car sputters. Paige sprawls over the console and has to brace a hand against the front dash. I grip the back of the driver's seat and hold on.

"You're going to get us killed," Paige says. "Move."

"You're sitting on the gearshift." He leans his shoulder into her, trying to push her out of the way. Ahead, a patrol car sits at an intersection. It starts to pull out, blocking our street.

Paige grabs the wheel, spinning it. I'm thrown against the door, and I swear we nearly flip as we make a wild left turn.

"Jesus Christ, Paige!" The driver rights the steering wheel, but once again, the car lurches.

"This isn't working." I grab the door handle. "We're going to have to run."

"Not if this asshole cooperates," Paige says. She gets her legs underneath her, then somehow maneuvers her way into the guy's lap. She's petite enough that she's actually able to fit under the wheel. From the backseat, I can't see what exactly happens next, but there's a grunt of pain from the driver, the gears grind one last time, then tires squeal as we take off.

Sirens blare beside us. I curse when I see the patrol car speeding toward my window. Curse again when Paige yanks the wheel, sending me across the backseat. I'm awkwardly wedged onto the floorboard when I'm flung in the other direction.

Adrenaline surges through me—I'm pretty sure we're going to crash any second—but when I manage to crawl back into my seat, I see that Paige totally has this.

She's shifting gears like a pro, dodging pedestrians and random medians in the road. She hasn't shaken the cops pursuing us, though. At least three vehicles are on our tail.

"You're on the wrong side of the road," the guy formerly driving the car says. He's maneuvered himself into the passenger seat. The tendons in his throat are tight, and he's holding on to the door and center console as if they're his only lifelines.

"Seat belt," I say calmly, yanking on the strap over his shoulder. I still tense with every close call and last-minute turn the car makes, but I keep my breaths steady and force myself to trust Paige's driving. She's doing better than I could, which is ironic because I know she doesn't have a license, and I'm fairly certain she's never even owned a car.

I grab my own seat belt and buckle in. "We're not going to be able to lose the cops. We need—"

"We'll go back to where we fissured in at," Paige interrupts. "Someone will find us there."

The someone she's talking about has to be a remnant. "Paige. We need to talk. What did they tell you? Do you know who they are?"

Her eyes meet mine in the rearview mirror. "Don't you mean *what* they are? They're fae. And I'm totally pissed you never told me about them."

Obviously, *they* told her about them. I'm grateful for that, though, and if they've convinced her that they're the good guys in the war, then they must not have hurt or threatened her. After seeing what they did to the Sighted humans, I'm grateful for that.

The former driver looks over his shoulder at me. "You know where a gate is?"

"North side of the river near the docks," I say. Then I add, "Who are you?"

I'm extremely curious. He and Paige obviously know each other. They must have both been with the remnants. They kidnapped Paige because of her connection to me, but I've never met this guy. I don't think he was one of Atroth's humans.

Atroth's *murdered* humans.

"My name's Lee," he says.

"He's the jerk who's using me to find you," Paige adds. Then she slams on the brake and spins the wheel.

I brace against the front seat again.

There's a squeal of tires behind us, then a crash as we lose a patrol car.

Paige sideswipes one of the city's signature red phone booths and keeps driving.

"Using you to find me?" I ask, a death grip on the back of the driver's seat.

"I'm just looking for my brother," Lee says.

"Who you need McKenzie to find." She makes a relatively controlled turn to the right. "Hey, I found the river."

"We need to go south," I say, taking a closer look at Lee.

He's facing forward again. The light from the radio high-lights his profile. His eyes are dark, and his black, spiky hair is meticulously styled.

"You're looking for Naito," I say, certain I see a few faint Caucasian features in his otherwise angular Asian face.

"You do know him," he says, peering back at me.

"Yeah," I say, but I don't elaborate. I had no clue Naito had a brother. He never mentioned one, but then, he never mentioned his father very much either. Understandably, since Nakano is the person who killed Kelia. Nakano leads the group of Sighted humans who attacked the rebels back when they held me captive in Germany. They loathe the fae and are determined to kill them whenever and wherever they can. We call them vigilantes, and they're a perfect example of why the fae hide themselves from human society.

"You have the Sight?" I ask. The Sight is supposedly hered-itary, but it's extremely rare for two immediate family mem-bers to possess it. For all three to have it, that's truly remarkable.

We cross to the other side of a bridge before Lee answers, "Yeah. I have the Sight."

That tells me nothing about his allegiance.

"Have you been with the rem . . . with the fae for long?" I ask.

"We met them a week ago," Paige says, swerving onto the road running parallel to the river.

"I can answer for myself," Lee says.

"Oh, really?" Her blond bangs fall into her face when she swings her gaze to him. "You don't need to consult—"

"I can answer for myself," he says again. This time, it sounds like he's gritting his teeth.

"What do you want with your brother?" I ask. If he's a vigilante, maybe I should find a way to ditch him.

"I haven't seen him in three years," Lee answers. "I want to talk to him."

"He hasn't mentioned you."

"We didn't part on good terms," he says, then he uses a button on the center console to move the mirror on his door. To focus on the patrol cars pursuing us, I assume. Five are behind us. One pulls parallel whenever he has the chance, but so far, they aren't being aggressive about forcing us to stop. Back in the U.S., some cities have a policy to just follow suspects. If we're lucky, they have the same policy here.

"So, the gate," Paige says. "How are we going to use it without a fae?"

"Someone will be waiting for us there." I *hope* someone will be waiting. This was Aren's plan. If we're separated, he'll bring an army to the gate to make sure I'm fissured out of this city unharmed.

If he has time to summon that army. If he wasn't killed back at the club.

Fear surges through me, making my throat close up. It's exhausting, worrying about him so much, and even though I'm still upset about his connection to Thrain—or, more precisely, about him not telling me up front about the connection—I can't make myself not care.

"Who's 'someone'?" Paige asks. Then she slams on the brake. The car fishtails on the wet pavement, but she maintains control, which is lucky for the humans standing no more than two feet away from the front bumper.

"Crap, people!" Paige yells. "You have to look before you cross the street!"

A patrol car pulls up beside us. The officer opens the door.

"Not yet," Paige says, her tone hard, determined. She pounds on the horn, shifts into first, then drives straight at the people. They scurry out of the way before she hits them.

Lee watches the officer as we speed away.

"You done this before?" he asks Paige.

"Star in my own police chase?" She shakes her head. "Nope."

The cops fall into pursuit behind us again. We're screwed if the rebels aren't at the gate. We'll be arrested. I'll most likely be charged with murder, maybe with grand theft auto, too, which is completely unfair. Every car I've climbed into in the last month might have been stolen, but they were all stolen by someone other than me.

Lee holds on to the oh-shit handle above his door as Paige

veers around a fountain, which for some illogical reason, is placed in the middle of the road. "Where did you learn to drive like this?"

She shifts, then, very deliberately, she meets Lee's eyes, and says, "I dated a guy who street races."

Lee's mouth tightens as if this is some kind of verbal jab. My gaze shifts back and forth between the two of them. Do they have a history together? I'd swear the last guy she dated was named Ryan. Or maybe Roger. I'm pretty sure it started with an "R." Anyway, if there is or was something between her and Lee, she has plenty of exes to throw in his face.

"Have you guys known each other for long?" I ask.

"No," they say in unison. Then Lee turns his glare on me as if my question offended him. "Where's the gate?"

Or maybe that look is because I'm asking questions that really aren't important right now, not with half the British police force on our bumper. And not with a roomful of slaughtered humans discarded in an apartment and one innocent girl stabbed to death in a club.

"We're getting close." I sink back into my seat, and the edge my adrenaline's been giving me fades. I don't think those deaths are the only ones that occurred tonight. The club was packed. Everyone was panicked. My gut tells me not everyone made it out of there okay. Shane might not have made it out okay.

I stare out the window. Lights from the patrol cars tailing us flash in my peripheral vision, but I block them out and focus on the buildings we're driving past. They're all big, blocky warehouses. London's gate was near the city airport. We're curving south. If we curve back to the north once we pass the warehouse ahead, I think we might be there.

"You're sure a fae will be waiting?" Lee asks.

"Yes," I say, praying I'm not lying.

We pass the warehouse. I think this is the right location, but a thin line of trees separates the road from the bank of the river. At the speed we're driving, I won't be able to see the blur in the atmosphere. Too bad Sosch isn't here now. He'd beeline straight for the gate and—

"There's Aren," I say, and my heart finally starts to beat

easily again. He's alive and he doesn't look hurt, thank God. He's standing on the bank of the river with two other fae. It's not quite an army, but it might as well be. Kyol is here.

Paige slams on the brake.

Unbuckling my seat belt, I say, "We have to make a run for it. Fast."

I don't have to tell them twice. They open their doors the same instant I do, and we're running, sprinting for the riverbank. I can hear the cops behind us, climbing out of their cars and yelling at us to stop.

I'm certain I can keep ahead of them—I have a little too much experience running for my life—but Paige doesn't. She loses too much time looking over her shoulder. A particularly quick cop grabs a handful of the back of her shirt.

Ten years ago, I left her at Bedfont House, and she took the blame for our escape attempt. I won't do the same again.

I stop so quickly the officer on my tail barrels into me. I have the foresight to drop to a crouch, causing him to flip over me. He lands spread-eagle on the ground, and I'm up again, sprinting toward Paige. I ram my shoulder into the cop holding her. Paige is fighting back. She's able to get loose. I grab her arm and pull her toward the gate.

But we're surrounded.

"Hands where we can see them," a female officer yells. All the cops have their batons out.

Light flashes in my peripheral vision. I turn that way, see Aren and Kyol step out of two fissures just outside the cops' circle. No one looks their direction. They're invisible to normal humans.

"This way," Aren says.

I start to tell Paige to run, but she's apparently already decided to make a move. She leaps toward the small gap between two of the officers. The officers close in, one raising his baton.

Aren bats the baton away when the human swings, causing it to narrowly miss Paige. The second officer's baton comes close to hitting me, but I duck. Then Paige and I are outside the circle, catching up with Lee, who's doubled back to help us.

"Go!" I yell at him, but he waits for Paige, steadies her when she trips. Then they're both running for Trev, who's waiting at the riverbank.

I'm right on their heels, but an officer is nearly on top of me. I don't slow down or look back, but there's a thump when he hits the ground just behind me.

"Faster, McKenzie," Aren says. There's no doubt the fae can keep the humans off us. Keeping them off us without them noticing that their efforts are being sabotaged by an invisible force is another question.

But we're lucky. We make it almost all the way to the bank without another problem from the cops. In fact, we'd probably make it to the gate and disappear from this world without another hiccup if Kyol didn't appear in front of Paige. She grabs Lee's arm and skids to a stop.

"They're rebels!" she says, eyes going wide.

Shit. She knows more than I thought she did if she recognizes the *jaedra* tree etched into Kyol's armor.

"I'm with them," I hiss, shoving her forward.

"What?"

No time for explanations. The river is a good five feet below the bank we're standing on. "Jump!"

But she's still backpedaling. Aren grabs her, yells at Trev to open a gated-fissure, then he throws her over the edge. Her scream is cut off by a splash.

Either Lee doesn't care whose side I'm on, or he'll go wherever Paige does because he jumps into the river after her without protest.

Trev goes in next. I make a move to follow them, but I'm tackled to the ground, and not just by one person. There have to be at least three cops on top of me.

I slam my elbow back, try to raise my knee to one of their guts, but an officer punches me. Another one slams a baton into my ribs.

My breath whooshes out of my lungs. I manage to keep fighting, to get my arms between my chest and the man pressing his full weight against me. I shove with all my might.

And he flies off me.

I'd love to take credit for that, but Aren is there, knocking off a second cop. The third one still has me, though. I twist, throw my hip into him, and manage to get about half an inch away.

Flopping to my back, I bring my right knee up, prepared to ram my heel into his chin, but fae arms close around me. I'm wrestled away from the human. We roll toward the bank of the river, stop at the edge just long enough for the fae to press an anchor-stone into my palm.

I close my hand around it.

Meet the fae's eyes.

"Hold on," Kyol tells me.

I wrap my arms around his waist and tighten my grip on the stone as he rolls us one last time.

We go over the edge. I catch a brief glimpse of Paige splashing in the Thames beside the gated-fissure before Kyol and I fall into the slash of light. The In-Between steals my breath away, but the shock of the cold, empty nothingness is muted beneath another shock.

The British officers never once saw the fae because they're invisible to normal humans. They're invisible to normal humans, but Paige knew they were rebels.

Paige saw the emblem carved into Kyol's *jaedric* armor.

Paige *saw* them.

Paige has the Sight.

SEVENTEEN

◆

KYOL AND I roll into the Realm. Into Corrist. I hear a shout go up from the wall, an alarm being raised, but the fact that we're both still breathing tells me we've fissured into a safe zone. Even if we hadn't, Kyol is on top of me. His arms are braced on either side of my body, caging me beneath him. They'd have to kill him before having a chance of harming me.

Kyol doesn't move immediately. Neither do I, mostly because the right side of my rib cage is killing me, but also because I can't with him positioned above me. He stares down, and his silver eyes look bright framed by his dark hair. He's looking into my eyes, which is totally understandable considering my face is right under his, but then—just for the briefest second—his gaze dips to my mouth.

Suddenly, I'm completely aware of our position, of the way the length of his body presses against mine. My right arm is around his waist. My left grips the tight muscles in his forearm and it's as if my thoughts trigger my *edarratae*. Lightning licks its way into my palm, up my arm and shoulder, and I feel my face blush with heat. I break contact immediately, but Kyol still doesn't move. He focuses on my eyes again, and doubt surges through me. Not doubt about Aren or the way I feel about him, but doubt about the way Kyol feels about me. I don't know if he told me the truth when he said he was okay with our breakup.

A throat clears to my left. "I can take her now."

Aren's voice breaks through whatever's holding Kyol frozen. He rises off me, acknowledges Aren with a nod, and steps back.

Aren crouches beside me. A frown creases his forehead as I slowly sit up. At first, I think he's searching for a reaction, trying to pick up my feelings toward Kyol. I know it still bothers Aren, my ten-year pseudo-relationship with him. I haven't been able to convince Aren that I would have left Kyol even if I didn't have Aren. I left Kyol because I wasn't myself when I was with him. I was careful with my thoughts, my words, and my actions. I tried to become someone I wasn't all because I wanted to be worthy of him.

I don't feel that way with Aren. If we work out, it will be because *we* work, not because we're changing ourselves to meet the other's expectations.

Aren doesn't say anything about Kyol, though. Instead, he glances toward the silver wall, then asks, "Can you make it to the palace? I shouldn't heal you out here."

"Do I look that bad?" I ask as I look down at myself. "Oh."

I'm still covered in the human girl's blood. I don't think any of the red stains on my clothing are mine. I have a few bumps and scrapes, bruises from being trampled at the club, and my cheek hurts from the remnant kneeing my face, but my worst injury is my ribs. One or two might be cracked. The officer landed a good blow with his baton there at the end.

"I've had worse injuries," I tell Aren as I stuff the anchor-stone I'm still holding into my pocket. His gaze moves to the scar on the right side of my throat. That's not what I was referring to—I don't remember the cut hurting at all, actually—but it throbs now, and it's difficult not to reach up to touch the raised skin. Aren put a sword to my neck three weeks ago. We were in Lyechaban, and I think that day might have been the last day we were enemies. He should have killed me then. The rebels were so close to losing the war, and Lena ordered him to cut my throat if I didn't read Kyol's shadows. Kyol had just captured Naito, and I was still stubbornly defending the king, but Aren couldn't do it. He couldn't slide his sword across my neck.

He swallows, and his silver eyes seem to darken with regret. They do that every time he looks at the scar. I've never actually told him that I forgive him for what he did. Maybe some part of me still holds it against him.

He offers his hand. As he's helping me to my feet, a flash of something white in my peripheral vision catches my attention. It's a chaos luster on Lee's skin. He's standing a few feet away. Water pools around his feet as he stares up at the wall of silver stretching into the sky. I can tell he's never seen it before. His eyes are wide. He's slightly off-balance. I've been in and out of the Realm enough to adjust quickly to the difference in the atmosphere. It has a lighter touch here, almost a buoyancy that can affect your equilibrium. It's clear Lee isn't accustomed to it. Has he been to the Realm at all before?

Has Paige? I have no idea where the remnants might have kept them and . . .

I look around. "Where's Paige?"

A fissure rips through the air in answer. Trev rolls out of it with my friend, my friend who is *not* supposed to be able to see the fae. She's soaking wet and pissed. Kyol and I fell through Trev's fissure before we hit the water. I don't envy Paige or Lee, going through the In-Between like that.

Trev tries to keep a hold on her, but she throws back an elbow, getting a lucky hit on his chin. She almost slips free then, but Trev grabs her ankle, keeping her from scrambling away. This time, he locks his arms around her like a straitjacket.

"Having trouble controlling your human?" Aren asks, grinning.

Trev glares back. "I was told this human didn't have the Sight."

Aren's grin fades. He looks at Paige, who's still struggling to get free. It's obvious she can see the fae holding her. It's obvious she sees Aren and the rebel swordsmen closing in on both sides of us.

Some humans with the Sight make it through their entire lives without knowing they have it. Fae rarely stay in the human world for an extended period of time, and when they do, they tend to keep to rural areas, away from tech and, therefore, away from humans. But Paige has met Kyol before. She's met Aren. They've both let her see them on occasion, and she acted like they were normal humans, like she couldn't see their chaos lusters. There's no way in hell she wouldn't have noticed the lightning.

"Paige," Lee says, moving toward her with his hand outstretched as if to say "calm down."

"They're rebels, Lee," Paige hisses.

"I know," he says, almost to her side. "It's okay."

"You know? It's okay?" she practically snarls.

"Paige." I walk toward her, too. I don't know how she can see the fae, but I don't believe she's lied to me all these years. "I tried to tell you before. They haven't been holding me captive." Not this whole time, at least. "I'm on their side. I'm helping them. The fae lied to—"

Lee kicks out without warning, landing his heel squarely on Trev's chin. Trev's head whips back hard enough to make me wince, and Paige wiggles free.

Lee grabs her arm and pulls her to her feet. Then he spins, putting himself between her and the fae swordsmen who've just arrived. His knees are slightly bent, and he's tense, as if he thinks he might really be able to take on the three armed fae facing him.

"Karate?" she says, crossing her arms. "How stereotypical of you."

"It's *jujitsu*, Paige, and you're welcome."

This guy might be connected to the vigilantes, but he's standing up for Paige. If he doesn't turn out to be a complete jerk, I might like him.

"They're not going to hurt you," I say, moving toward them. "Let's just calm down for a second."

"Could we calm down on the other side of the wall?" Aren asks with a pointed look at the row of buildings to my left. Anyone could be inside of them, and it's not just the remnants we have to worry about. Three humans in one place might freak out the more paranoid fae who are worried about the Realm's magic.

"You won't touch her," Lee says. "And I want to see my brother."

"Your brother?" Aren cocks his head to the side. He's speaking to Lee, but he hasn't taken his eyes off Paige. He knows she didn't have the Sight when he first met her. He's just as curious as I am to learn how she got it.

"Naito," I tell Aren. "He's Naito's brother." I turn back to Lee. "He's in the palace, and if you don't touch the fae, they won't touch you."

"You can guarantee that?" Lee asks.

Technically, I have no authority over the fae and what they do, but Aren and Kyol . . .

Kyol's gone. I have no idea when he left, but he wouldn't contradict me on this. So far, none of the rebels have gone against anything I've said. That might just be because they haven't had a reason to yet, but Lee doesn't need to know that.

"Yes. I'll kick their asses if they do."

Paige lifts an eyebrow my direction. As far as she knows, I wouldn't hurt a fly. Whenever I'm around her and her friends, I never step into their debates, never argue or contradict anyone else. She thinks it's because I'm extremely easygoing. Mostly, it's because I'm always distracted and thinking of something or someone else.

Lee shrugs. I take that as a sign of agreement and motion them to the right. Paige looks wary of the fae, but she starts walking.

Beside me, Aren says, "I won't mention to Lena the way you're taking control of her people."

"I haven't taken control of anyone."

"Everyone here who understands English will follow your order," he says. "No one wants to cross the *nalkin-shom*."

"You really have to stop spreading rumors about me."

He grins. I roll my eyes.

I feel good, though. Compared to the place I held in Atroth's Court, this is a welcome change.

It's the middle of the day in Corrist. The city isn't deserted like it was the last time I passed through it, but there's still a noticeable difference in the number of fae on the streets now compared to the number on the streets when Atroth was in power, and everyone we pass seems to be on edge.

Aren doesn't take back roads to the palace this time. He leads us down the Avenue of the Descendants. In the plaza outside the palace, guards question and search the fae who want an audience with Lena or with one of the high nobles. They have offices in the palace as well as in their residences, both here in the Inner City and back in their home provinces.

The guards let us enter after talking to Aren. We step inside the huge greeting hall in the palace's south wing. It's designed to impress visitors. Twin staircases arch up to the left and right, joining together beneath a chandelier lit with magic in the center of the room. The banisters are a shiny, untarnished silver. It's an extravagance. So are the silver drapes making waves on the high ceiling.

"Well, this is fucking beautiful," Paige says, stopping to take everything in. I almost smile. I've always appreciated her bluntness.

A fae approaches us, one of the guards Aren talked to when we entered. He hands two heavy cloaks to Aren, who then holds one out for Paige and the other for Lee. Both humans are drier than they were before, but the air in Corrist is cool. They have to be freezing.

Lee takes his, but Paige keeps her arms folded. "I'm fine."

"To cover the lightning," Aren says without a pause. It's a lie. We don't need to hide our chaos lusters in the palace, but it gives Paige a reason to accept the cloak without feeling like he's doing her a favor.

It works, and I give Aren a small smile when he returns to me. He didn't have to do that, but it was considerate of him.

"Paige has . . . an interesting personality," Aren says, as she and Lee trail the two fae leading the way deeper into the palace.

"Yeah," I say, watching her pull on the cloak while she looks around the greeting hall again. I recognize the expression she's wearing. I wore it ten years ago when I first came to the Realm. I was intoxicated by this world and its magic.

So is she, and it's weird, seeing chaos lusters on her skin. They seem to go with her personality, though. They're as spontaneous as she is, and they dart across her face and hands like they're accessories.

"She can see us," he says, sounding as if he's speaking more to himself than to me. He's just as confused as I am. Paige has the Sight; she didn't before. *Something* changed since the wedding. Something or someone gave her the Sight.

"Could a fae have done it?" I ask. "Maybe with a magic that's supposed to be extinct?"

"I've never heard any rumor of it. Humans are either born with the Sight or they're not." After a moment, he adds, "I suppose there's a chance it might be possible. What about the other human? What do you know about him?"

"Just that he's Naito's brother."

"Right. Trev," Aren calls. The other fae approaches. To me, he seems kind of reluctant, but when Aren orders him to find Naito and bring him to Lena, he nods.

After Trev leaves, I tell Aren, "I think the remnants told Paige you kidnapped me."

"Well, that's true," he says, throwing me a quick grin that makes my stomach flip.

"Yes, but all the time she's been around the fae, she thought I was being held captive and that she was with the good guys."

"You need to talk to her," he says, as we enter the northern wing of the palace.

"Alone, if possible."

He nods. "We'll talk to Lena first, then see what Naito has to say."

The huge, gilded doors to the throne room are closed when we get there. The smaller door set into the left side is cracked open, though. It's dark inside. The fae who led us here stop and motion for Paige and Lee to wait, but Aren ushers me forward.

It takes a second for my eyes to adjust. When they do, I see that fae are covering each of the room's tall windows with black cloths that are stretched between a series of long poles. Lena is sitting on the throne. She doesn't look comfortable there. She's sitting straight and staring at a fae clad in black in the center of the room. So are the nobles standing on either side of her dais. They aren't all high nobles, but I do recognize Lord Kaeth and Lord Hison. A few other important fae are here, too. Even the archivist, Kavok, has come out of his hole for this. Like Lena, they're all staring at the black-clad fae.

The fae doesn't leave his position in the center of the room, but his arms are almost in constant motion.

"I wish you could see this." Aren practically breathes the words. His gaze is riveted on the center of the room, but I was wrong about what the others are watching. They're not staring at the black-clad fae; they're staring at the illusions he's creating.

That has to be what this is. I've heard of fae who have the ability to turn a darkened room or an amphitheater into entirely different settings. Some tell entire stories with their illusions. Others are only strong enough to add special effects to a stage show. I think this fae is different, though. The way Aren's gaze sweeps the room, following an object to the ceiling, then back down again, makes me think this is pure art.

The fae's arms go still, breaking the spell he has over the throne room. The windows are uncovered then, and the nobles clap. Lena waits until they're finished before she says, *"Thank you, Daron. I will let you know."*

"Let him know what?" I ask Aren, keeping my voice low.

"Daron wants to be named Lena's Court Illusionist," he says. "It's a respected position and will signify he's one of the best illusionists in the Realm. I promised him he could perform for her if he created a lightning storm in Rhigh."

"He did that?" I look at the black-clad fae again.

Aren nods. "He's an old friend of mine."

The fact that he doesn't say more than that tells me they were friends back when Aren worked with Thrain. That darkens my mood.

At the other end of the throne room, Lena's voice rings out. *"You may go."*

Daron gives her a respectful bow. Lena watches him

retreat. Then she must see Aren and me standing here because she adds, *"You may all go."*

The nobles look reluctant to leave, but eventually, they make their way out. Kavok follows them, giving me a pleasant smile until he sees Paige and Lee waiting just outside the door.

"Are they shadow-readers?" he asks.

That's actually a good question. I look at the two humans, take a guess. "I don't think so."

He seems disappointed by that. I don't know if I am or not. It would be nice to have another shadow-reader just like it would be nice to have more Sighted humans. It would lighten my responsibilities, give all of us more time off. I might even have a better chance at getting and keeping a job. On the other hand, I don't want to bring anyone else into this war. I especially don't want Paige to be involved in it. It's not that she needs protection or can't handle this new world or anything, but she's been perfectly fine and happy before all of this. The only reason she's here is because of me, and I *hate* being at fault for that.

"Can I find you in the archives later?" I ask Kavok, before he leaves. Maybe he's come across a story in the Realm's literature or history about a fae giving humans the Sight.

"Of course," he says with a smile.

He and the rest of the fae exit the throne room, leaving behind only the guards, Lena, and Kyol, who's standing to the left of her dais. Aren dismisses the fae who escorted Paige and Lee here, then we all approach the throne.

"Obviously, it turned out not to be a false lead," Lena says, standing to study the two humans. *"A trap?"*

Paige rolls her eyes when Lena switches to Fae. She never would have worked for Atroth. There's no way she'd put up with his rules. I honestly don't know how I did for so long, now. Habit, maybe. In the beginning, I wanted to be near Kyol, the king was nice to me, and it felt good to be needed. I didn't understand the Realm and its magic, so I was willing to follow the rules just so I wouldn't harm it. All those reasons seem weak now; they didn't at the time.

"Atroth's Sighted humans were there," Aren says. *"They were dead."*

"Dead?" Lena asks sharply. *"Are you sure?"*

"Tortured and killed," Aren says. *"I'm sure."*

Beside Lena, Kyol straightens. *"It doesn't make sense for the remnants to kill them."*

Kyol is an expert at hiding his emotions, but his words are so monotone and spoken so softly, I know he's not unaffected by the news. He worked with all the Sighted humans at one time or another, and he recruited at least one of them. It's not his fault they're dead, but he considered protecting them one of his many responsibilities.

"It makes slightly more sense if they can make more," Aren says. Kyol and Lena focus on him, but he doesn't elaborate. He's looking back at the entrance to the hall. Naito's there, walking toward us with his hands in his pockets and his gaze focused on the strip of carpet beneath his feet.

I glance at Lee. He sees his brother, too, and turns to face him fully. Naito doesn't look up until he reaches us. He takes everyone in, lingering for a few seconds on Paige, then finally resting his gaze on Lee. We're all quiet, waiting for one of them to say something. Lee breaks the silence first.

"Naito," he says, his jaw visibly clenching and unclenching.

Not even a twitch from Naito to show he recognizes Lee. Aren looks at me. I give him a tight-lipped smile in return. Aren and Naito are friends. We both want him to get better, but neither one of us knows how to help.

Lena turns away from them, faces Aren. *"What do you mean, 'make more'?"*

"She didn't have the Sight three weeks ago," he says, motioning to Paige. *"Someone gave it to—"*

I don't know where the knife comes from. One second, Naito is standing there all still and sober, the next, he's closed the distance between him and his brother. Light from one of the hall's tall windows glints off Naito's blade as he slashes out.

EIGHTEEN

◆

LEE'S QUICK. NAITO aims for his heart, but he turns his body sideways and bends out of the way.

Naito's momentum takes him past his brother. He swings his left fist back, manages to hammer Lee in the face as he brings his dagger around a second time. But Aren steps in, blocking Naito's attack and disarming him in a move too quick to follow.

"Naito, stop!" Aren gets his arms around the human. "Stop!"

Naito struggles, trying to get at Lee. He hasn't been this animated since Kelia died, and it's as if he's unleashing all his bottled-up rage and pain at once until, all of a sudden, he stops.

Cautiously, Aren loosens his hold. "Are you done?"

"How did you get here?" Naito demands, his chest rising and falling as if it can barely contain his fury.

"Nice to see you again, too, brother," Lee says, running a hand over his jaw and working it back and forth.

Naito's nostrils flare. I swear he's about to launch himself at Lee again, but then, his forehead creases. He looks from Lee to Paige, then back to Lee again.

"Son of a bitch," he says. "He did it."

Lee's face hardens. He sticks his hands in his pockets but doesn't break eye contact with his brother.

"Did what?" Aren asks.

Naito remains focused on Lee as well. "He was trying to find a way to give normal humans the Sight."

Lena, who's been watching the interaction between the two humans with a mildly curious expression, suddenly appears to be *very* interested.

"What?" she demands.

"I should have realized it in Germany," Naito says. "Or in Montana. I thought my father had a lot of humans with him, but I didn't think . . ."

Lena takes a step toward him. "What do you mean?"

"Nakano gave them the Sight?" Aren asks, turning to look at both Paige and Lee.

"*Lee* gave me the Sight," Paige says. "I've never met his dad."

Lena grabs Naito's arm. "Why didn't you tell us this before?"

He jerks his arm free. "I didn't know. I thought most of them were firing blindly whenever they saw the underbrush move. That's what they've always done."

"Lena." Kyol speaks her name softly but firmly. A muscle in her cheek twitches then, all the emotions she shouldn't be showing in front of her guards—anger, worry, fear—vanish.

"How does he give people the Sight?" she asks, her voice cool.

Naito slides his hands into his pockets and says, "He was working on a serum."

"And you didn't think to tell us about this before now?" Lena is still calm but just barely.

Naito shakes his head, more in disbelief than in response to Lena. "I never thought it would work."

I glance at Paige. Well, clearly it did work. Paige's life has been turned completely upside down, all because Lee wanted to find me.

Lena's mouth narrows into a thin line as she looks at Paige. I know why she's worried. If the remnants know what we do, they'll try to get the serum. They might already have it. If they do, they have the ability to make an army of Sighted humans with who knows how many shadow-readers among them. Our illusionists will be useless. We'll be unable to fissure to safety. In short, we'll be screwed.

"Do the remnants know about this?" For some reason, Lena's asking Paige, not Lee. Maybe it's because Paige is my friend and, therefore, more likely to help us than the son of a vigilante, but Paige meets Lena's gaze, and says, "I don't know."

She's lying. One of her ex-boyfriends discovered her tell a few years back. He was a wannabe pro poker player, and he noticed she always jutted her chin out after a bluff. It's jutted out now, just the slightest bit.

"How do we get it?" Lena demands.

"You captured a fae yesterday," Paige says. "Tylan. I want to talk to him."

Lena raises an eyebrow. "Do you?"

It's the wrong tone to take with Paige. She squares her shoulders and doesn't look away. She has no clue how dangerous Lena is. She has no clue how dangerous all the fae are.

"Let me talk to him, and I'll consider telling you where the Sight serum is," Paige says.

"Paige." Lee takes her arm, whispers something into her ear. I can't hear it. The fae have better hearing than I do, but by the way Lena leans toward them, I'm not sure she picks it up either.

"We don't need her to tell us where it is." Naito's voice is cold. He meets Lena's gaze. "Send me back to Earth. I'll get it."

In my peripheral vision, I see Aren shake his head. Naito sees it, too. He rounds on the fae. "You should want him dead as much as I do."

"We're not protecting your father," Aren counters. He doesn't back away even though it looks like Naito's one second away from ripping out his throat. "People make mistakes when they're angry and mourning."

Naito's eyes are hard. "I won't make a mistake."

There's a harsh laugh from my right. Lee. His jaw is swelling, but it doesn't seem to be bothering him anymore.

He glares at Naito with eyes that are just as dark and angry as his brother's.

"Dad was right," he says. "You've gone native, and you aren't coming back. You're turning your back on your family."

"My *family*"—Naito practically spits the word—"turned its back on me first. I know why you're here, Lee. I was born with the Sight. That made me Dad's favorite. Now, you can see the fae, and you have Dad's blessing to kill me. You've been dreaming about this day for years, haven't you?"

Before Lee can answer, Paige's eyes go wide. She turns on him. "God, tell me that's not true."

Lee grimaces. That hits me as odd. There's major family drama going on here, and Naito's tone has been scathing this whole time. Lee hasn't flinched once. But at Paige's comment? I don't have much evidence to go by, but I'd bet everything I own that Lee has a thing for Paige. It's not a surprise. I can't exactly explain what it is about her, but she's the type of girl that all guys want. The way she presents herself draws attention. She's the life of the party, the girl you call if you need a friend to hang out with. In short, she's fun. I wish I could be half as lighthearted as she is—I was back in high school—but the last decade of my life has been spent reading shadows and seeing fae. Seeing so much death and violence kind of puts things into perspective.

"Paige, you don't understand," Lee says. "My father lost his arm—"

"'I haven't seen my brother in years.' 'I need to know he's alive.'" Paige's mocking imitation of Lee is actually pretty good. "I was helping you because I thought you *cared* about him."

"That's enough of this," Lena cuts in, descending to the middle step of her dais. She looks at Naito. "You know where your father is keeping the serum?"

"I can find out."

"I'll have Trev fissure you home," she says. "But you have to promise not to go after your father on your own. We need the serum first."

We need more than the serum, actually—all his father's notes and research, his backed-up documents, hell, maybe even his scientist—but something in the way Lena's talking about all of this bothers me. It's like she's hinging all her hope on winning this war on getting the serum. Or, more specifically, getting more Sighted humans.

"You know you can't actually use it, don't you?" I say.

Her head tilts ever so slightly. "We don't have enough humans to watch all portions of the wall and palace."

"I know, but who are you going to give it to?" I ask. "Most humans have no clue the fae exist."

"We'll introduce ourselves," she says. I can't tell if she's being sarcastic or not.

I shake my head. "You can't interfere with people's lives like that. They shouldn't be made to fight a war for you."

She exhales sharply. She's annoyed with me, but I don't care. I won't let her do this.

"I won't force them to help us," she says. "I'll ask. And with their help, this war shouldn't last much longer."

"So what are you going to do? Give the humans the Sight, then dump them back on Earth when you're finished with them?"

Aren steps forward. "Maybe we should talk about this later. We're all tired."

"I'm not," Paige says. "I still want to talk to Tylan."

Lena levels a cool gaze on my friend. "I don't know who you're talking about. We've captured a lot of remnants in the last week."

We've killed a lot of them, too, but I'm glad Lena doesn't go there.

I cut in. "They can stay for now in a room near mine—"

"*Two* rooms," Paige interjects.

"Two rooms near mine," I amend.

Lena's eyes narrow. "She can go when she answers my questions."

Questions, not question. Lena will turn this into a full-fledged interrogation if I don't get Paige out of here now. It's my fault Paige is mixed up in all of this; I have to keep her safe. And more, I want to talk to her. Alone. I need to convince her that the rebels aren't the bad guys. I look at Aren, hold his gaze long enough for him to know what I want.

"Let them go," he says to Lena. "McKenzie will talk to them."

I move too quickly to grab Paige's arm. My ribs protest, but I grit my teeth and pull her toward the exit before Lena gets it into her mind to object again. I half expect her to order us to stop or to put up a wall of air to prevent us from going any farther.

When we're almost to the end of the hall, Paige leans toward me, and says quietly, "I don't like her."

I give her a tight smile. "I didn't either."

"So why are you helping them?" she asks. "They kidnapped you, didn't they? Because you're the best shadow-tracker or something."

"That's what the remnants of the Court told you."

"Yeah. And they promised me they'd free you. It was one of those if-I-help-them, they-help-me things. I wasn't even sure you were alive, but . . ." She shrugs. "You are. They didn't lie about that."

"They just lied about me being a prisoner, still."

"I'm not sure if they knew what your status was."

Oh, they definitely knew. They've tried to capture and kill me enough times in the past couple of weeks that there's no denying it.

We turn down a hall, and I catch a glimpse of Lee behind us. He's quiet, walking with his hands in the pockets of his jeans. From his conversation with Naito, I take it he's anti-fae like his father, and I wonder if it's hard being here around the people he hates. I wonder if it's just Naito he's come to kill.

Lena must be concerned about that, too, because farther behind us is Trev. He doesn't exactly look happy to be stuck with this babysitting duty. I actually don't blame him. It seems like he's always getting put on the crappy assignments.

"The Court fae lied to me when I worked for them," I say. "They let me believe they were capturing the fae I tracked for them. They didn't. The king was brutal in how he tried to win the war. He manipulated things to keep himself in power. Lena isn't like that. She's been very open about what she's done and what she plans to do."

"What about Aren?" she asks. "He's the Butcher of Brykeld, right? You acted like you hated him at Amy's wedding."

I try to suppress a grimace but fail. I know how my relationship with Aren will sound, and, sure enough, Paige stops.

"Oh, God," she says, eyes wide. "McKenzie, tell me you didn't fall in love with your kidnapper. Is that why you switched sides?"

"No!" The word comes out harsher than I intended, but she's been aware of the fae no more than two weeks, and she's acting like she knows everything. "I told you why I switched."

"I thought you were smarter than that," she continues, as if I didn't say anything.

"I am," I snap back. Then I draw in a breath, trying to stay calm. If she's half as tired as I am, she's probably on a short fuse, too. I don't want to fight with her. I want her to see that the rebels are okay and that I am okay. Then I want her to stay out of this war.

"I'm trying to be," I say, softening my tone. "I'm taking things as slow as I can, but Aren . . ." This is awkward, talking about my love life. I've never done this before. "I don't really want to take things slow."

"You're not sleeping with him?"

I shake my head.

"Because," Paige continues, "if you *are* sleeping with him, I want details."

I almost laugh. Paige doesn't exactly agree with my relationship with Aren, but she's not holding it against me. Her ability to accept me for who I am, no matter how crazy I seem . . . that's why she's been my friend for so long.

"This lightning"—she holds up her hand, waits for a chaos luster to strike across it—"I bet it makes just kissing a fae explosive. By the way, I totally get why you never let me shake Kyol or Aren's hands."

I smile. "Yeah, sorry about that."

Something inside me loosens. It's nice to talk about

something other than false-bloods and war, and that little part of me—the one that was so much bigger a month ago—that wants to retire resurfaces. I'm trying to get a job so I can support myself and have something that makes me feel human, but balancing two lives never worked in the past. I don't know why I think it will work now. I could leave the Realm and the war behind. Lena would flip, but Aren would understand.

We enter a residential wing of the palace. My room is here, though I still don't use it very often. I prefer to stay in Vegas because I usually get more sleep there.

I stop suddenly. I share my Vegas hotel room with Shane. How the hell could I have forgotten about him?

"What?" Paige asks.

I look over my shoulder at Trev, ignoring the sharp pain in my side when my torso just barely turns. "Did Shane make it out of the club?"

A long pause, then, "Lena has someone looking for him."

They don't know where he is. Damn it, I should have stuck around, looked for him before I left, but the club was crazy, and I'd caught a glimpse of Paige. Then the police officer was there . . .

Shit. Shane was briefly in the building with the dead humans, too. His fingerprints might be there. He might be in a British jail.

But that's a better option than the alternatives. If he was trampled by the crowd or captured or killed by the remnants, I'll feel at least partially responsible. He wouldn't have been there if it weren't for me.

"McKenzie?" Paige says.

"It's nothing. Here. This one's empty." I open a door that's two rooms down from mine. It's bigger than where I stay, more luxurious, too. A freestanding desk and sofa are arranged on the left side of the room. Two beds with silver, wrinkleless blankets are on the right. In between them is an open doorway to a bathroom. It's dark in here, though. Only the light from the hallway allows me to make out the furniture.

"Trev, could you . . . ?"

He mumbles as he enters the room. It doesn't take more than five seconds for him to send his magic into the sconced orbs. They glow a soft blue, lighting up the room.

"Thanks," I tell him. "If you'll do the same in Lee's room."

"I'm staying here," Lee says, walking inside.

"The hell you are." Paige crosses her arms. Trev mumbles something under his breath, then moves down the hall to the next room, leaving me to sort this out.

"There are two beds," Lee continues. "I think I can manage to not touch you."

"I don't want to breathe the same air as you."

"Don't be ridiculous, Paige," he says. "These fae aren't your friends."

"You said the same thing about Tylan."

"And I was right about him," he says, his voice rising. "He lied about McKenzie being a prisoner."

"Who's Tylan?" I interject before they take each other's heads off.

"He's the first fae I met," she says. "After this asshole injected me with the serum, I went by your place just to make sure there wasn't any truth to his crazy talk about faeries."

"Fae," Lee corrects, taking off his cloak as if he actually thinks he's going to stay here.

Paige rolls her eyes, and continues, "I was going to file a police report, but when I was about to leave, Tylan fissured into your living room. He told me you needed help."

The way she says his name makes me think she likes him. Not in a romantic way but in the same way she likes all of her guy friends.

"My living room?" I ask, thinking he could be the ward-maker who booby-trapped her purse. "So what happened at your apartment? It looked like there was a fight there."

She juts her chin out in Lee's direction. "Him. He didn't ask if I wanted to be injected. He just did it."

"I get it, Paige," he says. "You hate me. You'll never forgive me."

She turns on him. Paige angry is a scary sight. She's a

good foot shorter than Lee, but she gets right in his face and very loudly lists every reason he has no right to expect her to forgive him. I don't blame her. If I knew nothing of the fae and someone injected me with something claiming it would let me see them, I'd be pissed off, too. But something makes me think there's more to this. Sure, they appear to hate each other, but the way they're staring each other down makes me think they're seconds away from a kiss, not from clawing each other's faces off. So, I focus on the ceiling, all but whistling, until I hear Paige say, "What are your daddy's orders now? That's who's been texting you, right? He told you to murder your brother. What are you supposed to do afterward?"

His dad has been texting him?

"Shut up, Paige," Lee says.

Could he possibly still have his cell phone on him? We had to make a mad dash to the gate. After we fissured here, I so brilliantly ordered the fae not to touch him or Paige. Neither one of them have been searched.

"Give it to me," I order.

Lee's face hardens.

Paige sits on the edge of one of the beds, wrinkling the cover. "He won't let anyone touch it."

"Give it to me," I say again.

"I don't have it," he lies.

I meet Paige's gaze. I doubt I can get his cell away from him on my own, but with her help . . .

She knows what I'm asking. "Go for it."

Now that I'm looking for the phone, I see the bulge in his left front pocket. My ribs aren't going to love what I'm about to do, but I reach for it.

As expected, he grabs my wrist. "I said I don't have it."

I brace myself then ram my shoulder into him. It takes him by surprise. He staggers backward and loses his balance when he hits the bed.

My ribs scream as I fall on top of him, but I get my hand in his pocket as he tries to fling me off. He's too careful about it, though. He has the opportunity to hit me, and doesn't take it. Kudos to him, having trouble hitting a woman, but I knee him in the side. He grunts, then grabs ahold of both my arms. That's when Paige darts in and gets his phone.

"Damn it, Paige." He releases me to go for her, but she tosses the phone over his head.

I catch it, then backpedal until I'm in the hallway.

"What's the problem?" Trev demands, drawn by the scuffling.

"Keep him back," I order. The phone is damp from Lee's fall into the Thames. I'm afraid it might not work, but the screen turns on. Drawing in slow, shallow breaths, I bring up Lee's text messages. I have to blink back tears to see the screen. My damn ribs *hurt*.

Trev scowls at the phone, but keeps both humans from leaving the room. A quick glance tells me Lee's given up the fight. Good. I can take my time reading.

It pays off. We don't need to send Naito back to Earth. His father—who does indeed want his brother to kill him—has a place in Boulder, Colorado. And I think I can make it easy for us to get it. I key in a text message. Lee doesn't use any capitalization or punctuation when he types—it's extremely annoying—but I force myself to leave out the commas and periods for authenticity's sake. I just need one more thing, a picture to attach.

"Where are you going?" Trev asks, as I walk away, holding my side.

"I'm going to go get Naito to play dead."

NINETEEN

⬥

I FIND NAITO in his room, flipping through a *jaedric*-bound sketchbook. He closes it when I enter. It looks nothing like the Earth-made sketchbook Lorn gave me in Nashville—the one filled with drawings of Kelia—but it reminds me of it just the same. I'm supposed to give it back to Naito. Problem is, it's still tucked into the pocket of the cloak Aren made me take off in Rhigh. Aren fissured out with it when he told me to count to thirty. Presumably, that's when he talked to Daron, the illusionist who created the fake lightning storm. Maybe it's with him.

I'm not about to mention the sketchbook until I have it in my hand, so instead I ask what Naito's reading when he closes the book. He says it's a collection of notes he's taken on the vigilantes, their names and where they've been seen before. I tell him about Lee and Nakano's texts and about Boulder, and when I explain my plan, Naito agrees to it with only a grunt. I actually expected him to protest more, but I guess he doesn't care because he'll still be going back to Earth. He still thinks he'll have a chance to kill his father. Of course, I don't tell him what my prewritten text says. I wrote that the fae are burying Naito in Cleveland, Georgia. It's kind of a random location, but that's where the rebels had one of their safe houses. Nakano went all the way to Germany to kill fae before. I'm hoping he'll want to do the same now and will leave his compound in Boulder.

That's what Naito calls it—a compound. He says it's an abandoned ski resort, but it sounds like a military outpost. Nakano's probably made it into one. He has the weapons, equipment, and camo to supply half an army. Add to that the fact that he and his people are extremely good at killing fae, and I'm a little worried about what we'll find there.

But we need to get to the serum and the research, so I slice open a *roguia*, a fruit with thick, bloodred juice, and squeeze it over Naito's neck and chest. The picture I take with the phone comes out grainy and perfect—he really does look dead—and I just need to tell Lena and the others my plan, then have a fae fissure me to Earth so I can send the text and picture.

I stop by my room first, though. I have to wash the human girl's blood off my skin.

I strip off my shoes, my clothes, the belt holding my dagger. The bath I take is cold—they always are unless I have a fae heat the water for me—but I don't linger long, just long enough to scrub away the bloodstains. I can't scrub away the guilt, though. The fae's war has affected my world too much this last month. The girl in the club and the Sighted humans next door to it weren't the first deaths. A little over two weeks ago, three humans died when King Atroth's fae attacked a neighborhood near Vancouver. The neighborhood was home to a group of *tor'um* who sheltered the rebels. They were sane fae, born without the ability to use enough magic to fissure, but they were shunned by almost everyone else in the Realm. They moved to my world to start new lives in a place where they would be accepted. Only a Sighted human would know they were different. They weren't harming anyone, but then Atroth attacked. He didn't care who was caught in the cross fire. The war used to be almost completely limited to the Realm. It's not that way anymore.

I step out of the tub and dry off, taking care not to put any pressure on the side where my ribs are an angry purple. My favorite pair of jeans is still lying on top of my chest of drawers. I slip into them, nearly sigh at their perfect fit. The best option for a shirt is a long tunic. It's white and dips low in the front, but with the jeans, it doesn't look too foreign. Besides, I plan to only be in my world a few minutes, just long enough to text Naito's father.

I stick Lee's cell phone into my pocket, then head to the throne room. Aren and Kyol are both there. So are Taber and a relatively large number of Kyol's top swordsmen. I'm halfway to the dais at the other end of the room when I notice the latter are surrounding a fae.

No, they're surrounding a *tor'um*. The *tor'um*. The one who mistook me for Paige back in Spier. The one who almost became Atroth's sword-master. She's standing there with her wrists shackled in front of her, rocking back and forth, heel to toe, heel to toe. Her long hair is pulled back into a ponytail, then into a tight brown braid that drapes over her shoulder.

As if sensing my presence, Aren turns toward me, and I swear his face pales. That's when I notice he's outside the group of fae. Like, way outside of it.

"What's going on?" I ask.

Aren's eyes close in a long blink. When he opens them, he looks at the *tor'um*, then back at me. "I'm sorry, McKenzie."

There's so much regret in his voice that I would have to be an idiot not to put the pieces together. I freeze before I reach the group, and the stabbing pain in my side dulls to a distant ache when I realize that Aren did this. Aren turned this fae *tor'um*.

When I first saw the woman back in Spier, Kyol told me she was made *tor'um* years ago. I assumed Aren had nothing to do with it because he wasn't fighting King Atroth then. I didn't know about his history with Thrain.

It's easier to ignore Aren's past when I'm not directly confronted with it, but seeing what he's done right in front of me and knowing that this woman isn't the only person whose life he's ruined makes me feel sick.

"McKenzie," Lena breaks into my thoughts. "I thought you'd be with your friend."

The *tor'um* turns to see who Lena is talking to, and when she spots me, her face lights up.

"There you are!" she exclaims. She takes a step toward

me, then stops. Her brow wrinkles in confusion and, in a completely different, almost disappointed tone, she says, "There you aren't."

She's looking for Paige, I realize, but the only thing I can think of to say is, "Why is she here?"

"She was found skipping outside the wall," Lena says. She turns back to the *tor'um*, her gaze taking the woman in head to toe. "Clearly, she wanted to be caught."

"Clearly!" the *tor'um* chimes in.

"Why did you want to be caught, Brene?" Kyol asks in Fae. His voice is low, but gentle, and I get the impression that this Brene is someone he admired, someone he's saddened to see in this state.

She looks like a child concentrating when she frowns. She even has a slight pout to her lips. *"I was looking for something."*

"Were you looking for me?" I try, thinking maybe the remnants sent her to find Paige. Aren did this to her, not me, and I know this is unreasonable, but I feel like I owe the *tor'um*, like I'm obligated to help her because I'm involved with the fae who ruined her life.

Brene squints at me, and I wonder if my pronunciation is off. Then, it's like she's looking through me. I glance over my shoulder, but no one is there. When I focus on her again, she shakes her head then tilts her head up to peer at the ceiling. Her demeanor feels off, more off than it was a second ago, at least. I think we might be losing her.

"Brene?" I try using her name. Maybe it will help her refocus.

Her coal gray eyes lock on me. "Un-Paige," she says. "Tell them I dislike the bracelets."

"Bracelets?"

She holds up her shackled wrists.

"Can we—"

"No," Kyol, Lena, and Aren say in unison. Their responses are short and sharp, like taking off the shackles is the worst idea ever. Apparently, they all think Brene is dangerous, even in her semisane state.

I'm not so sure they're right, though. Without warning,

she plops to the ground like a child and starts tracing the edge of the blue carpet runner. She's babbling in Fae, something about lightning not being able to tell the difference between skin and sky, but she's using such a singsong voice, I don't know if I'm translating her correctly.

Lena sits on the top step of her dais and watches Brene. Just for a moment, I think I glimpse pity in her eyes.

"From what we've been able to learn from her," she says, "the remnants don't know about the serum. Naito will have time to track down his father."

The serum. Right. That's the reason I'm here.

"Are you planning to use it?" I ask.

She draws in a slow breath, lets it out. "I would like to," she says. "It will benefit us. It would benefit you, too, but if you are completely against it? Then, no. I won't use it."

I don't like that answer. I can't be her moral compass. Kyol tried to be that for King Atroth, and he failed. He failed because the king had someone else whispering in his ear and because Atroth wanted to do what was expedient, not what was best for the fae. I need Lena to do what's best for the fae *and* for my people.

She must see my thoughts written on my face. "I know it's wrong, McKenzie. I won't involve your people unnecessarily. We still need to get the serum, though. The remnants might not feel the same way we do."

The knots in my stomach relax. "We'll need to find and destroy the research, too, or someone might be able to reproduce it. But we don't have to wait on Naito. I know where the serum is."

I show them the cell phone. No one gets close to it, of course, so I summarize the texts between Lee and his father. It's better to think about this, about what we have to do, than to think about Aren and what he did.

"All I need is for someone to take me to Earth, so I can send the text," I finish. In my peripheral vision, I see Brene lie down flat on her back.

"I'll take you," Aren says, stepping to my side.

"No." I don't want to be near him right now. I need time to think, to process everything.

"I'll take you," he says again, his voice harder this time. "It'll be a quick trip. I think you can stand me for that long."

"Kyol can take me."

"He can't heal you," Aren counters. "Come on."

He places his hand on the small of my back before I protest again. The warmth of his palm is familiar. So is the firm, but gentle pressure he uses to urge me forward. He's always touched me like this, even when I was doing everything in my power to get away from him, and I remind myself that he's the same person he was five minutes ago. He's the same person he was before I found out about his connection to Thrain. And, besides, I won't fight with him here in front of Lena and Kyol.

He trails slightly behind me as we leave the throne room and pass the palace's administrative offices. I use the time and space to gather my thoughts. I need to figure out exactly what I'm doing with him. Just when I think I'm close to accepting his past, I learn something new. It's a blow every time, and I don't know how many more I can take.

Outside, a bright sun warms what would otherwise be a chilly day. It feels good on my skin, and I soak it in, letting it ease some of the tension in my muscles. Aren moves closer to me now. Even though this is the most affluent area of the Inner City, it's not 100 percent safe. Most of the high nobles have homes here. The eaves of the buildings are silver-trimmed even though we're still inside Corrist's silver walls. It's purely something to show their status. They have money to throw away on things that aren't necessities.

We reach the silver wall without incident, then cross the terrace to the river. That's when Aren takes my hand, pressing an imprinted anchor-stone into my palm.

"If I could undo my past for you, McKenzie, I would. But I don't have that power. No fae does."

I watch my chaos lusters dart across the back of the hand he still holds. His touch is hot, tantalizing. I still crave it. "Why do I have to find out about your past like this? When you don't warn me, it's like you're trying to keep things from me."

"Do I need to name every fae I've made *tor'um*?" he asks quietly.

I meet his eyes, a little startled. "How many are there?"

"I do remember them. Every one," he says. Then, as if he's just hearing my question, he adds, "There were five. All but Brene were when I was under Thrain's tutelage."

Five. After seeing Brene, it sounds like so many.

Aren bends down to the river to cup water in his hand. He raises his palm to the sky, then the air rumbles as a fissure splits through the atmosphere. I feel like it's splitting through me.

"Ready?" he asks.

I nod, then let him pull me into the light.

The icy bite of the In-Between makes my muscles tense, and *that* sends a sharp lance of pain through my side. I hiss out a breath, or try to, but the In-Between has stolen the air from my lungs. When we emerge on the other side, I'm coughing, which makes my ribs feel oh so much better.

I double over, holding my side.

"McKenzie." Worry fills Aren's voice. He puts his arm around my waist to support me, and that only makes it worse. My knees hit grass.

"McKenzie," he says again, more anxious this time.

"Ribs," I manage to get out. I concentrate on drawing in a slow, careful breath as he slides my shirt up.

"Sidhe." He crouches beside me. "I know you don't want me to touch you, but you should have said something. I didn't know you were hurt this badly."

He places his hand over my bruised side. Heat sinks into me as he flares his magic, using it to heal my ribs. They must be cracked or broken because it hurts. It hurts almost as much as it did when he healed the arm Lena broke after I tried to escape the rebels in Germany. My hand clenches on Aren's forearm. I squeeze my eyes shut against the pain, but it only lasts a few seconds. Then, the *edarratae* take over, and the only thing I feel is a hot, delicious tingling.

Aren's hand is still on my side. His touch was clinical at first. It's not clinical anymore. The lightning affects him just as much as it does me, and I know he feels it gathering. What he said was wrong. I *do* want him to touch me. I want it so much, I can barely think.

"Aren," I whisper. His body gives a little shudder, and I half hope he doesn't regain control. He's always done this to me, made me want him when I shouldn't. I shouldn't right now. There's too much between us, too much that we need to talk about.

We move away from each other at the same time. I see him swallow, and his eyes have a wild edge to them. There's a glimmer of something else there, as well, though. Something that I've rarely seen from him. Fear. He's afraid of losing me.

I'm afraid of losing him, too. I almost feel that, if I take the time to sort through my thoughts, if I create a list of reasons to stay with him and reasons to go, the reasonable thing would be to go. We were enemies. He threatened my life more than once and killed fae who were just trying to protect me. The thing is, I don't want to walk away. No matter how illogical it might be, I want to be with him.

"You have a call to make," he says quietly. He runs a hand through his already disheveled hair as he straightens.

A text to send, but I don't correct him. I stand as well, shutting down my feelings for now as I slip Lee's cell phone out of my pocket. Then, for the first time, I take in my surroundings. It's dark, and there's nothing but a starlit river beside us. The shadows from our fissure have already disappeared, so I have no clue where we are. We're practically on top of a gate though, which is good. We can be back in the Realm as soon as I contact Nakano.

Aren watches as I send the text and slide the cell back into my pocket. That's all I need to do here—he knows that—but neither of us moves when I'm finished. We're both waiting for the other to say something.

Okay. I just acknowledged that we need to talk. Now is as good a time as any.

"What did you do for Thrain?" I ask.

"Is that where we're going to start?" His gaze locks on the river, though I don't really think he sees it. My stomach churns, waiting for him to answer.

"I did whatever Thrain asked," he says. His voice, which

is usually lighthearted and full of mirth, is so monotone, it could be mistaken for Kyol's. It doesn't fit him.

"If he wanted someone killed," he continues, "I killed them. If he wanted someone captured and hurt, I did that as well. Then I healed them and hurt them again. I stole from fae. I burned down their homes. I exposed them to tech." He draws in a breath. "I delivered humans to him, humans that I later learned he sold to *tjandel*."

My heart turns cold at the mention of the *tjandel*. Atroth's lord general, Radath, threatened to send me to one of those. It's a brothel that houses humans. I've never seen one—they were illegal even under Atroth's reign—but Radath made it clear most of the women didn't have the Sight, and that the fae who visit them get off on their screams. Knowing that they exist sickens me. Knowing that Aren helped make them exist . . .

A lump forms in my throat. My chest feels hollow.

"I'm not proud of what I did, McKenzie," Aren says. He's still staring at the river, and the starlight reflecting off its surface is mirrored in his eyes.

"What made you leave?" Now it's my voice that's gone flat.

"Lena's and Sethan's father." He turns away from the river to look at me. "I was an *imithi* before I met Thrain. The exact translation would be orphaned wanderer, but it's . . . It's more than that. It's a subgroup of fae, usually children, who have no family, no roots. It's not a healthy way to grow up. Fae can fissure from place to place easily, but not having somewhere to call home changes us. We don't follow the rules and customs of a region. We don't care if we anger or offend people—we can just fissure to another city. We break laws and cause trouble, and there are almost never any consequences."

A part of me—the weak, sensitive part—wants to reach out to him, but I force myself to keep my hands at my sides, and say, "That doesn't excuse what you've done."

I see him swallow again, and this time, it's not because he's struggling to control himself.

"I know," he says, and my chest aches, hearing the pain in his voice. "I'm telling you this because I want you to understand why I followed Thrain. We—me and the other *imithi*—all pretended to accept our situations, but in truth, we wanted roots. Thrain took advantage of that. Healing is a rare magic, so I was useful to him, and I wanted a mentor. It didn't matter who it was. Not until I tried to steal silver from the mines in Adaris."

Adaris. That's one of the provinces Atroth dissolved, the one where Lena is from.

"You stole silver?"

"I *tried* to steal it," he says. Then he gives a short laugh. He doesn't smile, though, and there's no light in his eyes. "It's not the smartest thing to do, and I didn't plan it. Briant, the elder of Zarrak, showed up. He lived there, so he had experience fighting with deposits of silver around him. I didn't. He slipped through my defenses and gave me a wound that would have sent me to the ether if he hadn't ordered Lena to heal me."

"I'm sure she loved that," I mutter, imagining her having to heal someone who had just tried to kill a member of her family.

"There was an argument," he says. This time, when he chuckles, he does smile. "Anyway, the Zarraks were already making plans to oppose Atroth. They gave me a cause to fight for—a good cause—and they gave me a home."

He takes an anchor-stone out of his pocket. "I've spent every day since I ended my association with Thrain attempting to make up for it. Briant was a good man. I wanted to deserve the home he gave me." He runs his thumb over the surface of the stone. "I want to deserve you."

Those words make my heart thud against my chest, erasing the numb, hollow feeling that was there.

"Aren—"

"You need to know something else," he says, stepping forward and pressing the anchor-stone into my hand. "I regret what I did to Brene, but I would do it again. Radath had Briant. Brene knew where they were. She wouldn't tell us. We had so little time and . . ." He draws in a breath. "By the time

I made her tell us, she was broken, and he was already dead." His gaze grows distant as he relives the moment. "Almost dead. Radath tortured him. He'd lost so much blood and . . . If I'd acted sooner, I could have healed him."

I bite the inside of my cheek until it hurts. Falling in love with someone shouldn't be this difficult. It should be something you easily slip into, like a bed with silk sheets, but I can't continue questioning why I'm with Aren. I need to decide if I'm going to follow my heart or if I'm going to follow my head. I followed my heart with Kyol for ten years. It was the wrong decision.

The phone in my pocket vibrates, startling me. I wasn't expecting a response to my text, especially not one so quickly, but I take the cell out and read Nakano's message.

"He took the bait," I tell Aren. "He and his team will fly out tonight."

"That's good," he says quietly. Then he turns back to the river and dips his hand into its rippling surface. I watch as he lifts his palm to the stars, letting the water fall between his fingers. A rumble vibrates through the air as the rain turns into light, a fissure safe for me to step into as long as I have a fae escort.

Aren turns back to me, holds out his hand. His chaos lusters leap to my skin when I take it. It's as if they know I'm struggling with a decision, and they're going to make it as difficult as possible for me to be clearheaded about it.

Aren pulls me gently toward him. "You told me you wanted time. I've given it to you, and I'll give you as long as you need, McKenzie. I love you." He tucks a lock of my hair behind my ear. "You're worth waiting a decade for."

He places the softest of kisses on my lips, then takes me into the In-Between.

TWENTY

◆·◆

WHEN WE STEP into Corrist, Aren changes. He's back to his usual, lackadaisical self. It's like our conversation never happened. His movements are relaxed, languid even, and, as we pass through the silver wall, he teases me about my tendency to get hurt—which I promptly point out is so not my fault. Fae keep trying to kill me, and I wasn't born with a sword in my hand like he and everyone else in the Realm practically were.

His voice is still light when we step out of an alley and the Silver Palace comes into view.

"You've been to the *Sidhe Cabred*," he says.

"Yeah," I answer, even though he wasn't asking a question. When we were back in Germany, he found the anchor-stone that proved I'd been fissured to the Ancestors' Garden via a *Sidhe Tol*. "It was three years ago."

"Lena's thinking about allowing anyone to enter it," he says. "The high nobles are against the idea."

Of course they are.

"They love their privileges," I say.

Aren nods. "It's beautiful?"

I shift my focus from the palace's silver-rimmed turrets to him. "You haven't seen it yet?"

"I've been busy."

True. That's why we've only seen each other a handful of times since Atroth died.

"It's beautiful," I tell him, remembering the vibrant green leaves edged in pinks and purples. "Even at night, the flowers are brighter and more alive than any I've seen in my world, and they're lit with magic. Their petals are soft. Their scent lingers on your skin and . . ."

I stop. The only reason I know that last part is because Kyol laid me down on a bed of *laubrin* at the foot of the *Sidhe Cabred*'s waterfall. I thought the flowers would be prickly and uncomfortable; they weren't. They were sleek and silky, and Aren doesn't need to know what Kyol and I almost did on top of them.

"It's beautiful," I say again. Aren's watching me, his thoughts unreadable in his silver eyes. He doesn't look away until we near the base of the palace. He calls out to the guards watching us through hidden slits in the wall, and the small doorway beside the big, elaborate gate opens, allowing us entry.

"You should try to get some rest before we fissure to Boulder," Aren says once we're inside.

Lena's decided to give the vigilantes time to pack up and leave for Cleveland, so we have a few hours before I need to be ready to go. Sleep isn't a bad idea, so I nod and tell him I'll meet him later.

I head to my room to get as much rest as I can, but when I turn down the corridor that leads to the second level of the residential wing, I see Paige scrambling across the floor on her hands and knees.

"Paige?" I say, walking toward her.

She's heading away from me, but she looks over her shoulder when she hears my voice, and her eyes grow wide. "It wasn't me."

"What wasn't—" I stop. In front of her, a fae lies unconscious on the floor. I'm not sure who it is. His face is bloody, and he has at least two bruises swelling up near his right temple. He didn't go down on the first hit.

"It was Lee." Paige rises to her feet. "He's gone after his brother."

I curse. More than one fae should have been watching their doors.

I start to move past her—I have to find Naito before Lee does—but she grabs my arm.

"Don't involve the fae," she says. "Please. I can talk to him."

"He's already involved them." I jab a finger toward the fae on the ground, who's beginning to stir.

She looks down. "I know, but we had a fight, and I said some things . . ."

"He's a vigilante," I say. "Do you know what that is?"

"No." She meets my eyes. "But he's not the person he's trying to be. I swear, McKenzie."

"Vigilantes hate fae. They hate humans who help fae." I start down the corridor again—I don't have time to stand here and have this conversation. Paige follows.

"Did the remnants not know what he was?" I ask when I reach a staircase. I take the steps two at a time.

"He's never acted like he hates the fae," Paige says, descending behind me. "He just thinks they're dangerous and he's . . . I can take care of myself, but he's looked out for me."

We reach the bottom of the stairs. They lead out to the arched covered walkway that surrounds the statue garden. Only a few fae are here right now. I spot a guard and head toward him.

"I thought you hated Lee," I say to Paige even though I suspected otherwise.

"I *want* to hate him," she says. "I met him at Amy's wedding. He asked to meet you, but you were with Aren, so we hung out. Hooked up. He's actually fun when he's not being an idiot."

"You said yourself he was using you to find Naito."

"And Aren is using you to fight the Court fae," she counters.

I glare at her, but she has a point. Aren and I started off all wrong. "He's not using me anymore." He loves me—I'm 100 percent certain of that—and he'd do anything for me.

I veer toward the guard. Paige notices where I'm heading immediately.

"*Please* don't involve the rebels."

I stop to look at her. She changed out of her wet clothes. Someone delivered new ones. The narrow-sleeved white top looks more like a jacket than a shirt. It's laced up the middle, and the two tails flow over her hips. The tan skirt is short—I think she ripped off the lower half—but she's compensated for that with boots that reach up to her knees. Everything is fae-made, but somehow, it all looks like something she'd pull out of her own closet.

This is Paige, I remind myself. My friend. She's never asked me for anything, and she's always been there for me even though I haven't always been there for her, but if anything happens to Naito . . .

No. I can't risk it just because she asks.

"I'm sorry," I say.

There's a glimmer of hurt in her blue eyes when she releases my arm. It's gone in an instant, replaced by a carefully neutral expression.

"I understand," she lies.

It feels like someone's stabbed my chest from the inside. *I'm going to lose my only friend,* I realize, and it's like I'm losing my last connection to my human life. Paige has always put up with my eccentricities and random disappearances. She's always made me feel normal. I guess I finally need to accept that I'm not. I never will be.

"I'm sorry," I say again, then I start walking toward the guard. It's possible Lee passed by here, and the fae didn't detain him. Under Atroth's reign, humans were hardly ever stopped or questioned as long as we stayed in the public areas of the palace. It was assumed that, unless the fae were told otherwise, we belonged here. I know Lena is suspicious of Paige and Lee—that's why she put a guard outside their door—but I don't know if she's issued a general alert to all her people.

I'm only a few steps away from the guard when I see movement in the corner of my vision. Lee leans against the wall in the covered walkway opposite the one Paige and I stepped out of. He slides down it, sinking to the ground then propping his arms up on his bent knees. Blood covers one of his hands.

Please don't let it be Naito's blood.

I hear Paige take in a breath. She moves toward him before I do, but I'm at her side a second later.

"Lee?" Paige says when we reach him.

He doesn't raise his head. "I couldn't do it."

Thank God. The blood on his hand is his own. I can see the cuts and broken skin on his knuckles.

"I should have been able to do it," he says.

Paige stares down at him. "Are you serious? You're talking about *killing* a person. You're talking about killing your *brother.*"

"I hate my brother." His words come out more like a question than a statement of fact. "I'm supposed to hate the fae. They've been trying to kill my father for years."

His father has been trying to kill *them* for years, but I don't correct Lee.

"I've been telling myself Dad just needs closure, that he just needs to kill the fae who killed my mother, but I'm as delusional as he is. Naito's right. Dad's obsessed. Insane. He has to be to order me to kill my brother. I have to be crazy to consider it."

"You're not crazy," Paige says. "You're an idiot. What happened to your hand?"

He finally looks up at her. "A wall hit it."

She sinks down beside him. "Like I said, you're an idiot."

"It was a wooden wall," he adds, a hint of sarcastic humor invading his tone. "I didn't expect it to break."

She rolls her eyes as she inspects his injured hand. Paige went to nursing school for something like two weeks before she dropped out, but she's still into things like blood and stitches and broken bones. There's plenty of that here in the Realm.

I lean a shoulder against the wall and look down at them, at the way he watches her face as she unties the ribbon that's playing the role of a belt around her waist. She uses it to dab at the blood on his hand. It's obvious Lee cares about her.

"Paige mentioned you were looking for me at her sister's wedding," I say after they stand. "You knew about my involvement with the fae. How? And how did you know to look for me at the reception?"

He raises an eyebrow in Paige's direction. When she nods, he says, "A fae told my father your name."

"In person?" I ask.

"Yeah."

"Do you know who the fae was?" Aren and Lena think Atroth gave my name to the vigilantes, knowing that they'd find and kill me, but Kyol has sworn that's not true. I don't know what to believe. Nakano's people did track my cell phone and attack the place where the rebels were holding me in Germany, and it's clear they had no problem with killing me, but I trust Kyol's word. He says Atroth wanted me back alive, not dead.

Lee shakes his head. "I never saw the fae. I didn't inject myself with the serum until Dad left for Germany. He called when they didn't capture you. He told me to check out your place in Houston, so I flew down there."

The vigilantes were *not* trying to capture me, but I let him continue.

"I broke into your apartment and listened to your answering machine. There were enough messages from Paige threatening to kick your ass if you didn't show up at the wedding that I figured you'd be there if you were able to. I found the invitation, went to the mansion, asked for Paige, and . . ."

He fades off, looking to the right. I turn. Lord Hison is there. He's watching us, walking slowly—even by human standards slowly—through the sculpture garden. He doesn't glance away when he sees me looking in his direction. He doesn't look any happier to see Paige and Lee now than he did when he passed us exiting the throne room. He'd rather this war be fought without human help.

"Let's go back to our rooms," I tell the others. I don't want to talk out in public like this. Besides, they look as tired as I do, and if I want to be useful in Boulder, I need at least a couple hours of sleep.

I escort them back to the residential wing. It's not until we reach the second level that I remember the fae Lee knocked out. He's not lying on the ground anymore. A new guard is here, and when I step into the corridor, his hand goes to the

hilt of his sword. Then Lee and Paige emerge from the staircase after me, and the fae's gaze moves to them.

I turn to look at them, too. Paige's eyebrows are raised.
How am I going to explain away what happened? I think Lee
is okay now, and I don't want the fae to be pissed at him.

"There was a misunderstanding," I try, facing the guard
again. "Is the other fae okay?"

The guard doesn't answer for a moment. It's long enough
for me to wonder if he speaks English. Finally, he nods.
"He's fine. I'm to take over his watch."

"Is anyone else looking for us?" Paige is whispering to
me, but fae have good hearing. The guard shakes his head.

"I was about to call for a search," he says.

There's no need for that now. "They're going back to their
rooms."

I motion for them to go.

"Paige—" Lee begins.

She takes his hand, looks into his eyes, and says, very
deliberately, "You can stay with me."

Apparently, Paige has forgiven Lee. Either that or she
wants to keep an eye on him. The guard doesn't seem to
mind them slipping into the same room. Neither do I. Hopefully, they'll get a decent night's sleep.

And, hopefully, I'll get at least a couple of hours of rest.

MY door slams open, jarring me awake.

"McKenzie!"

I leap out of bed as Lena storms into my room. My leg
gets caught in my blanket. I hit my knees, get back up.

"Where are they?" she demands, inches from my face.

I'm groggy and off-balance. It takes a second to focus on
her, and when I do, I take a step back. Damn. I haven't seen
this look on her face since she ended one of my escape
attempts in Germany.

"Paige and Lee?" I guess. I can't think of anyone else who
would make her this angry.

"Of course Paige and Lee," she snaps.

"They're gone?" Even though I know Lena wouldn't have

stormed in like this if they were safely tucked in their rooms, I can't keep the note of disbelief from my voice. Lee already surprised a guard and escaped once. The second guard would have been more alert.

Or maybe he'd be less alert because who would have thought he'd try to escape again?

Lena grabs a fistful of my shirt. "If you don't tell me exactly where they are, by the *Sidhe*, I'll ban you from the Realm."

I grab her hand, try to loosen it from my shirt. "Lena. I didn't—"

"I *thought* you wouldn't do this," she says, shoving me back. "But they're gone, McKenzie. They couldn't have made it out of the palace on their own."

"And I'm the only one who could have possibly helped them escape." Sarcasm probably isn't the best way to address Lena when she's this pissed, but I didn't do this.

"She's your friend—the only friend you think you have." There's a note of something in her voice. Is she suggesting *she's* my friend?

"Lena, don't!" Aren sprints into my room. When he sees me, he stops and visibly relaxes. "She didn't kill you."

I scowl. He's a little too lighthearted about that.

"They were both in Paige's room when I went to sleep," I say. "They had a guard."

"Their guard is dead," Lena interrupts. "Lord Hison saw you with them."

"But that was"—God, this is going to sound incriminating—"the first time Lee broke out."

Aren's eyebrows go up. I give him a shrug that says, "Yeah, I screwed up," but there's no apology in it.

I turn back to Lena. "Look, we're wasting time. How long until we're supposed to leave for Boulder?"

"A little over an hour," Aren answers.

"I couldn't have been asleep for more than twenty minutes, then."

Aren's posture changes, becoming more alert, more ready for action. "They haven't had time to leave the city yet."

Lena mumbles something in Fae.

"They'll try for the gate." I'm fairly certain of that. Otherwise, it's a rough journey through the Corrist Mountains to get to the Missing Gate on their northeastern edge. That's the next nearest place humans can safely fissure.

I slept in my clothes, so all I have to do is stuff my feet into my sneakers, then grab my sketchbook off the hook hanging beside the door, and I'm ready to go.

"We can intercept them," I say, stepping into the corridor. I almost barrel into a fae. Jacia.

She steadies me with a hand on my elbow. *Edarratae* pool under her palm until she releases me, then focuses on the two fae still in my room.

"The remnant, Tylan, is missing," she reports.

"I definitely had nothing to do with that," I say to Lena. She gives me a look that is extremely unamused.

"Notify Taltrayn," she tells Jacia.

Jacia acknowledges the order with a nod and departs. Aren and I leave right after her, heading the opposite way down the corridor. Aren's walking quickly even for a fae, so I have to run to keep up. I'm not at a full sprint, though—I couldn't keep that pace up for long—but we're out of the palace and in the Inner City in just a few minutes.

"You should run ahead," I tell Aren.

"I'm staying with you," he says. "Tylan is an illusionist. We need your eyes."

My side is starting to cramp. I concentrate on drawing air into my lungs, then blowing it out. I don't want to slow him down any more than I already am.

I'm sweating, but a cool wind blows from the south, chilling my skin, and I think I hear a rumble of thunder. The sky was clear before I went to sleep. It's not clear anymore. Thick, gray clouds are gathering above the Inner City.

"Wait up."

Slowing down, I look over my shoulder and see Naito running toward us.

Aren stops. "Why aren't you on watch?"

"Taltrayn told me to go to the gate with you," he says. Then he looks at me. "You're supposed to go to the *veligh*. Watch for remnants there. It's safer than this."

Aren mutters something in Fae about a fool. I can practically feel him seething beside me. He's probably taking this personally. I don't really blame him. Kyol has no business overturning Aren's decision.

My hand tightens on the strap of my sketchbook. "I can't get there in time to be any help."

"And I'm not letting you run back through the Inner City without an escort." Aren puts an arm on my shoulder, moves me toward the silver wall. "You're both coming to the gate."

It's less than a mile to the northwest portcullis. It's closed. Two fae standing guard watch us approach. Others are here as well, but hidden at their posts somewhere within the wall, watching the Outer City. After a few quick words from Aren, one of the swordsmen touches the wall behind him. A faint blue line climbs its silver surface. As it rises, so does the portcullis.

The other swordsman says, *"We haven't seen anyone approach the gate."*

Naito steps between me and Aren. "Maybe they haven't left the palace."

"Taltrayn will find them if they haven't," Aren says. Then he asks the swordsman, *"How many are on watch above?"*

"Eleven," is the reply.

"Send six down. Three to protect the humans and three with me." He ducks under the portcullis with a motion for Naito and me to follow.

"It's clear, I presume?" Aren asks when I reach his side again.

I scan the flat area of land between us and the river approximately two hundred feet away. The foothills are just beyond it. Theoretically, Paige, Lee, and Tylan could go there, hide out in the caverns or in one of the mountain passes in the distance. Then they could choose the time to fissure out of the city. It's what I would do.

Well, it's what I would do if I didn't know that the rebels knew about the serum and where to get it. I have to assume Paige has chosen her side now, and that she'll tell the remnants how she was given the Sight. I don't think Lee will stop her.

The betrayal hurts exactly as much as it should. We were friends. She shouldn't stab me in the back like this. She shouldn't ally with my enemy without asking me what this war is about. I'm going to kick her ass when we recapture her.

"McKenzie?" Aren says. He's focused on the row of shops to our left. They're a good hundred yards away and difficult to make out with the sky growing so dark.

"I don't see anything," I tell him. "Do you?"

"Maybe. Keep heading toward the gate."

The six fae he requested from the wall have arrived. He assigns three to Naito and me, then he and the others disappear into slashes of white light. I see their exiting fissures near one of the gray-bricked buildings. Aren's looking down the narrow walkway between them. He draws his sword, then—

I'm nearly blinded when a virtual wall of light opens up in front of me.

My guards react before I do, leaping between me and the newly arrived fae before the nearest one is able to take my head off. Instinct makes me drop to the ground anyway. I roll, and when I get back to my feet, Aren's back at my side.

"Diversion," he snaps out. "Stay close."

Tylan must have fissured for reinforcements. No less than two dozen remnants fill the clearing between the river and wall. We're outnumbered, but not for long. Other rebels join us—probably the rest of the guards from the wall—and they surround me and Naito, attacking any remnant who gets too close.

"We should go back!" Naito yells. I just barely hear him above the sounds of the fight . . . and of the thunder rumbling through the air. The sky is almost black with clouds. They shift as I watch them, and just when I realize that this storm isn't natural, the hail begins to torpedo down.

Each strike feels like a bee sting. My clothing offers little protection. The tiny pellets bruise my face, my shoulders, my arms. Someone's controlling this, concentrating the storm above us. If we . . .

There they are. Paige and Lee. They're sprinting toward the gate from the east, not from the row of buildings to the west.

"Aren!" I unsling my sketchbook from my shoulder, start to open it up, but I'm knocked to the ground.

Then Aren's above me, intercepting a remnant, keeping him away from me. I roll to my stomach, scramble forward to grab my sketchbook, but another remnant is there. His boot comes down on the center of a page. I grab the leather strap just as he lunges forward and yank it as hard as I can. The packed earth is treacherous, with the hail building up; the sketchbook slides easily, sending the remnant flying back on his ass.

He hits hard, nearly loses his grip on his sword, the sword that's just within my reach.

I throw myself on top of him, grabbing his arm before he brings the blade up, but I'm totally screwed. He's stronger than I am. As he turns over, he hooks his free arm behind my back, then slams me face-first to the ground.

I swing back with an elbow. Miss. Then I lose my hold on his sword arm and—

Warmth spills over my back. His weight disappears just before I'm yanked back to my feet. Aren steadies me as the remnant's soul-shadow rises into the air.

"Back to the wall," he grates out.

"They're here," I tell him, turning toward the gate.

Aren follows my gaze, curses, then fissures out.

"Get back to the wall!" Naito shouts, showing up at my side, but I'm useless there. I need to be close to read the shadows.

"Map the shadows of the injured fae," I tell him. When fae are hurt, they instinctively fissure to locations they're most familiar with. They might fissure home or, if we're lucky, back to the remnants' base of operations.

Naito protests, but I don't listen. I catch the attention of the three nearest rebels and order them to cover me as I run toward the gate.

I lose one of my escorts on the way. He doesn't enter the ether, but he's hurt. I have to fight the urge to help him. Keep running.

"Paige!" I shout when I'm less than twenty feet from her. She looks my way. So does the remnant who's with her.

Shit. It's the fae from the corridor, the one who was *supposed* to be replacing the guard Lee knocked out. I'm an idiot. A complete and utter idiot.

It has to be Tylan. He's pushing her forward, toward the blur at the edge of the river. I won't reach them before they fissure out so I open my sketchbook and drop to my knees.

This is always the hardest part of reading the shadows. I have to ignore the strikes of metal against metal and the shouts and cries of the fae. I have to block everything out, open to a blank page, and lock my gaze on the fae approaching the gate. I grab my pencil, putting all my faith in the rebels who are protecting me.

A fissure splits through the air, but it's next to the gate, not over it, and a fae steps out of it, not into it. I squint across the distance, focusing on the newcomer's face and . . .

And it's Kavok, the archivist. What the hell is he doing here?

I glance up at the sky, blinking as the hail continues to fall. *Kavok* is doing this? He's fully capable of calling this storm, but he's . . . He's . . .

He dips his hand into the river.

He's betraying us.

I have no time to let that soak in or to contemplate his motive; he steps into the gated-fissure with Lee. Shadows replace the extinguished slash of light, and I draw a long, curving line down the right side of the page. It hooks up toward the middle. A peninsula. They're somewhere near its eastern coast. I'm guessing it's Brith until I realize I'm not drawing the Realm. This is—

I can't block out the remnant who fissures in front of my nose. He's so close, he steps out of the light and onto my sketch. No rebel is near enough to intercept his attack.

I throw myself to the left, dropping my shoulder and rolling even though I know it's too late. Only, it's not too late. Something hits the remnant, spinning him around and throwing him so off-balance he loses his grip on his sword.

A fissure opens behind him. Lena steps out, crouches, then stabs upward, sliding her blade in beneath the remnant's cuirass. The fae goes pale an instant before his soul-shadow replaces his body.

"Finish it," she orders, taking up a defensive position to my right. She *so* shouldn't be out here, but I grab my sketchbook, pulling it back in front of me, then find Kavok and Lee's shadows again. They're fading. My map won't be very accurate.

Before I draw another line, Paige steps through those wispy shadows, escorted by Tylan, who dips his hand into the river, opening a fissure of his own.

I rip the page out of my sketchbook, start a new map when they disappear. I'm not even halfway through it when the sketchbook is whipped out from in front of me.

I look up, see Naito standing there. What? Does he want to be the one to map the shadows? He's not as good at it as I am, but he might be good enough.

He doesn't start drawing, though. He just stands there staring down at me.

"Naito," Lena says, pulling her sword free from another remnant. "What are you doing?"

"It's okay," Naito says.

"What's okay?" I ask, climbing back to my feet. If he's not going to draw the shadows, I need to. Now. They're going to fade away if I don't.

I try to take back my sketchbook, but he holds on.

"McKenzie," he says, keeping his voice low. "Kavok found a fae who can bring her back."

"He found a . . ." A *banek'tan*, he called it. A fae who can bring Kelia back from the ether.

"He's been helping me research. He traced the lineages. He found someone who can resurrect her, but he won't give me the name unless they all make it out."

"Finish the map." Aren's here now. He yanks back the sketchbook, shoves it into my hands.

"Don't do it," Naito says. His voice is low. It holds a warning I'd have to be deaf not to hear.

Could Kavok be telling the truth? Is this just desperation on Naito's part? It's clear he believes it. God, I want to believe it, too.

"McKenzie!" Aren snaps.

I stare back at the shadows. Shit, they're almost gone. I drop to my knees again, start to draw a bend in a river, and then Naito loses it.

"I'll kill you!" he snarls as he leaps at me. "I'll fucking kill you if you read them!"

Naito's almost on top of me when Lena steps between us. A slight wave of her hand, and a gust of wind changes his trajectory. He crashes to the ground just two paces in front of me. He's blocking the middle of the fading shadows, but Tylan's taken Paige to the same place Kavok took Lee. I've seen enough of both to finish the sketch.

"Please!" Naito screams. The desperation in his voice rips at my heart. I know how much he loves Kelia. He'll do anything to bring her back. I'd do almost anything to help him.

I watch as the last wisp of shadow disappears. It's been too long since Kavok fissured out. Aren won't be able to capture him; he'll have to kill him. What if a fae really can do what Kavok claims?

I want to let them escape. I want a fae to bring back Kelia. I want her and Naito to have their happy ending.

But I can't put that before everything else.

"Coen." The city's name is just a whisper, but it's loud enough for Aren and the nearby rebels to hear. They fissure out, going to the west coast of Australia.

"No!" Naito yells.

Lena places her hands on his shoulders, shakes him. "Look at me, Naito. Look at me! No one can bring fae back from the ether. Those books you read? Everyone knows about them. They're fables. They're fairy tales, Naito. Kelia is dead, just like Sethan is. Kavok tricked you."

"No."

"She's not coming back, Naito. I'm sorry. I'm so sorry."

"No." This time, the word cracks into a sob. I've never seen Lena do anything remotely tender, but she pulls Naito into her arms, holding him as he cries.

TWENTY-ONE

·◆·

THE HAIL STORM dispersed as soon as Kavok fissured out. A bright sun lights up the sky now, but it does little to warm the air. I'm waiting with Trev for Aren at the silver wall. Naito's here, too, staring at the ground. He hasn't said much since Paige and the others escaped, just that Kavok approached him this morning, offering the name of a *banek'tan* in exchange for help breaking Tylan out of prison. Tylan wouldn't leave without Paige, though, and the remnants need Lee if they want to get the Sight serum.

I still can't quite believe Paige is siding with the remnants. I knew everything wasn't perfect. She wasn't telling me the whole and complete truth, but I never thought she'd run off like this. I thought I'd have more time to ask her about the remnants and to tell her about the rebels. I mean, I *should* have had more time. I've been shadow-reading for the fae for ten years. She's known they've existed for, what? Maybe ten days? And she's just going to choose her allegiance without consulting me?

I can't help but be angry.

And I can't help but feel like a fool for letting Tylan steal her away. Never mind that it's not plausible for me to recognize every single fae who supports Lena, but I should have been suspicious. I should have picked up a clue when Paige interrupted Lee, telling him he could stay the night with her. It's not like Paige to forgive a guy without making him grovel a little.

I sag against the wall next to Trev. The betrayals hurt, Paige's and Kavok's both. I keep trying to make excuses for them. Maybe Paige was under the influence of some magic I've never heard of. Maybe the remnants found some way to blackmail Kavok.

"Maybe I'm just the world's biggest idiot," I mutter.

Beside me, Trev snorts. I throw a glare his way, a glare that doesn't faze him one bit. He's leaning against the wall with his arms crossed over his *jaedric*-armored chest. His sword is loose in its scabbard, not clicked more securely into place, and no less than three knives are within easy reach in their pockets in his belt. He might agree with my statement, but he's here to keep me safe. He'll be coming with us to Boulder, too. We're leaving for Nakano's compound sooner than we planned in hopes of beating the remnants there.

I tighten my grip on the strap of my sketchbook. If the remnants do make it to Boulder before us, there's a chance I might need to map their shadows. There's a chance Paige and Lee might be with them. There's a chance the rebels might have to kill them.

We haven't talked about that, Aren and I, but I know it's a possibility. This is a war. The remnants are our enemies, and it doesn't matter that I don't understand her decision— Paige has chosen her side. There are consequences to that. There are consequences to everything.

A lump forms in my throat. I swallow it down as Aren approaches. Nalst and the illusionist, Brenth, are with him. If we need reinforcements, one of them will fissure back for help. We don't want to leave Corrist vulnerable while we're gone. With Shane still missing and Naito and me going to Boulder, Lena's already short three humans, and even if everything goes perfectly at Nakano's compound, it will take Naito and me a while to get back to the Realm. Boulder doesn't have a gate, so we're going to rent a car—*rent*, I insisted, not steal—and drive to a small town called Wiggins. The nearest gate is on a reservoir near there.

"Are you sure you're okay to do this?" Aren asks, stopping in front of me. Whether he's asking if I'm willing to be involved in the death of my friend or if I'm physically okay and ready to go to Boulder, I don't know, but the answer is the same either way. I'm going to do what I have to do to help Lena secure the throne.

"I'm ready," I tell him.

"You don't have to go," he says. "Naito will help us get the serum and the documents."

I focus on Naito, who's still staring at the ground with his hands shoved into his pockets a few paces away. Neither of us knows how dependable he will be in Boulder. When Lena ordered him to go with us, he didn't respond at all; he just showed up when Trev and I left the palace.

"I'm going," I tell Aren. "And I'm sorry about earlier. I'm sorry I hesitated. I wanted . . ."

"I know," he interrupts. "I want Naito to be happy, too."

Aren wasn't able to capture or kill Tylan and Kavok because I hesitated. The fae double-fissured with Paige and Lee. It didn't surprise me to learn that. I was pretty sure the maps led to the gate in Coen. When fae are running from a shadow-reader, they try not to go to their final destination. Most fae have to wait a few minutes to recover from their first fissure, but some of them have conditioned themselves to be able to fissure quickly two or three times in a row. That's what Aren did when he abducted me from my campus. He didn't wait more than a few seconds before pulling me into another gated-fissure. Even Kyol can't pop in and out of worlds that quickly.

Aren never saw Tylan and Paige, but he saw Kavok. The archivist had to wait to recover before fissuring out with Lee. If my map hadn't been such an inaccurate mess, Aren would have spotted the fae sooner. He would have killed him, preventing the remnants from getting Lee back. Lee, who can lead the remnants to his father's compound just as easily—maybe even more easily—than Naito.

"We should hurry," I say.

Aren draws in a slow breath, nods, then turns to Naito. Naito and I are wearing normal, human clothes. We're hoping the vigilantes have all left the compound by now, but if they haven't, we don't want to show up wearing fae garb. That'll just invite Nakano's people to kill us.

Naito doesn't look up when Aren stops in front of him. I don't know what he's thinking; I just know that he hasn't been thinking since Kelia died. He's been trying to find a way to bring her back, not trying to find a way to deal with his grief. He's the one who helped Tylan escape. He kept me from accurately reading the shadows, first by trying to convince Aren and me that Kyol had ordered me elsewhere, then by physically interfering with my drawing. He has a lot to account for.

Softly, he says, "Kelia wouldn't want me to be like this."

"No," Aren agrees. "She wouldn't."

Naito's mouth tightens. He nods. Another silence stretches out.

"I've been to my father's compound before. That's where he . . ." He clears his throat. "He's held fae there before. He does research there."

He doesn't have to say more than that.

The fae take up position around us, and we leave the Inner City, walking beneath the silver wall, then crossing the plateau to the gate that Paige and Lee were taken through less than an hour ago. I wonder if that will be the last time I see Paige. How far will she go to help the remnants defeat us? Will she try to return to her normal life back in Houston? Will the fae let her?

King Atroth is dead. So is his lord general, but there are other Court fae who are as brutal as they were—the slaughtered humans in London prove that. Paige doesn't know what she's gotten herself into.

We stop by the blur on the river. After Aren opens a gated-fissure, he holds out his hand toward me. I hesitate. I want that opportunity to talk to Paige. If she's in Boulder using her newly acquired Sight to see through Brenth's illusions, Aren might be the one who's forced to kill her. There's already a long list of things I have to forgive Aren for. Can I forgive him if he takes my friend's life?

"McKenzie," Aren says gently. I think he knows the

direction my thoughts have gone. I have to bottle them up and push them aside to think about later. No matter what happens between us, we have to get to that serum before the remnants do.

I place my hand in his, take the anchor-stone he offers me, then let him escort me into the In-Between.

I'm not fully prepared for the soul-numbing bite of the cold. When we emerge into my world, I'm shaking. I should have made time to drink *cabus*. This is my third time fissuring in a little over three hours. My body is so not happy with me right now.

My knees buckle, but Aren's there. His hands are firm on my arms, steadying me while I convince my legs to hold my weight again. Aren's touch helps chase away some of the cold, especially when his chaos lusters find their way to my skin, sending enticing, tingling pulses of warmth through my body.

"I'm not doing a good job taking care of you," he says, as Naito and the other fae join us in my world.

"It's not your job," I tell him. I'm balanced enough now to step away and take in my surroundings. It's night here. Or rather, early morning. A full moon is still in the night sky. It's bright enough to see the individual pebbles beneath my feet. We're on the western edge of Boulder, on a hiking trail that leads up into the mountains. The trailhead isn't far away. A parking lot is there. It's empty. Hopefully, that means we won't come across any late-night hikers. They should all be asleep in the city below. It's still and beautiful from this vantage point, each tiny light a pinprick that looks as innocent as a star, not like a piece of tech that can distract a fae and weaken their magic.

Naito seems oblivious to its beauty. He doesn't give the city so much as a glance as he releases Trev's arm and brushes past me on the narrow trail. I follow him. The fae follow behind me.

It's not a bad climb at first. It's gorgeous here, and the tall grass on either side of the trail seems to soak in the moonlight. The bright, vigorous green darkens when the trail veers left, heading into a copse of pine trees. Even though I know we need to be watching for vigilantes and remnants, it's difficult not to be captured by the tranquility of the setting. The Realm is exotic and beautiful, but there are so many places in my world that are the same, so many places worth visiting.

I'm not sure how far we have to hike. Aren had to visit a stone-seller to get us to this location. The palace didn't have one for Boulder in the archives. I guess we're lucky it brought us to the west side of the city. If it had deposited us on the east side, we'd have a much longer way to go.

"We're heading up there," Naito says after a while, pointing up and to the left. Despite the size of the three-storied building, I wouldn't have noticed it if the lights from Boulder weren't reflecting off its tall windows. It looks like an old resort, one that probably went bankrupt in the recession a few years back. The green, sloping roof and wooden façade act almost as camouflage, making the building blend in with the deciduous trees surrounding it.

The path beneath my feet steepens. I'm in decent shape, but my legs begin to burn, and the thinning oxygen is making my breaths come in quick, shallow gulps. I concentrate on keeping a steady pace and distract myself by trying to spot the ground squirrels that I keep seeing scurrying through the grass or across one of the big white boulders that we pass. They're marmots, I think, and even though they look nothing like Sosch, they remind me of the *kimki* anyway with the way they dart from crag to crag or sit on their haunches, blinking at us with mildly curious expressions.

I keep climbing, letting my sketchbook hang behind me. It knocks against my butt with every step I take until we finally hit more level ground. Nakano's compound is about half a mile away. The building Naito pointed out from below isn't the only one here. Two others, both smaller but with the same green roofs, are nestled side by side farther back from the mountain's edge. Naito's father chose a beautiful location for his compound. I have to give him that.

When we're within a few hundred yards of the main building, I grow paranoid about the fae's chaos lusters. They're wearing long sleeves beneath their *jaedric* armor, but their faces and hands are uncovered, and even with the moonlight, the blue lightning looks phosphorescent and bright.

And it's becoming more erratic the closer we get to the compound. Nakano must be running a ton of tech inside.

We walk along the edge of the tree line for as long as possible then Naito and Aren kneel in the foliage. The lights are off, and there's no movement inside the building as far as I can see.

I crouch by Aren's side. "Do you think we beat the remnants here?"

"It's possible," he says.

"But unlikely," Naito adds. "They don't have a city to defend. They could have fissured out the second Lee and Paige told them about the serum."

"They would have to find a stone-seller to get here, too, though."

Naito shrugs. "Their stone-seller might have had an imprinted location even closer than ours."

I take in a breath, then slowly let it out. The only way we're going to know for sure is to get in there.

"Will there be an alarm?" I ask, wanting to know just how fast this search of ours is going to have to be.

"I can get us in," Naito says.

That's not quite an answer to my question.

Naito straightens, then says to Aren, "You should stay here. My father has made this place unpleasant for fae."

"We'll be okay," Aren says, standing as well.

"No, you won't be. You're already feeling the tech. You step inside that building, and you won't be able to think. He has a low-level electric current flowing through the walls, and the signals he broadcasts—they're designed to affect fae. The compound will let you walk in, but it might not let you walk out."

God, he makes the place sound sentient.

"What if the vigilantes haven't left?" Aren asks. "What if the remnants show up looking for the serum?"

"If the remnants come in, they'll be just as crippled as you would be," he says, turning his attention back to the main building. "And if the vigilantes haven't left, McKenzie and I will take care of them."

His voice is as cold as the In-Between, and goose bumps break out across my skin. I don't have to guess what he means by "take care of them." He fully expects me to kill a vigilante if we come across one.

Aren's looking at me, watching for a reaction. I don't give him one. I keep my expression and my voice carefully neutral, and say, "I have my dagger. We'll be fine."

"If you want to help us," Naito says, "check out the residences." He nods toward the compound's other two buildings.

Aren doesn't take his eyes off me. I'd feel more comfortable with him at my back, but I'm trusting Naito on this one. If he thinks going inside that main building is dangerous for the fae, then I don't want Aren going in. If something happened to him . . .

Just the possibility causes my throat to tighten up, making it hard to draw in air. Losing him would crush me. There's no doubt about that.

My fear is mirrored in his eyes.

"We'll make it through today," I tell him, and I don't know if my words are meant to reassure him or to reassure myself.

His jaw tightens, but he focuses on Naito, and says, "You have ten minutes. Then I'm coming in."

"Make them long minutes," Naito says, setting off across the clearing.

Long minutes, I think as I jog after him. Not a chance. The fae have good internal clocks when things are calm, but when they're waiting on the shit to hit the fan, they're as impatient as two-year-olds. We'll be lucky if we have five minutes before he comes in after us.

Miraculously, Naito and I reach the door of the main lodge without any hiccups. He reaches into his pocket and pulls out a set of keys. He selects one, then slides it into the lock.

"You have a key to this place?" I ask quietly.

"No." He grabs his dagger, then, keeping it safe in its

scabbard, he hits the end of the key with his pommel three times.

It's so fucking loud, but I don't see any movement from inside. A quick check to my right, and the other two buildings look quiet and still as well. So why do I feel like we're being watched?

It takes another two knocks for the key to turn. I have no idea how he did that, but I just tighten my grip on the strap of my sketchbook as Naito pushes the door open. Once we're inside, Naito goes straight to an alarm pad. He reaches up to type in the code, but freezes, his finger hovering above the buttons.

"It's not on," he says.

My heart hammers in my chest. "We need to know if the serum is gone."

He nods. "This way."

I follow him through the main room of the lodge, though it's hard to see that this place was once a resort. Only a wet bar in the back corner, the wide, thick wooden beams on the vaulted ceiling, and the huge stone fireplace toward the front of the room indicate its history. The rest of the area is taken up by long, plastic tables. On top of them are about a dozen flat-screen computers. They look out of place here, especially with the piles of old books in the back of the room. They're in tall stacks on the floor and on a sofa pushed up against the wall. I read one of the titles as we pass by, *Grennan's Guide to Faery*, and want to laugh. The fae are nothing like the winged creatures little girls dream of meeting.

Naito moves into a smaller room in the back of the lodge, but I pause in its doorway, looking back at the computers. The screens are black, but they're plugged in and, if the little green lights are any indication, they're on.

I walk to the nearest one. Move the mouse.

A box pops up, asking for the password.

I type in "vigilante" because, yes, I'm that uncreative. Plus, I'm stalling. Thinking. The details of how to make the serum might be on the hard drives. What other research could be here? Is it worth taking with us?

"Hey, Naito," I say, entering the next room.

"What?" he asks, but I don't answer immediately. He's standing in front of a safe, twisting the knob to the right, back to the left, and back to the right again. And again when it doesn't work. But that's not what's caught my attention. This room has been converted into a laboratory. Beakers are held in metal clamps, petri dishes sit beneath microscopes, and plastic tubing runs between bags of clear liquid and glass flasks. In short, this room looks like a fully equipped medical lab minus the sanitation.

"McKenzie?" Naito stops what he's doing to look at me.

"Do you know the password for the computers?" He acted like he could disarm the alarm with a code, and he obviously has at least some hope of guessing the combination to that safe, so maybe his father is overconfident and hasn't changed any of the vigilantes' codes.

Turning back to the safe, he says, "I might be able to guess it, but it'll take too long to . . . Finally."

He opens the safe.

I move forward, trying to see inside. "Is the serum there?"

He's shuffling through some things. Papers, stacks of money, more papers. He shakes his head. "No. It's not here."

Damn. "Is that the only place it could be?"

Naito closes the door, slips something into his waistband. A gun. I hate guns. It's not just that they're lethal and that one of them killed Kelia, but it feels like a bad omen to see this one. This break-in has gone well so far, but that could change in an instant.

"This is where it's most likely to be, but no," Naito says. "My father could have put it somewhere else."

His gaze sweeps the room. We don't have time to do a complete search of the compound—Aren's probably already losing patience—but we need to be sure we're not leaving it behind.

"I think Lee's already been here," Naito says. His mouth is pinched. It's his fault. There's no denying that. His grief blinded him, and he made a decision that could cost us the war.

But I can't find the will to be angry at him. Instead, I say, "We should get out of here."

He nods.

"But we can't leave the research here," I add. "Find a match or a lighter or something. We'll burn the place down."

God, I sound like an arsonist, but we have to make sure we don't miss anything that will allow the vigilantes to easily reproduce the serum.

I leave Naito to search the lab and head back to the main room. The wet bar catches my attention. There could be a lighter there, and alcohol is flammable. Some of it is, at least.

Ducking behind it, I start rummaging through the bottles. Most of them are red wines, mostly Pinot Noir, but there's some vodka and rum, too. Those might fuel a fire. If I can find a matchbook.

There's a shallow basket behind one expensive-looking bottle, but it contains nothing but old corks, a simple cork-screw, and some pocket change. Nothing to start a fire with.

"Did you find any . . ." Naito's voice fades out, and he tilts his head to the side. That's when I hear it, too, a whirling, clicking sound. I look to my left, where a staircase leads down to a lower level.

"Basement?" I ask quietly.

"Yeah," Naito whispers.

We should just leave—everyone knows not to go into the basement when unidentified sounds are coming out of it— but Naito's already heading that way. I mutter under my breath and follow him.

The basement isn't a dark, gloomy hole. It's brightly lit and is being used as an office. File cabinets line an entire wall, and a shiny, executive-sized desk is set up in the room's center. On the end of that desk, a laser printer spits out page after page. It's responsible for the sounds we're hearing, and as we reach the bottom of the stairs and turn toward it, a hand reaches up to grab the newly printed documents.

It's Lee. He's sitting on the floor, hunched over a tablet computer. He doesn't read the pages that just printed; he clenches them in his fist. He hasn't noticed us yet. His atten-tion moves back and forth between the tablet and the mess of papers that are strewn all around him.

I glance at Naito. His jaw clenches. The barrel of his gun dips toward the floor.

His gun. I didn't see him take it out, but as I watch, he seems to regain his resolve. He reaims at Lee's head.

"Naito," I whisper. Something is obviously wrong with his brother. Lee's eyes are puffy, bloodshot, and he's pale.

Naito lets out a breath and lowers his gun all the way. "Lee."

The other human ignores him.

"Lee," Naito says again, more emphatically this time.

Lee finally looks up. "I've killed her."

"What?" Naito takes a step toward his brother.

"I've killed her." Lee's gaze takes in the papers around him. "Paige. The Sight serum is fatal."

TWENTY-TWO

◆-◆

I FEEL THE blood drain from my face. My skin becomes cold and prickly. "Paige is dead?"

Lee stares at the papers around him, shaking his head. "They've all died. Within six months. They just . . . we'll just die. I didn't know. I swear to God, if I had, I wouldn't have injected her."

"Wait, Lee." I grab his shoulder as I crouch in front of him, shake it to make him meet my eyes. "Is Paige alive now?"

Tears pool in his eyes. "She'll never forgive me for this."

She's still alive. I let out a breath, but my chest feels tight and achy. If Lee's right about this, she won't be alive for more than six months. Neither will he, but he seems more concerned about Paige than about himself.

"Where is she?" I ask.

He runs a hand through his jet-black hair. "With the Court fae. I wouldn't let her come here with me."

"And where are the Court fae?" Naito asks, kneeling beside us. His gun is still in his hand. His finger runs across the trigger guard as if he's itching to fire the weapon.

"I'm supposed to meet them at the turnoff."

I have no idea how far away that is, but it sounds way too close. We need to get out of here.

"You have the serum?" Naito asks.

His brother's nostrils flare. He turns toward the desk, and as he reaches underneath it, I see a tiny glass vial that's rolled there. He grips it in his fist, staring down at the milky liquid inside. Then he stands and yells as he slams the vial down on the desk. It shatters, spreading the serum and Lee's blood across the desk's surface.

Well, that's one way to get rid of it.

"I told you our father is a heartless bastard," Naito says, straightening.

I rise, too, and glare at Naito. Now is *not* the time for the I-told-you-so's. His brother may be dying. My friend might be, too, my friend who never, ever should have become involved in the fae's world. I don't care if she's chosen to be on the wrong side of the war, I'm not going to just let her die.

My gaze falls to the mess of papers at our feet, then to Lee's tablet computer. I bend down to scoop it up, touch the screen to turn it back on. It's filled with long paragraphs of text and a few diagrams and scientific equations that I don't understand.

"Does this have all the serum research on it?" I ask Lee. He's staring down at his bleeding hand, which is still flat on the top of the desk.

"Yes."

"How do you know it's fatal?" I ask him, sliding the tablet inside my sketchbook. The *jaedric* cover just barely cinches shut.

"Dad told me."

I freeze. So does Naito.

"Dad's here?" he asks Lee.

"I'm here."

The gun goes off before I turn. It's loud and sudden, and I stumble back even though the bullet didn't hit me. It hit Naito.

"Naito!" I only make it a step before Nakano reaims at me.

"No," he says tersely.

"He's your son." My breath is coming in short, angry intervals. Naito's lying on the floor, his chest covered in blood. He's still alive, still conscious, but he needs help. He needs . . .

Aren. Naito and I have been in here more than ten minutes, and Aren would have heard the gunshot. He would have rushed in despite Naito's warning if he was able to.

If he was able to.

I feel rage building under my skin. I'm going to kill Naito's father.

"You sent the text," Nakano says. His voice is as cold as his eyes. He's wearing camouflage, head to toe, and what's left of his right arm is in a black sling. Kyol severed that arm when the vigilante aimed a gun at me before. He should have killed him, but Naito rushed to his side, trying to save his father. I know he regrets that now.

"You knew we were coming," I say, trying to ignore the gun he has aimed at my chest.

"You put a period at the end of your message," he says, and I don't know if the disgust in his voice is because of that punctuation—a stupid, single period I don't even remember typing—or if it's because he has to talk to me, a human who colludes with fae. "I sent men to Georgia. And I kept a few here just in case." He looks at Lee. "Can we use her?"

Use me? As in, make me give them information about the fae? I glance in Lee's direction, careful to keep my expression neutral. If Lee says no, that I'm not useful, I'm almost certain Nakano will fire that weapon.

Lee is still staring down at his brother. Slowly, he looks up. He focuses on me.

"Yes," he says.

"McKenzie!" Aren's voice rings out from above.

I close my eyes as relief pours over me. Nakano's men haven't killed him. He's okay. If he gets the hell out of here, he'll stay that way.

"Take care of it," Nakano snaps.

I hold my breath as Lee mechanically starts for the stairs, and pray I haven't misjudged him. When he chooses to walk in front of Nakano, not behind him, I move, throwing myself to the left just as Lee knocks Nakano's arm, redirecting the line of fire to the right.

The gun goes off, harmlessly hitting the back wall.
"McKenzie!"

Aren again. He's on the stairs now. He grips the banister,
sees Lee wrestling on the floor with his father, then his gaze
locks on me.

"Naito's hurt," I call out, scurrying forward until I'm at
Naito's side. The bullet went all the way through him, and
he's losing so much blood.

"Tell Aren to go," Naito manages to get out before he's
wracked by coughing. "The tech . . ."

I press my hands over Naito's wound—it's right in the
center of his chest—then look over my shoulder at Aren. His
edarratae are going ballistic, leaping over his skin in some
kind of chaos, and he's stumbling down the stairs more than
walking down them.

Nakano's gun goes off again, but Lee's wrenched it out of
his father's hand. He rises to his feet, points the barrel at
Nakano's forehead. He doesn't pull the trigger.

"You know what the demons did to your mother," Nakano
says, heaving air in and out of his lungs.

"That was twenty years ago."

"They kill. They rape." Nakano rises slowly to his knees.
"It's our God-given charge to eradicate them."

Aren reaches the basement floor. He's off-balance when
he crosses it, but he makes it to my side.

"Can you heal him?" I ask, not knowing if he's capable of
it inside this compound or not.

Aren places his hands over Naito's chest. The *edarratae*
give no indication that he's using his magic, but Naito gasps.
Healing a wound that serious will hurt.

I rise and turn toward Lee. His aim is wavering. He's still
warring with himself, trying to decide if he's going to murder his father. It has to be done—he's ruined too many
lives—but I can't imagine what it would be like to kill the
man who raised you.

I take a step toward them. I know what it's like to kill,
though. It's not something I want to do again. The fae I
sent to the ether in Belecha almost three weeks ago still

haunts me. Despite everything Nakano's done, his death will as well.

I reach behind my back, wrapping my hand around the hilt of my dagger.

Nakano rises from his knees to his feet. "Put the gun down, boy. Go back to that school of yours and ignore the war I've been fighting for you."

"I tried to fight it with—"

"And you failed," Nakano cuts him off.

"You have to stop this," Lee says. "The fae aren't anyone's demons but your own."

He lowers his gun, damn it. I'm going to have to do this.

"You're as weak as your brother turned out to be." Nakano's voice is dripping with disgust now. Lee's knuckles go white on the grip of his weapon.

Nakano notices that, too. He sneers. "You can't kill your own father."

A shot rings out, thundering through the basement. The bullet hits Nakano's shoulder, throwing him against the wall below the staircase. Lee didn't fire the weapon, though.

Nakano's startled gaze swivels to Naito.

"He can't kill you," Naito says. "But I can."

He fires his gun again.

I can't look at the shattered shell of Nakano's skull, so I focus on Aren as he helps Naito all the way to his feet. Naito is deathly pale—Aren's magic can't replace blood loss—but his eyes are determined and cold. Not satisfied, though. His father's death won't bring Kelia back.

"Let's go," Naito says. He takes an unsteady step toward the stairs. Aren tries to keep him balanced, but he looks just as weak as Naito.

I slide my dagger back into my scabbard and glance at Lee, who's staring at his father's remains.

"Help your brother," I order.

Lee looks up, blinking. He's shell-shocked, I think. We don't have time for that.

I grab his arm and shove him toward Naito. Moving seems to snap him out of his daze. He tucks his gun into his waistband, then puts Naito's arm over his shoulder. But Naito doesn't budge.

"You with us or the Court fae?" he asks.

Lee clenches his jaw. "Right now, I'm with you. Six men stayed here with Dad. They're—"

"They're dead," Aren says when I reach his side. He looks like hell. The *edarratae* are angry on his skin, and his eyes are as red as Lee's were when I first saw him. I have to get him out of here.

"Come on," I say, looping my arm around his waist. He doesn't lean on me, but he does let me guide him to the staircase. Lee leads Naito up ahead of us. We make it halfway before Aren's knees buckle. I'm there, catching him.

"Sidhe," he says. His voice cracks. What the hell is in this place? Tech gives fae headaches, makes it harder for them to fissure, or use magic. It doesn't weaken them like this.

"We just need to get outside," I tell him.

I try to move him forward again. He doesn't budge.

"McKenzie," he says, reaching up to cup my cheek. He doesn't say he loves me, but the words are there in his eyes. I *feel* them. This is the man who will do anything for me, even wait a decade while I decide if I'm going to let myself fall in love with him. But I have fallen for him. I can't deny that, and I can't walk away from him.

I kiss him. It's brief because we have no time, but it's deep. It's a kiss that says he's forgiven. It says I want him, and it says he better damn well survive this.

"Come on." I half carry him the rest of the way up the steps.

"Aren!" Trev's voice comes from the lodge's exit.

"Don't come in here!" Aren orders. We move past the computers and plastic tables. When we're almost to the door, Aren draws his sword. "The remnants?"

A quick nod from Trev. "Nalst brought back reinforcements."

I hear it as we step outside, the sharp clap of metal against metal. I don't see Naito or Lee, just dozens of fae fighting each other. They don't come near this building—Aren's an idiot for doing so—but they're everywhere. Their fissures brighten the night more than the moon. I'm going to have to make a run for it, try to get out of here before they spot me. We came from the east. That trail is covered in fighting fae, but Naito mentioned an older trail, one that will take me down to the same parking lot I saw when we first fissured here. I need to find it.

"Can you fissure?" I ask Aren.

"Not yet," he says, his voice pinched. He tightens his grip on his sword. "I'll keep them away from you."

Fighting without being able to fissure is a huge handicap for a fae, even for Aren.

I draw my dagger. This is all going to go horribly wrong.

A few steps out of the building, and Aren is able to walk without support, thank God, but his forehead is still creased. His *edarratae* are still going crazy.

His reflexes are slow, too. He doesn't react quickly enough when a fissure rips through the air in front of us.

If Naito didn't step to my side at that moment, if his gun weren't already in his hand, Aren and I would both be dead. As soon as the In-Between releases the remnant, his blade arcs toward us. Naito fires, and the force of the bullet knocks the fae off his feet.

Naito takes two more steps forward, fires again. A second later, the remnant disappears into the ether.

"Go," Naito orders. "I'll cover you."

"Where's Lee?" I ask, but Aren is shoving me forward.

Another fissure opens in front of us. Trev.

Aren mutters a prayer of thanks to the *Sidhe*. Then he's intercepting the attacks of the remnants who appear around us. Trev is, too, but I yell his name.

"Burn it down," I order when he turns.

He spares me a scowl, fissures, then, when he reappears, says, "Lena doesn't want—"

"Burn it down," I say again, not caring that Lena doesn't want to draw the attention of normal humans. "They'll make more serum if you don't." I have the tablet computer in my sketchbook, we need to destroy the rest of the research, and we need to get rid of the body in the basement.

As soon as I see the flames rise from his palm, I concentrate on finding the trail Naito mentioned. I spot it on the edge—the very edge—of the cliff.

"There," I point it out to Aren.

"Go," he says, then he turns in time to block a remnant's attack. It won't take him any time to catch up with me, so I head toward the trail at a full sprint.

And skid to a stop when a fissure splits the air in front of me.

The remnant is on me, tackling me to the ground as I draw my dagger. When I try to bring it around between us, he easily grabs my wrist.

I tighten my grip, throw my hip into him, and we roll. We stop just before we reach the edge of the cliff, and my heart's pounding. I'm not strong enough to fight off the fae; I'm buying time until someone can help me, but the remnant's bending my wrist back. If he bends it any farther, the joint will snap. I can either give in to him, or let him break my arm. Either way, I'm going to end up dead or the remnants' prisoner.

I glance at the edge of the cliff again, notice that there's a thin ledge nine or ten feet down.

It'll hurt like hell, but I think I can survive it.

"Okay," I gasp when my wrist is at the breaking point. "Okay."

In the split second he releases my wrist to confiscate the dagger, I roll, throwing us over the edge.

I manage to land on my back. The impact drives the air out of my lungs. I nearly lose consciousness when my head slams into the ground, but I'm lucid enough to shove up at the remnant. He's flailing already. I think that's the only reason my plan works. He tilts off me, hitting the ground to my right and rolling. His arms splay out, his hands reaching for something to grab onto, but this ledge is bare and sandy. He screams as he goes over the edge.

I don't move for a minute. I concentrate on drawing air back into my lungs. My head hurts. So does my back and the arm I landed on, but I can move all my limbs. I force myself to my side, then to my hands and knees.

Black spots smear my vision when I get to my feet. I wait for them to pass. When they do, I see my sketchbook lying on the ground just in front of me. I slip it over my shoulder, then look up the ten-foot drop I just took. Sometimes, I really am an idiot. How am I supposed to get back up there?

Fortunately, the answer is easy. The ledge rises steeply to my left, but it's not a sheer drop like where I'm standing, and I think it just might join the trail I was heading for. I shuffle that way, keeping a hand braced against the cliff face so I don't lose my balance. I'm still feeling dizzy.

When I reach the trail again, I look back toward the compound. The main building's on fire. Thick black smoke rises from its burning walls and roof. The fae are still outside it, still fighting. I think I spot Aren, but I'm not sure, and as much as I want to see him, to have evidence that he's okay, I can't stand here and wait. I need to press on before a remnant spots me.

The ground to my right becomes a cliff face, towering several feet above my head, and the drop-off to the left is at least a hundred feet straight down. I'm not afraid of heights, but the dirt under my feet is unstable, and this trail is fucking narrow. I keep my eyes forward, hug the cliff wall, and inch along. I can practically feel gravity pulling me down, making my legs feel like jelly and throwing off my equilibrium.

The trail widens in about ten more feet. I'm almost there, so I keep moving, shuffling my feet along at a slow but steady pace. When I'm just two feet away from being on sturdier ground, Aren screams my name.

He sounds so angry, so agonized, I almost slip off the ledge. I grab hold of a crack in the cliff face and whip my head around, looking back toward the compound, terrified I'll see a blade spearing his heart.

"McKenzie!" he screams again. He doesn't look injured. He's fighting his way toward the edge of the cliff beside the main building. He kills the remnants attacking him with proficient swings of his sword. White soul-shadows rise on either side of him, marking his path.

A remnant lands a kick to his side. God, it looks hard

enough to break ribs. I don't understand until he drops to his knees at the edge of the cliff, peers over the side, and screams my name one more time.

This has to be the work of an illusionist, a powerful illusionist. Aren thinks I fell. I open my mouth to call him—

And am wrenched off my feet before I have the chance.

I land on my back, my head hitting the ground hard. A fae is above me. A remnant. Tylan.

"Aren!"

His hand goes to my throat, choking off my scream. I cough, swing a fist at his face, then scramble back toward the narrow trail. Aren's pain is raw, desperate, like he's losing a part of himself. He's still peering over the edge of the cliff. I don't think he realizes he's surrounded.

"Aren!" My scream is a hoarse whisper.

Tylan flips me onto my back again. His knee presses down on my chest with the full weight of his body, then he raises his hand. I glimpse the rock clenched in it just before he slams it down.

TWENTY-THREE

⋅—◆—⋅

I T'S COLD, DARK except for the *edarratae* flashing across
my skin. I'm in a small room, sitting on a dirt floor. My
wrists have been bound with silver. The metal shackles bite
into my flesh, and I have other scrapes and bruises. Some of
them are from rolling off the ledge with the remnant I killed,
the others, I think, are from Tylan dragging me away from
Nakano's compound.

I've been unconscious for a while. I don't know how long,
but it's an hour's drive between Boulder and Wiggins, where
the nearest gate to the compound was. Tylan wouldn't have
driven me there, though—a remnant wouldn't risk being
trapped in a car for so long. So could Lee have taken me to
the gate, then? He might have helped Naito out of the compound, but I doubt the remnants would have just let him walk
away. They might have forced him to drive me to Wiggins.

Maybe one of the rebels saw me being dragged away.
Maybe Aren did . . .

My eyes sting, filling with tears. Aren was surrounded. If
he hadn't gone inside the compound to find me, he would
have been able to fissure, but the tech or whatever the hell it
was Nakano had inside that building crippled him. His *jaedric* armor might have stopped one or two swords from slic-

ing into him, but I don't think he could have fought off that many remnants.

I'm not sure he wanted to.

God, I hope I'm wrong about that. I hope he fought back. If he had time to think, I'm sure he would have—Lena needs him too much for him to give in to his grief—but the remnants weren't giving him time.

I close my eyes to hold back the tears, refusing to let them fall.

A tiny squeak makes me reopen them. It sounded like a door opening. I look left, notice a tiny gap between the wooden wall and the dirt floor. I don't know what's on the other side of the wall. I have no idea where we are, just that it's cold here.

And quiet. That squeak is the only thing besides the wind that I've heard since waking up. The remnants aren't holding me in the middle of a city, that much is clear.

I lean my head back against the wooden beam holding up the center of the shack. My hands are bound in front of me, but a silver cord links the shackles to a metal loop in the beam. I can't move more than two or three feet away from it.

I'm pretty much screwed here. The rebels think I'm dead; they're not going to be looking for me.

Lena will still be searching for the remnants, though. Maybe someone will tip her off to where we are.

Or where *they* are. The remnants might not have brought me to their camp. They might have stuffed me in some remote corner of the Realm, far away from other fae and far away from a gate.

I swallow down the lump in my throat, trying to fight off the panic and frustration threatening to take over me. This isn't the first time I've been held captive. My history with escape attempts isn't great, but that won't keep me from trying. I'm going to find my way back to Corrist, even if I'm stranded in the middle of the Barren.

I draw in a breath, let it out, then the door in front of me cracks open.

"McKenzie?" It's Paige's voice. My stomach knots into a mess of emotion. I wouldn't be the remnants' prisoner if she hadn't escaped. I wouldn't be sitting here trying to convince myself that Aren's alive.

But she wouldn't be here if I hadn't tried so hard to hang on to my human life. She wouldn't be dying.

"Hey," I say.

Soft moonlight spills inside when she opens the door wider. "Here. It's for your head."

She's holding something wrapped in a cloth. Ice, I realize when I take it from her. It's heavy and cold.

"The remnants don't have a healer?" I ask.

"Not one who will touch you," she says, a touch of annoyance in her voice. She looks completely at ease, though. She's comfortable with the remnants. She's comfortable with fae. I don't know how she's adjusted so well in a week. I'm not sure I was ever this relaxed around Kyol and the Court fae.

I put the ice to my temple. The pressure hurts, but it numbs the pain some, and the panic I felt a few minutes ago eases as well. Paige is here. A gate can't be that far away.

"How did I get here?" I ask.

"Tylan," she says and doesn't elaborate. "I'm sorry about your head."

I'm sorry you're dying.

She doesn't know. She wouldn't be this calm if she did.

Those knots in my stomach tighten further.

"Paige—"

"I know you're mad," she says. "But Tylan was right there at the palace, McKenzie. I didn't have time to think. He wouldn't leave without me, and the rebels would have killed him if they'd caught him again."

"You've only known him a week," I say, almost grateful she interrupted me. It's easier to talk about this than the serum. "He told you I was being held captive. All the remnants know that's not true."

"I know, and I've had words with him about that, but, McKenzie, the Court fae didn't kill the humans in London. We showed up there *after* the rebels."

She saw the humans. I wasn't sure she knew anything about them. Neither she nor Lee has mentioned them before now.

"The rebels didn't kill them," I tell Paige, pronouncing

each word so that she knows there's no doubt of it. "We received a tip saying you were there."

I expect at least a glimmer of surprise in her eyes; there is none.

"We received the same tip about you," she says, her tone and cadence matching mine. "I went to London to find you. The remnants didn't want to take me. They thought it was a trap, and when the rebels attacked us, they tried to force me to leave. They've been protecting me."

I remember the fae who wrestled Paige off the stage. She was trying to get away from the remnant but not for the reason I thought. She wasn't scared of him; she just wanted to find me.

Suspicions and theories turn over in my mind. The deaths of the Sighted humans bother me and not just for the obvious reason. The remnants convinced Paige to support them. Surely they could have convinced the others. What motive would they have for killing them? Am I being blind, not considering the possibility that it was someone else? It's been easy to blame everything on the remnants. They're the ones who have attacked Corrist, they dragged Paige into the Realm, and they want to punish the rebels for deposing Atroth, their king who had become increasingly violent and extreme.

But what if someone else is puppeteering this war?

That possibility seems like so much wishful thinking. I don't want Paige and me to be on opposite sides of this war, and I want to justify her choice, find a way that we can negotiate a peace. But that's the thing. Lena has tried to contact the remnants. Their leadership has an open invitation to meet with her—she's guaranteed their safety—but they've never responded.

They'd rather kill us than talk to us.

Something squeaks to my left again, but it's the door behind Paige that moves, swinging open all the way. Tylan steps inside. Another fae is with him. A brother, perhaps? They look enough alike. Both have the same shade of brown hair, the same deep-set eyes, the same sharp-angled nose. The other fae is shorter, though. Stockier. And he's also somewhat familiar. He's definitely a former Court fae. Kyol thinks one of Atroth's higher-ranked officers is organizing the remnants. Maybe this guy is him. He has that quiet confidence that comes from years of training and experience.

He stares down at me. Even though I hate craning my neck to look up at him, I don't bother to stand. I don't think the short cord between my shackles and the wooden beam will allow it anyway.

Eventually, he crouches down so that he's eye level with me. *"I should slit her throat and send her back to them."*

And I'm supposed to believe these fae aren't the blood-thirsty killers they've proven to be? Right.

I want to translate what he said for Paige, but I don't know if she'd believe me, and I don't want them to know I've learned their language, so I stay quiet and give no indication that I understood his words.

"English, Caelar," Tylan says beside him.

Caelar's lip twitches at the request. He doesn't repeat what he said, though. He just crouches there, glaring. I think he's contemplating the most painful way to kill me, and my stomach churns, remembering the skinned humans in London. With the amount of hatred contained in his silver eyes, I can believe he slaughtered them himself.

Finally, he says, "You and I worked together once before."

I give no reaction to that. I worked with a lot of Court fae off and on over the years, usually when Kyol needed to put distance between us.

"It was soon after you came to the Realm," he continues. "You were young and wary. The false-blood Thrain had starved and beaten you, but you wouldn't let our healers touch you. We thought you were broken, but you agreed to read the shadows for us. You hated Thrain that much. Given that, I don't understand how you can support the fae who is his prodigy."

He's waiting for a reaction, some sign of shock or outrage. I don't give it to him. I knew where this was going the second he mentioned Thrain, and the news doesn't blindside me. "Aren isn't Thrain."

"He is exactly like Thrain," Caelar all but snarls.

"We're looking for a fae," Tylan says quickly, taking a step forward. His posture is tense, and his gaze is on Caelar, almost as if he expects the other fae to carry out his wish to send me back to the rebels with my throat slashed. "Her name is Brene. She's—"

"Tor'um," I finish for him. Caelar's jaw clenches at the word.

"You know her?" Paige asks.

"She's in Corrist," I say, still watching Caelar. His silver eyes are angry and agonized.

Caelar curses, then stands, facing Tylan. *"You were supposed to watch her."*

"I'm sorry, I was busy being captured in Eksan," he says in English. Then, softening his tone, he adds, "If I'd known she was there, I would have made sure she escaped with us. You know that."

"She was there because you'd been captured. She wanted to help. She's . . ." I see the muscles in his neck tighten as he swallows, and I can't help it. My heart breaks a little for him. Brene means something to him, that much is obvious.

Paige clears her throat, mutters, "English, please," under her breath. She's demanding the fae speak our language. Please tell me this isn't why she trusts them. She's not a naïve sixteen-year-old. Surely she doesn't believe they're translating everything they say for her.

Caelar turns his back on me, walks to the door, and stares outside. I can't see anything past him.

"The rebels won't win this war," Tylan says, drawing my attention back inside.

I meet his eyes. "People said that about them taking the palace."

He lifts a shoulder as if to say, *That's true.* "The high nobles won't approve the daughter of Zarrak unless she hands over the *garistyn*. She's had two weeks to do that. She hasn't, and she's losing support every day."

I frown. *Garistyn*? I've heard that word before. Back in Spier when I was shadow-reading with Kyol, I think. Jielan mentioned it. It has something to do with a king or Descendant.

"They haven't told you about that, have they?" That's from Caelar. He doesn't add anything else, doesn't turn around or move. He just stands there, staring outside, and an uncomfortable feeling gathers in my gut.

"What's a *garistyn*?" Paige asks the question. I'm grateful. I don't want to show curiosity or weakness or anything in front of these fae.

"Kingkiller. You can't kill a king without consequences," Tylan says. "They're Descendants of the *Tar Sidhe*. You might call them 'holy.' The fact is, the high nobles won't approve Zarrak unless she turns the *garistyn* over to be executed. She's protecting the Butcher of Brykeld."

My stomach sinks. I'm almost dizzy because I think he's telling the truth. Lena mentioned it before. She was annoyed because the high nobles were insisting she tell them who killed the king. I didn't realize it was this important, though, and Tylan has it wrong. Aren didn't kill Atroth. Kyol did.

"Jorreb had nothing to do with the king's death," I whisper.

"Some people say the *nalkin-shom* killed him," Tylan continues. "The silver walls didn't protect him. She fissured into his bedroom. Her touch poisoned him, they say. She weakened his magic, and while he was distracted and vulnerable, she sliced open his throat with invisible metal from her world."

I attempted to slice open Lord General Radath's throat with shrapnel that was embedded in my arm. The silver walls didn't protect him because I was fissured to the palace via a *Sidhe Tol*. Someone's twisted up and mangled all the details of that day. I never even touched Atroth. I almost don't mind fae believing that I did, though. It's better than their knowing Kyol killed him.

"You're going to tell us how to get into the palace," Caelar says from the doorway. He leaves without giving me a chance to respond, not that I would have answered the way he wanted me to.

Tylan watches him go, concern in his eyes. It vanishes when he realizes I'm watching him.

"Paige," he says, extending his hand.

"Can I have another minute?" she asks.

He looks at me. "Just a minute. I'll be close by."

"He trusts you," I say, after Tylan leaves.

"About as much as I trust him," she says. "He'll be right outside."

I lift an eyebrow. That doesn't exactly sound like a vote of confidence.

Paige runs a hand through her perfectly chaotic hair, and an *edarratae* flashes across her face. She scoots closer to me, lowers her voice to a whisper that I can just barely hear.

"That's what I wanted to tell you before," she says. "I'm not relying on what the fae tell me. They don't know Lee speaks their language. He's translated what they've said in Fae. That tip was anonymous, and they honestly believe the rebels killed those humans."

"Lee speaks Fae?" I ask.

Paige nods. "I made a deal with him. If he told me what he overheard, I wouldn't tell the fae about the serum."

The serum again. She really doesn't know the consequences of what Lee did to her.

"Lena would have used the serum against Caelar," Paige continues. "I couldn't let that happen, so I told Tylan about it. Lee was pissed, but . . . Well, I convinced him to get the serum."

Is she *blushing*? There's not much light in here, and her chaos lusters make it hard to tell for sure, but I'm almost certain her cheeks are pink. When we were at the palace, she said she and Lee hooked up after her sister's wedding. In Paige-speak, that means they slept together. I think she slept with Lee again to convince him to get the serum. If there wasn't a hint of pink on her cheeks, I'd say that was a whorish thing to do, but Paige *never* blushes when she talks about sex. She really is into him.

She clears her throat. "Lee was supposed to just walk in and walk out with it. There wasn't supposed to be a fight."

"Is Lee here?" I ask, hating that any feelings she might have for him are likely to end very soon.

"Yeah, he's . . ." Her gaze flickers to the left. There's just a wall there, but I have the impression Lee's somewhere in that direction. "He helped Tylan bring you here. I'm not sure if that was his choice or not. He's not acting like himself. He's quiet and angry, I think. I need to talk to him."

"Paige," Tylan calls.

"One second," she says over her shoulder. Then she turns back to me. "Look, I know you wouldn't join the rebels just because you're in love with a guy, and I was thinking. I'm *certain* the Court fae didn't kill the humans in London, but I'll admit that there's a chance that *maybe* the rebels didn't kill them either."

"Paige," Tylan says again.

"I have to go, but . . . These fae aren't bad people, McKenzie. I promise."

TWENTY-FOUR

◆

I LET MY head fall back against the wooden beam. I'm so thirsty. The remnants haven't given me anything to eat or drink. They keep asking me how to get into the palace. They think I know the shifting pattern of safe fissure zones Kyol devised. I don't, and even if I did, I wouldn't tell them.

I think about what Paige said, that these fae aren't the bad guys, but it's hard to believe that with my stomach cramping from hunger and a headache pounding behind my eyes. The latter is from dehydration. The In-Between will do that to you if you're not careful, and I can't remember the last time I had something to drink.

I'm pretty sure it's well past 5 P.M. on Friday by now. I've missed my meeting with Jenkins. Maybe I can convince him something came up, that I came down with the flu or had a death in the family. Of course, before I can convince him of anything, I have to get out of here in one piece.

I'm staring off into space when there's a noise from a few feet away. It's the same noise I've heard more than once since I was brought here, a tiny little squeak. For all I know, we could be in the middle of a forest. It could be one of a million animals I don't know the names of, but on a whim, I make a clucking noise. Immediately, two bright blue eyes peer in the crack between the ground and the wall.

No fucking way.

"Sosch?" I whisper.

The eyes blink.

It's him. It has to be him.

I make a kissing noise. His whiskers twitch, and his head turns to the left, then to the right, as if he's checking traffic before crossing a street. After a quick *chirp-squeak*, he scurries under the wall and into my arms. Which is kind of awkward considering my wrists are shackled together.

"You don't have a picklock on you, do you?" I ask, scratching him behind the ears. He purrs, then rubs his furry face against my cheek. My nose tickles. Apparently, *kimkis* do shed.

"Did Aren send you?" I ask quietly though I don't know if *kimkis* can be sent anywhere. From what I've seen, they have minds of their own. Plus, Aren thinks I'm dead. Sosch has found me on his own before; my guess is he's done it again.

Sosch *chirp-squeak*s, then scurries out of my arms, dragging his long body behind me. He nestles down between my back and the base of the wooden beam.

"That's real helpful," I tell him, but he's warm. And I'm glad for his company.

I fade off. When I wake up, Paige is sitting against the wall beside the door. Sosch is still behind me. I don't think she can see him, but I try to make myself take up as much room as possible, just in case. I don't want the remnants to take him away from me.

When Paige doesn't say anything, I take a closer look at her, and immediately, my heart sinks. Her eyes are red, puffy, like she's been crying.

"You talked to Lee."

She draws in a breath, nods, then lets it out.

"I'm sorry," I say. "This is my fault."

She closes her eyes. "It's not your fault, McKenzie."

"I was trying to hang on to my human life," I tell her. "That's why I was in school. That's why I picked up the phone every time you called and kept agreeing to go on those blind double dates—which I hated, by the way."

"None of those guys were right for you." She smiles before she opens her eyes. "Sorry about that. I didn't know you preferred fae."

"I don't prefer fae, I just . . ." God, it must seem that way.

She shrugs, then she picks up the tablet computer resting beside her. It's so thin, I didn't notice it before, but the screen lights up when she touches it.

"I'm surprised this works here," she says.

"There's no way to charge the battery, but the Realm doesn't mess with tech." The tech just messes with the Realm, according to some fae. "Do the remnants know you have that?"

She sniffs. "Yeah, Caelar's not happy. He's making me take it back to Earth."

"He knows what's on it?"

She looks up from the screen, meets my eyes, and nods. "The serum's terminal, though. He's not going to use it."

But he would have. He'll do anything to kill Aren and get rid of Lena.

"It's funny," Paige continues, toying with the edge of the tablet. "I was in Bedfont House because I tried to commit suicide. Now, ten years later, I'm dying, and all I want is to live."

It's not funny at all, but it's just like Paige to underplay something like this. Back when we were roommates, she talked lightly about her deliberately reckless behavior—the street race that resulted in a bad wreck, the time she took a running leap off her roof and landed in the neighbor's pool. The bottle of cold medicine she downed that led to her being institutionalized definitely wasn't her first suicide attempt; it was just the first time her dad woke up and realized there was a problem.

I'm glad Paige is admitting she wants to live, though. The nurses and attendees at Bedfont House might have violated dozens of federal regulations, but the medicine and psychologists helped her work through her depression.

"Anyway," Paige says, clearing her throat, "I dated this guy named Rob once. He's getting his PhD in chemistry. I'm going to take the tablet to him, see if he can figure out what's wrong with us."

"You're going to tell him about the fae?" The last part of that comes out a little high-pitched, partly because it surprises me but also because Sosch shifts, snuggling closer to my back.

"I don't know why you didn't tell me about them," Paige says. "I would have understood."

"You would have thought I was crazy."

"No, I wouldn't have. I would have—"

"You thought Lee was crazy," I point out.

She deflates a little. "Well, I'll make Rob understand. I'm not letting this beat me."

Good. I give her a tight-lipped smile. Out loud, I say, "I've been thinking about what you said before, about the remnants not killing those humans. I think it's possible it could be someone else. If we could get Lena and Caelar to meet—"

Paige shakes her head. "Caelar won't negotiate. He won't even talk to the rebels because of Brene."

"The *tor'um*?"

"Yeah. They were going to . . ." She frowns, trying to recall a word. "Whatever the fae equivalent of marriage is. A bond or something."

"Life-bond," I say.

"Yeah, that. But then Aren captured her."

She doesn't need to say more than that. I know what happened afterward. I've seen her.

"You should see the way he takes care of her," Paige continues. "It's sweet. She's crazy as hell, but he loves her still." She draws in a breath, lets it out. "I have to admit, I, too, wouldn't mind seeing Aren dead for what he did."

My jaw clenches. I have to consciously make it relax. Aren's past is his past. He's not a ruthless, barbaric fae; he's a fae who wanted to save the life of a friend. I don't approve of what he did, but I understand it.

"Are you staying with the remnants?" I ask.

"I'm not going to let the rebels kill them," she says, tucking the tablet under her arm. "But I can't help them if I'm dead. I'm going back to Earth soon. I just wanted to make sure you were okay."

I'm not exactly okay, but things could be worse. "If you could talk the remnants into giving me something to drink, I'd appreciate it."

She stops midrise. "They haven't given you water?"

"No."

"What the hell." She straightens fully. "I'll be right back."

She doesn't come "right back," but she does eventually return with a wooden mug filled to the brim with water. The liquid sloshes over the edge when I take it.

"I'm going to try to talk some sense into Caelar before I leave," she says. "I don't know if he'll listen. It might help if the rebels send Brene back to him. It'd be a gesture of good faith."

"They don't know about Caelar," I say, but she's already closing the door behind her. I hear the lock click into place, sealing me in the dark.

Lightning flashes across the hand holding the mug. I lift it to my lips and something in it makes the tiniest *thunk*. I pause, midsip, and stare at the wooden bottom. My *edar-ratae* are bright enough to make out an object lying there submerged in the cold water.

I reach inside, pull out a key, a key that looks like it'll fit in the tiny lock of my shackles.

Paige just handed me my freedom.

PAIGE put our friendship before the Realm. When the rebels caught her, I helped them keep her prisoner. I even tried to help them recapture her when she escaped with Tylan. I spend half the night feeling guilty about that and waiting for the right moment to make my escape. If my internal clock isn't completely broken, something close to an hour passes without any sound or sign from the fae. I think they might all be sleeping.

Finally, I slip the key inside the lock and turn it.

The shackles fall from my wrists.

I'm going to need the biggest head start I can get, so I

don't waste any time. I crawl to the gap Sosch entered through and start digging. It's not as easy as I want it to be. I end up going back for the shackles to use them to gouge into the ground. That helps, but it still feels tediously slow.

"You could help," I whisper to Sosch when he makes an appearance to sniff at my work. His whiskers twitch as if he thinks he could do a better job, but he just curls up into a ball, resting his head on his front paws.

I don't know how long it takes to make the hole big enough to slip through. It feels like hours, but it's still night when I start wiggling under the wall. I barely fit. The wood scrapes against my skin, catches on the waistband of my jeans. For a good two minutes, I'm almost certain I'm going to get stuck. I've never been overly self-conscious or critical of my body, but I'm praying for smaller hips and a few less pounds when I finally—finally!—tear my way free.

And I do mean tear. My right hip is red and angry, the skin frayed and bleeding. I pull my jeans up, my shirt down, then rise to a low crouch, ignoring it while I survey my surroundings.

There's a reason why I've been freezing my ass off—the remnants are camped on the side of a mountain. For a moment, I'm disoriented, thinking maybe we're still back in Boulder, but the lightning on my skin and the lightness to the atmosphere proves otherwise.

Behind me, Sosch squeaks.

I turn around quickly, picking him up to keep him from making any more noise. Tents are set up around this shack, five within my line of sight. I assume there are more on the opposite side of my little prison. I'm sure remnants are guarding its door, too, or at least watching it.

I look into the wooded area that leads farther up the mountain. I am so not dressed for that hike. My jeans and long-sleeved T-shirt won't provide enough protection from the elements, and my hands are already numb from digging in the cold soil. I want to go *down*, but up will take me away from the remnants.

Sosch sluggishly climbs from my arms to my shoulders. I let him stay there, then I finger-comb my hair so that it's covering most of my face. After tugging my sleeves down over my hands, I have most of my skin hidden. I don't waste any more time; I silently jog to the woods.

Honestly, I shouldn't call it a woods. It's more like a few scattered trees that decided to brave the increasingly rocky soil. They don't offer much protection from the wind or from any eyes that might look this way, whatever this way is. The Realm has four mountain ranges. This could be any one of them, but . . .

But Paige and Lee are in the camp. There has to be a gate near here. Of course, a gate won't help me unless I find a fae I can trust to take me through it. I wish there was some way to know where I am, where I'm going, but there's not right now. All I can do is put as much distance as possible between me and the camp. When the sun rises, maybe I'll be able to orient myself.

Hours later, the sky brightens. I'm not going up the mountain anymore because I can't. The incline is too steep to attempt without a rope. As it is, there's a very real possibility of breaking my neck. I set Sosch on the ground because I'm worried about him falling or making me lose my balance. I'm weak, partly from not eating or drinking and partly because I'm just so damn worn-out.

Sosch chirps and scurries over the rocky ground. I let him lead the way because he's choosing a path I can actually follow. I feel bad, though, that he's stuck with me. Normally, he wouldn't be. Fae open fissures so often, he's almost always able to scurry into the In-Between and hop out wherever he wants. Guess being stranded is a downside of getting attached to a human.

I press on and try not to think because I don't want to face the truth: I don't know if there's any chance in hell that I can make it to civilization. The sun hasn't burned off the fog below yet.

It doesn't until midday. I'm staring at the dissipating clouds, trying to decide if I'm hallucinating or if there really is a city down there, when Sosch and I come across a stream. He's already there, lapping at the water, when I fall to my knees beside him.

Minutes later, I have to force myself to stop drinking—I'll make myself sick if I continue—then I turn back to the city below. It's huge, filling up the plateau between the base of the mountain and a large body of water . . .

Really?

I'm not hallucinating, but this isn't just any city.

"It's Corrist!" My voice is hoarse, weak, but I grab Sosch and hug him to my chest. He squeals, then scurries out of my arms. Once he's firmly back on the ground, he looks up at me with the *kimki* equivalent of a glare.

"Be happy," I tell him. "We're not going to die."

I'm surprised as hell that the remnants are camped so close to the Silver Palace. Lena sent rebels to search up here, but they found nothing. Either the remnants had their camp hidden by illusion, or they just recently moved into these mountains. Right now, I don't care which is true. The morning fog made the valley below seem deceptively far away, but now that it's cleared, I can see that we're not as high in the mountains as I thought. Sosch and I might even make it to the city by dark.

Reinvigorated, I lead the way back to civilization.

TWENTY-FIVE

$\bullet\!\!-\!\!\bullet\!\!-\!\!\bullet$

W E DON'T MAKE it by dark. We don't even make it by morning. Sosch abandons me around noon, and it's at least another hour before I reach the plateau that lies between the base of the mountains and Corrist's silver wall. The stream Sosch found joined another stream, then another and another until it fed into this river, the one that hosts Corrist's gate.

I'm too tired to worry about a rebel archer shooting me as I make my way to the wall. The air down here is warmer, but I'm still numb. My feet are moving only because I haven't let myself rest. If I stopped even for a minute, I don't think I would have had the strength to keep going.

A fae calls out from the wall when I'm within a hundred feet of it. My mind is just as numb as the rest of me because I can't seem to make sense of his words. It's not until an arrow stabs into the ground at my feet that I force myself to stand still, to think.

"I'm McKenzie." It takes three tries to get those words out.

No one answers. Not for several long minutes. I don't call out again or move from my current location. The fired arrow is evidence the fae don't trust what they see.

Finally, the portcullis begins to rise. Chaos lusters strike across the arms of the human who ducks under it.

"Naito!" I'm smiling and moving forward despite the fae drawing their swords behind him. He made it out of Boulder. I've been worrying about so many things, I didn't realize I was worried about him, too.

"She's not an illusion," he says, as I throw my arms around his shoulders. He staggers, probably because I'm not doing a great job of keeping myself upright.

He keeps his arms holding mine when he steps back and surveys me, head to toe. "What happened? Aren said he saw you fall, and he's . . . He's not doing well."

My heart thumps against my chest, aching and anxious, but relieved as well. Aren is alive. "Where is he?"

"In the palace," Naito says, guiding me under the silver wall. He calls for some of the wall's guards to follow us, and while we're walking through the Inner City, I tell him where I've been and where the remnants are. I don't know their exact location, of course, only that they're in the mountains overlooking the city and that they're being led by a fae named Caelar.

As soon as we step inside the palace, my legs start shaking. Now that I'm safe, it's like they've given themselves permission to give out on me. I need to sit, to sleep, but I need to see Aren more, so I force myself to keep walking, ignoring my body's demands to rest. I make it as far as the three steps that lead down to the statue garden before my knees buckle.

"Shit, McKenzie," Naito says, keeping me on my feet.

"I'm fine."

"You're not fine." He lets me go but keeps his arm raised, ready if I fall again. "Go to your room. I'll send Aren."

That sounds like a great idea, now that he mentions it and now that I know I don't have the energy to search for Aren myself. So, instead of following Naito through the statue garden, I turn left, staying under the covered walkway. It's not until I step inside the residential wing that I remember I'm going to have to go *up* to reach my room. I don't know how I'm going to make it, but I walk to the staircase.

And stop.

Aren's there, sitting on a step halfway up with Sosch in his arms. Aren's eyes are closed. His forehead is pressed to the *kimki*'s, and he's murmuring something I can't quite make out. With Sosch in front of him, I only see half of his face, but it's clear he's in pain, more pain than I've ever seen him in before. He looks haggard, and the way his shoulders slump toward the ground makes my heart break. I remember the way he screamed my name outside of Nakano's compound, and I know that I can't ever let him hurt like this again.

"Aren," I call out, placing one hand on the banister.

He looks up.

Our gazes lock.

He pales as if he's seen a ghost, and I pour all my energy into climbing that first step. I need to close the distance between us, touch him, taste him, tell him I want forever with him.

I climb another step.

He sets Sosch aside. I wouldn't have believed it possible, but he becomes even more pale. I'm not even sure he's breathing until he finally draws in a long, deep breath.

Then something goes wrong. Instead of relief or elation, fury takes over Aren's expression. He curses as he draws his sword, and that's when I realize my mistake. The fae don't believe in ghosts; they believe in illusions.

Shit.

He's on me before I can explain, grabbing the front of my shirt in his fist. If he was in his right mind, he'd realize that touching me would break an illusion, but he's in a blind rage right now. He's not listening to me.

Instead of trying to pull away, I move toward him, manage to lay my hand on the side of his neck. Thank God, my chaos lusters react instantly. I see the spark of heat in his eyes. He goes still.

"McKenzie?" His voice breaks. Confusion moves through his eyes. He saw me go over the cliff. He's believed I was dead for almost forty-eight hours.

"I'm not an illusion," I say.

He touches my face. Tenderly. Tentatively.

"McKenzie. *Sidhe*, I thought . . ."

He doesn't finish that sentence. Instead, he kisses me with

a fierceness that takes my breath away, murmuring my name over and over and over again. His hands run down my shoulders, down my arms. They rest on my hips, tighten, then one splays across the center of my back, all as if he's still not sure I'm here. I cup the back of his neck and kiss him harder, proving I'm not a dream.

I want to keep kissing him, keep touching him, but Aren presses his lips against mine one last time then takes a half step back. He looks at me, almost as if he thinks his hands are deceiving him. He needs to prove I'm alive with his eyes now, so he takes me in. The relief I was searching for earlier reaches his gaze. It doesn't completely chase away the shadows of his pain, though.

"I saw you at the edge of the cliff," I tell him. "I heard you scream my name, and it killed me." I loop my arms around him, pull him close again so I can rest my head against his shoulder. He's warm and deliciously solid. "I tried to get your attention, but Tylan had me. He . . ."

I lift my head. "He took me to the remnants' camp. It's in the Corrist Mountains." I draw in a breath to tell him more. "I told Naito—Paige is there. A fae named—"

"No, shhh." He lightly touches a finger to my lips. "Unless the remnants are going to attack the palace in the next hour, I don't want to hear a report. You're always putting the Realm before yourself. It stops now."

With that, he scoops me into his arms. It's sudden and unexpected, but I'm holding on to him instinctively. He climbs the rest of the steps and takes me to my room.

To my bathroom. He kicks on a lever, and water begins to fill the round, tiled tub. When Aren sets me on my feet, I steady myself by holding on to the black pipe that travels up into the ceiling. A reservoir of water is up there. A palace employee fills it every time it's drained.

"Don't take this the wrong way," Aren says, studying me, "but you look like you've crossed the Barren."

Crossing the Barren, a stretch of land in the Realm where no fae can fissure, is an idiom that basically means I look like shit, and damn it, I do. Dirt is packed under my fingernails, the sleeves of my gray shirt are torn and streaked with brown and black, and, when the *edarratae* flash across my skin, they look dim under the thick layer of grime. I don't want to think about what my hair must look like.

"God, no wonder you tried to kill me." I take my hands off him, step away.

He chuckles and pulls me back. "I wasn't in my right mind. Even like this, I want you."

A million chaos lusters somersault in my stomach, and when he kisses me this time, I'm undone. Nothing matters but him and us and *this*, the way he makes me feel like I'm everything to him. Sometime in the last month, he's become everything to me.

He pulls my shirt over my head, cups my face between his hands, and drinks me in. *Edarratae* leap from me to him in excited, frenzied bursts, and I decide then that I'm never letting him go.

"I never told you," Aren whispers against my neck. "How difficult it was." He plants a kiss on my bare shoulder, just to the right of my bra strap. "Not to touch you in Cleveland."

Cleveland? Too many thoughts are spinning through my head, too many sensations driving through my body for me to make sense of his words.

"You scared me then." His hands are between us, unbuttoning my pants. "I wasn't sure you'd wake up until I dropped you into the tub."

"Ohh." I mean that "oh" to be silent, but just when I realize he's referring to the safe house he took me to after Germany, he pulls my earlobe between his teeth. My entire body turns molten.

I feel him smiling against my neck, and I fall for him even more. I didn't think that was possible, but making him happy makes me happy, and all I want to do is make him smile.

Make him smile and moan and tremble when I touch him.

That's what he does when I start unbuckling his weapons belt. Then, he places his left hand over mine. His right touches my cheek.

"Again, don't take this the wrong way," he says, his voice sounding strained. "But I'm going to walk out of here."

The way he slides my pants over my hips suggests differently. I step out of my shoes and let him finish stripping me down to just my bra and undies. He's kneeling in front of me long enough that I have to run my hand through his already disheveled hair. I love how untamed it is, how untamed he is.

"Aren," I say. I mean to make his name an encouragement, to let him know that this is okay, that I'm not going to stop him, I want him, but my voice comes out just as strained as his, and when he runs his hands up my thighs, I can't manage any more words. My muscles quiver. I'm barely able to stay on my feet.

But then, he straightens, and, quickly, he picks me up and sets me in the tub.

I gasp when the ice-cold water bites at my calves.

"*Sidhe,*" he mutters. "Sorry."

Keeping one hand on my hip, he bends down to submerge his other hand beneath the water's surface. It warms immediately.

I raise an eyebrow when he straightens, then say, "That's one way to cool me off."

He laughs at that, and his smile and the brightness in his silver eyes makes my heart skip.

"Yeah, I . . ." He clears his throat, releases my hip. "Will you be okay? I'd stay and help, but I'd have to touch you, and if I touch you one more second . . . I think you need rest more than you need me right now."

That's extremely debatable.

"I'll bring you something to eat."

Or maybe he's right. Now that he's brought up the idea, my stomach decides to remind me I haven't eaten anything in almost two days. And it's probably not a bad idea to rest before I . . . before we . . .

God, I really want to be with him.

He gives me one of his crooked half grins, and his gaze and his posture tell me just how difficult it is for him to walk away.

And that's one more thing I love about him I realize as he's closing the bathroom door. I love that he needs me as much as I need him. Kyol always made leaving me look easy . . .

Kyol.

I almost slip in the tub.

He's the *garistyn*, the kingkiller. I don't think Tylan was lying when he said that's one of the reasons the high nobles aren't approving Lena. Whatever their opinion was of Atroth, they aren't happy he was killed. I just never realized how unhappy they were.

With shaking hands, I strip off my undergarments. I don't know if the shaking is because I'm weak and hungry or if it's because I'm afraid. I try to convince myself that Kyol will be okay. Lena needs him. She has to protect him, but I know him too well. He's too damn noble to let this go on for long. He'll turn himself in because it's what's best for the Realm and because he blames himself for not being able to find a way to save his king.

Naked now, I sink into the tub, letting the warm water swallow me. The only reason Kyol hasn't already stepped forward as the *garistyn* is because it's not the right time. He'll wait until he's sure Lena's place as the Realm's queen is secure. Then he'll let the high nobles kill him.

I clench my hands into fists. I won't let that happen.

TWENTY-SIX

•◆•

I DON'T INTEND to fall asleep, but climbing out of the tub and pulling on a pair of fae-made pants and a soft, loose top siphons my last ounce of energy. When I lie down on my bed, I pass out, sinking into two sets of dreams.

The first are my usual dreams. They're dark and terrifying and star more than one of my enemies. Thrain's face is foremost. It always is. He's the fae who dragged me into this world. He hurt me. He deliberately made me fear him. But I fear others too, now. Micid, the *ther'othi* who could walk the In-Between. Radath, the king's lord general who would have preferred to see me raped and broken in a *tjandel* rather than helping him hunt the Court fae's enemies. And there's a third face now, one that I can't quite make out in the shadows. I try to force Caelar's face to fit there, or Tylan's. I even try a number of the other false-bloods I've tracked down over the years, but none of their silhouettes fit.

I'm not sure I'd survive the first set of dreams if it wasn't for the second. Aren's in each and every one of them, holding me, touching me, kissing me. Sometimes we're in the Realm, my white lightning coiling around our bodies. Other times, we're in my world. He's taking my breath away against a brick wall in London or I'm kissing every one of his chaos lusters on the Strip in Vegas. And, every so often, we're in between worlds, making love as we disappear into a strip of radiant white light.

I hold on to every moment with Aren as long as I can, but I toss and turn no matter which set of dreams I'm trapped in until a warm body locks me against his chest.

Aren shushes softly beside my ear until I relax. It's only then, wrapped in his cedar and cinnamon scent, that I truly sleep.

HOURS later, Aren shifts.

I burrow closer against him. This feels good. It feels normal. I want this every single morning.

"Sorry," he whispers. "I didn't mean to wake you."

"I've been awake for a while." I grab his hand, intertwine my fingers with his.

"You've been asleep for a while," he says.

"How long?"

"A little more than half a day." His thumb rubs across my palm. "You've missed dinner and breakfast. Another hour and you'll miss lunch as well." He nuzzles my hair. "You smell better."

I grin, then roll to my back so I can see him. He hasn't been this relaxed and happy in a while, certainly not since we took the palace. He was more comfortable in the role of a rogue who disrupted the plans of the Realm's ruler; it's not quite as easy keeping the Realm's potential ruler in power. But I've always known this wasn't a fairy tale. If it were, everything would have been perfect the second we ousted the king.

I breathe him in, then draw my fingers along the strong line of his jaw. I forgave him with a kiss when we were in Nakano's compound. I realized I should have used words when I was being held by the remnants. I should have made it absolutely clear that I'm his forever.

So I make it clear now.

"I fell in love with you," I tell him.

He raises an eyebrow, gives me one of his half grins. "Just now?"

"No, 16.6 seconds ago." I lightly punch his shoulder. He laughs and pulls me closer.

"I don't know when," I say. "Maybe when you gave me that diamond necklace."

"Ah," he says sagely. "I've always heard humans could be lured in with sparkling rocks."

My smile widens. "You are so charming today."

"Aren't I?" He presses a kiss to my temple. I feel him shudder when a chaos luster leaps to his lips.

He sits up. Swallows. His eyes are a deep, steamy silver.

"You should eat now," he says, his rough voice sending a stroke of heat through my body. "You're going to need the energy."

At first, I think he means that Lena's going to need my Sight or shadow-reading skills, but the way his gaze locks on me as he brings my hand to his mouth indicates otherwise. His tongue tickles my palm before he releases my hand. Then he picks up a tray of bread and meats off the side table and sets it between us as if that's the only thing that can keep him apart from me.

My room has suddenly become hot. I have to concentrate on something besides the delicious ache that's settled low in my stomach, so I pick up a piece of bread, and say, "I'm surprised Lena isn't beating down my door."

"She's meeting with Lorn," Aren says. "Here."

He hands me a glass filled with a deep red liquid.

"Cabus?" I ask.

"Yes, *nalkin-shom*," he says with a sideways grin.

I make a face as I raise the glass then drink. It really is vile-tasting, but it'll make me feel better.

"Lena decided to let Lorn back into the palace?" I ask, returning my attention to the plate and trying to decide what will get rid of the taste of *cabus* the quickest.

Aren places a pillow between my back and the wall. "Only temporarily. He's still being difficult. He's helping less and less every day."

"He'd rather cooperate with a band of merry men than a potential queen."

"A band of what?"

"Never mind." I pick up the tongs beside the plate. They're wooden and similar to the kiddie chopsticks handed out at Chinese restaurants, but they're a standard fae utensil. I use it to select the stringy, dark meat sitting on the edge of the plate. I think it's *brive*. If I'm right, it's delicious, even though it looks incredibly unappetizing.

"Did Naito talk to Lena?" I ask. Then I nearly choke when I swallow down the stringy stuff. It's *not brive*.

"He did," Aren says, and something in his voice makes me forget about the horrible taste in my mouth. He's stiff, and his expression is guarded, almost as if he's waiting for me to lash out at him.

"You know about Caelar," I say. *And Brene,* I add silently. Aren's jaw clenches and unclenches, all but confirming my words.

I give him a tight-lipped smile, then grab a wedge of cheese. After another few seconds, Aren relaxes slightly, realizing I'm not going to make a point about his past.

"He's made this war personal," Aren says.

I nod. "That's why he won't negotiate with Lena. He wants you dead." I take another bite out of the soft wedge of cheese, then add, "He thinks you're the *garistyn*."

"Caelar told you about that." There's no inflection in his voice.

"He did," I say, using the same tone Aren did a minute ago. "I won't let Kyol die."

He gives me an insipid smile. "I know."

He retrieves the glass of *cabus* I set aside, starts to hand it to me, but almost drops it when someone pounds on the door. He's on his feet, reaching for the sword propped against the wall, when Trev calls out, *"Lena wants you."*

Aren lets his hand drop without touching his sword. He looks at me and doesn't say a word. What? Is he going to pretend he's not in here?

Trev pounds again. *"She instructed me to break down the door if you don't open it."*

Aren lets out a breath that's half sigh, half grumble.

"She'll want to know details about the remnants," I tell him, setting the tray aside and standing.

Reluctantly, he buckles his weapons belt around his waist. He starts to reach for the door but stops and looks back at me.

"I know I can't forbid you from helping us, but promise me you'll be careful."

"Promise me you won't be reckless," I counter.

"I'm never reckless." He grins, but only to hide his worry. We both know how easily we could lose each other.

He opens the door. Trev stands at the threshold, his fist raised to knock again.

"You couldn't have delayed her?" Aren asks.

"I did delay her," Trev says, sounding almost offended.

I think Aren was just harassing him because he gives Trev a brotherly pat on the shoulder as he passes. *"Dealing with Lorn makes her short-tempered, I know."*

"She's in the Mirrored Hall," Trev calls after us.

Aren waves his hand in acknowledgment, then places it on the small of my back. "Why don't you go ahead. Taltrayn will want to hear what you have to say, and I want Naito there, too. I'll bring them both to the hall."

I nod, but before he leaves, I ask, "Did Shane ever show up?"

Aren's expression tells me the answer. My heart sinks. Lena sent rebels to search for him, but London is a huge city. If he isn't at the gate or near the club, they're not going to just stumble across him.

"I'll need to look for him," I say. "He might have left a message at the hotel or he might be in a London hospital." Or a London morgue, but I don't let my thoughts linger on that.

He takes my hand, plants a kiss on my palm. "I'll take you back to Vegas after we talk to Lena."

He leaves me then, and I make my way to the Mirrored Hall on my own. I've never been in it before, but I've walked past it a time or two when the doors were open. Atroth only allowed entry to members of his Inner Court, which consisted of a few high nobles, his lord general and swordmaster, and a few other select, privileged fae. It definitely wasn't open to humans.

It's on the same floor as my room, but the residential wing of the palace is sealed off from the northern wing, which

contains the throne room, the administrative offices, and
Lena's apartments. I have to go down a flight of stairs and
through a corridor that parallels the statue garden. After I
cross the antechamber outside the throne room, I reach
another staircase. This one is elaborate, with silver banisters
and polished white marble steps. I'm halfway up it when I
see Lorn start to descend.

"Ah, so you do live," he says, his face lighting up with pleasure. At least, I think it's pleasure. It's always difficult to tell
when Lorn is being sarcastic. "I always thought humans were
breakable things, but you're proving to be quite resilient."

"Hello, Lorn," I say, veering to the right, so I can move
around him.

"You might want to delay your meeting with Lena," he
says. "She's in a foul mood."

"I'm sure you tried your best to cheer her up," I mutter.

He puts a hand to his chest as if I've wounded him. "Of
course I did. It's not my fault she expects so much of me."

I pause on the same step he's standing on. "Do you know
who's leading the remnants?"

He gives me his most charming smile. "I know everything, my dear."

Or he pretends to, at least. In this case, though, I think he
does know. If he didn't, I suspect he'd try to pry the information out of me. No wonder Lena's mad at him. He's not giving us the information we need to end this war. Who knows
what else he isn't telling us.

"Bye, Lorn."

"Have a wonderful day, *nalkin-shom*," he calls after me.

I roll my eyes. I want to like Lorn, but sometimes he
makes it difficult to believe there's a caring person beneath
the apathetic façade he puts up.

I climb the rest of the steps, then make my way to the
Mirrored Hall. The room is lit by hundreds of tiny glass orbs.
They hang from the ceiling, throwing their blue-white light
over the length of the room. Lena is the only one inside. She's
standing beside a long wooden table with her hands clasped
behind her back. She's not facing me or the doorway, but I
think she sees my tiny reflection in the mirror opposite her.

"I'll kill you if you hurt Aren," she says without turning.

It's an empty threat, but I tell her, "I'm not going to hurt him." I mean it.

A fae enters the hall from a gap that's almost invisible due to the gilded mirrors covering just about every square inch of the walls. He's carrying a silver tray with two bottles and an assortment of cheeses and fruits. Most of the latter is cut into cubes and covered with some kind of glaze. The fae sets it down, then asks if Lena wants anything else. She never once looks at him, just shakes her head no.

After he leaves, I say, "You should be nice to the waitstaff."

I expect her to protest, to say something about the servants being below her station or some other typical, I'm-a-noble-and-he's-a-peon crap, but she sinks down into a chair.

"I know," she says. She lets out a breath, and her shoulders sag. "I miss my brother."

She's staring at the silver tray, so she doesn't see my eyes go wide. She's confiding in me? What am I supposed to do with that? Never mind that I suck at girl talk, she's *Lena*. She's supposed to tolerate me only because she needs my Sight and shadow-reading skills.

"He'd know what to do with the high nobles," she says.

"He wouldn't have the problem of convincing them that a woman can sit on the silver throne."

"True." She looks up, and I think I see relief in her eyes. I understand it. It's like she's onstage every second of her life now. She can't be anything but confident when she's in public. Her supporters have to have faith in her. The high nobles can't see a weakness in her resolve. She shouldn't even let me see a weakness, but I'm not judging her. She's exhausted.

"The remnants let you go?" Lena asks, picking up an apple-shaped fruit.

I pull out the chair across from her and sit. "Paige let me go."

"Naito told us about the serum," she says. "He told us it's fatal. I'm sorry."

My gut twists. It's hard to wrap my mind around the fact that Paige is dying. She looked perfectly healthy.

"Will the remnants use the serum?" she asks.

"Paige says they won't. They know it's fatal now, too."

"She trusts them?"

I nod. "And she says the remnants didn't kill the Sighted humans in London."

She looks up sharply. "We certainly didn't kill them."

"I was thinking . . ." I draw in a breath, hoping I'm not just trying to justify Paige sympathizing with the remnants. "Maybe someone else is involved in all of this. Maybe we're not fighting the right people."

She turns the fruit she's holding in her hand, shining with the blue-white light of the magically lit orbs hanging above us. "Is it wrong to wish for that? If a false-blood was trying to take the throne, I think I could convince the high nobles to approve me."

"Before I went to London," I say, "you mentioned you thought you could force them to vote. Did that not work out?"

Lena gives a short, caustic laugh.

"I'm the one postponing the vote now," she says, setting aside the fruit as if she's lost her appetite. "I'm at least a vote short of what I need. I thought I had Lord Hison's support after you shadow-read in Rhigh, but he's blaming us for the riot at the gate."

"That started well before Aren and I were there."

"That's what I've told Hison," she says. "But his people continue to talk about the human who can call the lightning and walk unhindered through a crowd of rioting fae."

"They say the *nalkin-shom* is untouchable." That's from Aren, who's walking into the hall, with Naito at his side.

I am so not amused. "This is your fault."

"Mostly," he says with a devil-may-care grin. It's both annoying and extremely enticing.

Naito sits beside Lena, but Aren comes to my side of the table. He picks up one of the two bottles sitting on the silver platter in the center of the table and opens it.

"Where's Taltrayn?" Lena asks.

"He's at the silver wall," Aren says, retrieving one of the empty glasses. "When he returns, a swordsman will have him meet us here."

"Does he know about Caelar?" I ask, watching Aren pour a red liquid into the glass. More *cabus*, I presume.

Lena rests her folded arms on the table. "Yes. I mentioned Caelar's name when I told him you were still alive."

Still alive. Crap. I was primarily concerned about Aren when the remnants captured me because he was the one who saw the illusion of my death, but Kyol wouldn't have been unaffected by the news. He told me himself he cares about me. He still feels the need to protect me.

Aren sets the bottle of *cabus* down with a soft *thunk*, then slides the glass toward me without raising his gaze from the table.

"Did he have any insight on Caelar?" I ask.

Lena's silver eyes study me a moment before she answers. "Taltrayn respects him. He says Caelar is calm, charismatic, and calculating. But we have his weakness locked in a room underground."

"Brene," I say, and Paige's parting comment to me makes sense now. "We should let her go."

Lena raises an eyebrow.

"You want to talk to Caelar, don't you?" I ask. "It's a good faith gesture. Tell him you'll let Brene go when he meets with you."

"Brene might be *tor'um*," Lena says, "but she's still dangerous. She can fight, and she has information on the remnants."

"Information she's not telling us," Aren adds softly. Fae might not believe in ghosts, but his eyes are haunted. Are they haunted because he made her *tor'um*? Or are they haunted because he wasn't able to save Lena's father?

I cup the glass of *cabus* between my palms.

"Taltrayn has been asking her questions," Aren tells me. "No one's hurting her. She's being cared for."

He misinterpreted my worry; I didn't think they were abusing Brene.

Lena lets out a sigh. "We'll search the mountains again."

"It might not be their only camp," Naito puts in. He leans forward to grab a wedge of cheese off the tray, then pops it into his mouth. "And they probably abandoned it as soon as they discovered McKenzie escaped."

I still think they should let Brene go, but I don't voice that thought out loud again. Instead, I stare at the crimson surface of the glass of *cabus* I'm holding, and something tugs at the edge of my mind.

Aren pulls out the chair to my right and sits. "We need to persuade Hison to vote for you. When you're named queen, Caelar will lose support. He won't give up his war, but he won't be a threat to you anymore."

"He'll just be a threat to you," Lena says sourly.

I'm still staring at my *cabus*. If I didn't know what it was, I'd mistake it for a red wine.

"You're more important than I am," Aren says. "Besides, I'm fully capable of taking care of myself."

"He has to be killed or captured," Lena responds. "I won't allow him to plot my sword-master's death." They continue talking. I know I should be concerned about Aren's safety—and I am—but I block out their words. Sara runs a wine store that caters to people with expensive tastes. Lorn buys from her. He brings it back to the Realm and sells it.

"McKenzie?" Aren's brow is creased. He must see something in my face.

I look at Lena. "How did you find me?"

"What do you mean?" she asks, frowning.

"You found me on my campus. How did you know I was there? How did you find out my name?" The few Court fae who knew my name and where I lived on Earth were all trusted completely by Kyol and King Atroth. When the rebels found me, we were surprised they'd managed to learn who I was.

"A letter came," Aren answers. "It had your name and the name of your school."

"It was anonymous?" I ask.

He nods.

"Like the anonymous note that told you I was in Nashville?"

He nods again. "And it was like the letter that told us Paige was in London."

My heartbeat doubles its pace.

"We get dozens of tips every day," Lena adds. "That's how we get half of our information."

"Most citizens who want to help are worried about repercussions if the other side ends up winning," Aren explains.

"McKenzie," Lena says, "what are you thinking?"

It's clear she doesn't get it—none of them do—but the more I think about it, the more it makes sense. Atroth was a strong king. Sethan had a lot of support, but it was quiet support. The reason—the only reason—we took the palace was because we had Kyol's help. He told us the weaknesses in the Court fae's defenses. The rebels slipped inside, assassinating a few select guards to open up the way for Lena to lead in a whole contingent of her followers. Everything the rebels did had to be done covertly because they were no match for Atroth's Court fae in an open fight. No fae in the last decade, no matter how charismatic, has been a match for them.

"Kyol swore Atroth never gave the vigilantes my name," I tell them. "Maybe he was right. Atroth didn't give them my name. But somebody else did. It's the same person who arranged for Paige and me both to be in London and to suspect the other side of slaughtering the Sighted humans. That someone is pulling our strings, making us kill each other. Weaken each other."

"So they can step in and take the palace," Aren says.

"Or maybe it's just someone who wants the war to continue. He profits from it. He's even entertained by it. I think it's Lorn."

That statement is greeted with a long silence. I stare at my glass of *cabus* again. I don't want to believe it's Lorn. I want to believe he's a good person beneath his selfish exterior, but he hasn't been helping us since we took the palace. I could be misjudging him. After all, I misjudged Kavok.

"He lost Kelia in this war," Lena says, breaking the silence. "They had a life-bond."

"Lorn paid fae to protect her," Aren says. "She *should* have been safe."

"He wanted to sever the life-bond." Naito's voice is as cold and quiet as ice. He's as still as ice, too, and his gaze never wavers from the center of the table. I hate seeing him hurt.

"Lorn gave you an anonymous tip so that you'd find me in Nashville. That's how he works. Was the handwriting on any of the letters you received the same?"

"I don't know," she says. "They came months apart."

Of course, it wouldn't be that easy. I let my gaze sweep the hall, hoping I'll be struck by inspiration, an idea to prove conclusively that Lorn is manipulating things behind the scenes, but the mirrors don't offer any answers.

"I tracked Aylen to Eksan," I murmur, mostly to myself. She was an "associate of an associate" according to Lorn. Maybe it's more than a coincidence that she fissured to the same city Tylan was captured in.

"That doesn't prove anything," Lena says.

"I know." I let out a sigh and focus on the fae entering the room. He doesn't announce his presence. I don't find that odd until he's walking down the length of the table. My brow furrows when he's two chairs away from Naito, three away from Lena. Neither Lena nor Aren acknowledges the other fae's presence, and Naito is still staring at the table.

The problem doesn't click into place until he draws his sword.

TWENTY-SEVEN

◆·◆

"L ENA, MOVE!"
      My shout startles everyone into motion, and that's
the only reason she survives. Naito's chair flies back, barely
missing the remnant. The fae pauses long enough for Lena to
draw her sword. She swings blindly, completely missing him,
but Naito's grabbed ahold of his overturned chair.

He swings it as Lena backpedals, as Aren leaps over the
table, and as I grab the unopened bottle sitting on the silver
platter.

But I don't have to use my makeshift weapon. Aren knows
where the remnant is the second Naito swings the chair into
him. Aren slides off the table, his sword stabbing forward.

The remnant's *jaedric* cuirass stops the attack. He faces
Aren, but Lena steps left, then plunges her blade into his
side. He cries out, falls to his knees, but he's still alive. Still
breathing.

"How did you get in here?" Lena demands, withdrawing
her sword. The remnant's hand goes to his side, but he can't
stop the river of blood from flowing between his fingers. He
shakes his head as he gasps for air.

Lena's sword point reenters the fae's wound, and he
screams.

The room tilts, and I'm suddenly nauseous. Lena asks him

again how he got in here and what the remnants' plan is, then there's a shout from just outside the Mirrored Hall. Something breaks.

I sprint to the hall's open doors, step out onto the balcony that overlooks the huge antechamber below.

My breath catches in my throat. Blood spills over the smooth, polished marble floor. The remnants are everywhere. I don't know how. We're inside the Silver Palace, which is inside Corrist's silver walls. The only way for fae to fissure here is via a *Sidhe Tol*, but Lena has guards on all of them. It should be impossible for this many remnants to make it here at once.

Unless, of course, the remnants have retaken one of the *Sidhe Tol*.

As I back away from the railing, my gaze sweeps past the open doors to the king's hall on the floor below. Kyol's there. Remnants see him, too. They attack . . .

And he kills them as if they're afterthoughts. He's preoccupied, searching for . . .

He's searching for Lena, I realize.

"Kyol!"

I don't know how he hears me over the sounds of the battle, but he looks up. His eyes lock on me for two, maybe three seconds, then he's running, sprinting for the stairs that will bring him to me.

"Lena's in here," I say, when he reaches me. I expect him to immediately enter the Mirrored Hall. Instead, he cups the back of my head and pulls me against his chest.

His embrace is tight, and I swear I feel a shudder go through his body when he lays his head against mine. God, the news of my supposed death must have rattled him. He shouldn't be holding me like this—he should be rushing to protect Lena—but I lean into him, giving him a few seconds before I move back so that I can peer up into his face.

"I'm sorry," I tell him, though I'm not sure why. It's not like I wanted to be captured by the remnants. But I definitely didn't want to hurt him either.

I feel his chest rise as he draws in a breath, then he lets me go. Whatever he thought or felt when he pulled me into his arms doesn't show on his face. His expression is as hard and unreadable as a stone's.

After one quick glance at the fight below, he motions me inside the Mirrored Hall.

"Why are you here?" Kyol's voice rings out as we stride toward Lena. The remnant she was interrogating is gone. Into the ether, I presume.

"Privacy," she bites back.

He takes her arm when he reaches her side, starts pulling her toward the gap in the wall the servant entered and exited through earlier. "If you'd been in the king's hall or your quarters, you could have escaped by now."

"Escape?" She jerks free. "I'm not leaving the palace."

"You are."

"If I leave, I lose everything," she says, her tone scathing. Then, when Kyol reaches for her again, she adds, "Touch me again, and I'll kill you."

I think she might mean that.

"If you die," he counters, "the rebellion loses everything."

Her nostrils flare. She tightens her right hand around the hilt of her sword, then, her gaze steely, she lifts her left. In it, she's holding an anchor-stone. It's jagged and an opalescent smoky gray.

"A remnant had this," she says. "It will lead to a *Sidhe Tol*. A new *Sidhe Tol*."

"They found another?" I ask, alarmed. King Atroth knew the locations of only three of the Ancestors' Gates. Those gates allow fae to fissure into areas protected by silver. They're located in my world, and I know Atroth had fae constantly searching for others, but what are the chances that they found one *now*?

"We need to secure the *Sidhe Tol*," she says. The words are an order, and her rigid tone and regal posture say she expects it to be carried out, and quickly. She sounds very much like the daughter of a high noble, and it's apparently a queenly enough tone that Kyol doesn't argue.

His gaze remains on Lena. "Naito will go to the *Sidhe Tol* with Jorreb." His jaw clenches. "You'll stay with Lena, McKenzie. Make sure an illusionist doesn't assassinate her."

With that, Kyol turns and exits the hall.

"Looks like we have our orders," Aren mutters. He doesn't leave immediately, though. He turns me toward him, pulls me into his arms, and kisses me before I'm able to focus on his face. I feel more in his kiss than I'd ever see in his expression: affection, desire, and respect. Fear.

"Remember," he whispers, pulling back slightly. "Be careful. Please. I can't lose you again."

Naito goes with him, leaving me alone with Lena. She waits all of five seconds before she uses her foot to scoop up the dead remnant's sword. She catches its hilt in the air, then hands it to me with a terse, "Follow me."

I stare down at the sword. It's a long, slender weapon that looks elegant and light but is lethal and heavy. The blade is slightly longer than my arm, and the *jaedric*-wrapped hilt is grooved from the remnant's fingers. My hand is smaller than his, so the grip is awkward.

"Lena, we shouldn't—"

She's almost to the doors of the Mirrored Hall.

"Lena, wait!"

I manage to catch her arm before she steps onto the balcony. "You can't leave this room."

Cold silver eyes rise to meet mine. "You would rather me let people die than go out there and heal them?"

"They're fighting for you. I'd rather you stay alive, so it's not in vain."

"I'm not staying here, McKenzie." She shakes loose.

I blow out a breath and follow her.

She must have forgotten I'm human because I can't catch up, not until she stops at the top of the staircase, looking down at the battle below. Her face hardens. I think I know why: she's not used to seeing so many fae injured in the middle of a fight. They usually fissure out if they're hurt badly enough. They can't do that here. Her people are hurt. Without her help, they're going to lie there and die.

"Lena," Trev says, climbing the steps.

Lena descends the stairs, passing Trev without a word. His gaze locks onto my sword, and I swear to God I see his eyes widen.

Great, I look as ridiculous as I feel carrying this thing.

"Stay with us," I order as I go down the stairs two at a time, trying to catch up with Lena.

She kills a remnant before the fae is able to slam his sword into the rebel lying injured on the floor. His soul-shadow replaces his body. Lena passes through it, kneels by the rebel's side, and places her hands on his mangled leg.

Another fae approaches. Before I have to make a decision on whether I'm actually going to have to try to fight him, Trev engages him.

Thank God.

I turn back to Lena, but she's already moved on. Damn it. Kyol should have ordered *her* to stay with *me*. I can't keep up, and I really, really don't want to move farther into the fight.

I draw in a breath, start to move her way, when a cry to my left catches my attention.

It's Jacia. She falls back, barely deflecting a remnant's attack. The remnant's back is to me, and he swings at her again, then again and again, relentless in his attack. Jacia is barely holding him off.

And his back is still to me.

She'll die if I don't help her.

I pull back my sword as I step left, giving myself a straight shot at the remnant's side, where the bindings holding his cuirass together are tied. Putting all my weight behind me, I thrust my sword forward.

Only a few inches of the blade slide in, but those few inches hurt. The fae turns, screaming. He starts to lift his sword to attack me, but Jacia takes advantage of the distraction I caused. She swings her blade at the remnant's neck. It slides cleanly all the way through. Blood arcs through the air as the head and body fall.

Jacia nods her thanks.

A nod of thanks for helping her kill someone else.

I clench my teeth together, turn, but I've lost sight of Lena and Trev.

"Shit," I mutter. I have to find her. The illusionist in the Mirrored Hall was there because he was looking for her, and the remnants have other illusionists—Tylan is one. He might try to assassinate her.

Thinking about Tylan makes me think about Paige. Is she here? Is Lee? No other humans are in this antechamber, just remnants and rebels absorbed in destroying each other. Maybe Paige has gone back to Earth already.

My heartbeat thunders in my chest as I make my way to the wall, then follow it around until I reach a corridor that leads toward the eastern wing of the palace and the *veligh*, the waterfront. That's where we're the most vulnerable, so that might be where Lena's heading.

I keep my sword held ready, but try my best to make myself look small and uninteresting. I'm lucky. There are more rebels in this corridor than remnants. I'm able to make it all the way outside the palace without having to defend myself.

Things are worse than I thought they would be out here. It looks like the remnants had two goals when they fissured in: to assassinate Lena and to break through this portion of the silver wall.

Approximately a hundred feet lies between the palace and the wall. The silver plating is bent and cracked around a gaping hole. The interior of the wall, made up of stone blocks and wooden stairs and balconies for the guards to stand watch on, is clearly visible straight ahead. It was only a few days ago that the remnants almost broke through there. They lit fires at the wall's base while they pummeled it with rocks and boulders, some thrown by hand, others launched by magic. The rebels fought them off, but there hasn't been time to repair the damage.

The remnants are attacking the wall from both sides now. They're trying to chop down the beams of the scaffold that's holding it up. Kyol and a dozen other rebels are trying to fight them off.

I tighten my fist around the hilt of my sword and press my back against the palace, scanning the strip of land for Lena or Trev or some way to help.

My gaze goes back to the scaffolding. It's shaking and teetering, just barely holding out. Is there a way I can help there?

I push away from the wall, moving toward it, thinking I might be able to draw some fae away from it, when something in my peripheral vision catches my attention. A remnant stands far off to my right, focusing on the fight at the scaffold, too. He's gathering a ball of fire in his hand.

Dread traps my air in my lungs. He's going to throw it at the scaffold. The scaffold won't hold up. It'll fall. It'll crush Kyol and the other rebels and open up a huge gap in the wall. The remnants will be able to pour in.

"Kyol!" I scream, but even if he could hear me, he can't fissure. He wouldn't make it to the remnant in time.

The fire in the fae's hand turns blue.

My decision is already made. I'm already running, sprinting away from the palace. I have to get there in time. If I don't, Kyol is dead, half the rebels and remnants out here are dead, and the eastern wall will be in ruins.

I'm running as fast as I ever have before, but I won't reach the fae. I can only do one thing. If I fail, we're all dead. If I succeed . . .

I promised Aren I'd be careful. This isn't careful. I'm going to die doing this.

The ball of flame leaves the fae's hand, but I make it in time, leaping between it and the scaffolding.

There's a *whoosh* when the magic-wrapped flames slam into my right shoulder.

Shock stabs through me as I'm flying through the air. I expected the flames to be intangible; I didn't expect them to be as solid as a cannonball. My back hits the edge of the scaffold and something in my chest—a rib or my collarbone—snaps. I don't feel the pain of the fire until after my vision turns orange and red. Then some part of my mind notes that my skin is burning. My hair, my clothes, my shoelaces . . . they're all aflame.

Another part of my mind notes that I've hit a beam supporting the right edge of the scaffold. And a third part of my mind—the tiny, naïve part that believes I have a chance to survive this—chants, *Stop, drop, roll. Stop, drop, roll.*

I stop, drop, and roll to my back. There's a loud *crack* above me and a trembling in the wall. A section of it shakes loose. I see the stone blocks falling toward me just before my vision goes black.

I should be dead. I *want* to be dead. My leg is broken, my knee pulled up near my chest at a sickening angle.

"*Sidhe, no. No!*"

I can't move.

"McKenzie." Kyol drops down beside me. "*Sidhe*, don't move."

He says my name again as he scans me, head to toe. His hand reaches out like he wants to touch me, but he doesn't. I'm grateful. My skin hurts. Everything hurts.

"*Find Lena!*" he barks in Fae.

I squeeze my eyes shut, concentrate on drawing air into my lungs. It's a difficult thing to do with my throat closing up like this, but Kyol is trying to reassure me. He's trying to make sure I'm not afraid.

"You're going to be okay," he says. He's wrong. I can't survive this.

I concentrate and manage to lift my right hand. He sees it. Ignoring the blisters, he intertwines his fingers with mine, and suddenly, there's so much I want to say. So much I want to tell him. I want him to know that I don't regret the ten years I spent with him. I don't regret shadow-reading for him. I don't regret losing my family, my friends, my human life for him. I don't regret loving him.

I need him to know all of this, but more important than all of that is the one thing I do regret: leaving Aren. I wanted to have so much more time with him.

"Tell him, please." My lips hurt when I speak. They feel dry, cracked. Burned.

Kyol leans closer. I swallow, trying to work moisture into my mouth.

"Tell him . . ." Desperate to make him understand, I tighten my grip on his hand until he bends even lower. "I'm sorry I wasn't careful and—"

Kyol releases my hand. "No."

No?

"Please, Kyol."

"No," he thunders. "I won't let you die. You're *not* dying."

There's so much pain in his voice. I hate it. I hate hurting him. I hate how much I'm going to hurt Aren.

"Aren," I whisper.

"You're going to be okay, *kaesha*."

"*Kaesha*," I murmur.

SUDDENLY, the pain increases tenfold. I gasp, arching my back off the ground. I can't touch it anymore, can't touch anything.

I cry out again, draw in one deep breath after another after another until . . . I relax, my breathing slows, and I'm okay.

I'm okay. I know it's shock. My mind isn't able to process the pain. It's shutting down. I'm grateful for the reprieve, grateful that I can say to Kyol, "Let me go."

He shakes his head. Tears streak down his face. I've never seen him cry before.

I'll never see him cry again.

"It's okay. I don't hurt anymore. I'm not afraid."

"I can't, McKenzie. I can't." His voice cracks. "I love you. *Sidhe*, I know I have no right to tell you this, but I do. I always will."

I try to tell him I understand, but all that comes out is an incoherent mumble. I close my eyes.

"CAN you hear me? Say . . ." Something. Kyol wants me to say something. I'm too weak, too cold to do anything more than murmur a few syllables, but that's not enough for him. He demands me to keep talking. I try. I try until I feel my heart lurch and then . . .

TWENTY-EIGHT

◆

IT'S DARK. EONS pass.

MY heart is beating, but I feel wrong. Overfull. I'm distantly aware of someone above me. He's talking, demanding some kind of response from me.

Aren?

He wants me to open my eyes. He says my name over and over and over again.

"MCKENZIE." A different voice shatters the dark. *Kyol's* voice. I try to murmur his name, but my lips won't move.

"Open your eyes, McKenzie." His order is wrapped in fear and hope. They're such odd, conflicting emotions. I need to see his face. Need to see his eyes, his mouth. I need to see him.

I concentrate, pour all of my strength and willpower into the monumental task of opening my eyes.

It works. I see the blur of a ceiling high above me, a hazy silhouette nearer, leaning over me.

I blink until Aren's worried face comes into focus.

"Thank the *Sidhe*," he whispers. Then his lips are on mine. My mouth tingles, and chaos lusters spark between us as we kiss. I remember his touch, his taste, his scent, but I'm distracted. Something is off. I can't concentrate on Aren because Kyol is hurting. Was he crushed under the wall as well?

My chest is tight. I feel panicky. I need . . . I need . . .

"I'm here, McKenzie."

I turn my head, and he is there, crouched just behind me. We're in the small room hidden in the wall behind Lena's throne. The last time I was here, Atroth was still king. I was still on their side of the war.

I roll to my stomach so I can see him better. A mistake. Pain stabs through me.

"McKenzie," Aren says, his voice alarmed. "Don't move."

I don't think I'm completely healed, but I have to know what's wrong with Kyol. He's hurting more, now. I can see it on his face.

I try to push up. Aren's hands are on my shoulders, keeping me still. I ignore him, still struggling to rise until Kyol places his hand over mine.

"Rest."

That one, simple word makes me relax. I can't hold my weight up anyway. I let Aren settle me back down. He carefully places me on my back again. Everything hurts. My bones, my joints, my skin. Black spots blur my vision. I need to sleep.

I think I actually do. When I open my eyes this time, I feel more settled. I can focus on Aren.

"The fight?" I ask. The fact that someone brought me to this hidden room and not my bedroom might mean it's still going on.

"Most of the wall held. The new *Sidhe Tol* is protected."

I breathe a little easier. Something went right today.

"You look awful," I tell Aren. And he does. His eyes are bloodshot, and his face looks pale except for a smear of red on his cheek.

"With your injuries . . ." Aren's voice cracks. "I don't know how you survived long enough for me to reach you."

"You healed me?" I feel the question wrinkle my forehead. He was somewhere in my world, fighting at a *Sidhe Tol*. Lena should have been easier to find. "Is Lena okay?"

"I fissured directly to the *veligh* after we secured the *Sidhe Tol*. If I hadn't . . ." He swallows, re-collects himself. "Lena's fine. She'll be here soon." His touch is gentle as he brushes my hair back from my face. It's as if he's afraid he'll break me. He doesn't know how I survived. I don't either. When I blocked the flame, I knew I was going to die. I remember it hitting me, remember burning.

I remember Kyol.

I start to crane my head so I can see him, but he comes to my side, sparing me the effort. I analyze his face. He's wearing a perfectly impenetrable mask. There's no tension in his mouth or at the corners of his eyes. Something isn't right, though. I'd swear he's . . . anguished?

"What's wrong?" I ask him.

Kyol doesn't answer. That's weird. I mean, even if something's wrong, and he doesn't want to tell me, he'd say he was fine. Why doesn't he tell me he's fine?

"He's okay, McKenzie," Aren says. He touches my forehead. I feel his magic—I think he's trying to heal the headache growing behind my eyes—but I push away his hand and sit up.

That's definitely a mistake. Aren brought me back from the brink of death, but I am *not* well. A prickling sensation moves through my hands and feet, like they've fallen asleep and are just now waking up, and my muscles protest. I squeeze my eyes shut and lean forward, fairly certain I'm going to vomit.

"Lena," I hear Aren say. *"She's hurting, and I'm spent. Please."*

She says something back to him in Fae, but she's speaking too softly for me to make out the words.

Then, she's at my side. "Lie down."

I shake my head. I don't want to lie back down. If I do, I might never get up again.

"Lie down," she says, and this time, she puts her hand on my chest.

I'm not strong enough to fight her. I fall to my back.

She finishes the work Aren started, mending bones, re-attaching muscles and tendons, repairing my skin. It hurts, but I don't make a sound. I'm not sure if I have the energy to cry out anymore.

I must fade off again. When I wake this time, I feel better. Tired, but better.

Lena is still kneeling beside me.

"I'm glad you're alive," I say. My voice is stronger now.

"I'm glad you are as well," she says. I actually think she means it.

She moves aside, letting Aren take her place. He intertwines his fingers with mine, and I feel him tremble. Just for a second, and it's not due to my *edarratae*. Jesus, he's close to burnout because of me, and I've been focused on Kyol this whole time. What the hell is wrong with me?

"Are you okay?" I ask him.

He smiles. Then he bends down to kiss me.

It's only when our lips meet this time that I truly believe I'm going to live. He grounds me to this world, and I pull him more tightly to me. I make sure he knows I want him. I love him. Then, I'm suddenly aware that there are others watching us.

Kyol's watching us.

I pull back. Aren's eyebrows dip in concern. "What is it?"

"It's . . . Kyol."

There's no hurt or anger in Aren's expression now, just worry. Simultaneously, our heads turn to look at Lena's lord general.

And that's when his composure cracks. His shoulders slump and the silver in his eyes darkens with . . . pain? Why is he hurting so much?

"I'm sorry," he says. "I couldn't let her die. It was the only thing I could try."

Beside me, Aren stiffens.

"What did you try?" Lena asks.

Kyol looks at her. I don't think I've ever seen this much fear in his eyes.

"It shouldn't have worked," he says.

"What did you do, Taltrayn?" Her words are soft, almost consoling, as if she can ease the confession from his lips.

His gaze returns to Aren.

"I'm sorry," he says.

There's murder in Aren's eyes, in the way he draws in a slow breath, lets it out as he rises.

"You should leave, Taltrayn," Lena says, her voice still cool, still calm.

Kyol doesn't budge. Aren does. His hand clenches on the hilt of his sword as he takes a step forward. The muscles in his forearms and biceps tremble. It's like he's fighting a war with himself.

"Now, Taltrayn," Lena says.

Kyol's jaw tightens. He looks at me again, and my heart rips in two. It takes everything in me not to go to him, comfort him.

He winces, then starts for the exit.

Aren steps into his path.

"The only reason you still breathe," he whispers, "is because killing you would kill her."

I feel sick as I watch Kyol leave. It's not just because I nearly died today and not because I'm weak from being healed. Nothing makes sense right now.

I look at Lena. She seems to be the only sane person in the room.

"Aren," she says. "You should go to your room. Rest."

"I don't need rest," he grates out. He's staring at the exit Kyol disappeared through.

"Then you must feel well enough to heal the remaining injured," she says. "Go. And stay away from my lord general."

"Aren," I say before he walks away. He looks at the open doorway. There's determination in the way he clenches his jaw. I'm still sitting. I start to rise, knowing I can't do it on my own and knowing he can't help but come to me and help.

I hold on to the arms that hold me, but when I lean into him, he's rigid, and his expression is impenetrable.

He swallows. "We'll talk tomorrow, McKenzie."

I'm too shocked to stop him when he walks away. His words sounded like a good-bye.

"You can feel Taltrayn," Lena says. She doesn't say anything more than that. She's waiting for me to understand, but I already do.

"That's impossible," I say.

"It *shouldn't* be possible."

Kyol formed a life-bond with me. I can feel it, feel him. He's making his way through the statue garden, I think. I can't see what he sees, and I don't know his thoughts, but he's like a blur of emotion just beyond my reach. And now, he's angry and hurting.

"How did this happen?" I whisper.

"You wanted it to happen."

My gaze snaps to hers. "I didn't—"

"I'm not saying you wanted *him*, but a life-bond won't form unless both parties wish for it to. Kelia certainly didn't *want* Lorn. She wanted to hurt Naito."

"Hurt Naito?" Was that before they fell for each other?

Lena waves away my question. "You'll have to ask him about that. But in your case, it might have been that you just wanted to live. The bond connected you to Kyol. He connected you to this world. He allowed you to cling to life long enough for Aren to reach you."

I knew that fae share magic through life-bonds, and that the bond makes both fae stronger; I didn't know it could help hold someone from the brink of death.

"If he hadn't done what he did, or if the bond hadn't taken," she goes on, "I have no doubt you'd be dead."

Not every bond takes. I know that. The two people have to be compatible on some level, but that's just it. I'm human, and he's fae; we shouldn't be compatible.

"So, I'm the only human-fae bond?"

"*Sidhe*," Lena says. "You're not *that* special."

"That's not—"

"If Kavok were around," she says, starting for the exit, "I'm sure he'd love to tell you about the others. There were two of them, if I remember correctly. Neither life-bond ended well."

"Where are you going?" I ask, when she's almost to the exit.

She turns, and one side of her mouth tightens into a smile. "Back to my duties. I'm going to convince the high nobles that someone else is behind this war. Then I'm going to have Lorn arrested."

"With no real evidence?"

"Half the palace is in shambles. They'll be looking for someone to restore order. I won't mention Lorn's name until I'm certain he's guilty. The high nobles will assume I'm talking about a false-blood. That will cause a number of them to change their minds."

She leaves then, and I don't stop her. Kyol's emotions are becoming clearer, more potent. I don't know if the latter is because he's hurting more or if it's because I'm becoming more aware of the bond, but it's distracting, almost distracting enough that I don't catch the significance of Lena's words.

A number of nobles will change their minds *about her*. She thinks they'll approve her as the ruler of the Realm now. If they do, this war might come to an end. The remnants don't have a Descendant who can challenge her for the throne. They'll lose support; Lena will gain it. Some of them will fight on—Caelar, for example—but they shouldn't be able to launch the attacks that they have been these last few weeks.

There may finally be a break in the bloodshed.

ONE day passes, then another, and another. Aren doesn't come to me as he promised, and I'm afraid to seek him out. I'm afraid that I was right, that his last words to me were a good-bye. I don't want to confirm them, so I pass the time recuperating from my wounds and drinking *cabus*.

The high nobles approve Lena as the *interim* leader of the Realm. It's not what we were hoping for, but she's confident she'll eventually become the Realm's first queen. She has the power now to restore the provinces Atroth dissolved decades ago, and since she's technically the high noble of Adaris, she'll be able to cast a vote for herself. The nobles from the other dissolved provinces will be grateful for what she's done as well. She'll have their support.

On the fourth day, I'm close to my breaking point. The life-bond with Kyol has grown stronger, and his pain, his sadness is killing me. I don't know if I'll feel him less in my world, but I can't stay in the Realm, not until I find a way to block out these feelings. And not without having a damn good reason to stay.

So I finally seek out Aren, hoping he'll be that reason. He's on the roof of the palace, sitting on its edge and looking beyond the silver wall and out over the Imyth Sea. I think he knows I'm here, but he doesn't say anything.

Silently, I sit down beside him.

Minutes pass. I'm not exactly sure how many—ten, twenty, maybe a half hour—but the moon reaches its zenith and is well into its descent when I finally say, "I've missed you."

Starlight outlines Aren's profile, and a cool, gentle breeze ruffles through his hair. With the palace beneath him and Corrist's mountains in the background, he's exotically alluring.

He rests his hand on top of mine, squeezes it. Hope loosens some of the knots in my stomach. I watch my *edarratae* zigzag down my arm, but when they reach him, he takes his hand away.

"I can't do this, McKenzie."

My heart breaks. It's a tangible thing. The pain is deep inside my chest, slightly off centered and sharp. There's no way I can hide it from Kyol. I feel alarm pass through our bond, then understanding, I think, when he realizes I'm not injured. Guilt and sadness follow that. I swallow and try to block out his emotions.

"You're giving up on us?" I ask Aren.

"You don't understand, McKenzie. The life-bond . . . I can't compete with that."

"I'm not asking you to compete with it." I turn toward him, take his hand. His mouth tightens, but he doesn't pull free this time, not even when a bolt of white lightning skips from my skin to his. "I love you, Aren."

He draws in a breath. I move closer until I'm pressed against his side. Just over two weeks ago, right after we took the palace, he came to me in Vegas. He told me he'd fight for the chance to be with me, and I chose to give him that chance. I made the right decision. He might have a dark past, but he was strong enough to overcome it. He's become something good. He's become someone I respect, and if I have to fight for him now, I will.

I reach a hand up to turn his face toward mine. His expression is pained. I have to make that go away. I press my lips against his. He doesn't resist. The feel of his mouth against mine, the taste of his breath, it's an exquisite combination of the exotic and the familiar, and when he shudders, I deepen the kiss. I pour myself into it, ignoring the tangle of emotions sitting alone somewhere in the palace.

Aren murmurs my name. He murmurs it over and over as he gives in to me. His hands go to my hips. He pulls me away from the edge of the palace and closer to him. Pressed together like this, on our knees, with no space between our bodies, I can feel just how much he wants me.

The *edarratae* are alive inside of me. I move my lips to the curve of Aren's jaw, then to the base of his neck, transferring little shocks of lightning to him with my kisses. He's still so tense, though. I run my palms down his biceps.

"Aren." It's the softest whisper, but once his name touches the air, I've lost him. His grip on my hip isn't pulling me closer now, it's holding me away.

He puts an inch of space between us; it feels like a gulf.

"I love you," he says. "*Sidhe*, I love you, but I can't do this. You're his, McKenzie."

Those last words hit me like a physical assault. I'm still holding on to Aren's arms, but like him, I'm not pulling him closer anymore.

"Kelia wasn't Lorn's," I say. My voice sounds frigid to my ears.

"Kelia never loved Lorn." He releases me to stand.

I stand, too. "You're holding my past against me." He has no right to say who I belong to.

He faces the Imyth Sea. "You should talk to him."

"I want to talk to you."

"He could explain the bond," he continues. "You could work things out."

"Work things out?" I ask, feeling the coldness in my voice seep into the rest of my body. "What's that supposed to mean?"

He looks over my shoulder. His expression is closed off.

"You're pushing me into his arms."

"I'm giving you the freedom to choose," he counters. "You need time, McKenzie, to understand the bond."

"You've already given me all the time I need."

"Please, go." He says those two words as if they mean The End. My throat closes up. The Silver Palace is Lena's now. Aren and I should be celebrating. We should be in each other's arms, wrapped in lightning and loving each other. We should be laughing. We shouldn't be breaking up. But there's a finality in the way he turns his back on me to lock his gaze on the sea once again.

"This is your decision, Aren," I say softly. "It isn't mine."

I don't want to walk away from him, but I do, leaving the roof and heading . . . I don't know where. I half expect Aren to realize his mistake and to come running after me. That's what *should* happen. He's risked his life for me over and over again, but he's giving up on me because of this life-bond? I didn't ask for it. I didn't ask to be linked to Kyol like this.

I swallow as a wave of pain rushes over me. It's hard to tell how much of it is Kyol's and how much is mine. He lied when we were in Spier. He said he was okay, that he accepted and understood my decision to leave him, but he wasn't okay. Every second he's been near me, every second I've spent with Aren . . . I've been hurting him this whole time.

I bite the inside of my lower lip, focusing on that pain instead of the other. I'm not ready to talk to Kyol yet.

"McKenzie." Naito's voice pulls me out of a daze I didn't know I'd fallen into, but I'm not on the roof anymore, not even on the stairs leading back into the palace. I'm in the sculpture garden, and Naito is off to my left, sitting on the floor with his back against a square, ivory planter.

I walk toward him, and say, "Hey," when I sink to the floor beside him.

"You doing all right?" he asks. That's the question everyone's been asking him off and on these last few weeks. I answer the same way he does most of the time, with a shrug.

He toys with a frayed hole in his jeans. "Kelia said it was easier to ignore Lorn when they were in separate worlds."

Kelia said. Past tense. And there was a certain acceptance in the way he said her name. He's still hurting, but he's healing.

"I'm sorry we can't bring her back," I say.

"We knew there was a chance . . ." He stops, clears his throat. "I thought I'd be the one to die. She's fae. She could fissure out if she got into trouble."

I wrap my arms around my bent knees. "Do you ever wish you'd never come to this world?"

He gives a short, humorless laugh. "If I hadn't come to the Realm, I'd still be one of my father's pawns."

He doesn't regret killing Nakano. Good.

"What will the rest of the vigilantes do now?" I ask.

"The same thing a cult would do if their leader died. Some of them will find new lives. Some of them will continue to hate and hunt the fae. And, apparently, in a few months, some of them will die."

"Paige has the tablet I took from the compound. She's going to give it to a friend of hers. Maybe they'll find a way to live."

"I hope so," he says. "My brother . . . We never got along. My father all but ignored him because he couldn't see the fae. Lee went off to school a few years ago. I don't know why he went back home. He shouldn't have."

There are a lot of *shouldn't haves* when it comes to the fae, and to life in general.

"I'll let you know if I hear anything from Paige," I tell him as I stand.

"You're going to leave, then?" he asks, looking up.

"Yeah. For a while," I tell him. I wish I knew how long that while will be.

TWENTY-NINE

❧

LENA FISSURES ME to my Vegas suite. She's been meeting with nobles and merchants and normal citizens with complaints every hour since she was voted the interim ruler of the Realm. I think she's here because she needs a break, just a few minutes without someone beating on her door to remind her of issues and obligations.

She sets the anchor-stone we used to fissure here on the center of the coffee table. She's never been here before. She takes in the balconied window, the elegant pictures of the city—black and white except for touches of reds and yellows here and there—hanging on the wall, and the tech scattered about the room. Her gaze rests on the flat-screen TV a few steps in front of her. It's not on, but her *edarratae* register the power running through the cord. I keep unplugging it; the maids keep plugging it back in.

"What will you do?" she asks, turning her back on the tech.

I set a satchel down on the couch. It contains my photo album and a few other trinkets. I cleaned out my room at the palace.

"Sleep," I answer. "Enroll in a local college. Maybe look for a job. An apartment." Shane was looking for a place for us to live. He said he found a house for rent, but I don't know where. None of the fae Lena sent to London has seen him. "I'll try to find out what happened to Shane."

And I'll try to find a way to save Paige. I don't voice that out loud, though. If Paige and Lee survive more than six months, the remnants will know they worked out the problem with the serum. Caelar might decide to re-create it and use it. That could cause a problem for Lena's new Court. That's something I have to risk, though, because for me, Paige's life comes first.

Lena walks to a desk that's set against the back wall. A phone is there, a spiral-bound book with things to do, and a pad of paper and pen with the hotel's name on it.

"You'll help us if I need you?" she asks.

"Naito is your shadow-reader," I tell her. "You shouldn't need me."

A small lamp is mounted to the wall beside the desk. She taps it with her finger, watches the blue lightning spread across her hand, then taps it again.

She drops her hand to her side. "Aren is doing the right thing. The pull of a life-bond is intimate. It would be wrong for him to be with you now, before you understand how deeply it will affect you. You might not want Aren a month from now."

My jaw aches. I realize I'm clenching it, force it to relax. Lena and Aren both talk like they know how it feels. Neither of them has been bonded to another fae. They're repeating rumors and making speculations. They have no idea what it's like to have two sets of emotions twisting inside them. Kyol's feelings aren't as potent now that we're in separate worlds, but they're there. I know when he's alone and hurting, when he's numbing his thoughts by sparring with another fae. I know when he's thinking about me.

He's thinking about me now.

Warmth spreads through my chest. It's some kind of desire.

"What about the *garistyn*?" I ask Lena. I try to make the question sound casual, like an afterthought. The truth is, if I know there's a chance something will happen to Kyol, I'll return to the Realm without question.

"The high nobles should be appeased until a false-blood is found and killed."

"You think Lorn is innocent?" I ask.

"We've been . . . acquaintances for a long time," she says, her gaze turning inward. "I don't want it to be him."

I understand that all too well. Maybe I'm wrong about a third-party manipulator. If so, the war should be over soon. Caelar is already losing supporters. One of them will betray him to the rebels soon.

Lena returns to the present, shaking off whatever thoughts she let herself get lost in, then asks, "If you leave here, will you leave a message for Naito? I'd like to know you're okay."

She'd like to know where I am in case she needs me.

"Yeah," I say. "I can do that."

She gives me a small smile. "Thank you, McKenzie, for helping us. I know it wasn't easy to turn against the fae you worked with for so long."

She doesn't wait for my response to that. She leaves this world in a flash of white light. The shadows dance in my vision when she's gone, making my fingers itch to draw them. But I've officially retired. I'm beginning a new life now, the life I should have had all along. Without the fae calling on me, I might actually be able to get a job and finish my degree.

My gaze goes to the pad and pen on the desk. A few quick lines, a curve of shadow here and there, and I could relieve the need I feel to map her location.

I draw in a breath, let it out, resisting the temptation. I'm going to try my best to forget the Realm.

The suite has a minifridge in its small kitchenette. Inside are an assortment of cold snacks and drinks. I'm sure it costs an arm and a leg to touch anything in it, but I grab a Diet Coke and pop the top. Can't remember the last time I had one of these.

The fridge squeaks when I kick it shut. Sipping the Coke, I head back to the living area. My gaze sweeps the hotel, not knowing what's next. What would a normal person do now?

Shower. Order room service. Maybe go down to one of the casinos . . .

A squeak interrupts my thoughts. The same squeak I heard before, but it's not from the fridge; it's from the couch.

I'm behind it, so I walk around to the front, knowing what I'm going to find curled up on one of its cushions.

Sosch. Obviously, *he's* not going to let me forget the Realm completely.

"You're going to get me banned from this hotel," I tell him.

His big blue eyes blink up at me innocently.

I scoop him into my lap after I plop down beside him. His fur flushes silver. I scratch behind his ears until he purrs. And then, for the first time in ages, I pick up the remote and click on the TV.